DEAD
GIRLS

Also by Abigail Tarttelin

Flick
Golden Boy

DEAD GIRLS

ABIGAIL TARTTELIN

MANTLE

First published 2018 by Mantle
an imprint of Pan Macmillan
20 New Wharf Road, London N1 9RR
Associated companies throughout the world
www.panmacmillan.com

ISBN 978-1-5098-5274-1

1 3 5 7 9 8 6 4 2

A CIP catalogue record for this book is available from the British Library.

Typeset by Palimpsest Book Production Limited, Falkirk, Stirlingshire
Printed and bound by CPI Group (UK) Ltd, Croydon, CR0 4YY

Visit www.panmacmillan.com to read more about all our books
and to buy them. You will also find features, author interviews and
news of any author events, and you can sign up for e-newsletters
so that you're always first to hear about our new releases.

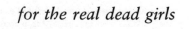

for the real dead girls

We were so wholly one I had not thought
That we could die apart. I had not thought
That I could move,—and you be stiff and still!
That I could speak,—and you perforce be dumb!
I think our heart-strings were, like warp and woof
In some firm fabric, woven in and out;
Your golden filaments in fair design
Across my duller fibre.

Edna St Vincent Millay

The walls are bare, cold, like a hospital. She paces to the locked door and then back to the wall.

The space is three-point-five metres wide, five long. Not really enough to live in. The window is barred, and sound-proof. It looks out onto a large courtyard surrounded by low office blocks, built in the seventies, pale-painted. Above them is the sky, blue and unmarked. She knows where she is, but not where the rest of the world got to. There is a bed, low and slender and hard. The mattress is thin.

She stops pacing; drops to the floor. Fifty push-ups, fifty sit-ups, repeat three times. Now the combinations. Front, reverse, backhand. Left hook, right hook, left uppercut, right. Front kick, side kick, roundhouse. She turns. Front kick, this time with the left leg, side kick, roundhouse. Left arm leading, front hand jab, reverse, backhand. Repeat. The temperature of the small room rises with her body heat. The sweat drips down between her breasts. Left hook, right hook, uppercut, jab.

The day the door opens, Thera will be ready.

She will be prepared.

We wanted to contact the dead, just to see who was around. It was a still, humid July day, the kind where the sweat trickles down your back under your T-shirt, and we had exhausted ourselves playing tig in the churchyard, amongst the graves. That must have been where we got the idea. We ran back to mine and dug out an old Ouija board from *J17* magazine that Billie and me had glued to cardboard and left in my bookshelf.

The five of us tramped across the wheat fields towards the copse. Around six o'clock, the wind suddenly got up. I watched the breeze move the wheat, and then lift the backs of Billie's and Sam's blonde hair. On Fridays, my village gang stay out through teatime and have supper late, so Billie, me, my little brother Sam, Hattie and Poppy were all there at the copse. We crawled on our bellies down the long entrance tunnel to the den and sat in a circle, our backs to the bushes. We must have all felt the significance of the moment, because we lit our candles in silence. My mum had dug out one for each of us before we left the house. 'Don't play with these,' she'd warned, handing me the matches.

I'd rolled my eyes, for show. Hattie was watching. 'Yeah, I know, Ma.'

We closed our eyes. I asked the spirits to come forth. We waited. Billie repeated my demand, louder. We opened our eyes, looked at each other, and felt a spark go between us. There's always been magic between Billie and me. We can make things happen. We opened our mouths at exactly the same time, and repeated the words Billie had spoken, together. 'Come forth, dead things, and speak to us your will!'

Suddenly there was a scream. It was Poppy, and then Hattie, and then Sam was screaming too. Billie and me were grinning at each other, but then I looked at Sam's face. He leapt up, staring just to the right of me, into the bushes at the far side of the den.

'Thera!' he shouted as Billie stood up too. I turned. It was just over my shoulder. A large black dog, snarling, baring its drool-slicked white teeth and mottled pink-and-black gums. It barked twice, loud and savage.

I froze.

I don't react like everyone else to fear. When everyone else is panicking, I'm in a little bubble of stillness. Once, when she was giving a presentation at school, Hattie fainted. I think she was nervous. I hadn't been paying attention because I was reading a book on my lap under my desk, but everyone else gasped, and that was when I noticed she'd fallen down. I stood up immediately, walked past our teacher, put Hattie in the recovery position and told Billie to fetch a glass of water.

The black dog was almost near enough for me to reach out and touch. Everyone else was screaming and running towards the tunnel, and crawling through it. But I was still as the ground I was sat on, watching the dog advance, thinking about how to defend myself against it. Scared but ready. Terrified, but with all my faculties at my disposal.

Sometimes I feel like I am built for the bad times, and that's a thought that does actually shake me up. Who wants to be built for the bad times? To know the right place for you is a place no one else wants to be?

In the end, I only moved because everyone else had already disappeared, crawling as quickly as they could back through the tunnel, and running until they got to a tree you could climb really easily. I was last, and even then before I left the den I turned back: I had this weird idea that the dog wasn't bad, that it was there to warn us about something, but when I turned I heard more barking. Behind the first black dog another sprang from the bushes, and then another, so I ducked into the tunnel and followed the others. The dogs were big, like Alsatians or Rottweilers, but they didn't look like any dog I'd seen before. Maybe they were what we had called forth with the Ouija board.

I ran until I reached the tree and then I climbed up it, past the others, right to the tip of one of the branches. I didn't hold onto anything, and I don't remember wobbling. The others said afterwards I looked like a witch, or a wood sprite.

'Did you see?' I said. 'There were more of them. Look, now there are four.'

I stood there and stretched my neck up to see into the empty den through the leaves.

'I can't see four,' said Hattie. She was sat on a branch,

a little higher up than the others. Maybe she could see into the den from where she was. 'I can only see one.'

I shook my head. 'There are four.'

I've never tried to contact the dead before, but I'm pretty sure savage black dogs are a sign that trouble is coming. Then I thought I saw blonde-brown hair through the trees in the den. It was a girl. I saw an eye. 'Look!' I shouted.

'What?' Billie, Sam and Poppy said together.

'Stop shouting, Thera!' That was Hattie. She looked down to the others. 'It's just the one dog. There's nothing else there.'

The girl with the blonde-brown hair looked at me, and then she was hidden by the trees again, and a voice, a cold whisper, murmured in my ear: 'Death is near, Thera.'

Until then, the week had been a normal one. On Monday me and Billie played that we were twins. It's a game we often play, because we look similar. We have long blondey-brown hair, blue eyes, and are the same height. Billie is prettier than me and I am smarter than her but we are both equally funny. On Wednesday we both raised our Nano Pets up to two years old. Nano Pets are the same as Tamagotchis. It's a little baby on a screen in this egg-shape thing you keep in your pocket. You raise the baby until it dies of hunger or pooing too much or until it gets to three, when it's completed. Then you get a new baby, which is zero years old. It occurred to me perhaps they're supposed to teach us to take care of something other than ourselves, so we talked about me and Sam asking for a kitten at Christmas, and then we made up imaginary pets and chased them all over the playground.

That day we had talk assembly. It was about bullying. Hattie turned to me and said that she was bullying Poppy. Bullying Poppy! I snorted. What about *me*, for heaven's sake? She's always mean to me because she wants Billie to be her best friend. Poppy wants Billie to be her best friend too. It mostly doesn't worry me because Billie and me are two peas in a pod but sometimes it worries me because

Billie is too nice to see what they're doing. Even Mrs Adamson likes Billie best out of everyone. She's our teacher. Billie always plays along with Mrs A liking her, but Billie and me think Mrs A is wet. She was stroking Billie's hair on Wednesday afternoon and making us late for home time, so I started singing our home-time song loudly, and Billie joined in and I pulled her out of the classroom, and we went to get our reading folders and coats from the cloakroom. Our home-time song goes: 'TIME to go HOME, TIME to go HOME, ti-i-i-i-i-i-ime to go home!' It's from *Watch with Mother*, which is a black-and-white video for babies.

Everyone wants Billie, but she's mine.

'Why are you bullying Poppy?' I asked Hattie in talk assembly.

''Cause she's annoying,' Hattie replied, then paused for dramatic effect. 'I don't think she deserves to be in the gang.'

I frowned. 'But *you* probably don't deserve to be in the gang because you're a bully.'

Hattie leant into me, hissing. 'She's sitting with us, the Year Sixes, and she deserves to be with the Year Fives, because she's a *baby*.'

I rolled my eyes, but not so she could see. I get so tired of her meanness that I go home crying some days. Most days I don't want to go into school. I just go in so I can see Billie.

At lunchtime on Thursday, Billie started to feel ill. I was telling her about how, when we say Grace, which we have to do before we eat, we say 'may the Lord make us truly thankful', and I love lunch so I was telling her I guess I'm truly thankful. Just as I said this, she sneezed on me. It was really funny, but she kept sneezing all day, and then she felt really tired. It turned out she had flu. I felt very sorry for her. I stood by her when she was putting things away in her drawer. I didn't know whether to ask her if I could do something. I felt silly just standing there.

So, apart from Billie being ill, this week was completely normal until yesterday, when the girl no one else could see spoke to me. And then today.

This morning, Saturday, about ten o'clock, I was up and dressed and reading on my window seat, waiting for Billie. From my window, I can see out over the fields, so when I saw her run down the hill into the field behind our house, I went downstairs to help her climb over the back fence. She put one leg over the top, and I pulled her dungarees until she rolled over to my side. Then she started falling and I wasn't in enough time to catch her, and we both fell kind of clumsily into the hedge.

'D'OH!' she yelled, like Homer Simpson. Did I mention that Billie is ridiculously loud?

When we went in the kitchen, Mum was there, taking food and cleaning things from Tesco's out of shopping bags and putting them away.

'What's for tea tonight, Mum? Can Billie stay?'

'Spag bol and yes.'

'Scrumplicious!' Billie yelled. 'I love spag bol.'

'I know you do, chicken.' Billie is round here all the time, so Mum is used to her loudness. She's like Mum's third child.

I don't know where Dad was this morning. I didn't think about it at the time. Probably out in the village, at his carpentry workshop. Billie and me were planning to play running away, but we made the mistake of telling Mum, and Mum said we had to take Sam. I whined a bit. It's a little annoying that he has to come everywhere with us when I just want some alone time with my best friend. But he's a good brother anyway, and he always plays the games we want to play. He's very amenable. Grandad taught me that word; he said it reflected better on me than me saying, 'He does everything I tell him to do.'

Billie had brought round her backpack, and I put mine on too. We packed them with two Rice Krispies Squares, our diaries, two pens (green and red), Dad's compass, our Nanos and three Ribenas (one for Sam, but there were only two Rice Krispies Squares). We ran away into the village pretending that the Huns were following us, but Sam started to whinge about how fast we were running and how he couldn't keep up, so we stopped on the corner near Hattie's. Billie said why didn't we go and see if she wanted to come out and play. I didn't want to, but I couldn't think of an excuse that wouldn't make me seem mean, so I followed Billie and she knocked on Hattie's door. Hattie opened it. Poppy was behind her, in the dark of Hattie's hall.

'Hi, butthead!' Billie said cheerfully, and then giggled for a long time. She's weird like that. 'Want to come out with us?'

Hattie slurped on her Um Bongo straw. 'Sure. What are you guys doing?'

'We're running away,' I said, a bit nervously but trying to sound nonchalant. Hattie always makes fun of my games.

She snorted. 'I won't do that, but we'll come out with you guys.'

It got a lot less fun with them there. We just wandered around, talking. They don't like to play. We went back to the den, but there was nothing there. No dogs. No girl. Hattie called me a liar. I got more and more annoyed. I hate how Billie doesn't see Hattie for what she really is.

About three o'clock it got really hot, and Hattie was complaining loads, so we stopped and drank the Ribenas and sucked sweet nettle juice out of the white bits off nettle plants in the hedgerows. That was when I saw the man.

We were on the verge near the school, lying on our tummies in the grass by the road. The horse field was behind us, and the air smelt of hay and flowers. The crickets were chirping loudly and Sam was trying to catch one in his hands. I was writing in my diary and Billie was ripping paper out of hers to make a paper predictor, so we would know who we were going to marry. We had split our Rice Krispies Squares and were just finishing off the last bites. Suddenly the man came over the stile.

'Get down!' I whispered, urgently.

We all put our heads flat in the grass. All of us apart from Hattie.

'Look at that man!' I said. 'He's alone, and in dark green. He looks like a German spy.'

'A Nazi, eh?' said Billie. 'Or maybe a Jap.' She had just finished the Famous Five book I had lent her. They were written in the war.

I grabbed her arm. 'Let's follow him! And document his movements!'

'His bowel movements?' Billie said crazily, and cackled.

'No, his spying movements, you dolt,' I said, and clapped her on the head.

'Mm, but it's so comfy and nice here on the grass,' Billie argued. 'And I'm getting that tanned back-of-the-neck that I've always wanted.'

'Yeah, I don't want to play, Thera; you're being dumb,' Hattie said.

'Yeah, I'm getting a nice tan on my neck too,' added Poppy. Poppy is rubbish at telling when people are joking. Billie doesn't care about getting tanned, or about make-up, or the other boring stuff Hattie and Poppy care about.

'Come on, butthead,' I said to Billie. 'When I get pulled out of school by MI5 and sent to a secret school for geniuses, you are coming with me. And you know the only way you'll qualify for that?'

She sighed. 'Fieldwork! Come on, Watson,' she said to me. 'We must be at our most vigilant!' She made imaginary binoculars with her hands. 'He goes that way!' She pointed down the road. We packed up our bags quickly.

'Let's follow him on the other side of the hedge!' I said.

'He'll never suspect a thing!' Billie crowed. 'Come on, Sam!'

Sam helped us collect our litter, but Hattie grumbled. 'Forget it, I'm not going to follow some stupid man. He's probably going to the pub.'

'Yeah, me neither; we're staying here,' Poppy agreed.

'One of us could go up to him and question him,' I said. 'Find out who he is while the others lie in wait!'

'Indubitably!' That was Billie.

Hattie sighed. 'I'm going to go home. You can come back to mine for dinner if you like,' she said to Poppy, as if she didn't care one way or the other.

'Okay,' said Poppy. I rolled my eyes.

They went in one direction and Billie, me and Sam ran in the other after the man, but stealthily, so he didn't see us. He was pretty tall, and had broad shoulders and brown hair, like Dad. You could tell he was quite muscular. We couldn't tell his age, though. We followed him down the lane to the bench on the green grass triangle in the middle of the village, where the roads intersect. He sat down on it and started to eat something. Suddenly the man looked over his shoulder. 'Hey!'

'Eep!' we squeaked and ducked down. A little way back, Sam hid behind a hedge.

'I can see you!' he called. 'Do you go to school here?' He laughed, shook his head, and turned away from us.

Billie and me were lying flat on the ground. We turned our faces to each other and grinned. Quick as a flash, I said, 'Dibs you go up to him.'

'Gosh darn it!' Billie cried theatrically. She shook her head at me. 'Why, I oughta . . . He's forgotten us now, look: he's a-lookin' at that there pub, wonderin' 'bout a whiskey or suchlike.' She nodded at the pub across the way.

But I felt naughty. 'I dare you to go up to him.'

Billie's always up for a dare, or an adventure. She'll go up to people on my command and start talking to them about the weather, or pretend she's lost something, or ask them why the sky is blue. She makes up elaborate backstories about who she is, why I can't talk to them ('A deaf mute,' she'll say. 'Can you believe the bad luck?'), why we we're out alone ('Running away.' She points to her stomach. 'I'm pregnant, see, and my pa don't approve.'). Most of the time, people believe her too. She can lie all day without stopping, looking someone straight in the eye.

'Well, now,' Billie replied, still in a cowboy accent. 'I surely can't refuse a dare. Then I'd be lily-livered.'

'Darn tootin'!' I yelped. We cackled into the grass. Billie jumped up and went off to talk to the man. I smiled to myself. I love our little games.

She was away for a while. I watched her the entire time, keeping my guard up. Maybe he really was a spy. He put one leg up on the bench and leant on it to talk to her. They were laughing. He showed her something, putting his arm on her shoulder for just a moment. Then she gestured to me, and he nodded. She ran back. I was still on the ground, holding my hands like a telescope. The Billie in my vision got bigger and bigger. When she reached me, she pretended to kick the end of the telescope with her foot, and then jumped on me.

'Gah!' I shrieked. I sat up and pushed her off me. We were laughing loudly. 'What did he say?'

'He's a walker. He wanted to know which way to go on a good walk. I told him to go to the woods.'

'What was he showing you?'

'Some pictures of his nieces 'cause they look like us.'

'Me and you?'

'Yurp. And he gave me some water 'cause I was parched.'

'Hmmph, I'm parched too.'

'He was fiiiiit,' Billie crowed, making the 'i' really long.

'Was he? Isn't he old?'

'Come on, he's basically the same age as Leo.'

'That's true. And I'm marrying Leo, so maybe you'll have to have this walker guy.'

'I think I'm in lurve. *Lurve*, I tell you!'

'Now I wish I'd gone up with you and seen him up close.'

'He said he was married, anyway. But maybe she'll die in an accident.' Billie touched her fingers together and did an evil laugh. 'Mwah-ha-ha-ha!'

'Dastardly,' I agreed.

'Are you guys done?' Sam shouted.

'Come over here and stop being a snozzbucket,' I called. We stood up and put our backpacks on. 'Come on, let's go to the churchyard and plan our devious ways.' We looked over to the bench. The walker was still watching us. We grinned at each other, and whistled at him from far away when we were leaving.

After that, we came home for tea, and then went out again, carrying on with our spy game.

Later – much later – Billie went home through the field. I wanted to go with her a little of the way, and told Sam he had to stay on the path.

'On my own?' he whined.

'Don't be a wuss.'

'I'm not a wuss! Fine, I'll wait. I don't care.'

'Cool. Good.'

'Good,' he said, but he still looked nervous. Sam is scared of lots of things.

I'm glad I left him on the road, though, because me and Billie walked through the wheat a bit (it's taller than us), and played with the predictor. It was nice to have some time alone.

'Pick a number from one to four,' said Billie.

I picked three.

'One-two-three. Pick a colour: red, yellow, green or mauve.'

'Mauve?'

'M-a-u-v-e. Pick a colour: sicky orange, blue, purple or pink.'

'Yuck. Sicky orange.'

'S-i-c-k-y-o-r-a-n-g-e. Hehehe, you got "poophead".'

'Does that mean I am a poophead or I'll marry a poop-head?'

Billie cackled hysterically. 'Dunno. Maybe both?'

I grabbed it off her. 'Let me do you. Pick a number.'

She picked two.

'One-two. Pick a colour: blue, purple, pink or sicky orange.'

'Sicky orange.'

'S-i-c-k-y-o-r-a-n-g-e. Pick a colour: green, mauve, red or yellow.'

'Yellow.'

'Hahahaha, you're going to marry a snot-nosed badger!'

We were laughing loudly, and it echoed around the fields. The wheat was suddenly a blinding gold as the sun got low in the sky and hit it. The sky had no clouds, and was purple-blue, like the bruises on Billie's arms from Chinese burns. I gave Billie the predictor back and she folded it so it didn't get squashed. It's origami.

'Later, alligator,' Billie said, and did a salute.

I waved back. 'In a while, crocodile.'

I turned back and she kept walking ahead. We both made dark paths in the gold, going away from each other, tramping down the wheat.

I retraced my steps to where Sam waited, and we got home at 9.35 p.m.

It is now midnight on Saturday night and I am in my room, sat in the window seat again. I'm trying to read, but I feel too distracted. I keep looking up from the book, out into the blackness over the fields. There must be clouds overhead; you can't even see the stars tonight, but the wind is so warm I have the window open a crack. I wrote up everything we did today, and this week, in my diary, after I'd had a bath and just before the police came. Billie's mum and dad know we write diaries, so the police came to ask me if they could borrow it. They asked me some questions at the kitchen table, and then I gave them it with the key left in the lock.

Billie didn't come home. No one knows where she is.

The black dogs return in my dreams. The four of them move into the den, sniffing around, snapping, and slobbering everywhere. They almost catch my feet in their teeth as I slither out through the tunnel. Why didn't they follow us? In my dream I get to see what they do when we leave. They circle the den on the inside, making sure all of us are gone, and then they stop and wait, more like guard dogs than murderous beasts. I realize they were chasing us out of the den. They are quiet for a minute, but I hear their panting, and then I feel it on my neck. It's hot and tickly, and then it becomes cold. I shiver. I try to turn around to see them, but I'm stuck. It's because I'm unconscious. I'm asleep, and so I can't move my body, but I suddenly know they are in my room, my real room, and one of the dogs is on my back while I lie there. I strain to look over my shoulder, but all I can see is hair. But it's not my own hair. It's the hair from the girl I saw in the den. The black dog has morphed into her. She's lying on my back, and I strain to turn around, and in my dream-that's-not-quite-a-dream I just manage to look over my shoulder at her wild and staring eyes. Suddenly her hand grabs my shoulder, and I squeal at its coldness.

'Thera!' Mum shouts. I open my eyes. 'Thera, wake up!'

'What? Why? What's happened?'

'You're screaming!' She is sat on my bed, and she hugs me tightly.

'Ow! Mum, get off!'

'It's okay, they'll find her. They'll find her, darling.'

'What? They'll find who?'

Mum pushes the hair back from my face and looks at me as if I'm nuts. 'Billie, sweetheart.'

'Oh.' I shake her palm off my head. 'Yeah, I know. She probably just decided to sleep outside under the stars. You know we like to do that.' I pick sleep out of my eyes. 'I wish she'd asked me to stay out with her, though.'

'You know curfew is nine thirty on Saturdays!' Mum snaps.

'That's probably why she didn't ask!' I counter.

'Urgh, Thera,' Mum says, and Dad calls something through the wall that neither of us catch. 'What did you say?' Mum sounds annoyed. She strides out of the room and they start arguing next door.

I scramble through my duvet and do a forwards roll off my bed, so I'm sat by the wall. I retrieve what I need from its hiding place under the bookcase. Billie and me like these books called The Mystery Kids by Fiona Kelly, and they use this trick to help them hear through walls better: you put the open end of a pint glass to the wall you want to listen through, and you put the other end to your ear. It really works. We used it once to listen to Billie's dad, but all he did was order fishing equipment. We made up a story that he was going to use it to garrotte someone.

We wrote it down. Hopefully the police don't find it and think Billie is a terrible person.

I'm still, with the glass pressed to my ear. Mum and Dad's voices sound like they are underwater.

'It could have been Thera,' Mum's voice says. I frown. What could have been Thera?

'Don't say that. What did she say?'

'Something something . . . sleeping out under the stars.'

'. . . might be right.'

'. . . told you I didn't want to move here, near your parents.'

I roll my eyes. Mum's from a city. She doesn't like the country.

'Something something . . . middle of nowhere,' she is saying.

'Can't supervise them all the time.'

'. . . surprised you're alive after your childhood.'

This almost makes me laugh. Dad used to do things like fix up old motorbikes with his friends and then drive them holding onto the handlebars while standing on the seat. That was when he was fourteen! Barely older than me. I cover my mouth so I don't make any noise laughing and then, when I take my hand off it again, I sneeze. Silence.

'Thera, are you listening?'

I take my ear away from the glass, and shout through, 'No!'

There are more arguing sounds, and then Mum opens the door again. I just manage to get back into bed in time.

'Dad is going to drive you and Sam to Nanny and Grandad's this morning so we can help look for Billie.'

'Can't I help look for Billie?'

'No, Thera.'

'But I know everywhere she goes. It makes more sense that I look for her than you do.'

'You told the police all those places last night, didn't you?'

'But—'

'I said no! I'm not having you out there in miles and miles of cornfields!' She yells this part so Dad hears it. She's wrong, though: it's all wheat and barley around our village. I know, because I'm a country kid. Not like Mum.

I grumble. Mum and Dad are always shouting at each other. 'It's not Dad's fault Billie ran off.'

'Thera! Billie didn't . . .' For a second Mum looks stricken. Her mouth is hanging open, like her unfinished sentence.

I frown. 'What?'

'. . . Nothing, sweetheart,' she says. 'Nothing. Just . . . get dressed. Dad's taking you in ten minutes.'

Nanny and Grandad live out on the North Sea coast. Dad drives us fast, with the windows down and rock music on loud. We all sing along to T.Rex and Badfinger and Led Zeppelin. When we get close to the beach, Dad turns the cassette tape off and makes us sing 'Summer Holiday'. Sam is singing loudly and off-key, on the same side of the car as the sun and the sea. He grins at me when he sees me looking at him, showing his gap where he lost a tooth last week. Sam's a bit of a wuss, but he's also the best little brother in the world.

Secretly I am pleased we have been banished to Nan and Grandad's, I think to myself, as we walk around from the car to their house. It's a Victorian house, five storeys tall counting the basement and the attic, and full from top to toe with books. Grandad writes novels and is interested in everything, so he reads all the time. He says he has 'intellectual curiosity', and that I do too, like him. He is a science-fiction writer, and when people ask him about it, he says he writes 'oh, pulp, yarns, pocket fodder'. He has three interests that he writes about a lot: the future, technology and spiritual stuff, like gods, dreams, souls and ESP. He could really help me out today.

Dad unlocks the big black door and calls out, 'Hello! It's me!' Nanny and Grandad are his parents. Dad has six brothers and sisters, but none of them live here any more. Still, me and Sam come round all the time, and Nanny says grandkids are better than your own kids because you get to buy them sweets and not worry about their teeth.

Dad goes down the corridor to the living room, and Sam and me follow him. Did I say every wall at Nanny and Grandad's is covered with books? The corridor is actually really narrow, because Grandad has built bookcases on either side, and they are filled with paperbacks and several big Roman-statue-type heads whose eyes follow us as we walk by. When we squeeze our way into the living room, Nanny is standing where she always stands: in the doorway to the kitchen, holding the teapot. When she sees us she squeals, 'Eeeee!' and runs over to give us big slobbery kisses and pretends to suck the juice out of our skin, so it fills up all the bits in between her wrinkles and she doesn't get old.

After we have finished giggling and being eaten, Dad says, 'Mum, could I have a word?'

Nanny looks at him and nods. 'You kids,' she says in her crackly Nanny voice, 'why don't you make the tea?'

'Okay!' We run through to the kitchen. Grandad likes his tea just so, and lukewarm. Nanny likes hers weaker and hot. Sam and me like ours golden-brown, like that Stranglers song Dad said is about tea. We don't have sugar at home but here we each have two. Nan and Dad are talking quietly in the other room. I'm not listening to them because I'm telling Sam to get the milk and stir the sugar in and stuff, but I can hear them in the background.

'What time are you picking them up tomorrow?' Nan says.

'Eight. Otherwise they won't get to school on time.'

'What did the police say?'

'Nothing much. They something something.'

I concentrate harder.

'. . . we're going to the station, and then I suppose we'll split into teams . . .'

'Did you talk to Paul and Rebecca?'

That's Billie's mum and dad. I don't hear Dad's reply because Sam is clinking the spoon in the cups too much. 'Shh!' I tell him.

He tuts. 'Stop listening!' Sam minds his own business a bit too much, if you ask me. Some people don't want to know anything. I do. I want to see and know everything about the world and my life and what's going on. It's intellectual curiosity, like Grandad says. I listen again, but Dad and Nanny are quiet.

'Well,' Nanny says. 'Have you got time for a cup of tea?'

'I better go, Mum. Frances is waiting for me.'

'Alright. I hope you find her, dear.'

'Love you,' Dad says.

'Love you, darling.'

I look through. They are hugging. 'Bye, Dad,' I say.

He waves. 'Bye, snoop.'

'Hey!' I grumble, but I'm joking. I *was* snooping. I better get better at it so I don't get caught next time.

'Let's have our tea here and then you can put your bags upstairs,' Nan tells us. We have our overnight bags with us.

'I have to take Grandad's tea up,' I say.

'Well, off you go, love,' Nan says. 'He's in his study.'

Grandad's study is upstairs. It's a big room, with small writing desks in all four corners. There is a light over each desk and a different-sized chair in front of it. There is also a big table in the middle of the room, covered with the books Grandad is currently reading, all open. The windows are long and large, with a balcony outside, but the room is dark because of the books on all the walls. When I push open the door with my toes, Grandad is sat hunched over the desk in the far-left corner, the one with the gold-and-green lamp.

'Aha,' he says, without looking up. I can hear the whisper-scrawl of his pencil on paper. It doesn't stop while he talks.

'Could that be one of my favourite grandchildren, bearing Indian tea?'

'It could!' I say, and pad over quietly in my socks. I put the cup down next to him, give him a kiss, and watch him working.

'Just one moment, Thera,' he says. 'Just finishing my thought . . . There we are.' He looks up. 'How is my clever girl?'

'Good.'

'I hear your friend has gone missing.'

'She's run off.'

'Ah.'

I chew my lip. 'Without me.'

Grandad nods. 'I think, in time, it will become evident that this indiscretion was not intentional on the part of your friend.'

'Billie.'

'Yes. Billie.'

I think for a moment and then I drag a chair over from the big table and sit on it. 'Grandaaaaad?'

He smiles. 'Do I detect in the tone of your voice that a favour is about to be requested?'

'Well, I had this dream.' I look at him seriously. 'And I don't know what it means.'

'I should think we can be of assistance.' Grandad puts down his pencil and beckons me to follow him to a dark corner of his study. He sits in an armchair there before another of the desks, and pulls out a book on dreams. 'What are we looking up?'

'Black dogs. Savage ones.'

Grandad leafs through the book.

'This tome suggests a dog is a symbol of protection. "The dream is warning you,"' he reads. '"You should attempt to protect someone or something in your life."'

'Hmm.'

'Was there anything else in your dream?'

'Er, cold hands?'

'Hands! Hands . . .' he murmurs, turning the pages. 'Ah. "Hands are rarely dreamt of, and their presence in a dream has a strong significance. They are a sign of taking control of our own fate, and of making an impact through our actions on another, or the world at large." Interesting. What was this dream?'

'I dreamt of a dog that changed into a girl.'

'My goodness. Not a prophetic dream, then.'

'Why not?'

'I would imagine even modern technology would find such a feat unachievable. Maybe putting a dog's heart in a young woman, although I believe it's thought pig hearts are more practical for the purpose.'

'Mm, yeah. It was a ghostly girl,' I add. 'And the dogs are from real life.'

'Are they?'

'They came forth from the spirit world and barked at us when we were using the Ouija board. In the woods on Friday.'

'Oh dear. Well, perhaps those dogs were warning you off playing with Ouija. It might not be the best idea in the hands of one so imaginative.' Grandad reaches past me and picks up a box on the shelf near my head. 'Still, you might enjoy looking at these, if you have taken an interest in the spirit world.'

'What are they?'

'These are a set of tarot painted by Lady Frieda Harris and designed by Aleister Crowley himself.'

'The dark-magic guy?'

'The occultist, yes.'

'They mentioned him on *Eerie, Indiana*.'

'I take it that's a children's television show?'

'Yeah. What do they do?'

'They can be read, to predict your future. Would you like me to read yours?'

I reach out and touch the pack, and suddenly I feel cold. I shiver. 'No. Not now. I better get back to my tea.'

'And I had best return to my work. Come back later if you need anything. And stop poking around in the nether-world. You never know what spirits you might disturb.'

'Got it.' I shiver again, and run out.

We spent all day playing with Nanny, and went into town to spend our pocket money. Me and Sam bought Tooty Frooties and ate them after tea, then tramped up the stairs to bed at 9 p.m. There are thirty-six steps in all, and Nanny says they keep her and Grandad healthy. They are basically like doing a Jane Fonda video. Bums of steel. Mum has that one.

Our bedroom is on the third floor and looks out over the main road. There are two single beds in here; Sam's is by the door and mine is closest to the window. Outside the glass is the main road. I like the sound of the cars going by all night, but the cries of the foxes scare Sam. I press my hands to the glass and look out. The sun has gone down, and the last birds are settling on the chimney pots on the houses opposite. I realize Dad hasn't called, which means they still haven't found Billie. Which is a long time for her to be away from home, even for someone as resourceful and fearless as she is.

'Don't fall out,' Sam says softly from his bed. He has climbed on it and is standing, looking at the books. We always pick out a book to read here, last thing at night. I know what I want to read tonight. I go into the next room. There are three bedrooms up on this floor, which

Dad and his brothers and sisters used to sleep in when they were little. Uncle Tony's bedroom has Star Wars toys from the seventies on the shelf above the radiator, as well as little ornament dogs and porcelain people and a smiley golliwog. The bookshelves in here are mostly filled with books about astronomy, because it's something Grandad writes about a lot. He has written ten books, and they sell pretty well, but he's not ginormously rich. It's very hard to be ginormously rich if you don't sell out, Grandad says. He was a teacher at the local college, but he retired when I was born because Mum and Dad had to go back to work very quickly, and Nan and Grandad babysat me every day for three years (except weekends), until Sam was born. That's why I love going to Nan and Grandad's so much: I practically grew up here. I love helping Nan flour fish, which I used to do as a kid. I love the plastic mats we eat on, and the woolly green tablecloth, and luncheon meat, and spam and beans and chips. I love the book-paper mustiness that the whole house smells of. I love the scratchiness of old blue and green book spines from the twenties and thirties and forties on my fingertips. Some-times I want to make a den out of books and disappear in it. Sam and me think it's funny that behind the books on the bookshelves in our room there is another row of books, like maybe if you kept pulling books out the rows would go on forever and ever.

Sometimes I wish I still lived here with Nanny and Grandad, and I didn't have to be eleven, which is almost a whole decade older than three, and much more grown-up. When you're eleven you have responsibilities. I have a responsibility to Sam, and Billie. It was my idea to use the Ouija board. Maybe Billie hasn't run away for fun. Maybe I conjured the black dogs and they came back for Billie and chased her away. Maybe she's lost.

Uncle Tony's teddies sit together on the bed. I know when I go out again they will start playing. I don't tell Hattie or Poppy that I believe these things, but Billie believes them too. She's not dead inside like Hattie.

I walk to the little staircase in the corner, and go up to the attic room, crouching so I don't hit my head on the eaves. This is the darkest room in the house, with the darkest books in it: the occult shelves. There is *Cunningham's Encyclopedia of Magical Herbs*, *Magic in Herbs* by Leonie de Sounin, *Myths and Symbols in Pagan Europe* by H. R. Ellis Davidson. I move my finger slowly across the spines, and even though I haven't looked that far ahead yet, it stops on the book I was looking for, *Ouija: The Most Dangerous Game* by Stoker Hunt. I remember getting it out last October, when we first got the Ouija board. I never read it, but now I will. I move forward to get it and bonk my head on a beam.

'Ouch!' I say, and then stop myself, and breathe quietly, listening. The room is icy cold. I hear a creaking from behind me, like a footstep. It's just the wind, I tell myself, but then there is another creak. I try and concentrate on what I'm doing. I notice the title of the book is in red lettering, like on the paper predictor me and Billie were using yesterday. My finger is shaking. There is another creak.

'Thera! Bedtime!' Nan calls.

I jump, turn to the door and bellow, 'Coming!' I grab the book and run downstairs. I don't dare glance back to see if there is anyone behind me, in the dark corner by the dirty round window, but I feel the presence of that cold, ghostly girl.

By Monday morning, Billie has been missing for thirty-six hours. Mum calls and tells me that she and Dad have decided we should stay at Nanny and Grandad's and not go to school while Billie is missing. We get in a row. I tell her I would have found Billie by now.

We spend the day in Cleethorpes, at the seaside with Nan.

At teatime, me and Sam have just sat down to eat when the doorbell rings. Mum doesn't have a key, only Dad does.

'Good evening, Frances, love,' Nan says throatily. She has never smoked, so I don't know why her voice is like that. It's Grandad that smokes. He has a cigar in the evening in front of *Match of the Day*. His intellectual curiosity also extends to football and horse racing, so he's in front of the races when Mum comes in.

'Hello, Betty. Oh, you've fed them.'

'Yes, well, it's quite late, and Arthur and I still have to eat afterwards.'

Nan and Grandad are going to have a pie out the freezer, but Sam and me got to have our favourite: luncheon meat, chips and beans!

'I helped cut the chips,' Sam says.

'How was your day?' Nanny says, but she says it in a funny way, with her eyes really wide, and nodding.

Mum puts her big black handbag on the arm of the sofa and hugs both me and Sam really tightly. 'Um, no, Betty, nothing,' she says finally. 'Do you want to talk in the . . . ?'

Nanny follows Mum into the kitchen. Mum is in her business clothes: a cream blouse, a black skirt and black shoes with small, chunky heels. My mummy is so beautiful, with a wide smile, big lips, medium-length brown hair and the same blue eyes as me. When she's upset you can tell because her whole face looks like it's being pulled downwards by tiny fairy hands. Mostly it's Dad that upsets her, because he yells. Then her bottom lip bulges out like a fish's lip. Tonight, her eye make-up is falling into the bags under her eyes in tiny pieces, like she's smudged it, or has been crying. With that thought, I leap up from the table.

'Thera!' Sam yelps, because I knock his knife on the floor.

'Mum?' I say, down the step into the kitchen. Mum and Nan look at me like I've interrupted them. 'There isn't something you know that you're not telling us, is there?'

'No.' She hesitates. 'If you haven't finished eating, you shouldn't get down from the table without asking, should you?'

'Don't change the subject! Are you lying to me? Is it about Billie?'

'Thera, sweetie, not now,' Mum says. 'Please.'

'Are you lying?' I say firmly.

Grandad says I have a very developed sense of right and

wrong. My theory is that you should be like Knights of the Round Table. This means you should be honest, loyal, trustworthy, kind, chivalrous, courageous, brave, tough, strong, righteous and true. You should never lie, especially to your family.

'Mum.' I narrow my eyes.

'I'm not lying,' she says. 'Now, *get back to the table.*'

They shut the door and talk really quietly in the kitchen. Nan makes her a cup of coffee, and we drive home at eight o'clock.

When we reach the limits of our village it's nine, but still bright. Our village is quite small, with only five hundred people in it, and it sits in a valley surrounded by fields. There is a police car on the side of the road, and bluc-and-white tape across a mud track that leads down to the fields. I have been leaning against the window, but I sit up, and so does Sam. There are police walking briskly along the main road. We turn in to our close and watch the police through the back window. For a moment, I think I see Billie, dead and in the arms of a police officer.

It's a trick of my eyes, of course. It's just a policewoman standing in front of a road sign. I shake my head hard, so the thought goes out of it. 'Billie's just got lost somewhere, that's all,' I say in my head. She's not dead.

Sam looks like he is about to cry and I take his hand. He holds on tight, and as we walk into the house together, I take Mum's hand too. Both of them squeeze me really tight, and I feel all the strength from deep inside me coming into the fibres of my muscles and quickening my blood to help me protect my family, if anyone should try to hurt them.

'Thera, Hattie is on the phone!' Mum calls up the stairs. She doesn't have to yell like Nan when she calls upstairs; our house is much smaller. I am just brushing the knots out my hair after my bath, so I come out of my room in my pajamas and dressing gown and see she has left the phone on the stairs with the cord poking through the bannister. I sit down with my back to the wall and my feet pressed against the other side of the stairs, and pick up the receiver.

'Hello?'

'I just saw on telly that Billie is missing.' Hattie sounds muffled.

'Yeah . . .' I pick my nails worriedly. Hattie doesn't say anything, just leaves a gap. 'Er, so . . . what's up?'

'So what happened on Saturday night?'

'Nothing! I left her in the field and me and Sam went home.'

'But Billie didn't,' she says, and I realize she sounds muffled because she's crying.

'Well.' I slump down the wall, unsure of what to say. 'No.'

Hattie sniffs. 'I asked Mum about it, and she said the police called last night and asked her questions about Billie. They asked who last saw her. She said you, because when I came in I told her me and Poppy left you guys together. If you did anything to her, I'll tell everyone.'

'What? Of course I didn't do anything to her! She's my best, true, forever friend!'

'You're a weirdo. A freak. You're jealous of her.'

'No, I'm not!'

'Yes, you are.'

'Am not!'

'I told Mum about that man. She told the police about him. Billie's mum is really worried about him.'

'What man?'

'The man you made Billie follow.'

'I didn't make her follow him. She wanted to.'

'You're always making Billie do things. Maybe you made her disappear!'

'Of course I didn't!' I hiss, my cheeks hot. 'You're so mean, Hattie!'

'There's something you're not telling me,' Hattie says, sobbing. She sounds crazy.

'Believe what you want to believe,' I say, and I lean through the bannister and put the phone back on the hook. I sit on the stairs for a while, kneading my feet into the carpet. The living room is quiet. Probably Mum and Dad were listening in. Hattie makes everything worse, always. But what if she's right? Two tears escape my eyes. What if something has happened to Billie?

And what if it's because of me?

At school I go around in a gang of four, with Billie, Hattie and Poppy. Our school has eighty-seven pupils, and there are only eleven of us in the top year, Year Six. This is our last year before we move up to the big school, in the town of Eastcastle, ten miles away. It's a long time since we started here as four year olds, but me and Billie have been best, true, forever friends the whole time. Hattie and Poppy are only our best friends, but most of the time Hattie isn't very friendly at all. Mum says her parents are going through a d-i-v-o-r-c-e so we should cut her some slack, even though she's such a massive bumhead some-times I want to punch her.

Things our gang has in common:

We love the Spice Girls
We all have Nano Pets
We like to sing and dance
We like to play imaginary games

We each have phrases that describe us. Hattie's phrase is 'Fabulous' because she heard it on telly and she thinks it suits her (it doesn't). Poppy's phrase is 'Let's eat sweeties!' She's really skinny but her teeth are rotten and she already has a filling. I'm the best at imagining and I come up with all our games, so my phrase is 'Let's pretend . . .' Hattie and Poppy aren't that great at making things up, but it's mine and Billie's favourite thing to do. Billie's phrase is 'Totally nutso'.

Billie is never mean, but Hattie and Poppy are. It's mostly Hattie, and Poppy just copies her because they are supposed to be best, true, forever friends, but Hattie really wants to be BTF friends with Billie. Honestly, I think Hattie wishes I was dead, so she could be friends with Billie without me. She does her best to make me feel rubbish, and she basically succeeds every day. I'm not good at being mean with words like Hattie is. Mostly I just want to smack her, but Dad says violence is never the answer.

We are doing maths right now. It's Tuesday, and Billie is still missing. Even though Mrs Adamson likes Billie best, she hasn't said anything about her not being in school. She has already told everyone what exercises to do, so we are supposed to be doing them, but Hattie is playing with her Nano Pet and whispering to Poppy about me, and Mrs A isn't stopping her because Hattie was crying earlier. I wish I could play with my Nano instead of doing maths. I think it was hungry when I left it this morning.

It only takes a week to get a Nano to three years old (this is when they are successfully grown up and you get a new one on the screen), but since Mum has banned me from taking my Nano Pet to school, mine usually die early. You have to feed them regularly and clean their world because otherwise it becomes overrun with poo and they croak. My fourth Nano baby is two years old right now but here is my list of dead Nanos:

> BOY – Jess – 0 yrs – *squashed (sat on in car)*
> GIRL – Alex Mack – 0 yrs – *died of hunger*
> GIRL – Lucy – 3 yrs – *grown up! Didn't die!*
> BOY – B – 2 yrs – *died of being overrun with poo*
> Right now, I have:
> GIRL – Elle – 2 yrs – *hasn't died yet*

I am sat on a table on my own, working through the maths textbook. Even though my table is next to Hattie and Poppy, and the boys in our year, they aren't talking to me because I'm in a higher maths set than them. There's only me in my maths set, so I have to work alone every lesson. I quite like finding ingenious ways to solve maths questions and being able to race through the book, but I feel left out when they're all talking and laughing without me.

I am very smart. People are always saying this like it's praise.

'Thera memorized four books of nursery rhymes, each with a hundred rhymes in, and one whole book about a field mouse, by the time she was two years old.'

'Thera did the SATs exam for thirteen-year-olds, as well as the one for eleven-year-olds. She also got ninety-seven per cent and ninety-nine per cent in the eleven-plus practice exams, and they told us her IQ was a hundred and sixty-seven, and she was scoring the same marks as the average seventeen-year-old.'

'Thera is so good at maths, she is in the top maths group *all on her own.*'

In reality, more people hate me because I am smart than like me. Especially people my age. They don't like it when I have finished all the work and I sit there and try to look busy, but Mrs Adamson notices and says, 'Thera's done everything. Haven't you all finished yet? Tut-tut, better get on with it, no talking', or when I finish so early she makes me stand up and walk about the classroom, correcting other people's spelling and full stops and commas. Hattie can barely write a sentence without making a mistake. She doesn't like me to point this out, but Mrs Adamson sends me over to help her, so I have to correct Hattie or Mrs Adamson will tell me off for not doing it, and then Hattie is incredibly mean to me at lunchtime. Sometimes I think even Mrs Adamson doesn't like me being smart. There are days when I put my hand up in class over and over again, and she never picks me. Eventually I keep my hand down, and then she will say, 'Thera, don't you know the answer?'

Billie likes that I'm smart. She likes all the games I make up. She likes when we make intricate maps and designs for our clubhouses, which we have several of throughout the village. We are sidekicks. She's Pinky, I'm the Brain. We're a team and we complement each other, to the point where one of us doesn't seem right without the other. I don't feel very good today, because usually Billie is sat right there, in the purple chair, making faces at me across the classroom. I can see her now, her cheeks puffed out. She pretends to float away like a helium balloon. I giggle. And then my mouth drops open because, instead of Billie, sat in her seat is another, totally different, girl. She's our age too, with blonde-brown hair and paler skin than I've ever seen. I blink, and when I open my eyes again she is gone. I look around. Hattie and Poppy are talking like nothing has happened. The boys are snorting with laughter over something. Did that happen? I rub my eyes. 'Billie?' I murmur.

Suddenly everyone turns to look at me, including Mrs A. They have all gone silent. I wonder if they heard me.

'Thera? Thera Wilde?'

At the door there are two police officers, a man and a woman. They are wearing neon-yellow jackets over black uniforms, and both are holding their hats. The lady police officer is older and she has curly hair. The man is about Dad's or Mrs Adamson's age (Dad is thirty-four) and he is saying my name like a question to Mrs Adamson, but the woman is looking straight at me. I saw her on the road yesterday and she looked at me the same way, like a hawk, with golden eyes. When I look right at her now she blinks, and then nods at me. I look down quickly and remember Hattie on the phone last night: 'There's something you're not telling me.'

'Leave your work for now, Thera,' Mrs Adamson says.

'But it's almost break time,' I say, not getting up.

'I can pack everything into your reading folder and bring it to you.' She smiles at me sadly, her eyes watery. She cried earlier, while she was hugging Hattie. 'Go on.'

I stand up slowly. I make the mistake of looking across to Hattie's table, where she is smirking at me and looking tearful at the same time. She looks away from me quickly and whispers something to Poppy. I tuck my chair in and walk over to the police. The man goes out the door first and I follow him, and then the lady is behind me, as if she is stopping me from running away. There is another policeman in the hallway. Mr Kent is standing by the staffroom door, holding it open. He's our headmaster. He speaks really softly, like Kaa the snake from *The Jungle Book*. He gives me and Billie the creeps.

'Thera,' he says, and puts his hand on my back, then sits down next to me. He makes me feel worse, poorly in my tummy, because of his hand on my back and his stupid, weird smile.

'Did . . . did you find Billie?' I say. It comes out a whisper.

'Not yet,' the policewoman says. 'Thera, I'm Detective Georgina Waters. You can call me Georgie. You are Thera Wilde?'

I nod. 'My name is Thera Leigh Wilde and I'm eleven years, three months, five days, seventeen hours and about thirty-two minutes old.'

She sits down and leans in towards me. 'And do you know Billie Brooke?'

Do I know Billie Brooke? Do I *know* Billie? How am I supposed to answer that?

Billie May Brooke and me have been best, true, forever friends since we were in the same antenatal class in our mums' tums when we were minus-six months old. We probably communicated in dot-dot-dot, dash-dash-dash (i.e. Morse code) through their womb walls. Billie's mum and dad moved back to here from London before she was born because both her grandparents live here, in East-castle, and they thought they might help with babysitting.

I was born a month earlier than Billie, on the first of April. Dad says because I was born on April Fool's Day, they must have sent a joke baby, and one day they will send the real one, and I'll have to go live on my own in a tent in the woods. He's just kidding, though. He tickles me while he says this. Billie was born on the first of May. I arrived early and she arrived late. This still happens.

For a few years after we were born we didn't see each other much, because tiny babies can't really have friends because they don't do anything. The first photo I have of us is from just after this time. It was Bonfire Night when we were three and a half, and I am standing up and looking into the camera, holding a toffee apple. Billie is crouching down on the left of the photo, picking up some snow, because it was a really cold November. It's funny because, even though we are really little, we totally look like us, and our faces and expressions look the same. Billie is talking, saying something about what we are doing, absorbed in the task like she always is when we play games, with her mouth open and her eyes looking down. I am more aware of what is going on around us than Billie, which is still true. I have noticed someone is taking a picture of us, and I am looking at the camera, and my face is white because of the flash, and my eyes are big and round. We are both in wellies and warm, colourful clothes and bobble hats. I think I can remember this moment, because the toffee apple was sticky and stuck to my hands, and I'm sure we were talking about putting snowballs down people's pants as we ran around the fireworks display, while everyone was looking up at the sky.

When we were three, Billie's mum and dad finally moved into their house now, which is a long nineteen-fifties bungalow with loads of light, in the middle of the fields on the outskirts of the village. In the living room, there is a glass wall and it goes up into a triangle at the top, and they have no attic, just the ceiling. Billie's mum and dad are a lot older than mine. They met each other when they were already old, almost forty, and they had to get the doctor's help to get pregnant with Billie. She's their miracle baby. Then they both retired when they moved back here so they could spend as much time with Billie as possible. Her dad was an electrician and made megamoney when they lived in London, and her mum used to be an interior designer. She did loads of famous people's houses, like Chris Evans's from *The Big Breakfast* and Stephen from Boyzone. She designed the inside of the house they have now, and the workers worked on it for almost three years while they lived in Eastcastle. The people who built it were from Yorkshire, and they had lost all their money in the eighties. They tore everything out of the house and sold all their things, and then they sold the house to a developer, but then that developer lost their money in a scam, so they left the house to ruin and it got all damp. Billie's mum and dad got it cheap because it needed lots of work. I have only ever seen it when it has looked really cool. Everything in it is from the fifties, apart from the telly, Billie's stuff and all the rubbish in Billie's mum and dad's bedroom, which is a total mess. On Billie's eighth birthday we played hide-and-seek, and me and Billie hid in there because Billie's dad said it was impossible to find anything in there. No one found us and they were searching for ages. We made a tent out of a shirt (Billie's dad is the tallest man I've ever met, and also quite wide) and ate Mini Rolls underneath it.

Once they had moved to the village, Billie's mum and dad would leave Billie at my house when they went to the shops, and when my mum and dad went out they left me at Billie's. Sometimes all our parents went out for meals together, and Billie's nanny and grandad would come over to her house and babysit Billie and me, or my nanny would come to ours and babysit. Then Sam came along, and my mum stayed at home for a year because Dad and Mum had good enough jobs by then, and after that year me and Billie started at playgroup. That's where we met Hattie and

Poppy. At playgroup we liked to play a lot outside, in the big tractor tyre, and pretend we were in a sinking ship and we had to bail out. We also played inside, in the little house that was made of big plastic bricks. I wet myself next to it once because I was too embarrassed to ask the teacher if I could go to the toilet. Billie also wet herself once at playgroup, but afterwards she just stood there with her legs spread wide apart, laughing her head off. 'Sploosh!' she kept saying, which was the noise it had made, and then laughing so hysterically that tears started to come down her cheeks, her legs gave way and she had to sit down in the puddle of her own wee, which she thought was even funnier.

We played dolls in the brick house. We liked the black and the Asian baby dolls, because they were the prettiest. We made a plan that, when we grow up, Billie is going to adopt an Asian baby and I'm going to adopt a black one. We're not going to have boyfriends, because boys are boring (apart from Sam) and just trump all the time (including Sam) or come up to us when we're playing and kick us and run away laughing. Mrs Adamson says this is because they fancy us (but I know she means they fancy Billie).

Hattie was already mean in playgroup, but no matter how mean Hattie was to me, Billie would never join in. She would just say, 'Come on, Thera, let's go and tuck the children in', like nothing bad was happening, and we would go and tuck in Denise and Melanie, which is what we called the dolls.

I remember how, on the first day of primary school, Billie was so scared she hid behind her mum the whole morning, until her mum said, 'Billie, this is getting ridiculous', and left at lunchtime. Later, Billie made a joke out of it, but I was the only one who she admitted to that she actually had been scared, and I promised I'd never tell.

I remember how she liked eating bees when she was about five, and you could see the little legs falling out the sides of her mouth, and her mum used to scream when she saw her do it, but she never got stung, not once.

I remember when Ken and Paul got married and we left them in their honeymoon bed, and Billie's mum found them and Billie said, 'What? They're making a baby. You love babies.'

I remember when we made our cookery show, *Baking with Barbary Apes*, because we had seen them on the television and Billie couldn't stop laughing because we had to pretend to be screaming monkeys and tell recipes to the video camera, like 'Eeeee! Eeeee! Oo-oo-aa-aa!' meant 'Weigh two hundred grams of sugar and add it to the butter', and she had eaten loads of Victoria sponge cake batter and she had some in her mouth while she was screaming instructions about what temperature to preheat the oven to, and then she started choking on the batter because she was laughing so much, and then she stopped choking and was sick all down herself and still couldn't stop laughing.

I remember when we did our eleven-plus exams, which is the test you do to see whether you can go to the good school or the bad one, and she was so nervous she had to take three toilet breaks, and one of the questions was

'Where on this chart does the foetus reach peak growth?' and Billie realized afterwards she had written 'No'.

I remember when we went to see the big school (the good one, which we both got into even with all the toilet breaks), and a boy laughed at me (we still don't know why), and even though he was like six feet tall, Billie turned back over her shoulder and yelled, 'Hey! Why does your face look like a bum?' and then burst out laughing, and I had to grab her and pull her into a run, because otherwise he would have caught us and beaten us up, and probably they wouldn't have let us go to the good school because they would think we were ruffians.

We go over to each other's houses at least once a week on schooldays and play together every weekend. Most weekends we also have a sleepover. We do art club and French club together, and we have been to see Tattershall Castle, Bolingbroke Castle and the London Dungeon in the last year, and we have the same T-shirt from the London Dungeon (on that visit we decided to try to contact ghosts, but we didn't successfully do it until the black dogs incident). Next term, when we are at the big school, we are going to do kung fu together in Eastcastle with a man called Gert, who Billie's dad says is a black belt.

Last year we both stabbed ourselves in the little finger so we could mush our blood together and be tied together for life. We agreed that, even if we had an infectious disease in our blood, it would be better if the both of us had it because then we would be shunned by society together.

Billie likes angel pudding, Australian accents, the tiniest orange in the bowl, playing conkers, her red yo-yo better than the green one, Um Bongo, monkey nuts, monkeys, pandas, the Secret Seven series by Enid Blyton, poo jokes, limericks, brown sugar better than white sugar, and Opal Fruits better than Fruit Pastilles. Purple is her favourite colour, she fancies Slater from *Saved by the Bell* and Randy from *Home Improvement* (I fancy Zack from *Saved by the Bell* and Brad from *Home Improvement*), her favourite book is *Black Beauty*, her favourite telly show is *Ren & Stimpy* (mine is *Clarissa Explains It All*), her favourite band is Hanson and her favourite food is blue Smarties. Ask me anything. Ask me literally any question about Billie, and I will be able to answer it, and if you asked her if I was right, she would say I *always* would be.

If I don't know Billie May Brooke, no one ever will.

I end up not talking for a few seconds while I'm thinking about this, and Georgie clears her throat. 'Your mum and dad tell us you're Billie's best friend,' she says. 'You remember you spoke about her to the police who came to see you on Saturday night?'

'Best, true, forever friend. Hattie and Poppy are Billie's best friends, but Billie and me are best, true, forever friends.'

The policeman smiles like I am joking, but Georgie doesn't.

'How long have you been best, true, forever friends?' she asks.

'Since we were babies.'

'And what's Billie like? How would you describe her personality?'

I chew my lip and then blurt out, 'Funny, bubbly and happy-go-lucky.'

'You must have lots of fun together. What does she like to do?'

'Play pretend games and draw. And listen to music. We like the Spice Girls.'

'Do you have any ideas about where she might be?'

'We always said we would run away to London and start a pop group.'

'You think she's run away?'

'Why else wouldn't she come home?' I hesitate. 'But . . .'

'But what, Thera?'

'Well . . . if she had run away, I don't see why she would have run away without me. We do everything together. I could understand if she was mad at me, but . . .' I stutter. I feel like I have to convince Georgie that we weren't arguing, she's glaring at me so hard. 'But we never fight, ever, and anyway, she was fine when I left her.'

'Was she?'

I nod. 'Yeah, totally. We were laughing. We were playing with the predictor, and—'

'What's a predictor, Thera?'

'Um. A bit of paper that tells you who you're going to marry.'

Georgie nods. 'We read about that in your diary. Can you show us?'

I pick up a piece of paper off the coffee table between us and tear it into a square, wetting the fold with spit. 'Billie's better at it,' I mumble, but I make her a predictor, folding the paper into a kite, then squishing it up into the right shape. 'And then you write the numbers and names on here.'

'Ah, yes,' she says quietly. 'I remember these.'

There are some quick footsteps outside the room. I hear a man's voice. 'Oh, Mrs—'

'Where is Detective Waters? They told me she was here.

She's in charge of the search and rescue and she isn't even out there fucking searching!'

'She's interviewing the girl who was with—'

'Do you people understand an eleven-year-old has gone missing? Every hour, every minute, something could—'

There are the sounds of footsteps dancing around other footsteps, and Billie's mum opens the door of the office. 'Georgina,' she says, looking at Georgie. Then Billie's mum looks at me. Her eyes widen like her eyeballs might fall out of her head. 'Thera!'

Georgie immediately goes out the door, and Billie's mum backs away, but the door is still open and I can hear what they are saying.

'Why are you interviewing her? I thought you interviewed her the night Billie disappeared? Do you have new evidence?'

'I'm not at liberty to say.'

'*Why?*' Billie's mum snaps. Then she says, as if she has suddenly thought of it, 'The police at the quarry said you had her diary. Did you find anything in it?'

'You shouldn't have been told about that, now—'

'I'm her *mother*!'

'Mrs Brooke' – Georgie's voice becomes steely – 'if you accost me like this, I can't do my work, and as you pointed out, time is slipping away from us.'

There is a silence.

When Billie's mum speaks again, she is just murmuring. I can barely hear her. 'Are you asking her about that man?'

'Rebecca,' Georgie says, calmer now too. 'I'll have to

report anything you say in Thera's presence to her parents—'

'Billie is missing!' Billie's mum snaps again, but this time it's different. This time it's more sad than angry. 'My Billie has been *missing for three nights*. She is *eleven years old*. Do you think I care that you'll *report* what I say to Frances? This investigation is . . . When you move to the middle of nowhere you think you'll never need the police and then – oh *god*!' She starts gasping loudly, like she can't breathe. 'Oh god, help me. Billie. Where is my baby? Billie . . .' She moans. I look at Mr Kent and the policeman. Billie's mum is crying. They sit there. Why aren't they doing anything? Billie's mum is right. They are useless.

'We're doing everything we can,' Georgie says.

'What did Thera say?' Billie's mum says, and then she adds, 'This could have happened to Thera, couldn't it? They were there together. If she hadn't dared my daughter . . . if she hadn't made her go up to that man . . .'

'Rebecca, you're in shock. You don't know what you're saying.'

'She has always been pushy. Bossing Billie around,' Billie's mum says. 'If it's her fault, I want to know, Georgina. She made my daughter follow him. She made her go up and talk to that pervert. Get her to tell you what happened. Ask her his name, for Christ's sake. Just do your job and ask her!' Billie's mum is shrieking now, and it's like her words have so much anger in them, the weight of it all has broken her voice. I'm sweating in my armpits, in my hairline.

'Officer Jones!' Georgie snaps, and the young police-man stands up and runs out.

'Don't touch me – don't fucking touch me,' Billie's mum growls. I feel sick and dizzy. Everything sounds like I am underwater, and my cheeks are burning.

I swallow down the sick. 'What pervert?' I must have said it quietly, because I barely hear myself, but Mr Kent turns to me. He puts his hand on my leg, trying to keep me sat down, but when he touches me I jump. Georgie and the young policeman stand in the doorway and look at us both weirdly. I address Georgie: '*What pervert?*'

Georgie comes back in the room, alone, and shuts the door. She is mad at me now. I realize she was only pretending to like me before. 'Thera, I need to ask you about your diary.'

It's my fault, Billie's mum said. My fault Billie went missing. It's true, it was my game to follow the walker. I make up all our games. If I hadn't dared Billie, if I hadn't thought it would be funny, maybe she would still be here. It was just a joke! That must be why they're here, questioning me. Because the pervert took Billie, and he's keeping her somewhere, and it's my fault. Maybe he drove her for miles and when he was done with her she didn't know where she was. Maybe he has her tied up somewhere.

'I'm sorry,' I blurt out.

'It's okay,' she says, but she says it snappily, like she doesn't mean it. 'You said in your diary that you met a man, someone who was out walking?'

I try to hold back the tears so I can be helpful for Billie. 'Is . . . is he a pervert?'

She holds her hand up. 'Let's not get ahead of ourselves. I just want to know if you remember anything more about him. What he looked like? How old he was? If he gave you a name?'

'No, he didn't tell Billie his name. At least, she didn't say he did. He looked older, but good-looking, so maybe about Leo DiCaprio's age.' I try to remember. 'He had stubble and a green jacket and big boots. And Billie said he had a wallet. But she said he was really nice!'

'I remember in your diary you said he showed you pictures of his nieces?'

'No, he showed Billie the pictures, because he said they looked like us.'

'Did he tell Billie their names?'

I shake my head.

'Can you remember anything else? Did he look like he was out walking?'

'I guess. I think he was wearing a greyish-black T-shirt and blue jeans. And the green jacket was light, because it was hot, and had a brown collar.'

'That's very observant of you,' Georgie says, almost suspiciously.

My cheeks are hot. 'We thought he might be a spy. We followed him for a while.'

'Through the village? Where?'

'From the school to the grass triangle at the crossroads near Brackerby Lane. He sat on the bench.'

'Good. That's very clever that you remember all of that, Thera,' Georgie says, but I figure she really thinks I'm stupid, because I introduced Billie to a pervert. I fight the tears back and try to keep my face really still.

'Was he carrying anything else?'

'Um, I think he had a sandwich.'

'Was it from a shop? Was it in plastic, or tinfoil perhaps?'

'I . . . I don't remember. I didn't see.'

'Okay, that'll be all for now. Thanks, Thera.' Georgie nods at Mr Kent. 'Thank you.'

'Not at all,' he says. 'If there's anything we can do . . .' Because I've been worried, I'd almost forgotten Mr Kent was there, but now I realize he has heard everything. That means soon Mrs Adamson will know too, and I won't be able to look her in the eye, at least until Billie escapes from the pervert.

Mrs A will probably say something in class. Sometimes Mrs A says things that are embarrassing, like when Hattie got her bra and Mrs Adamson commented on it, and said she didn't really have a chest yet but she supposed it was good practice, and young girls were growing up so fast these days. The rest of us don't have bras yet. When that happened, I could see Hattie was upset and I felt sorry for her, even though she makes me feel upset all the time. It was a mean thing for Mrs A to say. She can be mean like that sometimes. Another time, Poppy got her hair cut and it looked really nice, and Mrs A said she preferred it the old way and this way was too mature. If Mrs A says something in class about the pervert, then Hattie will know the police think it's my fault. Her meanness to me will be vindicated. Hattie will love that. She'll tell everyone in the whole world, ever.

Mr Kent lets me go to the toilets, and I sit down on the seat and let my tears out silently, wiping them into the cuffs of my sleeves. I really hope nothing bad has happened to Billie. She's incredibly brave and tough and feisty, more so than any other girl I know our age. Except me, of course. We're equals. Billie has got gumption. I think if someone attacked her, she'd just say, 'Well, I won't stand for that nonsense, you poopsicle!' Then she'd pretend to fence them, and they would find it so weird they would just leave her alone. Or she would give them a huge boot in the head.

Nothing really bad could ever happen to her. Even if a pervert grabbed her, I know she would fight him off and run and hide. Maybe that's what she's doing. She's hiding somewhere, and she's waiting for him to leave the area, and then she'll come out. Billie's not book-smart like me, but she's street-smart. Suddenly I remember something else, so I run out of the loos back to the hall. Luckily Georgie is still there, talking to Mr Kent. 'Have you found Billie's bag?' I ask her.

'Her bag?' Georgie says. 'Billie had a bag with her when she disappeared?'

'Yeah, she had a rucksack with Mickey Mouse on it.'

Georgie turns away from Mr Kent, forgetting him, and speaks urgently. 'Do you know what she had in the bag, Thera? Try hard to remember, it could be really important.'

'She had the predictor, her diary, a red felt-tip pen, two empty Rice Krispies Squares packets, an empty Ribena carton and a Nano Pet,' I say nervously, wondering if now Georgie will arrest me for withholding information, as well as following a pervert and getting Billie kidnapped. My heart is beating hard in my chest.

'Well done, Thera,' Georgie says, and then turns and

rushes out of the school, talking on the police radio attached to her shoulder.

My cheeks are burning when I walk back into class. Break is over and I sit back down, opposite Hattie this time, because now we have a history lesson and we don't get put into groups for history. The seat where Billie usually sits, next to me, is empty. I will her to be there with my mind. I even will the girl I don't know to be there, so I can ask her if she knows anything about Billie, but neither of them appear.

'So?' Hattie says in a low voice, while Mrs A is writing on the board and explaining we're learning about the ancient Greeks next. 'Did you tell them?'

'Did I tell them what?'

'Did you tell them it's all your fault?'

I look quickly down at my textbook, but not quick enough to avoid their faces – Hattie's and Poppy's. I'm not quick enough either to dip my head before the tears come. I wipe them away quickly. I have a promise to myself that I'll never let Hattie see me cry. I shouldn't be the one crying, anyway. Billie is the one that's missing. I'm the one who got her lost.

The lesson starts and I concentrate on the textbook in front of me and what Mrs A is saying, but it's all a blur, and when I press my pencil to my workbook I press so hard the lead breaks off.

I want to talk to the girl who was a black dog and ask her if she knows something about Billie, and if that's why she has been watching me. Sat on my bed at home, I stroke the red lettering of the book I borrowed from Nan and Grandad's house, *Ouija: The Most Dangerous Game*. I open it. I have already read the first chapter, about the history of Ouija. It is at least 2,500 years old. Many different cultures, including ancient China, Rome and Greece, created different versions, in the same way that different cultures built stone circles and worshipped the stars. Everyone wants to talk to the dead, because everyone dies. Well, everyone has died so far. Grandad says with stem cells they might be able to figure out how to keep people young forever, so I'm crossing my fingers that my generation will be the first to become immortal. I don't want to die.

I start reading again where I left off. I've shut the door to my room so no one sees me reading it. I'm scared to tell Mum and Dad about the dogs. They will think it was my fault Billie is missing, just like the police and Billie's mum do. The book says, in America, the Ouija board has always been very popular. In the eighties (when me and Billie were born), they sold more Ouija boards than Monopoly boards. Everyone I know has Monopoly!

The book says Ouija isn't just used to communicate with the dead. Some people use it to enhance their psychic abilities, making them better at mind-reading and predicting the future, and some use it to find people who are missing. Several missing-persons cases in America have been solved using Ouija boards. I look over at the board. I got spooked after the black dogs, so I folded it in half and stuffed it into my white bookcase. If I followed the instructions in the book, maybe I could contact Billie and ask her where she is. But what if an evil spirit does come through? In the book, it says if you don't perform the right rituals to send the spirit back to the spirit world, they can stay in the real world and haunt the person that brought them forth. Is that what happened with the dogs, and the girl? Is she a ghost, haunting me?

There is a creak by my window. I slowly turn my head. There's nothing there.

Holding my breath, I look back at the book.

There is a very interesting page about sceptics that makes me question everything. It says that some people think the Ouija board's messages aren't from dead people at all, but from the subconscious of the person operating it. The book says spiritualists believe that spirits talk through the board, but non-spiritualists think the person using the board is imagining it all.

Am I a non-spiritualist or a spiritualist? We go to a Church of England school, so we are supposed to be Christians, but what do I really believe? Do I believe I could talk to the girl/dog through the board? Do I believe it would help me communicate with Billie? Grandad always says belief is a powerful force. He says if you believe you can do something, you can.

'Thera!'

Suddenly Mum's voice is calling up the stairs, and I jump and scream. I guess thinking about ghosts is freaking me out.

'Are you alright?'

'Yeah!' I shout back, my heart thudding loudly. 'I'm fine!'

'It's bath time – go and start the hot-water tap.'

'Okay.' I look down at the book, shivering with fear. The next bit is about—

'*Now*, Thera.'

'I'm *doing* it!' I say, and slam the book shut, tucking it under my pillow.

At lunchtime the next day, Hattie and Poppy rush ahead of me to the playground, holding hands. I look around when I get there. No Billie. Sam and his friends are playing on the tyre at the back of the playground by the fence, and Hattie and Poppy are sitting on the climbing frame, talking. I slope over to them because I don't have anywhere else to go.

'Hey, guys,' I say hesitantly. 'Do you want to play a pretend game?' It seems awful playing a pretend game without Billie, but I want to at least try to be normal. Then the time will go quickly and before I know it she'll be back, talking in a funny accent and being louder than everyone else.

Hattie looks at me and sniffs. 'A pretend game?'

'Yeah. We could pretend we're in an all-girls boarding school. One of us has to be the matron.'

Hattie shakes her head. 'How can you even think about playing pretend games when Billie is missing because of you?'

My cheeks immediately get really hot because now she'll think I don't care about Billie as much as she does.

'It's okay if you don't feel like it,' I say quickly. 'We could play something else. Anything you want.'

Billie and me have the best playground games. I invent most of them, but Billie makes up loads. We have imaginary games, like families, or boarding school, but we have other games too. There's one called Batchelors Mug, where we wander around the playground singing the song, 'We always get together with a Batchelors Mug! Our job is making everyone happy in love, happy, happy, happy, happy!', and then we ask people what's wrong, and see if we can help them be happier. We do that one with both of us in the same coat, two arms down one sleeve. Then we have a dance to the *Animaniacs* theme tune that we do on the tyres, but we made up our own words, which go, 'We are the Animaniacs, and our bums are full of wax. My shoelace is undone, and I weigh a single tonne. We're the Animaniacs!' Hattie and Poppy think our games are childish, but they would never say that with Billie here.

'It might be dangerous playing with you,' Hattie says.

'Huh?'

'I might disappear!' She pretends to be frightened and Poppy giggles.

'Fine,' I say. 'I just thought maybe you might want to make up a dance routine, to do when we leave school, for the younger kids. We could do it in assembly. I bet Mrs Adamson will let us.'

'What to?' Poppy says. She looks interested. Maybe she wants to pretend everything is normal, like me.

I think about the songs Billie likes. 'Maybe like a Spice

Girls song. Or Steps. Or S Club 7. We could surprise Billie with it when—'

Hattie interrupts me: 'We don't want to do a stupid dance, thanks very much. Not with you and no Billie. You'd just boss everyone around and be annoying.'

'No, I wouldn't!'

'Billie thought you were annoying. She told me so.'

'No, she didn't!' I shout.

'And now she's missing.'

'She's not missing,' I say insistently. 'She's just . . . run away or something.'

'She's been gone for *ages*, you lame-o,' Hattie says. 'Where has she been sleeping?'

'Out . . . out in the wild.'

'She couldn't survive out there alone, she's only eleven.'

'So? She's tough.'

'She's just a little girl. Anything could have happened to her.'

The way Hattie says 'anything' is really spooky. It makes a shiver run down my back. 'Shut up!' I say. 'Stop talking!'

Her face takes on a pointy look, like she is directing all of her hate towards me. 'Who knows? Maybe she's lying dead somewhere in a ditch.'

'Shut up, Hattie, that's ridiculous!'

'All because you wanted to follow that man. Poppy and me told you it was a stupid idea, but you wouldn't listen.' Hattie looks like a queen on her throne, sat on the climbing frame. She makes me feel like her subject.

'Billie wanted to follow him too.'

'Yeah, but we know who's the bossy, annoying leader out of you and Billie, don't we? Who knows. You always wanted to *be* Billie, Thera. Maybe you got rid of her on purpose so you could replace her.'

'I don't want to be Billie!' I wipe my cheeks with a balled-up fist. 'She's my best, true, forever friend.'

'Maybe,' Hattie says, really cattily and nastily, 'you killed her because you're in love with her.'

Poppy sticks out her tongue at me. 'Gay.'

I'm so shocked I burst out crying. I rush at Hattie and put my hands under her bum and shove. Hattie falls backwards off the top bars, onto the rubber. It's quite a long way to fall, about five or six feet, but she manages to keep hold of one of the bars until her weight rips her hand off it, so she isn't badly hurt. She bursts out crying too, though, and grabs my leg and scratches it and I kick her in the head. I'm shocked at how powerful my boot feels driving into her skull. I didn't think it would actually do any damage to kick her in the head. I thought it would just be like a pinch, but Hattie is bleeding. One of the dinner ladies runs over, shouting my name, steers me out of the playground with a hand on my back and takes me to see Mrs Adamson. Mrs A takes me into our classroom and sits me down.

'She's SO MEAN! Hattie's so mean!' I scream.

'Yes,' Mrs Adamson says. 'I know she is. Mean people are awful.'

'She was making me scared about Billie,' I moan. 'I miss her.'

'I'm sorry, Thera.' Mrs A starts to cry. 'Don't you think I miss her too?'

I start crying, thinking about this. Billie is Mrs Adamson's favourite. She always gets her to deliver messages to other classes, even though Billie takes ages because she dawdles and gets distracted by the art projects on the walls in the hall. She makes Billie the lead in every school play, even though half the time she forgets the lines and I have to tell her them, and then she giggles and says them wrong anyway. Billie is always an angel in the Nativity, except for the last two years she's been Mary. I guess Billie is a lot of people's favourite, especially older people. They like her because she is pretty, always neat, and very good, although a bit dippy and easily distracted.

'We've got to try to think about other things, Thera,' Mrs Adamson says. 'It's not our fault this happened. You're only little and you can't help find Billie or anything. Playing with Hattie and Poppy is the best way to take your mind off things. So just . . . put up with it and, and . . . maybe Billie will come back.' A couple of tears fall down her cheeks.

'I don't want to play with them,' I say.

'Well, we all have to do things in life that we don't like. I have to do things I don't like all the time. That's part of growing up. Stop crying now, Thera. We're having a lesson after break about staying safe and keeping off the streets so nothing happens to you, so you'll have to pay attention to that.'

'I'm not crying for me, I'm crying for Billie,' I say. 'I

don't care what Hattie says, but Billie would be really upset with her for saying those nasty things to me.'

'We can't know that now she's gone,' Mrs Adamson says in a weird way, and I suddenly stop crying and start hiccupping.

The lesson about staying safe seems to be mainly about us not being allowed to do anything.

'Don't go out after school,' Mrs A says. 'Don't go out after dark. Don't talk to strangers. Don't take sweets off strangers. Don't dawdle on the way home. Don't wear anything provocative.'

'What's provocative?' I ask.

'Anything that shows skin.'

'Why?'

'Because if you show skin and the other girls don't, you'll stand out. Don't tempt fate.' She turns away from me and addresses Hattie in particular. 'Don't put make-up on. Don't answer back if a man harasses you in the street, just run away. Don't go walking in the fields.' Mrs A sits down behind her desk and looks unhappy. 'Don't talk to men you don't know. *Don't* flirt with anyone. Do you know what I mean? Don't engage. Don't say anything . . . inappropriate.'

'Like what?'

'I don't . . . I don't know, Thera,' Mrs A says really quietly. She puts her hand to her forehead. She looks really pale. Mrs A is already a pale person, really small and pale, and sort of pretty I guess, but not beautiful like Mummy.

She has a whiny voice and is always asking us not to do things: don't climb on this, don't all talk at once, don't breathe so loud. She sighs and has headaches a lot. She's not a great teacher. Mrs Kimberley, who we had in Year Two, was way better. 'It's really difficult to explain. It's so confusing, how these things just . . . happen.'

'Wait.' I frown. 'Do you know what's happened to Billie?'

She looks at me like I'm speaking another language.

'Are the grown-ups and the police keeping something from us?'

'No, Thera, no.' She shakes her head. 'Stop asking questions. You're just a little girl. You don't understand. You can't protect yourself. None of us can.'

Just then the door opens, and a black dog comes through it. It moves its head as if it is looking for someone, and then, when it sees me, it comes towards me, jumps up onto my desk, and turns into the ghostly girl. She bangs her hands on the table in front of me and looks into my eyes. She's so close I can feel the cold coming off her. I can't move, but my eyes are wide. She leans in towards me, so our noses are almost touching. 'She wants to talk to you,' the girl whispers.

That night, I dream about Billie. She is confused and lost out on the fields, calling for me. It starts to rain, and the drops are running in her eyes and for some reason she can't close them. (That was weird of me to dream, since it's been hot and dry all week.) I dreamt that finally she found my house and she was outside my window, but the window of my room at home is on the second floor so this was also weird. She tapped on the window and when I sat up in bed, I saw the ghostly girl was behind her. I yelled at Billie to turn around, or run away, but she didn't move, and the girl came closer. Billie just kept tapping at the glass.

When I wake up, a summer storm is raging outside the window, and the rain lashes the glass in a rhythmic pattern. The time on my clock says half past midnight – the witching hour. I go to my window and open the curtains. Lightning explodes in a massive crack down through the sky and the thunder roars a second later like it's angry. The storm must be right over us. The door flies open behind me, and Sam leaps into my spare bed and dives under the covers. I open the window and lean out, feeling the rain. Outside, our swing is swinging with no one on it. Beyond the fence, under the bright moon, the flowers in the fallow field shiver like waves on the sea, humungous lines where the wind presses down their stems in patterns. To the right, the pig field is empty; the sows are sleeping with their piglets in their sheds, their little half-circle corrugated-iron homes reflecting the lightning each time it strikes. They are arranged in two triangles, one above the other, in a way that looks like the letter 'B'. I frown at them, thinking it's a trick of my eyes, but they really do look like a 'B', every time the lightning lights them up. The trees on the horizon are black against the dirty sky. When the lightning cracks they look like cut-out puppet-theatre scenery. I squint. When the sky lights up, I think I see a figure walking beneath the trees.

'What are you doing?' Sam whines. 'The lightning'll hit you.'

'What if Billie didn't run away, Sam?' I whisper. 'Do you think she's out in this? Is she cold? Is she wet?'

'Stop it,' Sam says. 'Shut up.'

'Is she hungry? When we run away we always take Rice Krispies Squares.' I close my eyes and try to connect to her mind. 'Billie. Billie?'

'Stop saying her name,' Sam groans, hiding himself under the covers.

I open my eyes again and strain to see her on the fields. 'She's out there. I can feel her.'

Sam starts to cry. 'Thera, don't.'

I scan the horizon one last time. 'Don't be scared, silly. There's nothing to be scared of while I'm here.'

'You're not much older than me.'

'I'm your big sister. It's my duty to protect you with my life. I'd die for you if I had to. Mum and Dad would want it that way.'

'Billie doesn't have a big sister,' Sam says.

'She has me,' I say.

Suddenly there is something in the corner of my vision. I look down at the swing. For a fraction of a second, I see Billie. I gasp. Then she's gone. I strain my eyes and search for her in the dark.

Grandad has taught me about astral projection. If Billie is trapped somewhere by a pervert, she could be sending out a projection of herself to get someone to find her. And who would she send it to? No one else but me would both recognize her and believe it was true, because adults don't believe in things like the spirit world and being psychic, except for Grandad. Also, the Ouija book said that kids see and hear things adults don't, like bats and ghosts.

The rain touches my eyeballs. I blink the drops away, and they fall down my face like tears.

'Thera!' Sam moans.

I turn back to him. I want to tell him about Billie, but he's too scared already, so instead I shut the casing and the sound of the thunder gets quieter, and I climb into his bed. 'Shh, go to sleep,' I say.

'What if Billie never comes back?' Sam says, sobbing. 'What if she's lost forever?'

'She'll come back,' I say confidently. 'I'm going to find her. I'm her best friend, and I'm brave and tenacious.'

'What's tenacious?'

'Grandad taught me it. It means like a dog with a bone, not letting go.'

Sam sniffs. 'What?'

'Sam, go to sleep. I'll stay awake and sit by you.'

When Sam decides to go to sleep, he always goes quickly. He twitches and snuffles, like a hedgehog.

While Sam is sleeping, I think. I've been reading the Ouija book, and in the last chapter I read I learnt all about automatic writing. It's like Ouija, but it's easier to do on your own, and it can be used to contact missing people just as much as dead people. It seems less dangerous, because you're not releasing any spirits into the non-spirit world, you're just talking to a ghost that remains in the spirit world, like a phone call. You hold a pencil loosely in your hand, over a piece of paper, and the spirit or missing person takes hold of the pencil. The people who do it never know what they're writing until they're done, and the handwriting is different from their own, as if the ghost itself is moving the hand just like it used to write, in Victorian sloping script or whatever. Old people's handwriting, like Grandad's, elegant and joined up.

I slip out of bed and go to my bookcase. In my plastic art basket I find my A3 art pad and a 2B pencil, Billie's favourite. I sit cross-legged on my bed, with the pad of paper balancing on my knees, and hold the pencil loosely, like the book said. I close my eyes and think of her.

For a while, nothing happens. I hear the wind outside, and decide to open the window again because it might be easier for her to reach me, then I get back on the bed and wait. On the pad, I notice I've made a few little flicks of pencil, but on closer scrutiny they don't make any letters. They just look like a pile of twigs, like a little fire. I close my eyes again, and suddenly I feel the rain on my face.

It's not coming from the window. The window is too

far away. I feel cold and damp. I smell freshness, like the moors and peat and morning dew. She's outside. I feel my body stiffen up, like when Mr Kent put his hand on my knee. I feel like someone is holding my arms, and I know I have contacted someone. 'Billie?' I whisper, hoping it's her and not an evil spirit, but it doesn't feel like the ghost girl, or the black dog.

My chest tightens, and it's hard to breathe. I tremble, and shake so hard that all my muscles feel strange, and I search with my left hand for my heartbeat because I think it's racing. But it's not. It's steady and soft. Suddenly I splutter, like I'm drowning, and then I open my eyes, gasping for air, like Sam when he needs his puffer. I must have been holding my breath or something. My breathing slows down after I've been sitting for a while. I shiver. I look down at my paper. Nothing.

Hmm, hang on. I frown. It's dark and it's hard to see, but it looks like there is a scribble in the centre of the page. I take both sides of the pad in my hands, stand up and walk to the window, where the moon has just come out, making the world outside brighter than my room. I hold the piece of the paper out towards the night sky.

There, in pale grey, in handwriting different from mine, rounder and more spaced apart, like Billie's, are two words:

FIND ME

I'm going to tell you a story . . . about a little girl just like you. She is sweet and kind and good to her mother and takes care of her younger brothers and sisters. She is pretty and thin and has blonde hair. She tries hard to be good, and to do well in school. It's me. Before you ask. There are things she knows she is supposed to be, like bright and beautiful and fun and witty. But she always falls short. She's not quite clever enough to be top in her class. In a class of thirty, she comes out about tenth. What her mother calls 'borderline dumb'. She looks good with a lot of make-up on, but she's not allowed to wear it at school. They say it makes her look like a tramp. Without the make-up, she's on the average side of pretty. Not the pretty side of average, which would be a lot worse, but still. What her father calls 'good enough'. She isn't witty, but she laughs hard at jokes. She's fun but anxious. She's not wild like Jessica Urle, a busty firecracker in the same class who the boys all like. She's plain, sweet and not offending anybody, sitting there at the back of the crowd, laughing along with everyone and offering to chip in for a bottle of beer. (Other girls get their drinks paid for.)

She has had a few boyfriends, but she was too scared to do more than hold their hands, and they didn't like her enough to insist on a kiss. She's just not the kind to inspire that kind of pressure, or devotion.

Not yet. But then secondary school is over. And it is time for university. She gets into one; that she is relieved about. She knew she would, even though her mother doubted her. Of course, it's an average one. An average university for an average person.

Finally she can get away from home, away from the pain of being more invisible than other girls, less some-how. What was it about her that no one saw any real potential in her? People didn't feel that way about Jessica Urle. Or bold Nora Cunningham, who shouted when she spoke. Or wily Karen Vernon, with her brassy Bardot hair, who used her quick wit to mock the boys mercilessly. Well, they were beautiful. And she wasn't. Scrawny. No boobs. Too little. Were these the words that flitted through the boys' heads when she walked by? It set her cheeks on fire to think about it. They would all be laughing, having fun with Jessica or Karen as she walked past, and there it was, that horrible feeling, hovering right on the edge of lives well lived, always wishing, waiting.

Her body, heating up, responding to them, and at the same time clenching, withdrawing, confused by herself. And when they did talk to her, they teased her. Four Eyes, because back then she wore big, blue-framed glasses. Bambi, because she tripped once in assembly, in front of the entire school. Pink Pants, because that was what every-one had seen. The shame of it.

She kept her face very still at those times, still and smil-ing, when the boys all surrounded her but never spoke to her, when she had to pass through them on the way to class, clutching the straps of her school bag across her breasts.

School is out. She packs her bags over and over again. The summer heat is stifling. Mother keeps her in the house, like a maid, cleaning, cooking, the butt of Dad's sexist jokes. She waits on her single bed quietly while, even quieter than that, rage grows in the pit of her being.

We are running through the fallow field. It is the next day, a Thursday, after school. We have escaped from Nanny with cold Pop-Tarts in tinfoil and Um Bongo in our bags. I feel bad because Nanny was supposed to be babysitting us and we are not allowed out, so Mum will be mad at her, but we had to go. We are tracker dogs on a mission. Billie needs me.

We run over molehills and past reeds, getting small cuts on the sides of our legs. 'Come on, Sam!' I shout. He's lagging behind.

We get to the border of what we can see through the window and keep going, out of sight of the house. Our village is about one hundred and fifty houses in a valley surrounded by farmland: flat, wide, gold fields that go on forever. We run through a couple of fields and over a couple of tracks, and then we are almost at the top of the low hill. At the bottom is where we left Billie. 'Look for clues as we go,' I shout back.

'Like what?' Sam calls.

'If she's somewhere nearby, she might have dropped her bag, or something inside it. Or if it's the man . . .' I falter. 'If the walker we met has taken her and he's keeping her somewhere, he might have dropped an item of clothing, a watch, his wallet, maybe even a sandwich crust.'

We work quickly, parting the taller grasses as we go and running over the uneven ground. I push with my leg muscles as I near the top, willing myself to keep up speed. There is not a moment to lose. When I reach the top of the hill, though, I freeze. Sam is running so fast to catch up that he bumps into me. He looks around me, down through the barley field. 'Wow,' he breathes raggedly.

Below us, police cars and a crowd of people are gathered on the muddy track between the barley and wheat. A further line of men and women stretches all the way along the wheat field where Billie and me parted. They are moving through the field, away from us, towards Billie's house.

Sam passes me his binoculars, which he got for bird-watching on his last birthday. I put them up to my eyes. The police officers' heads sway from side to side as they walk, pressing down the crop with their hands, and bending over into it. I dip lower with the binoculars.

On the track, Farmer Rawley, who owns most of the fields on this side of the village, is scratching the bottom half of his face with one hand, watching them. He leans on the bonnet of his Land Rover and stamps his foot into the dirt.

The lady police officer, Georgie, is talking to a policeman. I blush, remembering our exchange, and take my eyes off the binoculars, feeling guilty.

'What is it?' Sam asks.

I gulp. I haven't told him about the police interview. He

knows about the walker, of course – he was there – but I haven't said that word, 'pervert'. I also haven't told Sam that Billie spoke to me through a psychic connection, or that it might be my fault that she is missing. 'Nothing.'

I am about to hand the binoculars back to Sam when there is a shout from the field below. One of the policemen sticks his hand straight up in the air and turns to look back at the police by the cars. I swiftly plug the binoculars back in my eye sockets.

The policeman waits, along with the others in the line, as a figure dressed in white, with a mask on, shuffles through the wheat. It comes on a diagonal, not crossing the policeman's path, and carries a few bits in its hands. It bends down in front of the policeman. They are near to the far edge of the field, where there is a thin footpath that leads past the field and off away from Billie's house. To get to her house, you have to cross over the footpath and walk straight through another two fields. The white-clothed figure holds up something to the sun. I leave Sam and race along the ridge, holding the binoculars against my face, to get a better look.

'Don't trip!' I hear Sam yell.

I refocus the lenses. The figure has a dainty nose. It is a lady, holding up something white between a pair of tweezers. She turns it over and I see the writing, in the red felt-tip pen Billie carried around all last Saturday. It is the paper predictor.

For half an hour after they find the predictor, not much happens. It's a hot day and we are impatient, drinking our Um Bongos, taking photos of them with my Olympus and watching them through the binoculars, both of us quiet and nervous. A few more people put on white clothes, and then they carry a white tent out to where they found the predictor. I don't understand why they're not moving further along Billie's path, now they've found one thing. That's what I would be doing if I were a policeman. Shouldn't they be looking for her? And not just her stuff? I gaze beyond all the tiny police people to the thin, raised footpath.

'Hey, Sam,' I say. 'I'm thinking.'

'What about?'

'Billie wouldn't have dropped the predictor. She knows not to litter. So let's imagine we're Billie. Maybe she dropped the predictor because she was scared, or distracted by something.' I look along the path and point. 'She dropped it on the footpath and it just blew back along the path she took through the field.'

'Maybe. It's not really windy, though.'

'It was windy at the weekend. I remember. We were walking to the den across this field on Friday, right? And

I watched the wind blow Billie's hair in the same direction as the predictor would have blown, if she had dropped it on the path. It was just like that on Saturday too.'

I look around the surrounding fields for the impression of Billie walking there. We always leave big tracks when we go anywhere, dark lines snaking into the field and back out again, but there aren't any in the next field, the one between the wheat field and her house, where Billie should have been going. There aren't even any circular impressions, where someone could have been lying down, or there could have been a fight. I frown. 'If there was someone out there, maybe they were walking on the footpath, and they made Billie jump, and she dropped the predictor. Maybe when she got on the path, she saw them.' I stand up and act surprised. 'And she was shocked! So she ran along the track, all the way to . . .' I turn, and then I realize. 'I know where she is.'

Sam looks up at me. He is sitting cross-legged on the ground. He bites his lip.

'Come on!'

I turn and start to run. I'm pleased with my intuition. The psychic bond between me and Billie must be strong.

'Thera!' Sam calls after me.

'I have to find her!' I shout.

I look back and he is finally following me. He glances across to the police, and speeds up. We run along the top, away from the police, parallel to the little raised footpath where Billie dropped the predictor.

'Where are we going?' Sam asks.

'Just trust me!' I shout. We run for ages, past two fields and some little trees, and then we turn and run down the hill through a fallow field, then a crop field. We come out onto the footpath, right by the entrance to the copse. Just at that moment, I think I see the ghost girl – a little flicker of hair – but then I squint, and she's not there. I can feel that she was, though, and that she's leading me to Billie. It was the ghost girl, after all, who told me Billie wanted to talk to me. I am starting to understand the game. Even though she's creeping me out, I'm supposed to follow her. Like a spooky version of Lassie.

The copse is a bit of land that anybody can go in. It's not owned by anyone. It has a small pond, with a bird hide, and trees all around it. Our den is at the back of it, just next to the caravan park on the other side, but no one knows about it because it is surrounded by trees. It looks overgrown, like an enormous bush.

'If Billie was scared,' I explain to Sam, 'she would have run to the nearest place she could hide.'

'The den!' Sam exclaims.

'That's right!' I say.

'Wait, Thera. What about the black dog?' he says worriedly. Sam doesn't like the woods. He's scared of lots of things: ET, and boys that are bigger than him, and what's under our beds. Sometimes I'm scared of what's under the bed, but I have to be brave, for Sam.

'Do you want to wait here, while I go in?' I suggest.

'No!' he protests. 'I'm fine. I'm not a baby.'

'Stay quiet,' I tell him. Low hedgerows surround us as we walk from the sea of golden wheat and barley towards the mass of green.

Suddenly Sam stops. 'The gate's open.'

I hesitate. 'Well, maybe somebody just left it like that.'

'You're not supposed to leave the gate open. The sign says.'

We exchange a look. 'I'm still going in, Sam,' I say. 'Maybe she's hurt. Maybe she can't walk.' I turn, and leave him picking his fingernails on the other side of the gate. I only have to keep walking a minute until I hear footsteps running up behind me. I take his hand.

We walk around the pond, poking our heads in the hide, just to check Billie isn't there. We reach the back of the copse, where the trees are closer together and it's darkest. This is where our secret den is. The den where we took the Ouija board. The den where we saw the dogs. It's made of a natural circle of trees that a bunch of vines and ivy have grown over, so you basically can't see inside. We have been making it better and better by pulling the vines into the spaces where you could once see in, so there really aren't any now. Hattie's sister showed us how to do it and she got showed by an even older girl, who's now eighteen, so it's been around for a really long time. To get into the den, you have to crawl under a thicket of bracken. We go up to the entrance, and Sam points.

'What?'

'Hair,' he says simply.

I peer close to the brambles, where he is pointing. There is hair there. Several strands of long, golden hair. 'That's Billie's hair,' I say. 'She's here.'

'Maybe she left it here when we did the Ouija board on Friday.'

I frown, and squat down in front of the entrance. 'Billie?' No reply. 'Billie?'

I get down on my belly to crawl through.

'I'm staying here,' Sam says.

I look up at him. 'Okay. If you see anyone, scream, and I'll come and get you.'

Sam gulps. 'Okay.' He turns his back on me. I leave him there, peering down the path, left to right, then over again.

I duck down and stretch my arms ahead of me, and crawl on my hands and knees through the thicket. The thorns tug on my hair, and my knees get cold in the dirt, which is always cold, even in July. When I get through to the other side, I stand up, and dust myself off.

As I walk into the clearing, I keep my eyes to the ground, scanning back and forth for something that might indicate Billie's presence. I don't see her right away. She isn't in the middle of the den, where we usually sit. Just past the entrance, the grass is flattened and ripped up a little. Half a muddy footprint has been left, even after last night's storm. It's bigger than mine, but not by much. I avoid the footprint, treading lightly on the dirt. The trees here are all deciduous – silver birches, beeches and oaks – so they have wide leaves, not like pines and most evergreens. My dad knows all the names, so I know them too. In autumn all the leaves will be gone, but right now the ground under the trees is shielded from the sun by lots of leaves and branches, so it's still damp from the storm. The leaves knit together above me, and the light coming through them makes everything green and eerie. It's quite dark. I am focusing on small details, on what is in front of me. It's like I'm too nervous to look around. It's like I know there might be something I don't want to see. The breaths I take are small, but they sound loud to me. I don't have to walk far in before I stop, realizing.

There is a ditch that runs along one side of the clearing that makes up the den. The water is higher than usual where I cross it, just past the entrance. There is too much water. I follow the line of the ditch. Now I notice the thing that is damming up the water.

The shape is to my right. It's a long lump covered in a dirty-white or maybe cream cloth. It comes into focus as I turn towards it. My breathing is getting quicker. I hear a crack in the undergrowth that makes me jump. I look around wildly, but I can't see anything moving. I inch slowly towards the shape.

The cloth is a sheet. The lump is a human.

My lips start to tremble. Tears come into my eyes but they don't fall. I keep my eyes wide to stop myself from crying. I look around again, then back at the lump. 'Billie?' I whisper. 'Billie?'

'Thera?' Sam calls from the other side of the bracken. 'Is she there? Have you found her?'

'Billie?' I force myself to move towards the shape. I tell myself Billie is my best, true, forever friend, and I have to be strong for her. I have to find out . . . I crack, and sob suddenly, then smack my hand over my mouth.

Maybe it's not her. It's not her at all. It's someone else. Or it *is* her, and she's alive, and I have found her just in time, and Sam runs to get the police, and they come climbing into the den through the back, and the ambulance arrives just as she wakes up, and everyone is so relieved that I saved her, and Billie is saying, 'That walker man said he was gonna kill me! But I knew Thera would find me if I concentrated on sending her messages with my mind. Indubitably! Phew!' and I will say, 'That's what friends are for', and just smile knowingly. It will be such a relief. Everyone will think I'm a hero.

I better rescue her now, then. But I still can't move.

'If she's alive, you have to rescue her!' I tell myself in my head. 'Look, she's lain on her back, so she won't have drowned.'

My legs feel weak and rubbery, but I step carefully towards the top of the lump. The slight crook in the last third of the fabric is the shape of Billie's knees, the way her legs always bend. That seems like a thing that wouldn't be personal, but I would recognize that bend anywhere. Billie's pointy elf ear is sticking out from underneath the cloth, the hair swept back from it like it always sweeps back from it when we are lying down. There is Billie's one freckle between her ear and her hairline. I haven't noticed myself noticing these things before, but it's funny how I know them so well. If you showed me any inch of skin, or hair, or even a tooth, I could tell you if it was Billie's. I lean over her. Holding my breath, I move my hand towards Billie's face carefully. As I do, I notice our friendship bracelet on my own wrist. I wear mine on the left; Billie wears hers on her right. I hesitate for a second. Some weird thing in my head rationalizes that if I don't pull it back, life will go on as it always has, and Billie being missing will all have been a big mistake.

It's a weird image, I know. This little eleven-year-old, four feet eleven inches tall, six stone two pounds, reaching out for a body in a ditch with an intent, slightly crazed look in her eye. I think I probably knew she was dead. I was never someone you could call stupid. I just didn't want it to be true. It was 1999, the precipice of a millennium, and I was eleven. My name was Thera Wilde. Thera the Wild. That's what my first name meant – wild – and my last name too. My mum had picked Thera, and made me double wild, intending it to mean something for me. I think about what it is to be wild a lot. To be wild is to be brave, and sometimes savage. Right then, I was neither of those things. But I think the terror of finding Billie entered my blood, and it would precipitate everything that followed.

I scream. Birds take off. Sam shouts my name. I stumble back, landing on my bum. The black dogs are back. There are five black dogs. They take a step towards me, then one by one they turn into girls. There is a cute little blonde one who is about five years old on my left. Next to her is one my age with dark skin, black hair and black eyes. To my right is the ghostly girl I've seen before. She has blonde-brown hair, wears school uniform and is the oldest of them all, about thirteen. The fourth girl is about nine, with a fringe, ginger hair and big eyes. In the middle of them is the fifth black dog, but as it walks towards me it becomes Billie. I scream again, and they're gone.

I crawl forward, on my hands and knees, to the body. Billie's eyes are open, like in my dream. I thought a dead person would look asleep, but she doesn't look asleep. She looks really, really dead, puffy and paler than I have ever seen anybody.

My body is shaking with unreleased sobs. It's holding them back without me thinking about it, so I can hear other things. I am on high alert, like an animal, for danger, for the walker. My ears pick up every tiny cracking sound in the woods. My eyes are suddenly like a powerful tele-scope, taking in all the details.

The voices in my mind feel like they are shouting questions over one another. I look at her body and then around me. How could Billie have been killed here, when the den is so hard to get into? The entrance is through the tunnel in the thicket, so you have to be quite small. The walking man would have been too big, wouldn't he? The only other way in is by running around the whole copse and coming through the back way, but there you have to cross a deep ditch filled with water, and then climb up a tall tree and through its branches. We're not big enough yet to leap across the ditch without falling in the water, so we always get in and out of the den using the tunnel. If the killer was chasing Billie, he would either have had to follow her to the thicket and then have Billie wait patiently to be killed until he came round the other side, or he would have had to know she would hide in the den, and be here already, waiting for her. Maybe that's what happened. Maybe he chased her, and when she went into the copse he just ran round, because he knew she would go to the den. But he would still have made a lot of noise, and Billie would have heard him and got away, right? It just doesn't make sense. Who knows about our den? It isn't visible at all from the outside.

Also, why didn't he bury her? She's just lying here, ready to be found by whoever uses the den next. If I murdered someone, burying them would give me more time to get away before anyone came looking for me. Maybe he didn't have time to bury her. Maybe he was disturbed. Maybe he was hoping that, if he left her out in the open, all the evidence would be eaten by a fox? And where did the sheet come from? I peer closer. There's something else weird about her too, but I can't put my finger on it.

'Thera? Are you okay? I'm coming, Thera.'

There is a rustling in the thicket and Sam's head pops through the entrance. I panic, wanting to stop him from seeing her, feeling protective of both of them, Sam and Billie, but my mouth isn't working. My lips are clamped together and trembling. If I open them, I'll start to cry. Sam crawls out of the tunnel. He is shaking, but my lovely little brother is coming to my aid, even though he is scared. Sam looks around. As soon as he sees me, his face changes into a mask of horror. He looks at me standing motionless above Billie's dead body, holding open the dirty sheet like a magician brandishing a cape, for about three seconds and then bursts out crying.

'Don't!' I shriek. 'The killer'll hear you!'

My yell only spooks him more. He stares at Billie, his hands knitted together at his waist, his face all red and his mouth open wide and wet. He cries loudly and babyishly, and I drop the sheet.

'I'm sorry for shouting, Sam, I'm sorry,' I tell him, running to him and putting my arms around him. His head tucks under my chin.

'Fetch the police!' Sam cries. 'What if there's a murderer in the woods?'

'That's why I want you to stop crying – he'll hear you,' I whisper, and he closes his mouth immediately, and whimpers through his lips. 'I just need a few seconds more. Then we'll get the police, I promise. Have you got a pen?'

'W-w-what?'

'Or a pencil.'

He continues to sob. 'I – I've got a pencil.'

'Give it here.'

'I don't know,' he mumbles, shaking.

'It's okay, Sam,' I say, even though it isn't. 'It's okay.' I search his pockets. His whole body is stiff and his arms are limp. Tears run down his face and he looks up at me pleadingly.

'I want Mum!'

'I promise I'll take you home,' I say. 'I promise. Just two more minutes here and then we'll get the police. Okay?' I escort him back to the entrance of the den, at the thicket.

'Okay,' he says, his mouth wide.

'Wait here. Don't look round. I promise I'll be right back.'

I run the few steps back to Billie and stand over her. Now I'm thinking of Sam, I feel braver. I have a half-full paper bag of sweeties in my pocket that Nan bought us on Saturday. I pour the rest of the sweets into my pocket and draw Billie's position on the bag. The sheet has been folded neatly over her in the ditch, as if someone took one last look at her before they covered her up. I have unfolded half. She is a bit sooty, the bottom half of her hair is gone, and she smells smoky and damp, like a bonfire the next day, but I don't think she is burnt badly enough for burning to have killed her. She is a bit mussed up. Her bright-pink T-shirt is rolled up on her tummy funny, her dungarees are halfway up her legs and her shoelaces are undone. Why would her shoelaces be undone? I note this down. I can't see any stab marks, and the water isn't bloody at all. Her face is a bit blue. She is cold to touch, but she isn't submerged in the water and she isn't wet on her face, so she doesn't seem to have drowned. I think about other ways to kill people. 'Maybe strangled?' I mutter.

'W-w-what?' Sam sniffs.

'Nothing! Don't look.'

I peer closely at her neck, but with the sootiness I can't tell if there are any marks or not. I sniff the air. It smells of burning, but there is another smell too, like a kitchen bin gone bad. There is a purple mark on her forehead, and a line of darkness along her neck where it meets the sheet, which is damp. I stare hard at her, marking down tiny details. When I reach the crook of her right wrist, I stop, shocked. 'Her friendship bracelet is gone.'

'Thera,' Sam moans. I barely hear him. 'Thera!' He chokes up little wet sobs. 'I want to go.'

'Coming,' I murmur. I cover Billie up and leave without disturbing the ground, casting my eyes about for the bracelet. When I reach Sam, we crawl through the thicket, and I take his hand and keep walking. As we walk through the trees, I get the feeling we are being watched. At first I get freaked out, and scan the woods all around us to see if we are being followed by an evil spirit, some frightening dead thing, but then I realize: Billie is a ghost now too.

I don't want to go talk to the police in real life because I'm scared of Georgie, so we ring 999 from the red phone box at the top of the hill, and tell the lady who answers that we have found a dead body, then we walk home. I have to drag Sam because he can barely move his legs. I lead him down the side of the house, around to the back door, and then let go of his hand.

'Thera?'

'Just tell Nan I'm out playing.'

'But . . . but she'll be angry at me. We were supposed to stay in the garden,' Sam says. He is still crying.

'No, tell her I made you leave. It's my fault. I won't be long.'

'Where are you *going*?' he wails.

'I just want to . . . see. I don't want to leave her there.'

'But the police will be there with her in a minute, Thera, you don't have to go!'

'The police being there isn't the same! I'm her friend. I have to go and take care of her, Sam, like I've just taken care of you.' He watches me as I climb over our fence. I run back, retracing our footsteps through the fallow field to the top road. My heart is beating hard against my chest. The police cars are already moving towards the copse, but the road they have to use is lumpy and longer than cutting through the fields. I know if I race along the top, roll down the side of the hill and run through the caravan park, round to the back of the copse, I could get into the den area quicker than them and hide, and watch them find her. I don't know why I want to. That intellectual curiosity, I guess. I don't want to leave her on her own, and maybe they will find how she died, or a really important clue, and I want to know about it.

When I get just past the copse, the cars are parking at the gate. I lie flat at the top of the hill and push myself down. The first field is fallow so I roll right over it, getting bruised and knocked about, but the second is crop and I have to stand and run, keeping low so the police don't see me. I get to the caravan park and run through the main entrance, past the caravans. Not many of the people who live here are out and about. They are probably all inside eating tea, or still at work. There are a few old men and women lying out in the sun, but they ignore me. I push through the hedge at the back of the field and only have a little way to go, across the corner of another enclosure, to get to the copse. When I get there, I hear them cutting through the thicket with a chainsaw. I take a run-up to the ditch and try to leap over. I trip at the edge, splashing my feet into the water. It's the same water Billie is lying in. This makes me upset and I stay, clinging to the bank for a moment to calm myself down. I feel my neck. My heartbeat is really fast. But I have to keep moving. I scramble up the bank and climb the tall tree on the edge of the den, right up into the thin branches, where I have a bird's-eye view of Billie. I still have the binoculars around my neck and I train them to the scene, watch Georgie push her way through the undergrowth, and try to quieten my heavy breathing. I'm panting like one of those black dogs.

The police are very hushed. First Georgie runs her eyes up and down Billie, then she calls over a man and a lady in white suits and they start to look at Billie too, lifting up the sheet and talking quietly to each other. Other police set up some tall lights pointing at Billie, even though the sun won't be going down for hours. One light is near me, so I slip even higher up the tree and jam myself in between a fork in the branches.

When I look back to Billie, I can't see her. There is a cluster of people around her, doing police stuff I suppose, like getting fingerprints. I peer through the binoculars. I catch glimpses of her as the police move, but I can't see her face. People surround her, touching her, lifting up her hands and her hair, and turning them over, studying them, and there is something I don't like about that. Billie is *my* friend. She belongs to me, not them. I feel sick and sweaty.

The sun is shining right onto me now, through the trees. I look up at the small streaks of fluffy cloud in the blue sky and start to cry, thinking about heaven. Is Billie there already? Will I never see her again? Or is she down here, with the dogs that turned into ghost girls? Will she stick around, or will they leave together for the spirit world?

Suddenly I hear someone clear their throat, very loudly, just below me. I look between my legs.

'Thera,' says my dad, looking up at me. I didn't see him come in the den. I guess I was watching Billie very intently. I am about to ask if I can stay a bit more, but then I see his face. 'Time to go home.' I scramble down the tree quickly.

The police watch as Dad and me walk out. All of their faces are sad, except for Georgie, who looks crosser than ever. There, just past Georgie, are Billie's mum and dad.

As we approach them, Billie's mum walks towards me, her mouth open, her lips trembling. 'I know it was you who called the police, Thera. How did you know she was here?' Her eyes are desolate and searching, but she speaks softly. 'Come here to me, sweetie, I just want to know.' Dad pulls me gently away from her, onto the other side of him. Then she tries to get around him, and Billie's dad puts his arm out in front of her, gently cupping the side of her waist. He's much bigger than her, and when she tries to move forward she just stops. She can't get past his arm. She looks shocked, then frustrated, then suddenly she screams at me. 'Thera, tell me how you knew!' The word 'knew' echoes through the woods. Billie's mum pulls at Billie's dad's arm, scratching it with her long nails. 'Let me go, Paul! Let me bloody go, Jesus Christ, let me go!'

'Rebecca,' Billie's dad says. He buries his face in her shoulder and puts his other arm around her too. 'Rebecca.'

'No.' She's whispering now. 'No.'

Georgie comes over to us all, and Billie's mum yells at

her. 'A child found her! A *child* found her! What have you been doing, you fucking—'

Dad puts his hands over my ears, then picks me up and carries me like a baby out of the wood, holding onto me so tightly that I can't see or hear or really even breathe. He is breathing funnily, heavy and hot, his breath steaming up my neck.

Lots of people are outside the gate, watching everything: police, a man with a big camera, people with notepads, the farmer, people from the village and people I don't know, from town I guess; all silent, with their arms folded. Some children are up on the hill. I look to see if Hattie or Poppy are there but the children are too far away for me to tell who they are. The only one I recognize is Nathan Nolan.

When I get home, the telly is blaring in the living room. A lady's voice is saying, 'The body of Billie May Brooke was found . . .' Mum runs out of the room and shuts the door, but I hear it loud over her shoulder while she hugs me. 'Police are looking for witnesses . . . a jeep seen leaving the area late Saturday evening . . . stationary vehicle in nearby layby . . . any additional information, please contact the local police force . . . number at the bottom of the screen . . .' I put my hands over my ears to silence it, and scream. The tears are coming now I'm home, now I don't have to look after Sam or keep watch over Billie. Dad takes me straight upstairs and puts me in bed. He sits on my bed for ages, but I can't stop crying.

I must have fallen asleep, though, because after that I keep seeing Billie, pale and dead. I see other faces too: the faces of the dead girls who morphed out of the black dogs, and I know now that they are murder victims, and Billie is one of them. In my dreams they have pale faces with cloudy eyes, and they are reaching for me and crying out like they want something, and I wake up, screaming, and Mum comes through and holds me and strokes my hair until the sun comes up. By dawn, I feel dried up, like all the water in my body has been cried out of me. I lie there unable to move, my lips and eyes dry and open, shocked to stillness. How can Billie be dead and gone, when I am alive and here?

Nathan Nolan lives in the village and he's two years older than us. We all met him on Bonfire Night last year and he scratched me for no reason while we were playing tig, which is what boys do when they like you. That, or they thump you. His parents are poor, though, so he lives in a caravan and he doesn't go to the grammar school, which is where Billie and me were supposed to go in September, along with Hattie, Poppy and a boy called Tim from my year, because we passed the eleven-plus.

Nathan is the same height as me. He has dark-brown hair in curtains, blue eyes and long, dark-brown eyelashes like a puppy dog. His family is Irish. That's why they live in a caravan. Poor English people tend to live in council houses (I learnt that from Hattie). There's something weird going on with his dad. I don't know what exactly; he's just the kind of person there are rumours about.

When we met Nathan on Bonfire Night, he was wearing a tracksuit like a townie, but when he goes to school he wears black trousers, and a black jumper with a small green emblem on the chest. His cuffs are snot-stained and chewed on. I haven't been up close to him in a while, but you can still tell from far away.

Sam and me are on our way to school with Dad at eight

thirty on the Tuesday after I find Billie. Since I found her, there have been tonnes of police about, wandering all over the village in their yellow jackets. It makes me feel tense and like I'm being watched, but Mum and Dad seem to like having them around. They even argued less this week-end, which is a miracle. We spent most of it gathered around the telly, watching our favourite films, like *The Land Before Time*, *The Jungle Book* and *Terminator 2*. Mum and Dad didn't want us to go outside, but me and Sam didn't feel like it anyway because we were upset about Billie. Dad walked us to and from school yesterday and he's doing it again today. I counted me and Sam as very independent before Billie went missing. Now I'm scared of leaving the house alone. I'm scared the black dogs will come back. I'm scared there's a killer out there. I think most of all, though, I'm scared of walking into the world and Billie not being there. She was always with us when we played outside, and when we went to school. Being out of our house without her feels so wrong it makes me shake.

Sam holds Dad's hand while we walk, and I walk just in front of them. There are a group of older kids at the bus stop. Nathan is with them, but he is younger than them. I hope he's not their friend, because they are bullies, really. They also go to the comprehensive. One of them has a light-up yo-yo. Hattie's sister is there. Sometimes we see the older kids on Saturdays, when we go to the super-market in Eastcastle. They just stand in the town centre, laughing really hard at their own jokes. Thinking about it, they were probably the group on the hill with Nathan, when Dad came and got me at the copse.

There is a policeman across the road from the bus stop, watching them.

When we walk past the bus-stop kids they all go quiet, including Nathan. He hasn't talked to me since Bonfire Night. He just stares at me most times I am walking past. Today, he waves.

He's never waved before. I look back over my shoulder and watch him through my hair. Then we walk through the kissing gate into the cut, and I can't see him any more.

The cut is a dark, leafy tunnel of young trees, bent over the top so you can't even see the sky through them. It's a quicker way to school than walking on the pavement. It also has a bend in it, so it's creepy to go down alone because you don't know who could be round the corner. We notice someone has started cutting down some of the trees. Sam asks why and Dad says it's because of Billie. Sam and me exchange a look but we don't ask what lopping off the treetops down the cut has to do with Billie. When we get to school, Dad squats in front of us and says, 'Call me from the school office if you're upset and need to be picked up. Don't leave school without someone with you, okay?'

We nod.

'And I don't mean each other.'

We shake our heads.

Usually we go to the playground in the morning, but it's empty today and the dinner ladies and police are standing there to shepherd us in through the double doors of the school building instead. When we are inside I look back. Dad is still there, his arms folded, watching us. It feels

109

awful to be stared at all the time. It's like they are expecting the killer to come back and murder every last one of us. Maybe they are. Grown-ups never tell kids what's going on, until it's too late.

Our names are called in registration, and it's strange when Mrs Adamson doesn't call Billie's name. She pauses for a moment, and I expect her to cry, but she just continues, seeming only a bit more moody and distracted than usual. I pick my nails. There is a hole in my heart like the hole in the register, like my chest has been punched straight through. Is no one going to mention Billie has gone?

After registration, we set up the chairs for assembly. Our classroom is where we have assemblies, so we have to stack the tables and chairs away. Everyone sits cross-legged on the floor, apart from the teachers, who sit on chairs along the sides, and Year Six. We sit on the long, wooden gymnastics bench right at the back of the room. There are eighty-seven pupils in our school, from my village and the surrounding ones, and Years Four, Five and Six are all in Class Three. This part of the school used to be the whole school in Victorian times, and they used to have a net above it all, attached to the ceiling, where the bad children were put. I'm not sure about that, actually, because it sounds false, but Mrs A said it once and I didn't think at the time that she might have been joking. Or lying, to creep us out.

Years One, Two, Three and Reception – the Littlies – troop in and sit in front of us. I turn to my left to remark on something and my words die away in Tim's face, because that's where Billie used to sit. I think he realizes my mistake, because he smiles awkwardly and looks down at his lap. I haven't seen Billie since I found her. Perhaps she just needed me to find her so she could go to heaven with the other dead girls. I feel my throat constrict at this thought. I don't want her to be gone. I want to be able to see her. I want her to come back and haunt me, so I won't be alone.

'Stop shivering. You're shaking the whole row,' Hattie says, but it's not as vicious as usual. Tears keep leaking out of her eyes. I'm glad. Maybe she actually liked Billie and didn't just want to hang out with her because she was pretty. That's what I suspected sometimes.

Mr Kent is taking the assembly today, which is weird. He clears his throat to start talking, and I stiffen up immediately because I realize what he is about to say.

'Good morning, everyone,' he murmurs, in his soft, creepy voice.

'Good morning,' we chorus back.

'I have some very sad news to share with you today. Some of you might already have heard, or seen it on television, but Billie from Year Six died the weekend before last.'

How does he know she died the weekend before last? Did he kill her? I stare at him.

Lots of the younger kids turn around to look at the spot where Billie usually sits, and then at me.

'We don't know how she died yet, but it is better for you not to focus on that. Billie was a bright, friendly girl who was known to you all, and it's normal for you to be sad. I know she got on with everyone well, and I liked her very much too.'

Billie hated Mr Kent. She thought he was two-faced and always had gross bogeys.

'The village church will be open on Monday night for a memorial service for Billie, and you can speak to your teachers or me about Billie if you wish.'

How come I didn't know about the memorial service? Am I invited? Or does Billie's mum not want me there?

'First lesson today is cancelled, and we will all have some time to make cards for Billie's parents . . .'

He keeps talking, but I turn away and stop listening. I don't like the way he's talking, as if he never said a harsh word to Billie, or shouted at her to stop running, or called her silly. My eyes blur with tears, but I don't let him, or anyone, see me cry.

In the playground at lunch a load of the younger children come up to me to ask questions about Billie. The really little ones, who are four or five, just come and hug me, and hold my hand, sucking the thumbs of their other hands. It's nice. It also makes me want to cry even more, and I really struggle to hold it in and be strong in front of them all, but I do, because I'm older and I have to be. Hattie and Poppy walk past while this is going on, and Hattie mumbles something about Billie.

'What?' I say.

'Nothing.' Hattie shrugs, but then she whispers something else to Poppy.

I turn around, still holding one of the Littlies' hands. 'What are you saying?'

'Nothing,' she insists. Her eyes are really red.

'Are you okay?' I ask.

'No. I'm sad about Billie.'

'I know. I was sort of asking if there was anything I could do.'

'Make the killer go away, so he doesn't come for us.'

I roll my eyes, realizing. 'Oh, so that's what you're worried about. Yourself.'

'Of course I'm sad about Billie too,' Hattie says. 'She was my best friend.'

Even though I know me and Billie are best, true, forever friends, and Hattie is only her best friend, something about this annoys me. But I'm really bad at comebacks, so I just shrug and stand there.

Hattie taps Poppy on the arm. 'Come on, Poppy. Better not talk to the last person who saw Billie alive – and the first person who saw her dead,' she says, and then sobs.

Poppy bites her lip, but goes to follow Hattie.

'You're a sheep,' I mumble at Poppy.

'You're a weirdo,' Hattie snaps.

'You're a . . . a nymphomaniac!' I say, which is an insult I heard on the telly that I've been waiting for a chance to use.

'You don't know what that means, Thera. Always trying to sound smart, even now that Billie's gone and you should be thinking about her.'

'I *am* smart, and I *am* thinking about her, all the time, and I'm going to find out how she died and do something about it. Not like you, just moaning and being a thicko!' I exclaim. Suddenly I stop. Hattie is sticking her tongue out at me, but I'm having a thought. Why would Hattie be attacking me so viciously? Unless she wants everyone's eyes to be on me, so they don't see what's right in front of their noses. Her. Hattie. A girl who is mean and cruel and evil to the core. What if it wasn't the walker who killed Billie? What if Hattie, a girl who wanted to be Billie's best friend so badly, decided that, if she couldn't have Billie, no one would?

I'd be off the hook. Billie's death wouldn't be my fault any more. It wouldn't bring her back, of course, but . . . at least I wouldn't have killed my best, true, forever friend.

Perhaps, on that hot summer night, Hattie doubled back from the village and found Billie in the field. Perhaps she asked Billie to be her best friend, and Billie, of course, said no. She coaxed Billie to the woods. Billie went willingly, because she was so nice, and she felt sorry for Hattie. Billie walked into the den, where she met her doom. I see it in my mind's eye so clearly that I suddenly truly believe it.

I slip my bag off my shoulder. With both hands, I swing it backwards, and then forwards, right into Hattie's head.

She screams, and falls down.

Over the other side of the playground, I see Sam clap his hands to his eyes. Both the dinner ladies and a couple of adults who are hanging about the playground (I think one is Daisy from Year One's mum and the other is Philip from Reception's dad) rush over, all of them shouting my name.

Mrs Stephenson, one of the dinner ladies, gets to Hattie first and looks at her face. 'She's bleeding!' She frowns at my hands. 'What have you got in that bag?' Before I can say anything, she snatches it off me. Usually we only take reading folders to school. They are fabric, A4, and hold our books, and they do up with Velcro on the top. But I've taken extra precautions because there's a murderer on the loose, so I brought an extra bag to school. You're supposed to do it with bricks in your bag, but I could only find blocks of solid wood at Dad's carpentry workshop.

Mrs Stephenson opens the pull-tie. She gasps, bringing out two pieces of wood. 'What in god's name—'

'I think Hattie's the killer!' I exclaim. 'Quick, grab her arms! Call the police!'

'For god's sake, Thera, Hattie can't be the killer – the killer's a man,' Mrs Stephenson says, telling me off.

'The killer's *definitely* a man?' I ask. 'How do you know?

'That's not something for silly girls like you to know.'

'Do they know who it is? Is it the walker?'

'They don't know who it is!' she snaps. 'But it's not Hattie! It's a man. So you just be careful what strange men you speak to. Of all the—'

'How do you know?'

Mrs Stephenson shakes one of the blocks at me. 'Your parents will be hearing about this, Thera.'

'My dad said I could borrow them.'

'Don't answer me back!'

'I wasn't answering— Ahh!'

Suddenly I'm knocked straight off my feet. It's Hattie, rushing me. My head hits the floor, and my eyes go fuzzy.

And then I see her.

Billie.

She is standing behind everyone, looking down on me, raising her eyebrows in that funny way she does, as if to say, 'Are you okay, bumface?'

I smile slowly, because even though it hurts to see her so pale and know that she is dead, I'd still rather see her than not. 'I knew you'd come back for me,' I murmur.

Billie scribbles in the air like she's holding a pen. I nod, understanding.

The automatic writing.

For the rest of the afternoon I miss Billie. Of course I also do schoolwork, history and geography, but mostly I miss Billie. I miss her jokes, I miss her doodles, I miss plaiting her hair.

On the way home I plan when I'll do the automatic writing. It'll have to be later, after bedtime, so Mum and Dad don't come in. I cross my fingers, hoping the walker isn't the killer. Mrs Stephenson said the police didn't know for sure. If it wasn't the walker, maybe Billie will tell me, when I am writing her words, that it wasn't my fault. Maybe she'll even tell me who the killer was. If I was stood in front of him, if he tried to attack me, I would attack him back with all my might for what he did to Billie. I am thinking about this, about what I would do to him, so intently I don't notice Nathan Nolan until he has hold of my arm. I scream loudly, because for a moment I think the killer has grabbed me.

'Thera!' Dad shouts, turning around. For a second he looks really panicked. Then he looks past me, at Nathan, and lets out a huge sigh. 'Jesus Christ.' He puts his hand on his heart. 'It's Nathan. Are you alright, son?'

'Er, yeah,' Nathan says, looking at Dad weirdly, as if he doesn't like him.

'If you want to talk to Nathan, Thee, Sam and me will wait for you by the pub.'

I frown. How does he know who Nathan is?

'Do you want to?' Dad asks.

'Er . . .' I say. 'Sure.' Dad and Sam walk off.

'Are you okay?' Nathan asks me.

I shrug, but I don't say anything.

Nathan shuffles from foot to foot and looks over to my dad, who is now sat on the pub wall holding Sam's hand. 'Your dad is big.'

'I dunno. Not bigger than other dads.'

'Is he alright?'

I don't know how to answer him. 'Erm. He's not ill or anything. We're all a bit sad.'

'I heard about Billie,' says Nathan.

'Yeah,' I say, because I don't feel like saying anything else.

'I heard you found her in the den.'

I frown suddenly. 'How did you know she was in the den? That wasn't on the news.'

'Huh?' Nathan says. 'Yes it was.'

'Hmm.' I search his face. 'You know, the murderer could be any man. Or boy.'

'Oh,' Nathan says. He screws up his face a bit. 'How . . . how do you know?'

'I just do,' I reply cagily. 'If it's not the walker . . .' I falter. 'That's this guy the police are interested in. Mum says they haven't found him yet, but they want to question him. If it's not him, it's still definitely a man. Mrs Stephenson said.'

'Well, *I* didn't murder her.'

'Okay . . .'

'Who's the walker?'

'I dunno. This guy.'

'Well, what does he look like?'

'Um . . .' I think, embarrassed. 'A bit gorgeous, dark hair, greenish clothes.'

Nathan bites his lip. 'That's good.'

'What's good?'

'That they know who he is.'

'They don't know for sure,' I say quickly. 'They just . . . suspect that it's him.'

'It sounds like . . . I mean, it might be, though.'

'Do you know him?

'No.'

Neither of us says anything for a minute, but I think Nathan knows more than he's letting on and, since I'm looking for alternative murder suspects, I decide to ask for an alibi. 'Where were you last Saturday night?'

'At home.'

'On a Saturday? Doing what?'

'Playing.'

'Playing what?'

'Cards.'

'Hmm.'

We stand in silence for a bit. Nathan looks nervous, as if maybe he really has murdered someone. 'Do you want to hang out sometime?' he says.

I frown. 'What? Like to play cards?'

'No, I just meant . . . whatever.'

'Like, come round to yours?'

'No, no, just hang out in the village. Have you got a football?'

'Sure. Sam and me have. I'll ask him if I can borrow it. Or maybe he can come? Mum likes him to come with me if I'm playing out.'

'Um . . .' Nathan says, looking up at the sky. He squints at the sun. 'I thought maybe it would be cool if you and me could be alone . . . together.'

My Nano Pet buzzes in my pocket, and then a bird sings at us from the hedge, like it's replying to my Nano. It makes Nathan and me both giggle, which is weird, because I didn't think I'd ever be able to laugh again, without Billie. She's been dead less than a week. This makes me feel guilty. As does the fact that I'm standing talking to Nathan Nolan like everything's normal and Billie hasn't just died. I realize I won't be able to go home and call Billie and tell her about this conversation. Unless . . . maybe I could tell her ghost about him. I study Nathan. His cheeks are a bit pink.

'So . . . do you think that would be okay? To hang out alone with me?'

I nod. 'Sure.'

'Oh, cool, that's . . . Maybe, like, Friday, then?'

'Let me check my diary.' I have my diary with me because the police photocopied it and dropped it back yesterday, so I open the padlock. I stare at it, but really I'm just trying to play it cool. It's important not to be too keen with boys, or they'll think you're a crazy stalker and you'll lose all your power. (Hattie's older sister told us so, when we were having a sleepover. She said in a good relationship the girl is always in charge. She should know about relationships. She's been out with all the boys at the bus stop. But probably not Nathan. She's fifteen, so way too old for him. He's thirteen.) 'Yep,' I say after a beat. 'Friday's good for me.'

'Cool!' He looks relieved. 'I get home from school about four twenty.'

'I'll meet you at the circle by the graveyard at four thirty,' I say. The circle is a roundabout of green grass. It's near the graveyard, but isn't near the triangle, where the walker was, so it feels safer.

'Okay.' He laughs. 'Spooky.'

'Don't worry, I won't be late, if you're scared,' I say. We wave bye, even though we're only two paces away from each other, and then I go over to Dad and Sam, and Nathan goes the other way.

Sam's rucksack makes a *fuh-lump, fuh-lump* sound as he jogs to keep up with my skipping. When we are a bit ahead of Dad, he whispers, 'Did Nathan Nolan ask you out?'

'No!' I shout, and run the rest of the way home, so Dad and Sam have to run to keep up with me. I imagine Billie is running beside me. Not her ghost, though. I'm imagining her alive.

At four thirty on Friday, I come through the cut that runs from the school towards the church, and see Nathan Nolan sitting on the graveyard gate. Dad walked me most of the way through the village, but he let me do the last bit on my own because there are so many police around anyway. There is even a policewoman behind Nathan, stood in the churchyard.

Nathan waves. 'Hi!'

'Hiya,' I call back as I walk up to him.

Nathan looks down at me. His lips are dark pink. Mine are a lighter pink. 'Cool football,' he says.

It's a Man United one, covered in emblems. I don't support any particular team, but if I did it would be Man United, because that's what everyone round here supports. I think it's weird, though, to support a team. What does 'supporting a team' mean, anyway? You don't send them money. 'Do you support Man United?' I say.

'I'm supposed to support Galway United,' he says. 'Because my mum and dad are Irish. But I support Liverpool. It's cool to have a ball with the logo on, though. It's official.'

'Aren't you Irish too?'

'No. I was born here.'

'Where?'

'England.'

'But what city?'

'I don't know. Maybe Coventry or Birmingham. We used to live around there. When Dad did . . .'

'When your dad did what?'

'Nothing.'

'It's weird to not know where you were born,' I say. 'I was born in Cleethorpes.'

He shrugs.

'So, you don't have a football at all? That's basically unheard of, for a boy,' I say.

'Well, I did have one, but it got a puncture last year.'

'Why don't you buy a new one?'

'I haven't got enough money. I'm saving up.'

'When's your birthday? Can't you ask for one for then?'

He jumps down from the gate and shrugs again. Nathan seems to be a big shrugger. He takes the ball out of my hands and kicks it around in a circle. He's pretty good. He kicks it back to me. 'The second of July.'

'That was only a few weeks ago! Happy birthday!' I frown. 'That's weird.'

'What?'

'Nothing.' I've just realized his birthday was the day we used the Ouija board and found the dogs. The day the ghostly girl warned me about death being near. It's a weird coincidence, but I'm not sure I trust Nathan enough yet to tell him. I don't know if it's significant yet. 'Happy birthday anyway.'

'Thanks.'

'What kind of party did you have?'

'I didn't have a party,' Nathan says.

I frown. Nathan is acting odd. 'Well . . . what did you get?'

'Just stuff. Do you know how to play football?'

'Yeah, I play with my brother. Open the gate, we can use that as a goal.'

We prop the gate to the graveyard open with Nathan's school bag. We play a few times and we have an equal number of goals, even though he's a boy and does football in school. Being a girl, I have to do netball, but I like both.

'You're pretty aggressive,' he says, because I accidentally kicked his shin.

'You have to be,' I say, thinking about Billie, which I have basically every minute since she died. I don't want to stop, in case she feels hurt, or in case I forget anything about her. 'Life's tough.'

'I'm sorry about Billie,' he says.

'You said that the other day.'

'Yeah, I know . . . Anyway, you've got a pretty good life otherwise, haven't you?'

I make a face. 'Well, Billie's a big part of why it's good. Was. And now I feel . . .'

'What?'

'Alone, I guess.'

'You've got other friends. Hattie an' that.'

I scoff. 'Hattie bullies me.'

He stops playing. 'Oh. I know Hattie's sister.'

'Are you friends?'

He laughs weirdly. 'Kind of. She's really bossy.'

'What does she boss you around about?'

He shrugs. 'Nothing. Just stuff. What's Hattie been saying? Does she hit you?'

'No. Well, today, but . . . not normally. She's not crazy. She's always bullied me, but now she keeps saying . . . saying I killed Billie.'

'That's mean.'

'Well, I didn't kill her but . . .' Suddenly I feel a bit rubbish, like I might cry. 'It might be my fault.'

'How would it be your fault?'

'I made her go up to the man who is probably the pervert. I left her in the fields to walk home. And it was my idea to spy on the walker in the first place. It's my fault. I know everyone thinks so.' I look at him, ashamed. It seems like he feels bad for me. He kicks the ball into the hedge.

'It wasn't your fault,' he mutters. 'I promise. It wasn't.'

I frown. 'But . . . how do you know?'

'I just . . . 'cause cause you're not . . . you weren't . . . you didn't finish her off.'

There's something weird in the way Nathan says 'finish her off'. I look at him suspiciously. 'But how do you *know* I didn't—'

Suddenly he forgets about the ball, and comes up to me and hugs me. I am surprised, and I don't know what to do for a few seconds, but then I put my head on his shoulder. He smells like chocolate and sweaty body odour and apples, and his neck is very warm. His school jumper is thin and waxy. How can it be that thin already, when it was new at the start of the school year? I can feel his hands, gently stroking my back just a tiny bit. I put my hands on his back. He is hard and bony, like a bird.

'It's not your fault, Thera,' Nathan says. 'You're a good person.' Then he pulls away and goes to get the ball.

'Mm.' I say. I've forgotten my train of thought. What were we talking about? Oh. Yeah. Hattie. 'Hattie probably won't bully me any more because we had a meeting with Mr Kent and he told us it has to stop. We've only got one more week of school and we have to be nice to each other.'

'I've got one week of school left too. Maybe we can hang out in the summer?'

'We're going to Majorca at the end of August, but I can hang out before that, and after.'

'Oh. When are you going?'

'On the twenty-eighth. Where are you going on holiday?'

He thinks. 'Maybe we'll visit my nan,' he says hopefully.

Now it's my turn to shrug. 'I guess that will be fun. I like my grandparents.'

'I like my nan.'

'Don't you have any others?'

'Grandad died ages ago, and my dad's parents are in Ireland.'

'That's sad,' I say, and then, because I don't know what else to add, 'Let's go in the graveyard.'

Nathan looks spooked, but he picks up the football anyway. The policewoman standing in the porch of the church watches us, her eyes following where we walk. It's creepy. 'Are you going to the memorial?' he asks.

'Huh?'

'They're having a memorial for Billie in the church on Monday night. It's on the noticeboard by the gate.'

'Oh yeah. Mr Kent mentioned it in assembly.'

'They had a candlelight vigil for that other dead girl on telly.'

'What other dead girl?'

'You know. Jenny Ann Welder, who went missing in March. It was on the news for ages.'

'I don't watch the news.'

'Why not?'

'Well, I guess it's kind of boring. To *me*, anyway,' I say, diplomatically. 'Also, we're not allowed to watch it at the moment, because of Billie. Does your mum let you watch it?'

'She doesn't know. She works 'til late, or stays out or whatever. I don't usually watch it but . . . I've been keeping up with the news about Billie. They did a big story about her every night this week on *Look North*.' *Look North* with Peter Levy is our local news programme. It comes on after the important news from London.

'What about your dad?'

'He doesn't live with us.'

'Why not?'

Nathan looks away. 'I don't wanna talk about him. He's a fucking bastard.'

I'm shocked by the swearing, so I don't know what to say. Poor, rougher people do swear more. That's what Nan says. She knows, because her dad was a navvy on the railways. Nathan probably doesn't know better, so I politely ignore it. 'Oh, right. So what do they say about Billie? Have they arrested the killer yet?'

'No, they haven't arrested anyone yet.'

'Not even the walker?' I say, dismayed. 'For questioning?'

'Nope,' he says, kicking at the ground and not looking at me. 'Anyway, did you want to go with me to the memorial?'

I wrinkle my nose. 'It's not a social event.'

'I know,' he says. 'You don't have to.' He sounds offended.

I think about it. I really want to keep my eyes out for Billie, but I like Nathan and, what with Hattie headbutting me in the stomach and everything, I don't actually have many friends any more. Well, not living ones. I have Sam, but he has to be my friend because he's my brother. 'Sure,' I say, eventually. 'Shall we meet at the gate?'

'Yeah, okay. Cool.'

We walk along the line of gravestones. I frown, thinking. 'Why would you kill someone?'

'I wouldn't,' he says quickly.

'No, but if you did. Revenge? Hatred? Anger? Jealousy? Maybe it's more complicated than that. Do you think it could be the same killer? He could be going after people with one-syllable middle names? Jenny Ann Welder . . . Billie May Brooke . . .'

We stop at a grave that has a little angel carved into the stone. Her name was Elizabeth Locke and she died in 1889. We pat the stone. 'You think it might be a serial killer?' Nathan asks quietly.

'A serial killer.' I swallow, nervously. 'Of little girls.'

He bites his nails and looks around, then twizzles the football on one finger.

I want to tell him about the ghost girls, but I don't know if I can trust him yet. Instead I say, 'Girls about our age die all the time. You always hear about them. Sometimes younger ones, and some that just go missing. Sometimes they're never found. And sometimes they're found dead.' I climb onto the edge of a stone tomb and walk along it, looking around at the countryside. It's a humid day, and the heat haze makes the fields in the distance fuzzy. Flies and bees buzz around us, and an occasional bird flaps by above. 'But why girls? And why *those* girls? What do they all have in common?'

'Well, they're all really pretty, aren't they?' says Nathan, absentmindedly.

I turn back to him, my eyes wide. The dead girls are all very pretty.

'That's a really good point, Nathan. But why would someone want to kill pretty girls?' I stroke my chin, as if I have a beard and I'm Sherlock Holmes or something. I do this thinking of Billie. All my humour is geared towards making Billie laugh, but she's not here to see it. Just Nathan, who doesn't seem to find it funny. He's jiggling his legs, like he needs the toilet. He tries to bounce the ball on the ground, but it just rolls. Footballs don't bounce.

'That's what pervs do, isn't it?' Nathan says.

I freeze. 'Billie's mum said the walker was a pervert.'

'Yeah.'

'Wait. How do you know it's a pervert?' A warning light is going off in my brain. 'You seem to know an awful lot about it.'

'I told you. I watch it on the news. Anyway, it's obvious.

Billie was pretty. She was found dead in a ditch. Pretty girls get killed by pervs and dumped in ditches.'

There is a strange feeling in my stomach. Pervs do weird things to girls, like have sex with them. Did the pervert do anything to Billie? Did he have sex with her? Or did she die before he could? The thought makes me feel really sick, like I'm about to throw up. Suddenly I want to be out of my physical body, so I can't be killed or touched too.

Nathan is watching me. He pats me on the back, consolingly, then goes back to messing about with the football.

I feel like, if I open my mouth, vomit will come out. But I have another question. 'Have you ever felt like that about a girl?'

Nathan frowns. 'What? Wanted to kill one 'cause she was pretty? No!'

'Good,' I say quickly. The vomit is settling on the bottom of my stomach. 'Okay, good.'

Nathan wrinkles his lip and turns away from me. He mutters something.

'What? I can't hear you.'

'I've fancied girls before. Obviously. That's normal.' He mumbles this, still with his back to me.

'Have you had a girlfriend before?'

'Sort of. I've done things. With Lauren, mainly.'

Now suddenly the sick feeling is back. 'Hattie's sister? What things? Kissing?'

'Stuff like that. Whatever she wanted.' Nathan turns

around and shrugs uncomfortably. 'I told you, she's bossy. Sometimes we went to the den and I touched her boobs.'

I feel physically sick. Hattie's sister is awful. Now Nathan is tainted. 'Do you still?'

'No. I never really liked her, she just liked me. She said she'd say things to people at school about me if I didn't.'

'What things?'

Nathan is chewing his lip and not looking right at me. He kicks the ball up into his hands. 'I better be going now.'

I follow him back to the gate. I don't want him to go. 'Do you have to be home for tea?' I ask, hoping he's not gone off me. 'We have tea at five thirty.'

He looks at me weirdly, almost meanly. 'Yeah,' he smirks. 'I'm sure Mum will have tea waiting on the table when I get back.'

'Me too,' I say uncertainly. Nathan hands me the football.

'You can borrow it if you like,' I say. 'You can bring it back at the memorial.'

He smiles, considering it, but shakes his head. 'Thanks. But I don't think I could keep it neat.'

We walk back to the end of my street. Nathan has to keep going, to the caravan park. When we get there, I say, 'So, maybe a serial killer killed Billie. Why do you think Mrs Stephenson would know for sure it's a man, unless she had something to do with it? I'll have to think about that. Find out if other people think it's a man—'

'It's a man,' says Nathan, nodding.

'How do you know?' I say suspiciously.

He looks back at me blankly, and shrugs for the ump-teenth time today.

'Because . . . Oh!' I realize. 'Perverts are men?'

'Yeah,' he sighs impatiently. 'Because men are perverts. Men like girls, don't they?'

I nod. Nathan must think I'm really slow. Of course the killer is a man. Because whoever it is, whether it's the walker or not, if someone kills a pretty girl and leaves her in a ditch . . . then that's a pervert. And perverts are men. 'Right. So I'm looking for a male pervert, possibly a serial killer.'

'Well, the police are.'

'Um, yeah.' I blink at him. 'The police are.' I'm not sure whether today with Nathan went well and I feel like he wants to leave, so I say, 'Bye', and start to walk off.

But then I hear him calling after me, and when I turn he runs up to me, and hugs me, with his hands on my back. It's not a bear hug like Dad, it's like the one Nathan gave me before, really gentle. He pulls out of the hug, but then he darts in and kisses me on the cheek, a big smacker. 'Bye,' he says quickly, and then he runs away from me, around the corner down the main road. I watch him as he runs. I press my hand to my cheek and get the kiss on my fingers, and then I clasp my hand to my heart.

Oh, boys. They are so weird.

And then I take my hand away. For a minute, I forgot about Billie. It's a minute too long.

I failed when I tried automatic writing again the other night. I felt ashamed of myself. I wanted to talk to Billie, but when I did it everything went unnaturally quiet, and then I felt an icy breeze on my neck, and then, I'm not sure if I was mistaken, but I heard a low growl. I leapt up screaming. Dad came in and asked me what I was doing. I said, 'Nothing.'

He frowned at me for a moment and said, 'Just get back to drawing nicely, now.' I looked at my pad and pen, and put them away. I try again the night I meet up with Nathan, but there is no icy breeze, and no growl, and no word from Billie. I hope it's only because she is disappointed in me after the other night, and not because the walker is the killer. If he is, I definitely led her to her death. I pray to her, and whisper to her that I'm sorry, and I'll be braver. I swear to her that if I led her to her death I didn't mean to, that I would switch our places if she wanted me to. I say I hope she's okay, wherever she is. Tears fall down my cheeks and I wipe them away with the cuff of my T-shirt. Billie's not okay. She's dead. I sit in the dark for a bit, imagining how I would have saved her if I had been there. After I've stopped crying, I go down to the kitchen to get supper, and accidentally overhear Mum and Dad talking.

'. . . make sure they aren't affected by it.'

'. . . total overreaction,' says Dad. 'I'm not sending Thera to a psychiatrist.'

'Christ! It's just a counsellor. She's clearly disturbed by what's going on. And Sam.'

'Sam's doing alright.'

'He's started wetting the bed again.'

'You didn't tell me that.'

'You're never here, you're always at the workshop.'

'I have to be, it's a new business!' Dad shouts, and then Mum shushes him.

'I found a book in her room about Ouija boards,' says Mum.

I almost gasp. What was she doing snooping round my room?

'Thera has always been . . .' I strain to hear, but Dad mutters it, whatever it was.

'I think . . .' Then Mum mutters something.

'She's just different!' Dad exclaims in a burst. 'She's different from other children.'

There is a long pause. I sit down against the door, my back to them. I want to tell them: I like that I'm different. Billie always liked that I was different. Billie was the only one who ever understood me. I was pathetic not finishing the automatic writing. I should try harder, for her.

'We've got to shield them from the details of the investigation,' Dad says. 'That's all. Mitigate their exposure to it.'

'Agreed,' Mum says, 'but we're keeping so much from them at the moment.'

'Whatever's going on between us has nothing to do with them.'

What's that all about? I shake my head. I don't like being kept in the dark. It's not in my nature. I like to know everything. I make a decision. I'll do the automatic writing and I won't be scared. I want to know what happened, even if it was my fault Billie died.

I crawl slowly back up the stairs, and then clomp down them loudly and ask for some milk and cheese on toast.

After supper, Mum and Dad tuck me in, and then at midnight I get back out of bed. I hold the pencil loosely over my drawing pad. The light is off and I've opened the windows again, so everything is how it was the first time, when it worked. I whisper Billie's name and I ask her to come to me, for her spirit to enter my body and use my hand, and tell me about the night she died. The iciness comes and slips around my neck. I tense, and struggle to breathe normally. The cold is inside me. It creeps down my arms and sits in my fingers.

I have no memory of the pen moving. The cold grips me for a few minutes and then disappears. When I open my eyes, I see one of the black dogs in the corner, squatting down by the bookcase. Its haunches are muscular and its short fur shines in the moonlight. The dog growls, and I have to hold my lips shut to keep from screaming, but then it becomes a girl. She turns her head to look at me, and it's so creepy I can't help myself: I jump up and run to switch on the light, but when I look back she's gone. It was the one who was about nine, with the ginger hair. I look down at the paper on the floor. My eyes widen. There are letters written on it. None of them spell words, they are not Billie's handwriting and I don't remember writing them, but there are loads.

T H G O O I E O M T N A W
S E A D H I E L K I M L E U N T H W L O D
A G S T T C P R A O E E Y O U T M S E N J T N H I E

Now she's off to university. The freedom of the halls, and the possibility of a new beginning. Sweaty-palmed, she tries to make friends. She sits in the library. She is meek. She is boring. Her opinions are not interesting. She is not well educated. There comes the slow, sad realization that she is still the same person. Still weak as water. Still a B student.

And then. Him.

He walked into the room. It was a party, at the student halls of residence, but it could have been any room in the universe. It was fate. He was tall, handsome, with almost-blonde hair. He was charming. Everyone loved him. But in this room, as he walked in, he looked at her. Their eyes met, right away, and reflected back in his perfect blue irises there she was, the right one. The girl in his eyes was an angel, still quiet and pale and fragile, but adored. He came over, said hello, offered to get her a drink. Later that night he told her there was something inside him that recognized something in her, some need he could not yet articulate. It was so fast it was frightening. Everything she ever wanted to be she was to him, in the instant they met. Everything she was crystallized in that moment, and she was never the same. (How right it felt, what a relief it was, after a lifetime of being lost, to find myself. I wasn't even broken. I was whole and perfect.)

She is eighteen and has nothing else to hold onto. Her parents never call, and when she comes home for holidays they ask her why she hasn't found a place she can live over Easter, why is her father paying so much for 'halls' when she can't even live there outside term time? He's not paying, the government is, but she knows he'll come after her with the hand that carries that glass of whiskey if she says anything. They complain she is taking up a bed they now use for her sister. She sleeps on the floor, in the living room, so Ginny can be rested for her exams. She is up by six every day so she doesn't anger Dad. She makes breakfast, she sits in their small garden. She tends the vegetables. She uses the old outdoor toilet. She avoids her parents. At university, she wanders the corridors like a ghost. She's not even teased any more, just a ghost of the girl who used to be teased.

When he looks at her now, and he murmurs to her, and he tells her how extraordinary she is, she feels like she has miraculously been thrown a life jacket in a sea empty of other people, where she was drowning.

She can't let that version of herself walk out of the room. She can't let the man who sees her, who sweeps her up without touching her, who knows her beauty and caresses her body with those intelligent, piercing eyes, leave.

She'll do anything to be with him. Anything.

'Why do you think ghosts haunt people?' I ask Hattie on Monday at school. We are eating our sandwiches in the playground at lunch, and talking about Billie. I haven't told them about the dead girls yet. I think Hattie would just think I was going nuts.

'Because they have unfinished business. Duh.' She always has to make me feel stupid.

'I thought so. But what if you think their business is finished?'

'You're wrong. They probably have some unfinished business that you don't know about.'

'Like . . . seeking revenge on their murderer or something?'

'Yes. Do we have to talk about this? It's morbid.'

School is ending soon, so we are making an effort to be friends. Or we'll grow apart when we grow up and are married. I guess that would be kind of sad. If Billie were here, we probably would all stay friends naturally, because we would all want to be friends with Billie. It's good, at least, when I am with Hattie and Poppy, that I can talk about Billie, because I can't stop thinking about her anyway, and about those letters. What did they mean? Were they a code?

We are quiet for a few minutes as we all feed our Nanos, and a thought occurs to me. 'Guys.'

'Yup?'

'Just . . . What's a pervert?' Hattie rolls her eyes and I put my hand up. 'I know, I know. A pervert is an old man with a white van, who tries to snatch girls into it. And I know they are, like, creepy,' I say, uncomfortably. 'But what about the other stuff? Why specifically did he pick Billie? What did he want?' I hesitate. 'What . . . what stuff did he do to her?'

'I don't know!' Hattie exclaims. 'It's horrible to think about that. Stop being weird.'

'You should know about this stuff.'

'What? Why would I know?'

'Because of your sister,' I blurt out.

Hattie frowns. 'What's my sister got to do with it?'

'Nothing,' I say, thinking of Nathan. I grit my teeth and try another tack: appeasing her. 'You're really grown-up, Hattie, I bet you know more than me.'

Hattie looks around, to see who's listening. 'I don't mean to be really protective, but they are too young to hear this.' She points to the Year Fives, who are sat nearby. They are only ten.

I nod, and we stand up, walk over to the hopscotch corner and sit down next to each other on the big rubber tractor tyre.

Hattie puts her Nano Pet on the ground with her lunch-box. Even Hattie seems a little shaky as she says, 'You know what perverts do, Thera.' Then she spells out the word rape, mouthing the letters without saying them. R-a-p-e.

Afterwards we all shiver, as if a cold wind has blown through the playground.

'We don't know that's what happened to Billie, though,' I say quietly.

Poppy replies with a hushed voice, though. There is a sense from all of us that we shouldn't be talking about this; that we should miss Billie without speaking about what happened to her. 'I think it did. I heard my parents talking about it.' My cheeks start to heat up. 'I hope she wasn't in too much pain,' Poppy adds.

I scoff. 'Any pain is too much pain.'

'I meant . . .' Poppy shakes her head.

We are silent for a minute and then Hattie murmurs, 'My mum and her boyfriend said Billie got killed because she was the prettiest.' She looks at me and Poppy. 'You know, of all of us. I heard them talking. They said it was a shame she was so pretty, because that's why he took her.'

Poppy picks her nails. 'I guess I'm glad I'm not pretty, then.'

There is an awkward pause. 'You *are* pretty,' I tell her. But Poppy is definitely not anywhere near as pretty as Billie.

'No, I'm not, I'm fat,' Poppy says quickly, and pokes her belly.

Hattie kicks a pebble and looks out over the playground. 'You can't argue over whether you're pretty or not, you just are or aren't.' She says this absentmindedly, without her usual venom. 'Billie was *so* pretty, with her long blonde hair. You are quite pretty, Poppy,' she adds.

I hesitate. When I was in Year Four, a boy two years

older than us kissed me on the cheek for a dare. His friends must have thought I was ugly if they dared him to kiss me. And the pervert didn't choose me, did he? The evidence speaks for itself. 'Nathan Nolan said that too, about being pretty. He said all the girls who are our age who get killed are pretty.'

Hattie frowns. 'You've been talking to Nathan Nolan? Why?'

'He asked me to play football with him.'

She makes a face. 'I wouldn't go talking to Nathan. He lives next to the woods. He could have killed Billie.'

'No! He . . . Nathan's nice,' I say uncertainly, thinking back to my conversation with him in the graveyard. He knew things, like the fact that I didn't 'finish her off', and that it was a pervert that killed her.

'You don't know him. He's rough.'

'He's just a boy.'

'Um, *yeah*.' Hattie is still muttering, but her usual mean tone is coming back, like she thinks I'm an idiot. 'A boy, i.e. a man, i.e. a possible pervert and killer of Billie.' She shrugs. 'I'm just warning you for your own good.'

'Well . . . you're wrong.'

She shrugs. 'Okay, fine, hang out with him, then.'

'He has an alibi, anyway,' I say, remembering. 'He was at home, playing cards.'

'That's not an alibi – not if he was alone. Was he gambling with other people?'

'Like his friends?'

'No, like with the other Gypsies from the park.'

'Nathan isn't a Gypsy,' I say, then, frowning, 'Is he?'

'Duh. He lives in a caravan. Also, Mum said his dad's in prison.'

'Why's his dad in prison?' asks Poppy.

'Mum won't tell me, but he's been in there for a really long time, so . . . you can guess.'

'D'you think he could have killed Billie?' I ask nervously.

'No, he's still in prison. But . . .'

'But what?'

'You never know. Like father, like son.'

I shake my head, but I feel frightened. 'He didn't kill Billie. He wouldn't. He likes me and she's my best, true, forever friend.'

'Anyway,' Hattie continues darkly, 'Nathan wanted to meet up with me, but Mum won't allow me to, because he's rough and older. He asked me, though. So he must have moved on to you.'

I blush. I wish Billie were here. But then, she never did hear it when Hattie was mean. Billie's not mean at all, so she doesn't understand it when other people are. Didn't. 'I bet he only asked you first because you live near the caravan park, and because he was finished with your sister,' I whisper.

'She finished with him,' Hattie says. 'Did he tell you he finished with her? Don't be nuts. Anyway, it's obvious why he'd prefer to spend time with me than you.'

'Why is it obvious?' I say, my voice getting louder. 'I'm much better at playing pretend and football and playing games than you are.' I drop to a mutter again and say to myself, 'Billie always thought so.'

Hattie rolls her eyes. 'You're such a child. No one our age but you makes up things, or has imaginary friends, or *plays* any more.' She uses bunny ears when she says 'plays', like it's not a real thing. 'That's not why boys ask out girls. Nathan obviously asked me first because I'm prettier than you. And if Billie was here . . .' She presses her lips together.

'If Billie was here, what?'

'Nothing. Forget it.'

I look down at the ground, feeling tears coming. 'You're not prettier than me,' I whisper. But maybe she is. I haven't thought about it before.

'Yes, I am. I'm the next-prettiest in the group, after Billie. That's why Mum says I have to be really careful about the murderer too.'

'It's not a competition to see who gets killed first! The murderer could come for any of us.'

'Yes, but he's more likely to come for me. Or maybe Poppy, but she's flat-chested.'

'What's that got to do with anything?'

Hattie looks at Poppy and they both snicker, like they have a secret I don't know about.

'He could have taken Billie because she was funny, or kind,' I say quietly. 'It's not always about being pretty.'

'Er, yes, Thera,' Hattie says. 'With the male species, I think you'll find it is.' She looks tired, as if our conversation has exhausted her. I know she is thinking about Billie, and that she misses her too, but she can't overlook the chance to be mean. She turns to Poppy. 'Nathan's going to be running back to me after hanging out with Thera. She clearly doesn't know anything about men.'

Just then the bell rings, and we have to go in. I stand up and look down at her. 'You're trying to make fun of me, Hattie, but men aren't a *species*. So clearly you don't know anything either.'

'Oh *god*,' Hattie exclaims, and drops her head into her hands, like she has given up on me. Poppy giggles uncertainly, always trying to keep on Hattie's good side. I walk away on my own.

We have reading time in the afternoon. I go in the library, where it's nice and snuggly, and bagsy a beanbag. I feel awful inside, but outside I try not to show it. I think about my dad, and how he always says I should be brave when I fall over or cut myself.

But then I think about rape. It's sex. But the man forces the woman.

Sex is what mums and dads do.

It's what boyfriends and girlfriends do too, like Hattie's older sister and her new boyfriend. Hattie told us they had already done it. Did she do it with Nathan too? I shake the thought away.

What if the girl doesn't want sex? What if the man just goes ahead and rapes her if he wants to?

I wonder, if Nathan was a rapist, if he would rather rape me or Hattie.

And then . . . do you die from it? Or do they kill you after? Do they kill you 'cause they think it's sexy? How long after you're raped do you die?

Boys prefer girls with big boobs. Billie didn't have big boobs. But that's why a pervert is a pervert. He likes children. Right? Or is that a paedo?

I've read every book we have in the library. I finished all the reading stages and went on to Free Readers when I was still in Year One. I have been bringing my own books into school since I was in Sam's year group. Now I'm reading *Anne of Green Gables*.

I open the book and pull out the bit of paper from automatic writing. It's all mumbo jumbo. I haven't been able to work it out so far. I look at the last line.

A G S T T C P R A O E E Y O U T M S E N J T N H I E

I pull my pencil out of my pocket and circle the letters P R A and E. Then I reorder them to spell 'rape'. I stare at the rest of the letters. Suddenly I start. I circle the letters S T T C O S H I, and reorder them to spell 'Scottish'. Jenny Ann Welder was Scottish. I asked Hattie about her. She brought the paper in to show me. It was comparing Jenny's disappearance to Billie's, and it has Jenny's picture in. Jenny's body was never found. After 'Scottish', I'm left with:

G A E Y O U T M E N J T N E

I play around with the letters a bit, and then I write down:

> *Jenny*
> *Get*
> *Me*
> *Out*
> *(spare A)*

I don't know what that means. Then I realize. It's 'Get me out Jenny'. Maybe the A is supposed to be a comma. It was all quite scribbly. I work on the first two lines, now I've figured out they are anagrams. After five minutes, I sit back, satisfied, and spooked. The message reads:

I want to go home
He said he wouldn't kill me
Get me out,
Jenny

Maybe the ginger girl's name is Jenny, and she's a spirit, stuck somewhere she shouldn't be. Like, on earth.

'Thera?'

I jump, and shut the book on the paper. 'Mrs Adamson!'

'What are you doing?'

'Nothing. Reading.'

Mrs Adamson oversees the library for reading time. She always used to plait Billie's hair at reading time, and sometimes Billie plaited hers. Mrs Adamson always has her hair in a ponytail. It's ginger, like Jenny's. Mine and Billie's hair was the same, long and blondey-brown, but hers was silky and mine has loads of knots in it. I hesitate. I want to ask Mrs A something, and I think I trust her, although she can be lame sometimes. But she's a teacher, and she really liked Billie too.

'Mrs Adamson?'

'What is it, Thera?'

'Do you watch the news?'

'Yes. Why?'

'Is it definitely a pervert who killed Billie? I mean . . . did he do things to her?' I shift my bum uncomfortably. It makes me feel physically ill to talk about this.

'Oh my god, Thera,' she whines. 'Why would you ask me that? There are some things you don't need to know.'

'But . . . if Billie knew those things maybe she'd still be alive.'

She looks at me sideways. 'What?'

'Maybe all the dead girls would.'

Mrs Adamson stiffens. 'All of them?'

'Yeah, Jenny Ann Welder, and the one last year in pieces in the rubbish bin. Other . . . other ones,' I say, thinking of the ghost girls.

She gives me a strange look. 'Why are you thinking about them?'

'Is the killer definitely a pervert?' I ask. 'Based on the news?'

'Well,' she says sadly, 'it certainly seems like that's why he was interested in her, doesn't it?'

'How can you tell a pervert from just a normal man?'

She blinks at me. 'You can't.'

'Not at all?'

She thinks. 'No.'

'Would all men kill a girl if they could get away with it?'

She sighs. 'I think people do what they can get away with, and I think men have a voracious . . . a voracious . . . appetite. But you learn to make allowances. Sometimes the compromise, to be with the man you love, is a big one, but I know I . . . I couldn't live without my husband.' She shakes her head. 'I couldn't live without him.'

'What?' I say, confused.

'Oh, nothing.' A tear falls out of her eye.

'Are you sad because you miss Billie?'

She wipes her cheeks with a tissue from her pocket and is silent for a while. Finally, she says, 'Yes, that's why.'

I hesitate. 'There was a walker that we met while we were out. Do they think he killed Billie?'

She looks at me. 'Have you been watching the news?'

'No. I'm not allowed.'

'It's probably someone who was passing through, Thera, like a long-distance lorry driver. They probably won't catch him now. He'll have left the area.'

'But . . . but it's their job to solve crimes! How can anybody ever be safe if he's not caught?'

'The police aren't all they're cracked up to be, Thera. But don't tell your parents I said that. Anyway, you're just a little girl. You shouldn't be asking or thinking about anything like that – men and everything. You should be playing. I'll tell your parents if you keep on this tack.'

'Can I just ask one more question?'

She sighs, like I'm really annoying. 'What?'

'Um . . . How does a pervert kill a girl?' I ask, as politely as possible. Mrs Adamson always rewards politeness. That's another reason she liked Billie. Billie would go along with anything with a smile and a happy attitude. 'You know,' I say, 'after he . . . touches them?'

Mrs Adamson is staring into the middle distance. She doesn't answer.

'Mrs Adamson?'

'Get back to your book now, Thera,' she whispers. 'And

stay away from men. They're all bad for you, one way or another.'

I am about to ask what she means, but then there is a sudden creak at the door and Mrs A and me look up quickly.

Mr Kent smiles at us. His head extends into the room, like a lizard, and he licks his lips with his gross, meaty tongue. 'Just checking in on you,' he hisses softly, his eyes darting from me to Mrs A and back again. 'Just seeing how you both were.'

'What do you want in your sandwiches?' Dad asks after school. He is next to the counter, buttering bread, and Mum is stood next to him reading a letter. Our dad is the best, and the strongest man I know. He works in the village. He has his own carpentry workshop, and at home he does the washing-up, mending stuff and cooking. I wonder if he could ever be a rapist. Mrs A seemed to say all men would be, if they could. The thought makes a big knot in my stomach. I wonder if rape looks different from normal sex. It's a lot more violent, I guess, which is horrible to think about. Maybe that's how you die? Also, I wonder if you can get a baby from rape. You must be able to, if it's sex. Is that why it's better to die of it, because you'd be pregnant? Billie and me always thought babies were gross. I close my eyes as it hits me – again – that she's not here with me any more. Well, not alive, anyway.

'Thera?'

'Beetroot, mayonnaise and cheese,' I say.

Sam nods. We are sat squashed on the little sofa in the kitchen next to the back door, shoes shined, hair spat down, and ready to go to the memorial. 'Me too. Is that your favourite sandwich, Thera?'

'Yeah, probably.'

'Mine's tuna with onion and lettuce.'

'That's a good one. What are you having, Mum?'

'I don't know, Thera.'

'Are we having a roast tomorrow, when Nan and Grandad are here for tea?'

'I don't know.'

'Can we have chicken kievs?' Sam asks.

'We should have fish in a bag,' I say over Sam. Neither of us like roasts much. Broccoli tastes exactly like dirty, lukewarm dishwater.

The real question is: If the killer wasn't the walker, could Dad have raped Billie? When I asked him where he was that Saturday, he said he was in the pub the night she died, but I haven't actually checked to see if anyone saw him there. If the only reason for being a pervert is being a bad man, and nobody can tell a bad man from a good man . . . It could be any man at all. Or boy, like I thought with Nathan. I look at Sam. How young does that go to? I'm pretty sure it means older boys. Like Nathan's or my age, and up. I can't imagine anyone younger than me would know how to rape someone.

Dad puts my sandwich plate on my lap and I pick up a square and take a bite absentmindedly. Dad always cuts our sandwiches in squares, and Nan does triangles. I don't know which I prefer. I guess squares. I keep jiggling my leg. I think both Sam and me are nervous about tonight. We have been talking non-stop since we got home from school. I don't know what will happen at the memorial. Will I have to get up and make a speech about Billie? I don't think I could do her justice. I don't want her to be disappointed in me.

'Can I have a Club as well as a sandwich, Dad?' Sam asks.

'If we've got some left.'

'Me and Thera had three each at the weekend and there are ten in the packet, so that leaves four.'

'Dad, are you ever violent?' I ask.

Dad looks at me weirdly. 'What makes you say that, Thee?' Dad calls me Thee. He always says Thera is too long, but he's joking.

'I'm just checking.'

He puts Sam's sandwich plate on his lap and fetches him a Club chocolate bar. He puts it on the counter. 'For afters,' he says to Sam. Then he turns around and starts making his own sandwich. 'All animals have the capacity for violence. But I believe a civilized man should never partake in such base behaviour.'

Dad's clever. So is Mum. They didn't grow up with as much money as we have now, so they are a carpenter and a businesswoman. Sam and me have a better start in life, so we can be anything we want to be. Sam wants to be a baker. He loves iced buns. I go back and forth between astronaut and pop star like the Spice Girls.

'So it goes against your beliefs?' I say.

'That's right.'

Mum leaves the room.

I swallow a lump of sandwich, watching her go. Dad is lying to me. He is violent, sometimes. One time he shoved me in my room when he was grounding me. Another time, he banged on the table really hard when Sam and me were arguing in the living room. He argued with Mum once, and he smashed a lamp, and she came and got Sam and me out of bed and put us in the car and drove off. She parked the car on the road and we were crying really loudly, so she turned around and came back, and we went back to bed, and there was no more arguing.

I put my sandwich plate onto the sofa and excuse myself with my mouth full. 'Back in a minute.'

I follow Mum upstairs, quietly, and slip into her room. She sits at her make-up table, looking sad. 'Mummy?'

'Oh, hi, big baby,' she says. That's another of my nicknames, but only Mum says that one. She turns around and opens her arms, and I climb right onto her lap for a cuddle. 'My lovely, lovely girl,' she says. 'My wild girl.'

I smile. But then I frown again. 'Mummy, why did Daddy lie about being violent?'

She doesn't say anything. Just cuddles me.

'Do you think he could be the killer?' I whisper.

'Oh god,' she pulls me back and looks into my face. 'No, Thera, no. Your dad is always going to be . . . around to protect and love you. And he loved Billie too. And he's so sorry she died. There is a big difference between shouting loudly and waving your fists about sometimes, and the violence it takes to' – her voice goes soft – 'kill someone. Sometimes men . . .' She sighs deeply. 'Men are bigger than women, so it looks scary when they throw their fists about. And it's part of . . . It's sort of a male thing, to get into fights. Dad doesn't like fighting, but sometimes he loses his temper and acts stupidly.' She cuddles me. 'Maybe your generation will be better.'

'Is that why you argue all the time?'

'No, Thera.' She pushes me off her and walks out, saying, 'Sometimes we don't see eye to eye, that's all.' I hear her feet on the stairs.

I gulp, thinking about other men. If Dad smashes lamps, and he's much better than them, what kinds of things do other men do? What did Mum mean? Mr Kent. Billie's dad. The chief of police. Farmer Rawley. Nathan's dad. There are loads more too, that live in the village, and in Eastcastle. Men are everywhere. If I ran away from here, there would be more men all over the world, men who punch and rape and kill girls like me. Or, at least, pretty girls. I look at my own reflection in the mirror. There is nowhere to hide.

I take Mum's nail scissors off her table, and I raise them to my hair. One good chop is all it would take to make me really ugly. I stare harder. I have a fierce look on my face when it's in neutral that I can't get rid of, and my eyes are intense and staring. If I'm not pretty, then I don't have to worry about being raped. But on the other hand, if I cut my hair and make myself even more ugly, Nathan will like me less. Maybe everyone will like me less. What do I want to be? Pretty or ugly? I close the scissors on the strand of hair in front of my face, and it falls on the make-up table.

'Thera!' Dad is yelling up the stairs. 'We're off!'

Poopsticks. 'Coming!' I yell. I turn back to my reflection. I've chopped off the front-left bit at chin length. With no time to chop off all my hair, I hold out the front-right bit and chop that off too. Now I look like Ginger Spice.

Sam was very specific about which candle he wanted to take to light at the memorial. He wanted it to smell like cinnamon, because it was one of Billie's favourite smells. I said I didn't remember her saying that, but he started crying and said she did so say that, so I hugged him better and Mum bought him the candle. He was just trying to do the right thing by her. I chose a purple candle. Billie's favourite colour. Tonight, when I take the cellophane off it, I realize it smells like lavender: Billie's favourite plant. 'I know you're here with me,' I whisper, a tear running over my cheek.

'Come on, sweetheart,' Dad says. 'We don't want to be late.'

We walk through the village to the church. It's 7 p.m. and still very light. We look very smart, and I am proud of us. Dad is wearing a suit, and so is Mum, except she has a skirt on, and Sam is wearing smart black trousers with a shirt and a tie. I am wearing a purple velvet dress over a long-sleeved lacy white top. It's quite warm, but Billie had the same thing and it was our favourite outfit. I also have new shoes I got just before Billie went missing. They are black, in canvas, and I begged Mum for them. She finally bought them for me because the platforms aren't as high as the ones that broke Baby Spice's ankle. I think she was worried that I couldn't run in them. Now, with Billie gone, I realize why I might need to run well in all my shoes. An attacker could come at any time. I think Mum thinks it could easily have been me that was killed. I should tell her it couldn't have been me, because Billie is prettier. Was. But really, still is. Even though she's dead. Maybe Mum wouldn't be so upset then.

We don't use the cut when we walk to the memorial; instead we go the proper way, through the village. The police are all around us. They nod at us as we pass. Going the main-road way means I can see Nathan for ages before we get close to him. He is standing by the fence, but a little way away from the gate, because lots of people are going in. His arms are folded and he is also looking quite smart. As we get closer I realize he is wearing his school uniform, but just the shirt and trousers, without the jumper and tie. He doesn't look like a murderer. He looks like a normal, really cute boy.

'Hi, Nathan,' I say as we approach.

'Hi,' he says. He looks at my dad warily.

'Are you coming in with us, Nathan?' Dad says. He told me he knows Nathan because he works in the open, out in the carpentry yard, and the village kids walk past it all the time.

'Um,' Nathan says, awkwardly. 'Yeah, if it's alright.'

'Of course.'

'This is my friend Nathan,' I tell Mum.

Mum smiles at him, but Nathan blushes and looks down. I nudge him and he says, 'What?'

When we get into the church, I see there are hundreds of people there. Dad decides we will stay near the back. I nod quickly. Billie's mum and dad are up front and I blush, thinking about what she said about it being my fault. I hope they don't turn around and see me. I think about that Saturday, how I led Billie off to meet her killer. Possibly. Depending on if the pervert is the walker. I start to cry, silently, but then I brush my tears away. Like Hattie said, if Billie is haunting me it's because she has unfinished business. That business could be that her killer is free. I have to try not to cry so I can focus on the people around me. On telly, the killer always comes back. Maybe he's here right now. If I could just interview Billie properly, I could solve this thing. But her ghost hasn't written to me since she wrote 'Find me', and I haven't seen her since the playground. All I have is that message from Jenny.

We shuffle into one of the church pews and, just as I am getting in place, I look up, and there's Billie. She is standing next to her mum, with her arm around her. Her blondey-brown hair falls in a long plait down her back, with wisps of curls coming out of it. Billie's mum looks at Billie's dad, and her face crinkles up with tears. Billie sticks her nose right between them, but they don't notice. It must be so sad for Billie, that her mum and dad don't see her, and so scary to be dead. Billie turns and looks straight at me. She makes a face, like 'Oh poop.' In life, Billie never got really sad, or really mad, or anything negative. She would just say, 'Oh poop' at things. Even when she was ill, she just told me, 'I feel like a bum.' In death she is exactly the same: brave and funny and weird. As I'm watching her, Billie scans the crowd as if she is searching for someone, and then one of the four other dead girls walks out from another aisle. It's the Asian one, with the long black hair. She walks towards me. I grab the end of the pew, wondering about running. She looks so pale and frightening. Behind her, Billie nods at me, and taps her nose with her pointing finger. She wants me to understand something. I look at the girl again, frowning, and then, as she gets near to me, suddenly she becomes a black dog and leaps for me. I jump, and then I feel Nathan's hand on my arm.

'What's wrong?'

The black dog is gone. I stare at him before I get myself together. 'Nothing.'

Nathan's hand slowly slips off my arm, but I can feel the grip even after it's gone. He is stronger than he looks. I sense his boyishness. He has short, choppy hair, because no one cares whether he is pretty or not. He has scabbed-over scratches on his knuckles. He smells different. Sweatier.

I look around us. There is no sign of the dog. Instead, along the pew behind Billie, I spy Farmer Rawley, who owns the fields around the copse where Billie was killed. Where was he that night? There is creepy Mr Kent, stood next to Poppy's mum and dad. Poppy's mum darts a look at him. Is she frightened? I frown. She moves slightly away from him. I am the only one who notices. Poppy's dad is a big man. He mends cars. Hattie's mum's boyfriend is a man. I don't know what he does. Hattie's sister's new boy-friend is here too. He is seventeen, and is much bigger than her. He could kill her while they were having sex easily. He could just put his hands around her neck and squeeze. I wonder if strangling kills you because the man squeezes your throat until there's no hole for air to go through, or if, one by one, all the tiny thin bones in your neck break, and they all puncture the air hole until it can't work any more, and you die. I feel my neck. I look around. There are men literally everywhere.

'I don't trust them,' I whisper absentmindedly.

Next to me, Nathan leans in closer. 'Who?' he murmurs.

'Men.'

'Good.'

'What?'

'I wouldn't. Especially if I were a girl.'

'I've seen Billie's ghost. She's with other dead girls. They're haunting me.' I wait for his reaction. I tell him so I can see it, then maybe I'll know whether he is the killer. He doesn't look at me, but stares ahead at the service. 'Nathan?'

Nathan wipes his forehead and I notice it's really sweaty. He keeps looking at the vicar. His skin has gone pale.

Nathan is silent all the way home from the memorial. When I quietly ask him if he's alright, he nods his head but still doesn't talk. He seems terrified, which could indicate that he feels guilty. I would imagine he would be just sad, like the rest of us. Hmm.

Sam was very brave in the memorial. I was proud of him when he went up all by himself to light his candle without crying, but he has been wiping tears off his cheeks all the way back. It makes me feel worse.

When we reach our house, Dad says he will walk Nathan home.

'Nah, I'll be okay,' Nathan says uncomfortably.

'It's after dark, son,' Dad says softly. 'And the caravan park isn't the safest place at the moment.'

'What trouble is Nathan going to get in?' I say, thinking about all the men at the service. 'He's a boy.'

There's a pause where Mum, Dad and Nathan all look at me funny, and then Dad puts his hand on Nathan's shoulder. 'We'll talk about this later, Thera. Come on, mate.'

They walk off together. Nathan doesn't look happy. I don't think he likes men either, from what he said in the church. He looks like he's worried Dad might kill him. I hope Dad's not bad. I watch through the glass panels in the door as he and Nathan walk away.

'That was a bit insensitive, Thera,' murmurs Mum, over my shoulder. She is leaning against the wall, patting underneath her eyes with a tissue.

I frown. 'Why?'

'Oh!' Mum sniffs, and walks into the kitchen. She leans over a chair at the kitchen table, like she's about to collapse and needs the support. She shakes her head. 'Just go to your room, sweetie, please.'

I do, because I hate it when Mummy cries. I crawl into bed, feeling tired already, but my mind doesn't want to sleep. It's going over everything from tonight, thinking.

Something was up. When Billie tapped her nose, she wanted me to know something about the other dead girl. Why are these ghosts in a group together? Why do they keep changing into black dogs? Are they doing it to protect themselves? In that case, maybe the pervert really is a serial killer. Maybe he has killed all of them, and now Billie too. I keep thinking back to what Hattie said about unfinished business. Two things are obvious:

1. She is still here, so she isn't at peace.
2. She is giving me clues through the other dead girls. Their deaths are linked. But how?

When Dad gets back, he and Mum come into my room with supper. Sam and me always have the same supper: cheese on toast, and milk. Billie used to have it too. I sit in bed, holding my book I got from the library in town at the weekend (*How to Do Automatic Writing* by Edain McCoy) inside another book (*Leonardo DiCaprio: The Unauthorized Photobook*) to disguise it. Mum puts the plate on the bedside table.

'Are you alright, sweetheart?'

'Yeah, I'm okay.'

She sits down on the end of my bed. 'It's okay to be sad. We all are.'

'I know.' I discreetly shut the book. 'What's up?' They never both come in my room. There must be something wrong. They look at each other, and Dad sighs.

'I walked Nathan home to make sure he got there safely, Thera.'

'Okay.'

'You seemed to think I didn't need to.'

'Well. He's a boy.'

'Boys get attacked too,' Dad says.

I frown. 'By perverts?'

They exchange a glance.

'Don't use that word,' says Dad.

'Nathan is only two years older than you, Thera,' Mum says. 'You never know what might happen.'

'So at what age do boys stop getting attacked and start attacking people?'

'What?' Mum shakes her head. 'Sweetheart, you have to stop fixating on these awful . . . Let's think about Billie in a nice way. Let's not think about what happened to her.'

'Someone has to.'

'Yes, but the police are doing that, darling. You just

remember all the lovely times you had, playing together. That's the right way to honour her memory. Okay?'

'Okay,' I murmur, but I'm not sure I agree with Mum. It honours Billie more to try to figure out what her ghost wants.

'Thee,' Dad says, 'what did you tell Nathan about ghosts?'

'Uh . . . nothing. Why?'

'He was spooked on the way home. He said you said something about a ghost?'

'I can't remember,' I lie, shrugging. 'Guess it was an offhand comment or something.'

'We want to tell you something about Nathan, Thera.' Mum looks at Dad again, and he nods. 'We're really pleased you've made friends with him, but we want you to be sensitive. He doesn't have a house like you, or nice things, or presents on his birthday.'

'Oh,' I say, confused. 'Why doesn't he have presents?'

Mum looks uncomfortable. 'You are not to repeat this. Some children are really lucky to have lovely parents, like yours. Daddy and I both love you very much. Some children, like Nathan, aren't so lucky. I think it would be good for you to be extra-nice to him, because he doesn't get a lot of hugs and love like you do.'

'Hattie said his dad was in prison. He's a bad man.'

'Yes, but Nathan is not his dad, is he?' Dad says. 'So best not to judge.'

'Hattie said, "Like father, like son."'

'Well, we don't believe that kind of backward rhetoric, do we?'

Grandad taught me what 'rhetoric' means. I nod.

'We judge people on their actions.'

I nod again. But I don't know what Nathan Nolan's actions have been.

'Thera,' Mum cautions, 'will you be careful with what you say around him?'

'Because he's poorer than us, and his dad isn't nice, and it might upset him?'

'Don't say that to Nathan,' Mum says quickly.

'I *know*, Mummy, I'm not stupid.'

They kiss me goodnight, and both give me long hugs. After they leave, I hear them go through to Sam and ask him how he is feeling. Dad reads him a story. I fall asleep listening to Dad's deep voice softly murmuring through the wall. I want to get an early night, because I have something to do.

My watch beeps in the dark. I reach over quickly and turn off the alarm. It's an Action Man watch, with a glow-in-the-dark face. They're for boys, but I wanted one last Christmas. I guess maybe somewhere in my mind I was planning for just such an occasion as this. The time is twenty-five minutes past midnight. I reach under my bed and find my torch, flicking it on. I have to get up at a time when everyone in the house is asleep. Not even Sam can know about my plan. He is much too young.

I pull two pillows that I took from the spare room earlier out from under my bed and stick them under my duvet to look like me, and then I put my big china doll from my other nan on the top of them, and arrange the hair so it looks like I am asleep. Then I put on my hoodie, trainers and rucksack, and sneak out of my door. Luckily it's always left ajar so the hall light can get in. I'm a bit afraid of the dark. Or I used to be, but I am getting braver. I have to be, for Billie.

I let myself out the back door and climb over the fence. The moon and stars are quite bright tonight, so I can see my way across the fields. This also means that a murderer might be able to see me, so I keep low to the ground. It's colder than in the day, but it's still mild. The weather will probably break again soon, because it's been so hot. I run up the hill and over the ridge. There is a police car a little way along, so I get off the road again and move away from them. There is another police car by the copse, with the light on inside it. I can see two police officers in there, a man and a woman, drinking something steaming from a flask. I decide to run further on, through the caravan park, and enter the den from the other side of the copse.

Some of the caravans still have their lights on. I wonder what they're doing up at this hour. I can hear a telly when I go past one, and people laughing on it. Nathan lives in one of these. There are some small ones, and there are some that are longer, or have tents coming off them. I run through them, and over to the trees.

I listen for a moment. My ears feel like they can hear absolutely everything, and my eyes feel like they have widened so they can see more. I climb into the den, shimmying up the tree to jump over the undergrowth. I land right in the middle of the den, and crouch low. I wait. I look all around me. I listen. No one is here.

Quickly I unzip my bag. I brought everything I would need with me. I take out the candles and matches and the paper, and put the candles down on the four corners of the paper so it doesn't blow away. Tonight I am going to be a proper medium. A medium is called a medium because they are the messenger existing partway between the spirit world and the living world. Which is neat.

I still get spooked when I'm doing the automatic writing, but because I've been practising I'm learning to pull myself together and not be so jumpy. I had an idea at the memorial. Normally a spirit would haunt a graveyard, but Billie hasn't been buried yet. And why would she haunt some morgue somewhere far away from me and her parents? So maybe she haunts the den most days. It must be the centre of her power, because she was killed here, and it's roughly halfway between her house and mine. I couldn't have come in the day, though, because the police are still guarding it. I had no choice but to come under cover of darkness.

I light the candles and lean over the paper, holding the pencil loosely in my hand. 'Billie,' I call softly. I hear a quiet laugh. 'Billie?' My hand isn't moving yet. There is a chill in the ground, seeping through my pajamas, and a funny smell. It doesn't smell like Billie. I gulp, and whisper, 'Jenny?'

Suddenly my hand darts to the page in front of me and starts to scrawl. I close my eyes and try to let the spirit wash over me, whoever it is. Within seconds, the chill at my neck is savagely cold, far worse than last time. I gasp, wondering if I have raised an evil spirit by mistake.

My hand keeps going, but I'm not really aware of it. Then my neck snaps backwards really far, and it feels like it's being pulled down towards the ground behind me by my hair. I no longer have control of my own body; I am possessed by something. The cold is affecting my breathing. My whole chest is pushing out, then collapsing in, in deep, gasping breaths. I open my eyes to try and look at the writing, but they seem to want to roll back into my head. Then my head falls forward and I let out a shout. It feels like someone has punched me in the stomach.

When I lean down towards the paper, there is a long story written on the page in front of me, and my heart is beating really fast. I press my fingers into my neck to feel my pulse. I freeze. Someone is standing by the entrance to the den. I look up. In front of me are five pale girls, including Billie. I know they are ghosts, but they look as solid as you or me. They glow a luminescent white, like clouds backed by sun. They start to walk towards me.

I'm trembling. I inch backwards on the ground, and then there is a crack from behind me. I whirl around. An old Gypsy man with missing teeth is standing in the bushes. He speaks with a smoker's cough. 'Alright, dearie?'

I scream. All the terror inside me gets let out. He puts his hands over his ears. I don't know what happens to the girls. My emergency mode takes over, and I blow out the candles, shove everything into my rucksack, and run past him, scrambling over the tree, tumbling into the ditch, running up the bank out of it, and then through the caravan park, my heart pounding somewhere in my throat. Several dark figures are opening caravan doors to look at me as I go by.

'What's going on?' one man says. Another tries to grab at me. I scream louder and angrier, all the spooked, jumpy energy leaping out of my throat, almost like roaring at him, and I pelt as fast as I can all the way home, as the barks of savage black dogs rise from the woods. They are the voices of the dead girls, calling me.

I run in and lock the door. I don't think the police saw me on my way back, because of my dark clothes. But I can feel the dead girls. The Asian one, and the one in school uniform. It was them in front of the others. They are still coming to me, following me, spirits flying over the fields, lengthening as they speed over the soft heads of the wheat, crying out my name. I stumble through the house and shut myself in the living room. I take the paper out my bag. The Asian one spoke to me first.

My dad said I was bad. Then he was being nice to me again, and said, 'Haadiya, we are going away for a treat', but it didn't happen. He told my friends I got on a plane and went to live in another country, but I didn't. He took me to his mate's house and beat me until I thought I would die. I didn't have anything to fight back with. I managed to escape out a window. I was homeless for a while, then a man let me stay at his house. I thought he was kind, but later he did the things to me my dad had accused me of in the first place; ugly

173

things. My mother still looks for me, but she knows where I am.

Written beneath this is another message, in different hand-writing, blocky and neat. It's a message from the oldest girl, the one in school uniform. She was the first one who appeared to me that day we did the Ouija board in the den, and told me death was near.

A SMALL RED CAR SLOWED DOWN NEAR ME. I WAS COMING HOME FROM TESCO'S, EATING A FREDDO. FUCKING WEIRD THING TO REMEMBER, BUT I LOVE FREDDOS. I'VE STILL GOT THE TASTE OF IT IN MY MOUTH. I WAS TWO MINUTES AWAY FROM MY HOUSE. I CLOCKED THE CAR TO MY RIGHT, AND HE OPENED THE DOOR. IT WAS THE BLOKE FROM SCHOOL, THE TEACHING ASSISTANT. GOD, WE ALL FANCIED HIM. I THOUGHT HE WAS WELL FIT. I'D HAVE GIVEN AN ARM AND A LEG TO SNOG HIM. IT WASN'T WORTH WHAT I HAD TO GIVE, THOUGH.

I THOUGHT HE WANTED DIRECTIONS. HE SAID HE'D DRIVE ME HOME, I SAID IT WAS JUST AROUND THE CORNER. HE ASKED ME – IN A WELL CHEEKY WAY – IF I WANTED TO COME FOR A DRIVE ANYWAY. JUST FOR FIFTEEN MINUTES. I SAID OKAY. I WAS THIRTEEN AND I'D PLANNED TO BE HAVING SEX WHEN I WAS FOURTEEN, BUT I DIDN'T MIND IT BEING EARLY FOR THE RIGHT PERSON. IT WAS EXCITING, AND HE WAS BEING REALLY NICE. HE DROVE ME TO HIS HOUSE WITHOUT ASKING. WE TALKED THE WHOLE WAY AND WHEN HE PARKED HE SAID DID I WANT TO COME INSIDE, JUST

FOR A CUP OF TEA. *NO SHENANIGANS, HE SAID, AND HE LAUGHED. I SAID OKAY. WE STARTED KISSING IN THE KITCHEN. HE SAID HE COULDN'T RESIST ME. HE TOLD ME HE'D WANTED ME FOR A WHILE. HE WAS LEAVING THE SCHOOL SOON AND HE HAD TO MAKE HIS MOVE. I STARTED TO FEEL SLEEPY AND SEXY. NOW I THINK THERE WAS SOMETHING IN THE DRINK. I WOKE UP ON HIS COUCH, ACHING. HE TOLD ME WE'D ALREADY HAD SEX. HE LOOKED SURPRISED THAT I COULDN'T REMEMBER IT, AND THEN HE SAID I MUST BE ILL, AND HE TOOK ME UP TO HIS BED. HE WAS BEING REALLY SWEET AND WE ENDED UP HAVING SEX AGAIN. IT HURT A BIT BUT HE MADE ME FEEL BAD FOR COMPLAINING. HE HELD ME DOWN AND DID IT AGAIN. HE WAS MUCH STRONGER THAN ME. HE KEPT ME THERE. HE KEPT MAKING EXCUSES. HE SAID HE'D CALLED MY PARENTS. THERE WAS A LOT OF SHOUTING DOWNSTAIRS THE NEXT DAY AND THEN HE PUT A BLINDFOLD ON ME. THERE WAS A SILENCE AND I CALLED HIS NAME. THEN I WAS STRANGLED. I WAS NAKED. I DON'T LIKE TO REMEMBER IT. I WAS MY FAMILY'S ONLY GIRL, THE ELDEST OF FOUR. I WAS A TOMBOY AND TOUGH AND DIDN'T TAKE ANY SHIT FROM ANYONE. I THOUGHT I COULD HANDLE MYSELF. NO ONE EXPECTED IT TO HAPPEN TO ME.*

I kneel down on the carpet. My legs feel weak and my armpits are sweaty. All I can think is they must be giving me clues.

One of the girls mentioned a car. I remember something from the police report, about a jeep. I figure there's also something in the messages about weapons. The first girl warned that she didn't have anything to fight back with, and the second said the man was much stronger. Perhaps Billie would have gotten free if she had been armed or if we had already started at kung fu. The second girl was clearly killed by a pervert, because he had sex with her loads. So maybe the serial killer is a pervert.

I turn slowly towards the telly. It's just the right time to do some research, because the sexy shows are always on in the dead of night. I pick up the flickerdeefloo, switch on the telly, press the mute button and find Channel 4. A blonde woman talking fills the screen. *Sex and the City*. I sit down on the carpet and watch some sex, but I can't really see what's happening. After the programme finishes I watch *Eurotrash*. This is more like it. On it there is a man in a black suit with only a zip at the mouth, someone who is trying to have sex with chickens, and a lady with bigger boobs than her own head. I'm pretty sure I watch some rape, with the suited man and a lady, or at least something like it, because it is really violent, fast and angry. It's as if the man is trying to kill the lady with sex. I shuffle close to the screen and peer at where their bodies are hitting against each other. I can't really get a good angle to see what exactly is happening, but I stare anyway. 'Hmm . . .' I whisper to myself.

'Thera!' I hear suddenly. I jump, thinking it's the dead girls, but it's Dad, in his pajamas. '*What* are you doing?'

Dad drags me to bed by my arm. He says something

about not thinking about these things, and it's sad but don't go poking around for answers on your own, and 'If you want to know, just ask.'

That's not me, though. I always want answers. I have intellectual curiosity. Anyway, from his attitude, and his and Mum's conversation in the kitchen about withholding things from me, I know Dad doesn't want me to know anything. I can't talk to Mum or Dad. They might lie to me.

They want me to stay innocent, but I suspect the time for that has passed.

After school the next day, me and Sam are in the back garden, playing Barbies and Action Men. We have made some of the Barbies into dead girls using Mum's make-up. I haven't told Sam about them yet. I don't want to scare him. He's making the Action Men fight them, and I'm thinking about ghosts.

At the memorial, a lot of adults got up and talked about Billie. The things they said irritated me, saying she was so sweet and innocent, and killing a child was like taking a life before it was a life. But Billie had a life. And Billie wasn't an angel. She was a whole human being, and she was my friend. Afterwards the vicar talked about heaven, and I thought about the dead girls and what the Ouija book said about spiritualists and non-spiritualists. I haven't thought much about god until now, but I feel like it's quite a simple question-and-answer when I do:

Question: Do I believe there is an old man in the sky, who decides what happens to everything and everyone?
Answer: Nope.

I guess, whenever they tell stories from the Bible in assembly, I've assumed that they are sort of like fables: made up to teach you stuff.

I don't find the question about god particularly interesting, but whether magic and ghosts are real plays on my mind a lot. Maybe Billie has got a lot of people wondering about this, because Sam brings it up just as I'm thinking about it. He's using Action Man's triple-action knife to pretend to slice Sindy's head off, when he says, 'Do you believe in heaven, Thee?'

'Um . . .' I run over Action Man with Barbie's red convertible. 'Do you?'

'I think so.'

I look up into the sky. 'I think people are in the clouds,' I say. 'When people die, they see a bright light at the end of kind of a long tunnel. We mistake it for heaven, but actually it's a cloud kingdom. Everyone's up there, and they can look down on you, except when you're naked. My imaginary friends live up there too.' I frown, wondering about all the imaginary friends I've had over the course of my life. Were they dead girls too?

'Why can't they see you when you're naked?' Sam asks, his brow knitted. 'Thera?' Sam nudges me with his foot.

'Huh?'

'Why can't they see you when you're naked?'

'That's private.'

'I don't mind them seeing me naked.'

'You will.'

'You think you know everything because you're older.'

'Well,' I said, 'I know *more*.'

'Hmmph.' He strokes the hair of a ghost-Barbie and whispers, 'Do you think Billie is in the clouds?'

I think before answering. 'Sam, can you keep something a secret if I tell you?'

'Yeah.'

'Promise? You can't tell anyone.'

'Cross my heart and hope to die.'

'Billie's not in the clouds. I've seen her.'

Sam's eyes open wide. 'Where?'

'In my room, and in the woods, and at the memorial. She wanted me to find her body at first, but she's still here, trying to tell me something. I don't know what she wants, but I think she can't go to the cloud kingdom until she gets it.'

'Well' – Sam looks distressed – 'you should find out what she wants.'

'I'm trying,' I say. 'Maybe you could help me.'

'How?'

'I don't know yet. But I'll think about it.'

I decide not to tell him about the other dead girls. He looks spooked enough thinking about Billie.

'Do you think she'll come and visit me?'

'I don't know. It's me that's her best friend, though. That's why she's visiting me. She hasn't visited Hattie or Poppy, or they would have said something.'

'Have you told them?'

'No. But Hattie and Poppy couldn't wait to tell me something like that, to make me jealous. I'm not like them.'

'When you find out what Billie wants and give it to her, will she go away?'

'I don't really want her to go away, but yeah, I guess she'll go to the cloud kingdom after we've sorted out her unfinished business. She might come to visit occasionally, but she won't be stuck on earth like she clearly is now.'

'But she won't visit me?'

'Do you want her to visit? I could ask.'

'Not really. I'd be scared. That's not bad, is it?'

'No, it's fine. She'll make new friends in the clouds anyway.'

'Do you think she'll make a new best friend?'

'No, I'll always be her best friend, and she'll always be mine.'

'How do you know?'

'I just do.'

'Who's your best alive friend?'

'Mm . . . I guess you.'

'I was hoping you'd say that. You're my best alive friend, Thera. And Tubby.' Tubby's real name is Charles. He's a white polar bear that sleeps in Sam's bed.

'Thanks, Sam.'

We go back to playing Battle of the Barbies.

I wouldn't discuss Billie and the dead girls with any adults, even Mum and Dad. They don't believe in stuff like that, and I doubt they would want me talking like that around the house anyway, because Sam would be scared, and they clearly don't want me to know or think anything about Billie. Adults don't believe in things like ghosts, or teddy bears being alive, or guardian angels being real. Maybe it's because children are nearer the spirit realm, having only recently come from it, so we can see these things.

I have a guardian angel. He's blonde and beautiful and sometimes he holds my hand. Agewise I'd say he's probably a teenager, but I expect he's actually as old as time itself. I won't say his name because it's a secret.

Our school is a Church of England school, which means we have Advent calendars, Easter eggs, the Lord's Prayer, harvest festival, Christingles, the Nativity play and BBC hymn books. It's the type of Christianity that isn't time-consuming. You don't have to go to church much, and the vicar has a family and listens to the Rolling Stones. Catholic priests don't have children or families, and they probably listen to classical stuff. My mum's mum and dad are Catholic, and I've been to church with them before. The priest is always Irish and goes on forever and touches your face with his big, soft sausage-fingers. Then Nan and Gaga have a bit of bread.

Dad says Christianity is a fairy story invented to make you put money in the collection tin. His parents were Catholic and they almost chucked him out because he refused to go to church. But then Auntie Mary and Uncle DJ refused to go too, and you can't chuck half your kids out, so they didn't. Now they don't go to church and Grandad is an atheist. He says religion's first mission is to self-perpetuate so they'll say all sorts of crap.

Most people are going off religion now because it's a bit old hat. It was bigger when people didn't know anything, but now we know how the world works it's obvious that you can't have a baby with immaculate conception, and dung beetles don't roll the sun up every morning (that's what the ancient Egyptians believed, so they prayed to the dung-beetle god). Christianity is all about believing in something that isn't real. Most people say the same about ghosts, but I disagree. With so much life in her, wouldn't that energy all go somewhere when Billie died?

'Do you believe in god?' I ask Sam. We are burying the dead from the battle now, in the sandpit.

'No.'

'Me neither. We're godless people.'

Sam nods. 'Yep.'

When we have finished and it's teatime, I stand and give the sky one last look before we go inside. There is a big cumulus cloud (we learnt about them in school) in the deep cornflower blue. I have always had imaginary friends who live in the clouds. I have one called Thomasina, one called Roberta and one called Cleopatra, who looks like Hawaiian Barbie. They live in a beautiful cloud kingdom like the castle before Disney films, and when they come to see me, wisps of cloud form steps that they walk down. Hattie and Poppy think having imaginary friends is babyish, but Billie never did. Billie didn't actually have any human imaginary friends, though, she had imaginary animals. Maybe I could always see Thomasina, Roberta, Cleopatra, and now Billie and the other ghosts, because I have a gift. Maybe Tom, Bobby and Cleo were really ghosts too, and maybe these dead girls have been visiting me for a long time, to prepare me for what is coming. For what I have to do for Billie.

After tea (shepherd's pie – yum, yum, yum), I make a list:

What I believe in

Ghosts

Ghouls

Witches

Angels

Elves

Banshees

That heaven is basically living on the clouds, and we can't see anyone up there because we are below them.

Three urban legends: the blood in the shower one, the ghost woman on the road (so if you hit someone with your car on the road, don't stop! It might be a poltergeist. Just call the police), the one specific to our village about the dogs, poison, luncheon meat and the hanging.

That Billie and the dead girls were all killed by a bad man, and they can't cross over to heaven until someone enacts bloody revenge.

I know why I would hang around if I were dead and my killer was still out there. If a man has killed Billie, and maybe some of these girls, the girls still living in the world would be safer for his not being here. If it were me, I would want him gone.

The girls are asking me for something. Not the police.

Me. I look from where I am sitting, cross-legged on my bed, at the five ghost girls. They have come to visit me, and they sit like they are at a vigil, quietly staring at me. Each holds hands with the next one, lined up along the wall of my room. Billie is in the middle. Her expression is more vacant than usual, as if she feels faint. They terrify me, but I am trying to be okay with them and not to scream and run out the room like I long to do, because I know they are in so much pain and they need my help.

I hold up my diary, where I have written down all my thoughts. 'Is this what you want me to do?'

The one next to Billie – the one who told me the story about the car – smiles.

Mrs Underwood's shop is in half of a terraced house. It's really tiny and it sells sweets and Panda Pops and orange Calypsos. You can buy the sweets in a 10p bag or a 20p bag. In the 10p bag usually you get ten one-penny sweets, but in the 20p bag you might get ten one-penny sweets and five two-penny sweets. She mixes them up, though. It's always a surprise.

Nathan and me both buy a 10p bag at the counter on Wednesday after school. Mrs Underwood is ancient, with white, whispery hair. She could be a witch. But a good witch, though. A white witch, only doing good magic.

'I think I'm going to get a strawberry lace as well,' I say. They're 5p. 'Do you want one, Nathan? I'll get it for you, as a present,' I add, remembering what Mum and Dad told me after the memorial.

Nathan mutters back weirdly: 'Um, no – I'm alright.'

'Thank you, Mrs Underwood,' we both say politely.

'Goodbye, Thera – goodbye, Nathan,' she says, and we wave at the door and walk towards the fields the main-road way. We go past my house and then cut across a farm track and walk down into a pasture that sometimes has a horse in it. The horse is there now, tied to the fence, eating. We go and pet it. It's a Lincolnshire shire horse, with shaggy hair over its hooves. It's black and cream. Normally they are just cream. Then we go and sit on the fence, a little way away. Lincolnshire shire horses are ginormous. We don't fancy being eaten, and it might want our sweets. Horses are always desperate for mints. I'm not sure if they love gelatin, but I'm not taking the chance and losing the rewards of my hard-earned pocket money. (I occasionally load the dishwasher and get ten pounds a month for it.)

'What have you got?' I ask Nathan.

'A coconut mushroom, a shrimp, chocolate mice . . . some pink-and-blue sour fizzies.'

'They're my favourites. Do you have two?'

'I've got three. Do you want one?'

'I'll trade you for my spare cola bottle.'

'Is it fizzy?'

'Yeah.'

We sit quietly, breaking the sweets in two with our teeth and chewing for ages.

'Would you have sex with me?' I ask Nathan.

His head snaps towards me really quickly. 'Like . . .' Nathan's eyes are wide and he looks me up and down. 'What?'

'Do you like me enough to have sex with me? I mean, I'm just thinking about why the killer chose Billie. You know, because she was pretty. So, I was thinking, if you *had* to rape someone, like, you absolutely had to . . . would you choose me?'

Nathan swallows, looks uncomfortably at his sweets and rips the head off a coconut mushroom. 'Yeah, I guess. You're pretty.' His voice is getting low and croaky.

'Cool.' I bite my lip to keep from smiling loads. 'Do you . . . do you think I'm prettier than Billie?'

'Yur,' Nathan mutters.

I grin broadly. This is the best news! Nathan can't be the killer because if he likes me more than Billie he would have killed me, wouldn't he? I swing my legs happily. This means I can ask Nathan for help with figuring out who the killer is, which is great because I have something I want to ask him to do. (Also I am so excited Nathan Nolan thinks I'm pretty. I think I would like him to be on top of me, like in sex, when we're older. I like it when he hugs me.) I break a piece off my strawberry lace with my teeth.

'Do you fancy me too?' Nathan says quietly.

'Yes. I'd definitely pick you to marry if you were at my school when we played Will You Marry Me.'

Nathan smiles. 'Really?' He eats the stalk of the mushroom. 'That's cool. I guess it's kind of the same thing.'

'Not really. People who are married don't get raped.'

He looks at me sideways. 'How do you know that?'

I talk while chewing my lace in my mouth. 'It's true, isn't it? Right?'

He opens his mouth, and closes it, then shrugs.

I finish my lace and spit on my hands to wipe the stickiness off. 'Nathan, I want to find Billie's killer.' Nathan's face goes pale at this. 'But to do that, I need to understand how and why he murdered her, and that means doing some research—'

'You really think you can find her killer?' he says, kind of meanly. ''Cause you're such a smarty-pants, aren't you?'

I frown. 'I'm intelligent, if that's what you mean.'

'Bet you're top of your year.'

'It's not hard. There's only eleven of us.'

'Think a lot of yourself, do you?' he says, kind of funnily.

'Being clever doesn't make you a better person,' I tell him. 'Trying your best to right wrongs makes you a better person.'

'Is that why you're so interested in Billie?'

'She's my best friend. I have to do something. I have to at least understand' – I bite my lip – 'what happened. Maybe I can stop it from happening to anyone else.'

'You'll never make her alive again. She'll always be dead.'

I frown. 'Why are you being so negative? Do you not want me to find Billie's killer?'

'I'm not being *negative*.' Nathan says this like it's a really long word and I'm showing off. 'Smarty-pants.'

'What are you talking about? The word "negative" only has three syllables. A baby could say it. You're changing the subject on purpose by teasing me.'

'No, I'm not. I don't care whether you find the killer.'

'You don't care that there's a killer on the loose?'

'It won't make her alive again, that's all I'm saying. What's the point?'

'She's not quite dead,' I say.

'Huh?'

I look in his eyes. 'Well, she is dead, but . . . I see her.'

'Like at the memorial?'

'No, like pretty often.'

He looks around wildly then back at me, and narrows his eyes. 'Is she here now? When have you seen her?'

'Outside my window, before I found her. In the playground. At the memorial. In the copse, the other night.'

'You went back to the copse?'

I nod.

'You shouldn't hang out there!' he says, panicked.

'I'm not scared.'

'She can't be a ghost,' Nathan says miserably. He stares into his bag, and then picks out the fizzy cola bottle and chews off its cap. 'She's not a ghost,' he says finally, as if he's trying to convince us both.

'Yes, she is.' I rip another bit off my strawberry lace. Nathan is still pale. 'Are you afraid of ghosts?'

'No!' he says quickly. 'Not unless . . .'

'Unless what?'

'Well, if I . . . if I had done something bad to her, I'd be afraid. Because she might be back to get me. Has she said why she's back? Is she here for revenge?'

'Revenge.' My eyes widen. 'Yes, I've been thinking about that – because if her killer was gone, it would redress the balance of good and evil, and protect other—'

'I don't believe in ghosts anyway,' Nathan suddenly says. 'You're wrong.'

I frown at him for interrupting me, and saying I'm wrong. 'I'm not wrong,' I say darkly. 'In fact, I'm rarely ever wrong.'

'Huh.' Nathan puts the rest of the cola bottle into his mouth, but he looks sick and sweaty again, like in the memorial. 'I hope she doesn't come round here.'

I swallow my lace and watch him chew. He yaps. He obviously hasn't been taught to eat with his mouth shut. But that makes sense, given what Mum and Dad said. Nathan looks afraid.

'I need to know what happened to her, Nathan,' I ask. 'Her ghost wants me to find out.'

He looks at me sideways. 'Do you think she will go away if you do?'

'Yes. So you'll help me, right? Can you pretend to rape me?'

Rape is the worst thing that can possibly happen to you. It's even worse than being dead, because it hurts so much and you're haunted forever by it. People who are raped are empty shells . . . That's what I'm told. Or maybe I wasn't told. I don't know how I know that, but that's how I understand it; that's what everyone believes. Here's what I have a problem with, though: if that were true, it would mean Billie is better off dead. I don't want her to be dead, and I don't think Billie would want to be dead. Billie really enjoyed fun, and that's something you can't have if you can't move your own body and you're stuck underground, and the only sound you can hear is the bugs slithering and making tiny scratching noises outside the thin wood of your coffin, and you know one day they'll break through and eat you, but until then you have to listen to them and know that that day is coming, for about fifty years. I imagine this a lot. It stops me from sleeping.

If I'm going to understand what happened to Billie, and solve her murder, I'm going to have to understand what perverts do, *better* than most people would. So what does it feel like? Why would they want to do it? How do you die from it? Why is it so bad that you're better off dead? And, most importantly, how could you escape from it?

Nathan looks at me with his mouth open, and then his face screws up. 'You want me to pretend to rape you?'

'Yeah.' It occurs to me too that Nathan would be very close to me when we do it, which makes me feel excited. Maybe he will kiss me again.

Nathan looks nervous, though. 'Mm . . .'

'Come on.' I leap off the fence. 'Let's go to your caravan.'

'Why can't we go to yours?'

''Cause my nan's in. And Sam.'

'Oh,' Nathan says, still sat on the fence. 'Okay.'

'What's the matter?' I say, starting to feel embarrassed. Maybe he doesn't really want to touch me, because he doesn't find me pretty after all. Maybe he was just saying it to be nice. 'Don't you know how?'

'Yeah! Of course I do,' he says, annoyed for some reason. He puts his sweets away in the pocket of his school trousers and grabs my hand roughly. 'Come on, then. I'll show you what happened to Billie.'

We tramp through the field, towards the caravan park. Behind it the copse looks dark and ominous. When we get across one field, we push through a hedge. It's a shortcut. In the caravan park there is a creaking of something metal nearby, as if a door is swinging off its hinges, and a few ratty dogs wandering around sniffing things, but beyond that the park looks deserted.

Nathan's caravan is one of the nearest, and medium-sized compared to the others. It has a washing line outside and some rusty crates by the door. He unlocks the door with a key that looks like our car key, and I follow him inside. My eyes adjust to the darkness after the bright sunshine outside. It's cramped, and sort of musty-smelling. There are dirty dishes in the sink.

'It's not . . .' Nathan mumbles. He picks up an empty packet of Pop-Tarts and puts it in the bin. '. . . that nice.' He picks up a cloth that smells and wipes the little table down. It's a plastic table, with bench seats either side.

'It's okay,' I say charitably.

'Bet your mum cleans your house really nice,' he says.

'Mum works. We have a cleaning lady that comes once a fortnight. And Nan does the laundry.'

'A cleaning lady? You're well posh.'

'Not really. Not compared to most people. Where are your playing cards?' I ask.

'Huh?'

'You said you were playing cards the night Billie died.'

'Oh. Yeah. They must be around here somewhere.' He picks up a bunch of empty baked-bean cans and puts them in the bin, and pushes the dishes into the washing-up bowl.

'Who were you playing cards with?' I ask.

Nathan doesn't answer.

'Your mum?'

'I was playing solitaire, Thera,' he says, kind of mechanically.

I look around. The only bedroom is at one end. The door is open and I can see a double bed, and then the caravan stops. 'Where do you sleep?'

He turns to what I thought was a cupboard and pulls a sliding door back to reveal a bunk bed. 'In here.'

'You've got teddy bears.'

'Everybody's got teddies,' he says.

'I just didn't expect it. You're older. And a boy.'

He just looks at me.

I nod to the little ladder leading to the bed with a duvet on it. 'Get on the bunk, then.'

Nathan wrinkles his nose, then bites at the cuff of his jumper and pulls his sleeve down, and then the rest of the jumper off.

'So that's how your cuffs get so shredded.'

Nathan is quiet. He throws the jumper on the bottom bunk, which is just a big pile of clothes and schoolbooks. 'You go up first.'

194

'Why?'

''Cause you go on the bottom.'

'Oh. Okay.' I clamber up the little ladder, and scooch into the small space. I can press my toes on the ceiling. It's not much bigger than a coffin. Nathan's head pops up next to me. Suddenly he's really close and I can smell his breath. It's fizzy-cola-smelling. His eyes are huge, and blue-grey like the North Sea. His eyelashes are dark and long. He slides on top of me.

'You're squashing my tummy,' I say.

'Open your legs. I'm supposed to be in between.'

I part my legs and my foot dangles off the bunk. 'Your eyes have a gold circle around the pupil.'

He blinks. His cheeks are red. His face is really close to mine. His chest is pressed against me and is rock-hard. He must be really muscly underneath his T-shirt. 'Okay. Just don't move for a second.'

'Okay.'

He takes my hands and puts them behind my head, with his hands on them.

'Ouch. You're hurting my wrists.'

'That's what's supposed to happen.' Nathan starts to move forwards and back, our stomachs rubbing together.

'Do we kiss?' I ask, watching his eyes. They are really wide, and staring into mine.

'No.'

'Oh,' I say, disappointed.

'Do you want me to talk to you?'

'Like . . . chat?'

'No, like, call you names.'

'What names?'

'Like . . . "slut" and stuff.'

'Is that what men do?'

'Some of them.'

'How do you know?'

'I, um . . .' Nathan hesitates. 'I saw a video. Just rub on me.'

I move my body a bit like he's moving his, but it just makes it more bumpy, and I'm sad that he had a chance to kiss me and didn't take it. I start to feel hot and uncomfortable. 'Can you let go of my wrists? You're hurting me.'

'I'm supposed to hold you still,' he grumbles, but he lets go and I put my hands on his back.

'That's much more comfy.'

'Should I do it harder?'

'Why?'

His voice goes really quiet. 'I'm going easy on you.'

'Don't go easy on me!' I hiss. 'I'm not a wimp. Do it properly.'

'Um, okay.' He moves forwards and backwards faster, our groins banging together a bit painfully. His whole body feels hard and like you could smash me up with it.

'Ouch, it hurts.'

'Sorry,' Nathan says. He is breathing heavily, and he looks confused and like he's in pain too. And then he looks away from me, like he doesn't want me to see his face.

'Put your hands around my neck,' I instruct.

'What?' Nathan gasps breathily. He doesn't get it.

'Put—'

Suddenly there is a shout from the open window by the door.

'Jan, I've got them dresses sewn up for you! I'll bring them round after dinner.'

Nathan jerks suddenly upwards and off me. He bangs his head on the ceiling, then races quietly down the ladder and runs into what I guess is the loo, slamming the door.

I sit up, climb down and stand in the middle of the caravan. 'Weird,' I mutter. I smooth down my clothes.

The door opens. A lady comes in. She must be Nathan's mum. She is a bit chubby and dressed in old, baggy jeans, and a very dirty kind of lab-coat-type thing with red smears all over it that look like blood. She has a fag burning in her hand. 'And who are you, then?' she says, looking me up and down.

'I'm Thera. I'm one of Nathan's friends, Mrs Nolan.'

'And where's he, then?'

'In the toilet.'

'Nathan?'

'Coming,' he mumbles, and the toilet flushes, and he comes out.

'What have you been up to? You look as guilty as your father.'

'Nothing,' he says, putting his hands in his pockets. His face is totally red and he is looking down at the floor. He does look guilty. I nudge him to make him stop it. He's not acting very cool, and she seems suspicious already. 'I was just showing Thera the van.'

She whips her hand forward almost so fast I don't see it,

and whacks him on his side. 'What-have-you-been-doing?' she says, fast.

'Nothing!' he whines.

'Don't hit him!' I say. 'That's abuse!'

Nathan's mum squints at me. 'You'd better go on home, Little Miss, I'm not feeding another ungrateful little shit.'

'That's okay. We're having spag bol for tea,' I say. She turns away and ignores me as I head for the open door. 'Thanks for having me, Nathan. Bye!' I smile at him to cheer him up, but he doesn't look at me, even though I defended him. He just stands there, blushing and staring at the floor.

It's making me feel a bit better to be doing something productive about Billie's death, so I decide it's time now to start getting into shape. The dead girls said it was important to be strong. I take off around the village, running. Last night I saw the dead girls in my dreams again. They were playing ring-a-ring-a-roses to amuse the little one. She's the cutest, tiny and blonde and sweet. I think about them as I jog along the main road, through the village and past the church. The police watch me wherever I go, so unless the killer is a police officer, I'm safe. When I get out onto the school playing field, I do fifty press-ups, one hundred stomach crunches, one hundred star jumps, and half a pull-up on the bars in the kiddy playground. Pull-ups are hard. The policewoman guarding the playground waves and shouts, 'Training for Sports Day?'

'Um,' I say, 'yeah.' She keeps watching me, so I smile at her and she goes away.

I practise my kicks and punches, like Billie and me would have learnt in kung fu. Maybe I'll still go when all of this is over, if I make it through. I run all the way home afterwards, and collapse in a sweaty mess on a deckchair in the back garden. Sam comes up to me.

'Hey, Thera.'

'Hey.'

'Want to play Tekken?'

Sam's been staying indoors on the PlayStation a lot in the past two weeks. He's scared to leave the house.

'Why don't we go and play on the field?' I suggest.

'No. I don't want to go looking for clues again.'

'We don't have to do that.'

'Don't we?'

'Well, I'll keep an eye out. But you don't have to.'

He rips some grass up and splits it down the middle. 'Hmm. No thanks.'

'How about we play tig?'

'Is it just going to be about whether I can catch you again?'

'That's the game of tig!'

'Thera,' Sam whines. 'You only want to play weird games now. Like battling ghosts. All your games and stories are all scary. And!' he exclaims, louder, 'I don't want to be strangled—'

'Shh!' I sit up. 'Nan will hear you!'

'I don't want to be strangled,' he whispers.

I tut crossly. 'I only did it once.'

Poor Sam. I didn't think until afterwards that I shouldn't have practised strangling on an asthmatic. But Poppy said in school that Billie was definitely strangled to death. Her parents were watching the news and she overheard. I wanted to get Nathan to do it on Wednesday, but his mum came home. It's still good, though, to know a bit about what rape feels like. It's important to figure out exactly how Billie died. I watched seven taped episodes of a police telly show last night, just to find out more about rape and strangling. (I fast-forwarded through the episodes where the victim died of different causes.) There were only two stranglings, but the evidence for them was very similar to how Billie's body looked – bruised necks, pale faces. They had peh-tee-kee-al (don't know how to spell it) hem-orr-radging (don't know how to spell that either), which is dots in their eyes, but I didn't know to look for that then. There was only one episode on rape, but they didn't show the rape itself, which I thought was a bit rubbish.

The other day, I got Sam to strangle me, and then I fought him off in several different ways. The best way of stopping someone from strangling you is to put both your arms straight up outside of their arms, then bring the right one down over both their arms, all the way until they have to let go of your neck, then elbow them in the face with your right elbow (which Sam got a tiny bruise from that we covered with make-up). Yesterday evening we also played some other games designed to get me strong and prepare me.

1. I made Sam tie me up and then I wriggled out of the ropes (we don't have rope, so we used dressing-gown cords).
2. I took the Swiss army knife Dad gave me a year ago for camping, and we stabbed into a pillow to practise how to stab someone, and how far it might go in.
3. Chasing (tig).

I made Sam promise not to tell Mum and Dad. It's good for him too. We have to learn to protect ourselves. In battle, I can imagine myself as a leader. In fact, I am a leader. I'm the leader of Sam, and I was the leader of me and Billie, when she was alive, so I have to keep being a brave leader now one of my troops has fallen. She still needs me. So does Sam.

'All this stuff is making me uncomfortable,' Sam says, picking his fingernails. 'I don't think I'm old enough to do those things and I think you're being a very bad big sister. I keep thinking you're going to want to try and kill a cat or something, to see if you can. I know you're upset about Billie, but this is getting silly now, Thera.'

Sam can sound very sensible at times. I nod, but I'm thinking about what he said about the cat. I did actually wonder about killing a cat, because the neighbour's cat is evil so it wouldn't be so upsetting to sacrifice it for research purposes. It's a horrible ginger hissing thing, and it eats all the little baby birds, just like a murdering pervert, picking on the weak.

'Thera, you're not paying attention to me,' says Sam.

'I'm sorry I've been a bad sister,' I say. 'I just have to catch this guy. We're not safe until I do. And my preparation is going well—'

'It's the policemen and -ladies' job to catch the killer, Thera.' Sam sounds just like Dad.

I bite my lip. 'Maybe we should be pooling resources. I've had this idea—'

'You're just little, Thera! And a girl! You can't—'

'Girls can do anything these days. That's what girl

power is about. And Billie is visiting *me*, not the police.'

He looks annoyed, so I take his hand and say, 'Sam, if somebody killed me, wouldn't you want to know who?'

'I gue-e-ess . . .'

'And wouldn't you want to avenge my death?'

Sam sighs. 'No, but I think I would have to or you would come back and haunt me and be really annoying about it.'

'I'm not annoying.' I frown. 'Am I?'

'Also, if I didn't, I suppose I would feel like I had let you down.'

'Exactly. So I have to do what I have to do, and if you want to play with me right now, you're going to have to play catch the killer.'

'Okay.' Sam nods at me. 'I'll help. As long as I'm not busy with Tekken or Gran Turismo.'

'Good. Now get on my back. I'm going to do more push-ups.'

Later, I look it up in the dictionary. It's petechial haemorrhaging.

Sports Day is on the last Tuesday in term. The wind has picked up and it sounds like screams coming from far away. Every race I run, I think about running away from a killer. I run until my legs are like Play-Doh, with no bones in them, and my heart is pounding. When I go through the red tape at the end of the seventy-metre race, everyone else is miles behind me. I look around at all the faces of the parents and adults who are supposedly relatives. But are they? If I were the killer, would I come back to gloat? Is he here now? I search for the walker. My breath is raggedy, so I lean over with my hands on my knees and scan the crowd, trying to work out where I have seen every face. I am going to be like a superhuman, always alert, always ready. I'm not going to die because I wasn't prepared, because I hadn't exercised enough or because I wasn't aware of what was going on around me.

'Thera? Thera!'

I turn around. The woman at the scores table is calling me over. I give the crowd one last look and then go over to her to tell her I came in first and get my badge. Next is the sack race, and then the egg-and-spoon race, and then the mums' race.

It's fun cheering on Mum. She comes in second. She

goes to stand with Dad, Nanny and Grandad again, and Dad looks at her nicely, which is unusual. He's usually moody, and so is she, but they haven't fought all day. It's a Sports Day miracle. In the dads' race, Dad runs faster than everyone and wins. It's nice to know he's fit, because if the killer broke into the house, at least I would have back-up in fighting him. As long as he isn't the killer . . . I have a plan to find out for sure about that one.

Afterwards we have a family party at home, with home-made curries. Grandad sits on the wall Dad built around one of the flower beds to smoke his cigar after teatime, and I sit on his lap.

'You believe in ghosts, don't you, Grandad?'

'I certainly believe in spirits, and souls, although how to reconcile that with my atheistic tendencies is another question.' He thinks for a minute and I wait, because he always tells stories just after he is quiet. 'There was a young man – I believe his name was Harry Martindale – working as a plumbing apprentice in the cellar underneath the Treasurer's House in York in the nineteen-fifties. Have I told you this story?'

'No.' I snuggle into his shoulder.

'It's a very famous one. While he was working, out of the darkness strode twenty men, dressed in Roman uniform. They looked very tired and dejected, as if they had lost a battle, and Harry remarked specifically that he could not see their feet. Their calves were beneath the floor, as if they were walking through deep snow. It transpired that the path of the old Roman road ran beneath the building, fif-teen inches lower than the level of the cellar floor. Harry kept his story to himself for quite some time, I believe, but later on it began to be believed by certain experts, when he reported details of their appearance that he could not possibly have known to be true. Who knows what battle those men had come from, what friends they had lost, what young loves they had waiting at home, or when they died.'

'Perhaps shortly after they walked down that road,' I suggested. 'And maybe that's why they haunt it. Because if only they had gone the other way, they wouldn't have run into trouble.'

'Perhaps. It has rarely been said that ghosts are unreasonable. Alas, for many it must be far too long since they passed from this world for us to know why they linger.' He takes a puff on his cigar and blows the smoke away from me.

'Grandad?' I ask.

'Yes, Thera?'

'Why do ghosts hang about?'

'Largely, I suspect, because they have unfinished business.'

I smile slowly. Grandad's always right. And he has confirmed what I suspected.

'Why do you ask, my lovely, inquisitive granddaughter?'

I shrug and play innocent. 'No reason.'

Just then, everyone else comes out into the garden, Dad and Sam call me to play football, and Nanny exclaims how beautiful the sunset is.

Two days later is our last day at primary school ever. I still can't quite believe Billie's not there for it. In the morning we have a talent show, which she would have loved, and we do a choreographed dance after all, to 'Bring It All Back' by S Club 7. Mrs A helped us put it together. We'd normally do something special like that anyway, but I think this year the teachers thought it would be particularly good for us to have something to focus on instead of Billie's death. It just reminds me of how much Billie liked to dance about and sing, though.

I bring a bag of sweets from Mrs Underwood's shop to school, and at lunchtime I throw them around in the middle of the playground and the little ones run around catching them. I get everyone to sign my shirt. I get three presents and lots of goodbyes. The Littlies tell me they will miss me, and I will miss them, but I promise to visit on my Baker days – which are like bank holidays for kids. They all tell me they love me and Billie, which makes me sad, but is also nice. I'm not sure they really understand that she isn't coming back. But then again, since they are so young and close to the spirit world, maybe they see Billie too, which is a nice thought. I say goodbye to them all. It's funny – when I pass school people from now on, they will be like, 'Hi, you're from my school', and I'll have to say, 'No, I'm not any more.' I've never been to school anywhere else in my life.

I'm looking forward to the grammar school, except that Billie won't be coming. The induction day there was really cool. We did assembly, form time, a tour, break, English, science, IT (which is computers), lunch, PE and home time. We met three friends I can remember the names of: Freya and Morgan, who are identical twins, and Tammy. I don't know what it will be like without Billie, though. We had so many plans, like starting a club that meets in the big library to read spy books, and me slipping her answers to all the exams so we both get to go to Oxford.

I'll miss Billie so much. It's weird. She should have been coming with me to the grammar, but now she is trapped forever in this time, maybe doomed to haunt only the places where she went in life. (She came to the induction, though, so perhaps she will be able to haunt the grammar and come and hang out with me.)

We all go into the girls' toilets and change into non-uniform for the Year Six barbecue in the afternoon. I change into a party dress in the loo cubicle. We used to all change outside the cubicles together but Mrs A doesn't allow that in her class. She says we are too grown-up for that now. The dress is not the kind of thing I would usually wear. In fact, Billie and me planned to wear our bright-green cords and our stripy green-and-orange tops together, but it didn't seem right without Billie, and Hattie got me all worried again yesterday that Nathan thinks she is prettier than me, and since there is a chance his school bus might get in about the same time as we leave for the cinema, I don't want him to see us both and decide to go and play with Hattie instead. My dress is still babyish, though, compared to what Hattie is wearing. She points it out, but I know already. My dress is white, with a tiny bow on the collar. It comes down to my knees. Hattie is wearing a black crop top that shows her big boobs, and black shorts so small they only just cover her bum and a tiny bit of thigh. She is staring at me too.

She makes a face. 'You don't wear a bra?'

'Why would I wear a bra? I don't have anything to put in it. Not like you.'

'Poppy wears a bra,' Hattie says.

I turn to her. Poppy is wearing on denim pedal pushers with a matching denim shirt. 'Do you?'

Poppy nods. 'I have three white ones. I'm an AA cup.'

'I don't believe you,' I say. 'Why would you need one? There isn't anything to push up!'

'Show her,' says Hattie to Poppy, leaning on the sink.

'No,' Poppy says uncertainly.

'Go on! What is your problem?' Hattie says.

So Poppy shows us her bra.

'Okay, now show us your boobs,' I say.

'No!' Poppy shrieks.

'Lesbian,' Hattie says to me.

'I'm not a lesbian. I like Nathan.'

'Then why do you want to see Poppy's boobs?'

'Because I don't believe she has any! If I were a lesbian, I'd ask to see Mrs Adamson's boobs – they're actually *there*!'

They both laugh. 'You want to see Mrs A's boobs!' Hattie teases.

I roll my eyes. 'I'll show you mine,' I say to Poppy.

Hattie suddenly stops laughing. 'Interesting,' she says. 'How big are yours? I bet you don't have anything there yet.'

'Whatever, I don't care,' I say, and lift my dress up.

Hattie lifts her top and bra up at once and shows us her boobs, and so does Poppy. I'm right: there is nothing there. 'You're cutting off your circulation for nothing,' I say to Poppy, and then I turn to Hattie. 'Yours are smaller than they look with your clothes on.'

'It's a *Wonder*bra,' Hattie says, like I'm supposed to know what that means.

'What's it do?' I ask.

'Make boys like you more than other girls.' She smirks, and flounces out of the bathroom.

I stick my tongue out after her, but I can't be bothered to fight. I've felt like that a lot since Billie died. It's because I have bigger fish to fry now. Later on Hattie cries, and hugs me, and says we will always be best friends. She's such a hypocrite.

The barbecue starts at two o'clock, and Mr Kent cooks sausages and burgers. I eye him suspiciously, and listen to him and Mrs A talking. Mrs A is helping him, but she's really just standing about and pretending she can't do stuff so he'll do it for her. She keeps acting like, because she's a woman, she can't make a fire or cook meat. This is one of those times Mrs A seems lame. She smiles at us as we walk over.

'Hi, girls! Who wants to help me get the party plates from my car?'

'I will!' I sing-song. I want to ask her a question. 'Mrs A?' I say when we are out of earshot of the school garden. 'Do you like Mr Kent?'

'Pardon?'

'Do you think he's nice?'

'Oh. Yes, of course.'

'So . . .' I hesitate. 'Do you think he can be trusted? You know, not to be involved with Billie's death?'

She turns and gawps at me, then she puts her hand over her mouth for a moment, as if she's thinking what to say. 'Thera, I don't want to talk about that any more. Let's think about other things, okay?'

'But what about Mr Kent? Couldn't he be a suspect?'

'The police are dealing with that.'

'But do you trust him?'

She looks back at Mr Kent. 'Oh my gosh,' she murmurs. Finally she says, 'You know what I said about men, Thera. You can't trust any of them. And you can never be too careful.' We exchange a look, turn and walk towards the car.

Billie usually did things like this for Mrs A, going to get things from her car and running errands and everything. Mrs A unlocks her jeep.

'Would you go around the back, Thera, and get the plastic cutlery from the boot?'

'Sure.' I walk round and open the back door. There's a lot of crap in there: a spade, a canvas bag, cleaning stuff, rope. I'm pushing things around, when I suddenly stop.

Mrs A has some matches. I open the canvas bag. On the outside it's covered in dirt, and on the inside there's some gardening stuff, and some plastic gloves. The rope looks like the rope around Billie. Why would a primary-school teacher have rope in her car?

'Thera, have you got it?'

'Coming!' I shout. I grab the plastic bag with the cutlery, and then I think about it and pick up the matches. 'Do you want these too?'

'No, why would I want matches?' she says in her light, tiny voice.

'What do you normally use them for?' I look harshly at Mrs A.

'Well, if you must know, Miss Nosy, I occasionally smoke.'

'Oh.' I put them back in the boot. 'That can kill you, you know.'

'Well, it's my husband's fault,' she says. 'He used to smoke and he liked how it looked when I did it. Don't tell anyone, though. It can be our little secret.' She looks at me out of the corner of her eye. 'Do you know how to keep a secret, Thera?'

'Sure.' I pretend to zip my mouth up. 'My lips are sealed.'

'Good. Come out of there, now,' she says. As she closes the door of the jeep, I am still thinking about the stuff in the back of it. Can it be a coincidence that Mrs A has all those things? But why would she kill Billie? And anyway, she's not a man. So she can't be a pervert.

The party goes well, and Hattie is actually being nice.

Afterwards Mr Kent takes us all to the cinema to see the new Star Wars film. We go to the Kinema in the Woods. It's famous in our area because it's the only back-projection cinema in the country. It's really cute. A man always pops up at the interval and plays the organ. The organ comes up in the middle of the stage, and he plays old songs like 'I Do Like to Be Beside the Seaside', and there is a glitter ball that turns and makes lights go everywhere in the whole cinema. I buy a packet of Skittles. When we sit down I'm next to Poppy, on the end of the row.

I look along the row at my year, one by one, but in the eleventh chair, because now there are ten and not eleven of us, there is Mr Kent, who is watching me.

When you fall in love with someone instantly, you don't exactly fall in love with them. *You fall in love with an idea. You have to; you don't know anything about them. Everybody falls short of an idea, because an idea has so much space to stretch into. It can be infinite and so perfect it makes you cry. It's such a great solution to the problem of loneliness, the idea that lightning could strike. I mean it did, for us. But then you have to deal with the consequences of accepting that type of love.*

I was shy. Stereotypical never-been-kissed. He started inviting me out. Proper dates. He opened doors for me, figuratively and literally. For the first time, I was able to see myself having status; able to see myself as a wife, as a mother, as someone important and valued enough to justify a man marrying me. I had never been on a date before our first. He treated me like a princess, moving my chair so I could sit down, paying for me, ordering nice things. But I would get a little embarrassed, because he always wanted something afterwards. The first time it was just a kiss. He didn't even touch me. He said I was too pure to defile. I took his breath away.

The next time we were kissing, softly, gently, on the lips. He started to get more forceful, and then he pulled my body to his and held me so hard that the next day I had bruises on the skin over my hips. I cried out his name when he bit at my tongue and he stumbled away, shocked. He was so sorry to hurt me. He said he couldn't help himself. I thought it was sweet. I thought it was exciting how much he loved me. He couldn't help himself because of me? I had never imagined that could be a reality – a man driven wild by me, my small, ugly body, my pale, dull beauty.

The third date he asked me to hold his penis. He said my hand looked so small around it that it made him look bigger. It was warm and hard. He started to move it. I was excited but also petrified. Scared of doing something wrong. I thought about the boys at school, how none of them would have wanted this from me. Jessica, Nora, Karen, yes, but not me. I should be grateful. And yet, the way he instructed me to hold still made me shiver. I held onto him tighter, cuddled into his chest, my hand still around him. He came on my hand. I had never seen that before, or felt it. He apologized that it had happened so quickly. He said again what he had on our previous date: he couldn't help himself.

I had a meeting with Mr Kent yesterday. Just me and him. It was weird. I don't know why he called me in, but he came to the classroom to do it. We were practising for the talent show with Mrs A. He opened the door and we all stopped giggling and went quiet.

'Thera,' he said, 'I'd like you to come to my office.'

Hattie and Poppy looked at me. We all hate Mr Kent. He makes us feel weird. If we go into his office, we always go together.

'She has to practise for the talent show,' Mrs A whined quietly. I think she was worried we weren't going to get the routine right. I don't know why. I thought we were really good.

Mr Kent ignored her and nodded at me. 'Thera?'

I shrugged at Mrs Adamson apologetically, and followed him out of the classroom and into his office. He gestured to his sofa. 'Sit down, Thera.'

So I sat down. He sat next to me. Our knees were touching so I pulled back.

'Would you like a sweet?' he said, and held out the bowl.

They were Opal Fruits, the fruity chew. I held my hand over the basket and tried to decide between flavours.

Lemon was sharp and the most tasty, but strawberry was a classic. Of course, purple and green were the best-tasting, but which one would I pick if I could only eat one?

'Thera, make a decision,' Mr Kent said.

So I took a lemon one.

'You've been happy at this school, haven't you, Thera?'

I thought about this. The honest answer would be: Well, no, not really. I've been bullied throughout my seven years here by Hattie, Mum says the work isn't challenging enough for me, I don't like it when Mr Kent yells at us, my best, true, forever friend died, and now I feel totally alone and afraid we will all be killed.

'Thera, you like it here, don't you?' He put his hand on my arm. I froze, and looked at it. He took it back.

'Um, yeah,' I said. 'Sure.'

There was a short silence and then Mr Kent said, 'I'm sorry about Billie.'

I frowned. Why was Mr Kent sorry? Did *he* kill her? I looked down in panic at the sweet wrappers. Mum always said never to take sweets from strangers. Was it because they were perverts? Was Mr Kent? I stared at him. He was quite big and broad. I shrank back in the sofa as he leant forward.

'What is it, Thera?'

I shook my head. 'Nothing. I'm great. Can I go now?'

'Not yet.' This time he put his hand on my knee, firmly, as if to stop me leaving. 'I'm sorry about Billie, but I hope it's not going to change your opinion of your time with us. What happened to Billie isn't related to our school. It shouldn't cast a bad light over your time here.'

I didn't understand what he was getting at, so I just nodded.

He reached out and proffered the basket to me again. 'Another sweet?'

'No, thank you.'

'Thera, have another one. It's rude not to.'

So I took a strawberry.

'Do you know what happened to Billie?' Mr Kent asks.

'Yes.'

'You do?'

'Uh-huh.'

'She was led away by a stranger. Probably the stranger has moved on now.'

I kept shtum. If Mr Kent was the killer, he would definitely say the killer has moved on now so that I wouldn't suspect him.

'Well, the police don't have any suspects, in any case.'

'Um. Okay,' I said.

He leant in, so I could smell his foul breath. I tried not to shrink back or show any fear. His hand was still on my knee. I suddenly thought, why are people always touching me? Everybody does it, hands fiddling with my hair, hands on my back steering me places, hands on my shoulders. As if to hold me down. As if I belong to everyone.

I stayed stiff and didn't say anything.

'You're safe here, Thera,' he said softly, looking into my eyes. 'You're safe with me.' He didn't stop looking into my eyes. I felt funny in my body, kind of like I felt with Nathan, but like I didn't want to feel that way. Then, suddenly: 'You may go now,' he said.

So I got up and he opened the door for me, and I stepped out.

Mrs A was standing in the corridor, looking worried.

'Eve,' Mr Kent said, and nodded to her before he closed the door.

'What did he say?' Mrs A asked me.

I chewed my lip. 'I don't really know.'

Mrs A frowned. 'What do you mean you don't know, Thera? You can't remember what he said just now? You're supposed to be really bright, aren't you?'

'Yes, but—'

'Did he say anything about Billie?'

'Not really. Just that probably her killer was a stranger. Why?'

She put her hands over her eyes and spoke to me without looking at me. 'Nothing. Go back to the classroom. I'm going to get a drink of water.' She walked over to the staffroom (it's a tiny school, so this was about three steps) and shut the door on me.

It now occurs to me in the cinema, as the Star Wars theme tune starts, that if Mr Kent and Mrs A were in league together he would have access to all the suspicious crap in her car.

It's still light when we get back from the matinee at the cinema. We are dropped off at the school and then everyone's parents pick them up, except for me, Poppy and Hattie. We walk home together, and then I'm the last one walking. The idea was that there was only a tiny stretch of road between Poppy's house and mine, but I am taking a quick detour and enacting part of my plan today.

I walk past the river, with the little bridge over it, and keep walking until I reach the pub. It is an old medieval pub, called The Shepherd's Arms. Our whole village built up around this one pub. We did it in a school history project. It used to be an inn with rooms in the sixteenth century, and travellers used to stay here on their way from the castles to Lincoln. There are two castles nearby, Tattershall and Old Bolingbroke, but one is just ruins. I try the door handle and push hard. The door is heavy, wooden and painted black. As soon as I open it up, I hear music.

'Hup! Hup!' a man shouts.

I walk around a wooden beam that goes from the ceiling into the stone floor. Behind it is a circle of men. One is on a banjo, and one has a shallow drum in his hand and a stick that looks like a two-ended pestle. They are shouting things back and forth. A third has a guitar. Some men are clapping and some are just sat there, nodding along to the music. The musicians look happy. They have shaved heads and earrings and one has a tattoo. The banjo guy has a tooth missing. You could lose a tooth if a girl punched it out of your mouth while you were killing her. There are a lot of other men in the pub who look unhappy. One man behind the bar looks at me grumpily. There are unhappy men hunched over at the bar, or sat in the corner, talking to each other with their arms folded. They are telling each other things. 'This is how you . . .', 'What you want is a . . .', 'I'm telling you . . .' I hear around me.

'So this is the world of men,' I murmur. 'I'm in enemy's territory. In the belly of the beast.' I narrow my eyes and study them. I hate men now. They are all scary. I'm over average height for my age by a centimetre, but they are a lot taller than me. A large hand clamps down on my shoulder. I jump and whirl around. 'Don't touch me!' I cry out accidentally.

It's the man who was behind the bar just a minute ago. His face and head are all covered with the same stubbly black hair, and his whole body looks sweaty. He takes his massive paw off me and wipes it on a rag. I stare at the rag, looking for blood. I can't tell in the light. 'Hello, young Miss Wilde.'

'How do you know my name?'

'You're Andy's daughter, ent'cheh? He comes in here to play darts.'

'Yeah, I know. He tells us when he's going.'

Suddenly the music stops. The band players are looking at me. It seems like all the men in the pub are looking at me. When I turn my gaze to the banjo player, he smiles at me. I imagine him doing what Nathan did to me. Would he crush me? I look at his big body. Is *that* how you die from rape? The barman touches me more gently now, on my back, at the top, near my neck. I jump away. See? Everyone touches me. The musicians have started up their playing again. I turn back to the barman, remembering why I'm here. I need to tie up a loose end for my plan.

'I need to ask you a few questions, if that's alright.'

He nods solemnly. He must know why I am here.

'Can we talk behind the bar?'

'Only over-eighteens allowed in there, legally.'

I fold my arms so he can't see I'm shaking a bit. 'I'm here on business.'

'Oh, are you?' he says, and he looks up and winks at someone behind my back. I'm being watched. I gulp. 'Come this way. What was your name? Andy's said it before, but I can't remember. Mira, or something?'

'Thera,' I say, but it comes out a whisper. 'Can I borrow a pen and paper?'

'Oh, sure you can.' He gives me a waitress's pad and a biro, and leads me through a little archway by the bar, into the back room. It's a restaurant, but it's empty.

'Why is there nobody here?' I say quietly.

'We only serve food Fridees, Saturdees and Sundees,' he says, pronouncing the days funny. He sits down at a table for two and I sit opposite him, careful not to touch his legs with mine underneath the table.

'First let's start with you.'

'Okay.' He laughs.

I look behind me, instinctively whipping my head around to catch the person watching me. But there is no one there. It's just him and me. I look at his hands. They could break my neck. I steel myself. If I have to be, I'll be brave to the end.

'What's your name?'

'Sam Peeves!' he says with a flourish.

'Occupation.'

'Well, I own this pub, love. I live upstairs.'

'Where are you from?'

'Here!'

'But you've got an accent. Where were you born?'

'Alright, then – Yorkshire.'

'And how long have you been living in the pub?'

''Bout seven year. Enough to call myself an old-time Lincolnshire boy.'

I raise my eyebrows. 'I've lived here eleven years. By that logic, *I'm* an old-timer. You be straight with me,' I warn him.

He holds up his hands, still smiling. 'Ooh, alright, missus. I'll play ball.'

I narrow my eyes. 'Are you in league with my dad?'

'Pardon?'

'Is that a no?'

'No, I don't think so. What do you mean?'

'You don't know what I'm talking about? You're not running black-ops from this pub? Is this pub a cover for murders?'

'Gordon Bennett!'

'Who's he?'

'Would you believe it!'

I stand up, pushing my chair back, put my palms on the table and lean in, like the police do on telly. 'Is Gordon Bennett the one who did it?'

'No, no, no, Gordon Bennett is just a saying! Like "Christ alive".'

'Don't swear in front of me,' I say sternly. 'I'm only eleven. Now, I'm going to ask you a very serious question.' I leave a silence to make him sweat. 'Were you working on the Saturday night that Billie Brooke died?'

'Yes, I was. I work every Saturdee night.'

'Do you remember that evening well?'

'Yes, I do. We had the musicians in, and the darts players—'

'Ah-ha! Was my dad here?'

'Of course, he comes in most Saturdees.'

I leave another beat. 'Are . . . you . . . sure?' I ask slowly.

'What's this about, love?'

'Don't patronize me. Just answer the question.'

'He definitely was, because your mother called the pub to get him to come home when the police came round. I gave a statement to the police to say so, on the Sunday.'

'Oh, good!' I say in relief. Dad's not the killer! Definitely, definitely not. I wanted to make one hundred per cent sure he didn't do it. I know it was probably the walker or a stranger (or maybe the walker is a stranger?), but I was secretly a bit scared that it might be Dad. After all, he knows Billie. She would have gone with him if he had asked her to come to the woods. He might have even said she was going to meet me there. But he didn't. I lean my head on the table, suddenly dizzy. Daddy didn't do it. Phew.

'Are you alright, miss?'

I sit up abruptly. 'Yes! Yes, I'm fine.' I look down at the notes I've taken. 'Hey, do you remember who else was here that night? Like maybe a quite attractive guy in green?'

'Ooh, well, I couldn't say for sure. There were lots of the boys in, though.'

'Gee,' I roll my eyes and quote a telly show I watched the other day: 'Could you vague that up for me?'

He shakes his head and looks concerned. 'Now, why are you worrying yourself about things like this? A pretty girl like you, you should be off having fun—'

'Wait,' I stop him talking by holding up my hand. 'Why did you say that?'

'That you should be off having fun?'

'No. You said I was pretty.'

'Well, yes, but—'

'You think I'm pretty?'

'Certainly! Very pretty! Very striking!'

He keeps talking, but I don't wait to hear him say more. I rip my notes off the waitress pad and stride back out into the main room of the pub. The musicians keep playing, but they all look at me. The men at the bar look at me. The men sat at the little tables in the corners, eating crisps and drinking big pints of beer, all look at me.

I realize finally why the men are looking at me: it's not just Nathan who thinks I'm pretty.

When I get back home, I run straight up to my room and shut the door.

'Thera, is that you?' Dad calls.

'I'm just doing something in my room!' I yell.

'Will you come down here?'

'Just give me two minutes!' In front of the full-length mirror in my room I take my dress off. Then I take my knickers off, and kick my shoes and socks off, and study myself naked. I sorely need boobs, and my tummy pokes out a little, but the rest of me is okay. I have bruises on my legs. I don't know where any of them come from, but I always have bruises on my legs. My legs look quite thin and muscular – from running around over the fields, probably. I turn to my side. I am pretty slim, but my bum pokes out. I bet if I brushed my hair, that would look better too.

The more the dead girls appear to me, the more I think about being a girl, and the more uncertain I am about it. There are some things I really like about being a girl. I like long hair and I like that my clothes are more colourful. But I don't like: periods, boobs or the fact that someone might kill you just because you're a girl. The only way a girl is different from a boy is how they look naked, and apparently that makes all the difference to perverts. I expect some perverts like little boys, but most prefer girls like the dead girls.

There are other things I don't like about being a girl. I don't like that I'm supposed to be pretty and polite and to behave, and that when I think about all these things they just seem like things that would make killing you a lot easier. I don't like that I have a vagina. I poke at it. I found it the other day. That's where the boy's thingy goes in with sex. I saw it on a video, but I had no idea what they were talking about. I realized when I found it. Boys don't have a vagina and girls don't have a willy, so when they threaten you with rape, you have nothing to threaten them back with. I don't like that even though my body is pretty strong now, it's going to get comparably weaker to all the boys my age when they grow taller than me. I'm scared I won't be able to fight back. I think about Billie, and imagine that if she were only a foot taller or a bit stronger or if we'd done a boys' sport like football or martial arts, then she would know how to kick the man so hard he would cry and fall to his knees. I imagine her running out of there and calling to me across the field. Suddenly she is here, in front of me, with the other dead girls.

So far, I have received automatic-writing messages from three of them. The littlest dead girl has not spoken yet, and Billie only said 'Find me', and that was ages ago.

'Don't worry,' I tell them. 'I'm going to make it right. I've been preparing, and I know how to do it now.'

And I *do* know how, finally. I realized in the pub, with all the men looking at me. I am pretty – it isn't just

Nathan that thinks so – and that's going to be my weapon. The thing I use to catch the killer and avenge Billie's death.

Just then, a load roar comes from behind me. 'Theeeeer-aaaaa!'

'I'm coming!' I turn around and shout, but my dad is in the room behind me. I recoil immediately into the corner of the room.

'Thera, put some bloody clothes on and get downstairs for supper right now!' Dad yells.

Mum comes up the stairs. 'What is it?'

Dad is on the landing now. 'She's naked and muttering weird stuff.'

Mum comes in, and I grab my big Disney T-shirt nightie and pull it over my head. 'Thera, what are you doing?'

'Nothing! I was just seeing if . . .' I trail off. The dead girls are standing around Mum. Sometimes it's really hard to make people understand you when they can't see ghosts.

'What are you looking at?' Mum casts her eyes about, but she looks over their heads. 'Thera, I understand if you're exploring feelings . . .'

I frown, confused. 'What?'

'But the sort of, um, nakedness on the television programme Dad says you were watching the other night is not normal, and—'

'I'm not "exploring feelings"! I'm figuring out how Billie was murdered!'

'Enough!' Dad roars from outside. 'You've got to get off this topic, Thera. Stop thinking about it, it just makes you and everyone else upset. You're going to Nan and Grandad's for the whole weekend. I'll take you tomorrow.'

'You can't banish me, you pig!' I yell back. I can't believe I spent all evening finding an alibi for this piece of poo.

He bats my bedroom door open with one hand. 'I can send you away to Nan and Grandad's for the whole summer if I feel like it, so watch your mouth.'

'I have things to do here!'

'You're upsetting Sam, talking about death all the time. It's gruesome.'

Sam is crying in his room, but I think that's got more to do with Dad yelling than anything else.

'Andy, calm down!' Mum shouts, and walks him out, shutting my door. 'Of course she's talking about death,' Mum mutters, as if I can't hear her right outside.

'You're the one who doesn't want her here,' Dad hisses. That hurts. Mum doesn't want me here? I think Dad means that she wishes we lived somewhere else. 'Her friend was killed. What do you expect? With everything going on, it would be better for her to be at my parents'. You know she's hard to watch, she's got a mind of her own. She's too curious about this. Her teacher said she was asking weird questions.'

Urgh, bums. I should have known Mrs A would dob me in.

'Well, if you hadn't encouraged them to play anywhere they liked, in the fields, in the—'

'Oh, so it's my fault now, is it? I suppose we should just coddle them like babies forever.'

'Oh, stop it, Andy.'

'We have to make some sort of decision about what we do with the kids. They're on holiday now, we can't just give them no rules because we disagree.'

'Exactly, so what's the point in arguing and name-calling?'

'I didn't name-call.'

'You sound like a schoolyard bully, getting at me all the—'

I put my hands over my ears and sink down to the floor. I hate it when they fight. Maybe it would be better for me to go to Nanny and Grandad's.

On Friday morning my alarm goes off at six thirty, and I run out the door at seven. I don't tell Sam where I'm going. I know Nathan is already off school for the holidays, though. I run all the way to the caravan park, and then creep around his caravan and look inside the grubby windows. I can't see any movement. I put my hands around my eyes and squint. It looks like he is asleep. Either that or there's another pile of junk now on the top bunk to match the one on the bottom. I go round to his side of the caravan, reach up and knock near where his head is. I wait for a minute and then I do it again: dum-dum-dee-dum-dum.

There is a little pause, and then I hear a quiet tap-tap.

I race back round to the front. He has rolled over in the bunk and is squinting at the window. It must be pretty impossible for him to see through too. I wave and make a lot of movement so he can tell I'm outside. He looks like he's getting out of the bunk.

I put my hands to the window again. Yep. He's getting out of the bunk. He's only wearing boxer shorts. His chest is very flat. He is pulling jeans on. They are blue and normal-looking. Now he is taking a T-shirt out of the washing basket, which is on the table. He pulls it on and his hair shakes around. He doesn't have those flat curtains boys get when their hair is really thin. Nathan has nice hair, thick and soft. There is a click, and he opens the door.

'Hey, you alright? What are you doing here?' he says sleepily.

'My parents are sending me away to my grandparents' for the weekend, so I wanted to tell you I can't come and hang out.'

'Oh, okay. What time is it?'

I show him my watch. 'Seven twenty-five.'

'Urgh, I only went to sleep at two thirty.'

'Why? What were you doing up that late?'

'Just watching telly.' He stretches and groans. 'Mum'll be up soon. She has work at eight thirty.'

'Where does she work?'

'In a factory.'

'What do they make?'

'Some sort of food?' Nathan says, like I would know the answer.

I nod, as if maybe I do. 'Were you okay last time?' I ask.

'What d'you mean?'

'When your mum got home.'

'Oh, yeah.'

'You were acting a bit weird.'

Nathan chews on his lip and looks across the fields. 'I felt funny. I don't like this thing about ghosts, Thera. I've been having nightmares all week. Mum's annoyed with me.'

'Why?'

''Cause I keep getting spooked an' stuff. It wakes her up. She needs her sleep 'cause she works earlies.'

'Are you okay? Do you want to talk about it?'

'No.'

'Okay,' I say. 'Do you want to try again?'

'At what?'

'Duh. At what we were doing when we were interrupted.'

'Um,' says Nathan, and looks down my body and then back up into my eyes.

'See, I have this plan.' I clear my throat. I'm nervous about telling Nathan the exact plan because I don't want him to laugh at me, but I have to have someone on my team, and Sam's too little, and he's scared of everything. 'The plan can only go ahead if I can pull some things off while I'm at Nan and Grandad's. But I need to practise with you now, so I can work out how to be raped and not die. So you have to start, and then I'll attack you while you're doing it and fight you off, okay?'

'I don't know . . .' Nathan says hesitantly. 'I don't want to hurt you again.'

'Don't worry, I'm tough,' I say. 'A few bruises are nothing. We could try it naked.'

'Um . . .' Nathan says again. 'Naked?'

'I mean with our clothes off. 'Cause Billie's clothes looked like they'd been taken off and put back on,' I add quickly, embarrassed. I don't add that Nathan wearing only boxer shorts was interesting to see, and that I wouldn't mind seeing him without them. Two birds, one stone.

'Yeah, I got that.' Nathan gulps. He looks over to the closed bedroom door. 'Mum's in.'

'We can just lie down in the wheat field,' I say, nodding up the hill. 'It'll be easy.'

Nathan looks where I'm pointing.

'What do you think?' I ask.

He screws up his face. 'Okay. Sure.' He goes inside and sits on the pile of junk on the bottom bunk and pulls his trainers on, without socks. When he comes out, we walk up to the wheat field. I skip ahead and jump onto the crop, flattening it out all around me.

'Wheat angel!' I call out, like Billie and me used to do.

'You're not supposed to do that!' Nathan exclaims. He looks around. 'We could get in trouble with the farmer.'

''Fraidy-cat,' I say, and he looks annoyed.

'Okay,' he says. He glances around and jumps in next to me. He lies on his side, gazing at me, and suddenly things get quiet. He swallows again. 'Take your clothes off then,' he says.

I sit up and lift my T-shirt over my head.

Nathan gapes at me. 'Wow,' he says, like he's breathing the word. 'Nice boobs.'

'I don't really have them,' I say.

'Almost,' he says, nicely.

'Now you.'

He takes off his T-shirt too. His chest is gorgeous, tanned and muscly with perfect red-wine-coloured nipples. I put my hand on it.

'Your heart's beating fast.'

'No it's not,' he says awkwardly. 'I've done stuff like this before.'

'Have you? Naked?

'Um, no, just top half. Now take those off,' he says, and points to my jeans.

'Let's both do it at the same time,' I say.

''Kay,' Nathan says. He seems almost shy, which is crazy, because he's older.

'One, two, three.'

We both unbutton and unzip our jeans, and pull them down at the same time, with our knickers and boxer shorts. Nathan's face suddenly goes dark red when he looks at me and his mouth opens. He looks up at my face, then quickly away, as if he's just realized I'm watching him, and bites his lip. He regards himself, between his legs, and then puts his hands over it.

'Are you okay?' I ask.

'I'm just . . .' he says. 'I'm not, like . . .' He shakes his head and stands up, almost falling over because his jeans are down around his knees. I see his thingy. It's pointing upwards. It's bigger than Sam's. I'm staring at it, when Nathan pulls his jeans up, grabs his T-shirt and runs away.

'Nathan?' I yank my jeans up and run after him, tugging my T-shirt over myself. He's waiting for me back at the horsey field. 'Are you okay?' He nods, but he's half-crying and looks like he's going to throw up. He brushes away some tears angrily. 'Was it me?' I ask. 'Am I ugly naked?'

'No!' he shouts. 'Of course not! Don't be a fuckin' idiot!'

'Don't swear! And I'm not an idiot!'

'Well, for a smarty-pants you certainly don't get some stuff.'

'Like what?'

'Nothing!' he says, annoyed. 'I don't want to pretend to . . . *you-know-what* you again, okay? I mean I do, but I . . . don't,' he says lamely. 'I'm not like those men.'

'What men?

He kicks the fence. 'Pervs.'

'Um, okay.'

'Aren't you weirded out doing this? If Billie is a ghost, then what if she's watching?'

'She knows why—'

'I don't want to think about Billie any more! I live right next to the woods. You don't have to see them and think about her every day.'

'You don't think I think about Billie every day?'

'Can we just stop talking about it for *one fucking second, I don't wanna think about it*!' Nathan shouts. He leans against the fence and looks away. I try to think of something to talk about.

'Hattie said your dad was in prison.'

'Did she?'

'That's sad.'

'Do you really think I want to talk about that?'

I feel my cheeks blush. This is what Mum and Dad warned me about. Maybe I am an idiot. 'Sorry.'

After a while of silence, Nathan says, 'He's not any more. They let him out.'

My eyes widen. 'When?'

'A few months ago.'

I frown, looking over to the caravan park, right next to the copse where Billie was killed. 'Does he live with you?'

'No. He's come by, but . . . Mum won't have him in. For now,' Nathan adds darkly. His arms are folded, his legs crossed, his head down, and his face is still red.

'Don't you want him to come home?' I ask.

He shakes his head.

'Why not?'

'He's a bad person.'

'What did he do?'

'Beat someone up really badly.'

'A girl?'

'No. Not this time. It was in a bar.'

'So . . . he's beaten up girls before?'

Nathan sticks out his bottom lip and shrugs. His eyes are all blank and staring, but at the ground, not me.

'Do you think he might have killed Billie?'

He lowers his head even more and looks away from me, so I can't see him properly.

'Nathan?'

'Nah.' He turns back to me, and looks alright again. 'Nah, I don't think he killed Billie.'

'You don't even suspect a little bit?'

'Nah.'

'But if he's back, maybe—'

'Do you think I'm a bad person?' he says suddenly, as if he's been holding it in and really wants to say it.

'No. Why would I think that?'

Nathan's face screws up. 'When we were . . . when I was on top of you in the caravan, and out in the field . . . I got an erection.'

My eyes widen. 'Oh.'

He sees me and looks away. His cheeks are back to red again, like before. 'And then, today, when I looked at you naked . . . Whoever . . . killed Billie is a really bad person, Thera. Men like that, they're really bad people. And I wanted to . . . I wanted to do . . . what they do.' He wipes at his eyes, even though they seem dry. 'There was this other time,' he whispers, 'this other thing. That I did.'

'What? When?'

'I can't tell you.'

'Why not?'

''Cause I'll get into trouble. With the police. And Mum'll be angry.'

'Is it . . .' I frown. 'Is it about Billie?'

'I can't . . .' he says miserably. 'You'll . . . you'll hate me.'

'I won't hate you.'

'I really like you, Thera,' Nathan whispers. He comes close to me and hugs me again, but this time he hugs me from the side, and puts his head on my shoulder. 'I think I'm in love with you.'

I hesitate. I can feel need pouring out of him. The only person Nathan has in the world is his mum. I feel hot and pressured. I chew nervously on my bottom lip. 'I can't think about that right now, Nathan. My best friend is haunting me and I have to find out why.'

'Sorry.' He stands up straight and roughly brushes his hand across his face, but it's so dirty, probably because his mum doesn't make him wash it, that I can see the tracks tears have left on his grubby cheeks. I don't blame him. I don't like washing either, and I probably wouldn't do it if Mum and Dad didn't make me.

'Come on, don't be sad,' I say. It's sort of scary. I feel like, if I say anything bad to him, even that I don't know if I love him yet, he'll be really upset. And yet he can tell me he doesn't want to be naked with me and I'm supposed to just not talk about it. I feel confused and annoyed.

'I'm sorry,' he mumbles again, his lip trembling.

'So,' I say, 'what did you do?'

He shakes his head. His eyes are squished together and his whole body is stiff.

'Nathan?' He's not looking at me. I put my hand to his chin and then the other to the side of his face and pull it upwards, forcing him to look in my eyes. 'What did you do?'

'Get off, Thera!' he shouts, his voice breaking, and pushes my hands away. I almost fall over. He's strong, for just being thirteen. He starts to run again, across the field, towards the hole in the hedge. Why is he so upset? Does he know something about Billie?

I race after him and jump through the hole a few seconds after he does. But then I slow down, because I see his mum. She's next to the caravan, putting out laundry on a line. 'What is it?' she snaps sharply.

As he nears her, he almost stumbles backwards, but then he shakes his head and goes for the caravan door. She grabs him by the neck of his T-shirt and looks at him, then me, then back at him. 'What did you do to her?'

'Nothing!' I hear Nathan cry, and then his mum shoves him in the caravan and shuts the door behind them both, leaving the laundry basket out on the grass.

As soon as I wake up at Nanny and Grandad's, I normally run downstairs for toast and tea and then read the papers, but today I get to the mirror near the door to my room, and stop. My pajama bottoms are shorts, and now I've grown a bit they are really quite short, and almost show my bottom, and I am starting to get very small boobs so they look like bumps under my top. Looking at my body and thinking about what a pervert would think of me makes me feel sick. I don't want Nanny and Grandad to think of me as someone who a pervert would have sex with, so I get dressed. I put on my long denim shorts with the pockets (they are actually Sam's but he's not big enough for them yet) and a vest top, and then a T-shirt over the top. I am now too hot but you can't see the bumps any more. It's eight by the time I pull on my socks, sit on the top stair and bump my bum down all three flights.

'Good morning!' I sing, poking my head around the door of the back living room, on the ground floor. The entire room looks dark with the books, but there is a ray of sun from the window and small pools of yellow light created by Grandad's many reading lamps. Nan is sat under one at the dining table, and Grandad is beneath another, in his armchair. As he does every day, he reads the *Telegraph* in his blue silky pajamas and dressing gown. Grandad likes to read about history, culture and politics, and Nanny likes to read the gossip stories about street fights and people raising money for palliative care at the hospital.

Grandad taught me that word. He teaches me to spell five words every time I come to see him. This weekend they are: 'uncharacteristically', 'monotony', 'post-prandial', 'liturgy' and 'enigmatic'. I have to recite the spellings on Sunday, before I go home. He says I might be a writer too, one day.

'Oh, you're up!' Nan says, turning around and reaching for me to squeeze my hand. Her hands are soft. I think it's because she always does the washing-up.

'Good morning, Thera,' Grandad says. 'Help yourself to breakfast. I believe there's toast, jam and fruit on the counter.' He says the same thing every time I'm here.

'Okey dokey!' I say, and skip into the kitchen. I fill the kettle and put it on to boil, and then dump out the old teabags, rinse the pot and put in fresh ones. 'Do you guys want tea?' I shout through.

'We'll both have another cup, dear!' Nan calls back.

Grandad tuts. 'My, my, Thera, you appear to have inherited your grandmother's lungs.'

I get the milk out of the fridge, then put some toast on. I prefer white toast, but brown toast is healthier, so today I'm having brown. The kettle boils so I fill the teapot and close the lid, and then the toast pops so I spread Lurpak butter and Robertson's blackcurrant jam on it.

I cut it into triangles. That's how Nan does it, but Dad cuts it into squares. I don't do that today, because I'm not talking to him. He's a bully, yelling at me. He's like a killer anyway, even if he didn't kill Billie, because he yells at me and Mum, so maybe he is evil. Maybe there are loads of men that are evil, only not Grandad. Or Sam. Or (hopefully) Nathan. I sigh sadly. Life is so complicated now. For a moment, I wish I could forget about finding Billie's killer, but then I remind myself that I promised her and the other dead girls. How could I live with myself, anyway, if I didn't find him? I would be a terrible friend.

I carry my plate through to the table and open my latest book, taken from Grandad's study, on historical ghost stories.

'Do you want to go to the seaside on the bus today?' Nan asks.

'Yeah, that sounds great. Um, could I go shopping on my own tomorrow?' I say nonchalantly, so she doesn't think it's suspicious.

Nan sticks her nose up in the air and pretends to be snooty. 'Does madam not want her nan with her?'

I giggle. 'No . . . I just wanted to be independent.'

'Ah, I understand.' She jerks her thumb towards Grandad. 'I often think I want to be independent of him.'

Nan giggles and Grandad huffs. 'Be my guest!' he says.

'Are we looking for anything special?' Nanny asks.

'Just a dress.' I can't say 'Nothing', because that would be weird. 'Maybe from Tammy or Internacionale?' I say.

'Are those shops?' Grandad chuckles.

I turn in my seat, eager to change the conversation topic. 'Are you going to write today, Grandad?'

'I might have a bash at it, yes, my dear.'

'Cool! What are you going to work on today?'

Grandad's books are for grown-ups, mainly, but I've read the seventh one, which is for children. It is called *Dark Zoid*, and the main characters were based on Sam and me. It's an adventure story about two kids who meet an alien robot over a beta version of an expanded, futuristic internet. Grandad's stories are often about how technology will affect our humanity in the future.

I take a bite of jammy toast and wonder if, one day, technology will make human beings able to live forever. Could technology be fused with a biological body, like in *The Terminator*? Could someone who was dead be brought back to life? How much rotting would they have to do to be too rotten to be brought back? Nathan Nolan sort of looks like Edward Furlong, who I've fancied since I saw *Terminator 2* for the first time. Suddenly I realize Grandad has been talking and I haven't been listening.

'Wait!' I stop him. 'Could you say that again? I wasn't listening.'

Grandad shakes his head and opens his paper up again. 'The aged are invisible.'

'Sorry, Grandad. I was just thinking about *The Terminator*.'

'I was saying – I'm sorry if it bored your none-too-literary sensibilities – that I'm going to take a bash at a first draft of the chapter introducing Tashi Sangpo today.'

'Is this the Chinese thing?'

'No, it's the Tibetan thing. One is not engaged in a "Chinese thing".' Grandad doesn't normally say 'one', but he is being uppity because I was accidentally ignoring him. Grandad's vocabulary is enormous, though, and his books are very imaginative. He is also the wisest and most intelligent person I know. I think I take after him. 'Tashi Sangpo is an impoverished Tibetan monk who wins a competition. The prize is to have his brain wired into "the cloud", a futuristic form of the internet whereby he can control everything in his home and around him via brainwaves, but the price is his soul.'

'Like he can order Chinese food and stuff?'

'I'm not sure a Tibetan would feel the need to order Chinese food, but technically, yes.'

'Grandad?' I say quickly. Nan has left the room to get dressed. I figure Nan won't like this question, so I have a limited amount of time to ask it, but I need to, because Grandad is so smart and knows everything.

'Yes, Thera?'

'Um . . .' I go and lean on his armchair, and whisper, 'I know Billie was raped and then strangled, but do you know exactly why the man killed her? Did he hate her?'

Grandad clears his throat and speaks without looking at me, folding the paper up noisily. 'I would suggest that a man who committed sexual assault on a child would have no scruples in doing away with his victim to avoid being identified by her and subsequently imprisoned. Now, I think I shall get dressed.'

I pick at the threads on his chair without responding, then ask another question. 'Why was she a bit burnt?'

Grandad, now on his way to the door, turns and narrows his eyes. 'How do you know that?'

'Because I found her.'

'She was wrapped in a sheet.'

I dip my head so I am hiding behind my hair. 'I had a quick look.'

Grandad doesn't say anything for a while.

'Never mind,' I sing-song in a high voice. Sometimes when I can tell people feel uncomfortable around me I do a baby voice, or a prettier, high voice. I've been doing it a lot lately. 'I'll go get ready for the seaside.' I walk past him, but Grandad calls after me.

'Thera!'

I turn back at the door.

Grandad pushes his glasses further up his nose. 'Burning eliminates DNA evidence.'

'Eliminates' was one of my words from a few weekends ago. It means 'destroys'.

In the morning, I make a list. I sit on my bed, with all my money from my piggy bank (one hundred and eleven pounds), and a piece of Grandad's paper in front of me. The bed next to me is empty. Sam is at home. I miss him. I take the lid off Grandad's fountain pen that I borrowed from his study and I write my name and the date, and then I start thinking.

Shopping list

Sealed plastic freezer bags like the sort Mum buys for lasagne

Nylon cable ties like on police show

Wonderbra like Hattie's

Lip gloss

Pretty dress

Heels?

Big rings? (to put on fingers so when I punch someone it really hurts)

Mini tapes for Mum's mini tape recorder

Batteries for mini tape recorder

Small sharp knife

I sit back when I'm done writing and look at my list. I'm nervous, but I know I have to do this. I think some more, and then I hunch over the paper again and write:

Why do I have to do this?

I dip into my Tooty Frooties. I'll just have one more before tea and biscuits at elevenses. A purple one.

Because Billie and the dead girls want me to do it
So more girls won't get killed
So the dead girls will be at peace and stop freaking me out
Because it's my fault Billie was killed

Which is true even if it's not the walker; even if I just left her alone in the field and didn't keep my eyes peeled for someone that might kill her.

I guess I'll also have a green Tooty Frootie. I munch on the sweetie.

Like Grandad and Hattie said, ghosts only haunt you when they have unfinished business. They also only appear to people who can help them. My plan is already in motion, but so far I haven't decided on the final aim. Does Billie want me to find her murderer to enact revenge, or does she want him to be killed so he doesn't get anyone again? Or does it matter? It reminds me of a conversation me and Billie had a long time ago.

We were at Billie's house, having a sleepover, and we were about eight. We had spent all day playing Sylvanian Families, and we were in sleeping bags together on the floor, eating marshmallows and watching our imaginary fairies dance across the room, commenting on what they were doing. We decided they were best, true, forever friends, just like us.

'We should write a convent of friendship,' I said. (When we had finally written it and I took it to Grandad, he corrected my spelling to 'covenant', but I was eight so I was really little and didn't know better, when we were talking, than to say convent.)

'Whazzat?' Billie said.

'It's basically what best, true, forever friends do.'

'That's a SPECTACULAR idea!'

'Shush, Billie!' Her mum's whisper came through the wall from her parents' bedroom.

We made the covenant of friendship up in our heads first, then wrote it down the next day, and Billie added illustrations. We made ten sentences that made up a BTF friendship. Number one was total honesty. Number two, I'm pretty sure, was that you would die for them. Number seven was that you could scream for them and they would come running immediately.

Billie chortled. 'Ahhhhh, Thera!' She let out a bloodcurdling cry.

'Billie!' Billie's mum hissed again.

'I'll always protect you,' I said to Billie.

'With your kung fu fighting, da-da-da-da-da-da-da-da-daaaaa?' Billie sang, and karate-chopped the air. Then she pretended to stroke her chinbeard. 'Or with your big old brain?'

'My brain, Pinky. Innnndubitably!' I said. (Thinking about it, this is kind of what I am doing now.)

We started to chant the theme tune from *Pinky and the Brain*, which is on Nickelodeon. 'Pinky and the Brain, Brain, Brain, Brain, Brain, Brain, Brain, Brain, Brain, Brain, Brain, Brain!'

And then we added number eight, which was that, if we did get murdered, we would avenge each other's deaths.

'Thera!' Nanny's voice yells up the stairs. She really has some lungs on her for being seventy. 'Elevenses!'

I race to the landing and lean over the bannister. 'Coming!' I shout back as loudly as possible.

Then I go quickly back to the mission notes and write down one last thing on the list of whys:

<u>Because I promised her I would</u>

I underline it. Twice.

In the afternoon, I went on my shopping trip, and got everything I needed. I spent half my savings: fifty-four pounds and thirty-six pence.

The Wonderbra was the most difficult thing to get on my list. The knife was hard enough. The man in the first shop was old and grizzly-looking, and it was a small shop. He didn't have a lot to do, and thinking back I'm pretty sure it was a mistake to just walk in there, test the points on the knives, then say, 'Ouch! That's perfect', and put the sharpest, longest one on the counter to buy.

He frowned at me. I looked up from counting out my pounds and knew he was onto me immediately. I smiled to make him feel comfortable (earlier Nan said I was starting to get an intense look about me, and I needed to flex the corners of my mouth a little bit), but he came around the counter anyway. My smile dropped away as he came towards me. I looked at the counter. I wanted the knife, but he was a bit scary and he had knives in his shop. I gulped and clutched my money tight, ready to run. 'Come here, dearie,' he said, and he frowned more, like he was about to do something horrible to me, and I screamed and ran out of the shop, my rucksack making a *fah-lump, fah-lump* noise on my back. My scream was so high-pitched

I'm surprised it didn't break all the glass in the shop windows. He didn't run after me. I flew across the pink and blue tiles into the heart of the shopping centre, the sound of my trainers slapping against the tiles startling everybody I ran past.

Next I decided to try and get the bra, so I went into BHS and poked their boobholders. They didn't really have anything like I wanted, and then the saleslady came over and made me jump.

'Do you need some help?' she said.

I thought about it. My cheeks were bright red. I could feel them. I didn't know it would be this embarrassing to look at bras. I guess it's because they are about sex. Anyway, I said, 'Nope' really quickly and laughed, and got on the downwards escalator.

Next I went to Marks & Sparks. They had a much bigger selection. No one was around, so I put one on my head in front of the mirror. It looked like a flying helmet. I tied it under my chin with the bits that go over your shoulders. Now I looked like a pilot. I made pilot goggles by putting my thumbs and pointing fingers together on both hands and tilting them back so my palms were on my face.

'Hello,' a little lady said suddenly.

I guess I was still geed up from the knife man, because I jumped.

'Oh my goodness, you look terrified!'

'You startled me!'

'Am I that horrifying?' she said, and pulled down her eyes so she looked gross and older. I laughed. 'Are you looking for a bra?' she said.

'Um, yeah, I guess,' I said casually.

'Have you been measured?'

I frowned. 'No.'

'Well, you have to be measured.'

'I do?'

'Yes. Come with me,' she said, and she took my hand between her hands and left me no choice but to follow her across the shop. People were staring at us. I frowned back at them.

'You might want to take that off,' she whispered to me.

'What off?'

She looked puzzled and patted my head.

'Oh! Oh yeah, I forgot.' I yanked at the bra on my head and the elastic straps catapulted it away from me, across the shop, where it hit the aisle and then slid further along the slippy floor, down to where some ladies were shopping. They looked at it like it was a bit of disgusting poo.

'Jane will clear that up,' the lady said, and waved to another lady in the shop uniform. 'Don't you worry.'

'I wasn't,' I said quickly.

Then she took me through a door. It was like going into the bowels of the shop, but it turned out to be a special changing room for bras. She shut us in a small space with curtains around us. 'Take your T-shirt off,' she sing-songed.

'What?'

'I have to measure you, don't I, silly?'

'Oh.' I felt weird, but I took off my T-shirt. Maybe this is how someone made Billie undress.

'Now let me just . . .' She whipped out a measuring tape and pulled it round me.

'Ow! It's cold!'

'Just a minute.'

'It's freezing.'

'Turn around. Let me get . . . Just another . . .' She kept pushing me round in circles, pulling on me with her tape. 'Wonderful! I'll just go and get you some bras in your size and we'll see how they are looking. Stay there!'

'Wait! Why—?' I started, but she went out. I wanted to pick the bra. Instead, she came back with three white training bras, like I was some sort of tiny ballerina. 'I want a Wonderbra,' I said.

'You don't want a Wonderbra! You want one of these!' she said happily, and flapped them about like she was modelling them on telly.

'No, I want a Wonderbra,' I said icily. 'I have to look like a man would want me.'

'Er . . .' she said, and her cheeks went red.

'If you don't go and get it for me, I'll get it myself,' I said, and went to pick up my T-shirt.

'No, no! I'll get one, I'll get it,' she said, and rushed out. A minute later, she rushed back in and pulled it on me roughly, tutting the entire time. 'Well, I never' and 'Goodness me,' she said.

Finally, she let me go off and buy the stupid Wonderbra. I only want it to catch the pervert anyway. I don't like it. It hurts like somebody trying to strangle my ribcage.

When I get home from Nan and Grandad's it is the summer holidays and there is no one to supervise me, which Mum and Dad don't like, but is ideal for my purposes. Dad is at the workshop in the village all day. He calls up the stairs to tell me so at breakfast time and asks if I want to go with him, but I ignore him because I'm still not talking to him, and he says, childishly, 'Suit yourself.'

Sam is at his friend Barry's for the day, so I decide to put the last touches to my plan before the day of action. I've upgraded it to a mission now, rather than a plan. That means I've made charts and instructions and stuff.

In the morning, I go into the village to see where all the police are. Hattie and Poppy are hanging out with Hattie's sister and her friends on a bench. Nathan isn't there, but the police are nearby. I walk right up to Hattie and the others and say hi, then stand there for ages. They are talking about how the village has a murderer in it and the police are like their personal bodyguards. It's true. Sometimes, when I'm walking around, a police car will drive slowly behind me for a bit, then turn off. Sometimes I don't even look back, I just know they're there because of the engine. It's changed in Eastcastle too. When we drove through on the way back from Nan and Grandad's, there were lots of police cars, and lots of people in the town centre.

'What's that?' I asked Mum.

'It's a protest, sweetheart.'

'What are they protesting?'

'Um . . .'

'Mum?'

'They think the police should have caught the killer by now. They think they're not doing a good job.'

'What do you think?'

'I think they're a small force. They're doing the best they can. Detective Waters is smart.'

'Georgie?'

'Yes, Georgie.'

In the village, Hattie's sister Lauren is saying how her friend Michelle, who lives near the caravan park too, isn't even allowed out any more, but her brother is.

'That's so unfair!' I say.

They all ignore me and then Hattie says, 'That's so unfair!' And they all agree.

None of them look at me at all, and I stand there for ages, listening to their conversation and nodding and laughing at their jokes. In the end, it's obvious they have sent me to Coventry, which is when you ignore someone and don't talk to them. I try not to care, but I suddenly feel like crying, so I turn and walk away quickly. Behind me I hear them say, 'Did you hear she—' and then I don't hear any more, but it sounds like they think I'm embarrassing and weird and I feel my cheeks going red and my eyes welling up. At least they acknowledged my existence. I hope Hattie hasn't told them about my plan. I told her about it when it was just coming together, when I thought I needed someone else to help me carry it out. But I don't need her. I don't need any of them.

I start to run through the village, past Dad's carpentry workshop, and I only slow down when I get to the caravan park. I haven't seen Nathan since Friday morning. I wonder if he misses me and I am really hoping he isn't still mad at me. I can't see Nathan hanging about around the field so I knock on his door.

His mum opens it.

'You!' She looks very lazy, in dirty clothes and with her hair not brushed.

'Hello, is Nathan here?'

'You can't play with my son any more.'

'Why not?'

'I know what you did, filthy girl. Leading my son astray.'

I huff. 'Me, filthy? Nathan's always covered in dirt! You should clean his clothes, like a good mum!'

For a second Nathan's mum looks livid, then she comes out of the door and hits me on the head with the cooking thing she is holding. It's like a wooden spoon but with slits in it, and it hurts loads.

'Ouch!' I yell, and put my arm up across my face. She thwacks me with it, over and over.

'You dirty little girls, all sluts these days. I see you. I see you!' she keeps saying.

'I'm just *one* girl, you crazy person!' I say. She keeps

hitting me, so I retreat from the caravan and run a little way away from her. 'I'll be back,' I say, like Arnie.

'You come back here, there's no telling what I'll do,' she says.

I narrow my eyes at her. Maybe Nathan's mum is just as much to be feared as his dad. And that means . . . I look over to the copse.

'Don't want to end up like her, do you?' she says.

My eyes widen. 'I'm telling,' I say. 'I'm telling on you.'

I run off home and decide to do one of my planning jobs, so at least it's a productive day, even if I don't have any friends who are allowed to speak to me.

I cut my hair. This doesn't seem like the most important job on the list, maybe, but I have been thinking about it and I made a list of reasons why I should. What it comes down to is: I think, with half my hair, I will be pretty enough for Nathan to like me, but not pretty enough for the killer to kill me. Also my hair will be long enough for me to be obviously a girl, but not long enough to grab and hold onto (if someone were to chase me and try to kill me). This is a fine balance, but I think it's one every woman must achieve.

Afterwards I go outside, and practise defending myself. I use Dad's axe that he chops the logs for the fire with, and which I intend to take on my mission, along with the vegetable-cutting knife that I eventually managed to get in the supermarket, pretending Nan needed it urgently to make barbecue kebabs.

The axe is heavy, but I figure out how to hold it so it feels right in my hand. Then I chop a few logs from different angles, so I can defend myself if I'm grabbed different ways, and then I practise throwing it. I've seen people throw axes on telly. The difficult thing is getting the blade to hit the side of the shed, rather than the handle. Unfortunately, the sixth time I throw it, the handle side hits again and knocks the blade out towards me. I jump to the side and it lands where my feet were. I try but I can't fix it because the wood is broken, so I hide it behind the logs at the back of the woodshed, and hope Dad thinks he's just lost it or something.

Then I take a shower to make myself smell nice for tomorrow. In the bathroom, I take all my clothes off and look at myself in the mirror. I'm pleased now I know other people think I'm pretty, but personally I can't tell if I'm pretty just by looking. The bags under my eyes make me look old, and there are lines on my forehead that look like wrinkles. My boobs are still only almost, and my belly is poking out loads because I ate a whole packet of Maryland cookies this morning. I'm sweaty and tired and I feel like all this preparing would be actually fun if Billie were here, but she's not. And I'm not looking forward to meeting her killer.

I look at myself in the mirror. My hair is cut off up to my chin on my right side, and to my collarbone on my left. 'Hmm,' I grumble, and then suddenly I realize it doesn't look like Billie's hair any more. We have always had identical hair. I have to choke back a huge, exhausted sob.

I miss her so much, but I pull myself together and tell myself I have to be tough for her now. Suddenly she walks through the wall behind me. I draw my breath in quickly but try not to look shocked. I don't want to upset her.

Billie sticks out her tongue sideways at me in the mirror. She must have known I needed her. She shakes her head, meaning, 'No tears, loopy.'

'I wish you could talk to me,' I say. 'Properly, in your own voice.' She takes my hand. It's so cold it makes my blood cold, and I can feel it running all around my body. 'And I wish you wouldn't always be with the dead girls,' I whisper, feeling guilty. 'I know they were killed too, and I feel really sorry for them, and I think I know what you guys want me to do, but we're never just us any more.'

She puts her finger to her lips. The girls must be close by and she doesn't want them to hear.

We look in the mirror together. My cheeks are pink and my hair is short and wild and curlier than before. Billie's skin is white and her hair is still long.

She squeezes my hand. She raises her other hand and makes a cutting motion in the mirror where my hair is cut weird. I nod miserably. I go and get Mum's kitchen scissors and hold my hair at my chin, and cut across the jagged bottom, making it straight again. Then I do the same to the other side, until my hair is chopped to my chin, but the sides are equal length. It looks okay. Definitely not as pretty as long hair, though. What if I made a mistake? What if I over-calculated my prettiness, and now I've made myself ugly and Nathan won't want me? It's so hard and confusing to think about trying to make Nathan like me and at the same time trying to be *not* likeable enough that I don't get killed. I wipe my eyes, and Billie makes fists in the mirror, and so do I. We are telling each other to be strong. Then she leaves. And I have never felt more alone or less strong in my short life.

But when I get into my bedroom, someone else is there to keep me company. She takes my hand and I feel a dead girl that's not Billie for the first time. She's cold, and tiny. We sit on my bed, against the pillows, and I write down what she is telling me in my journal. She doesn't just speak. She draws her My Little Pony and her mummy and daddy. It's the littlest dead girl, and her voice is high and cute.

Hi Thera, my name is Ellie and I'm five. My favourite colour is blue and my favourite toy is my My Little Pony. She's a unicorn and her name is Sasha. I saw her on the television and she galloped all the way to my home for my birthday! Mommy and Daddy are still looking for me, but I died a long time ago. We drove across the whole country to a place that was nice and sunny and Mickey Mouse was there too! A man said my mommy said I had to come with him. I followed him for so long, and then I was really, really tired, so we got in his car so we would get to Mommy *quicker, but I fell asleep! When I woke up I felt funny and sad so I cried and he gave me some juice and I went to sleep and I never woke up again. I miss my mommy and daddy. Will you help us?*

Mum cries when she sees my new hair.

'What's wrong, Ma?' I ask her. She comes in the door with her work bag, and immediately goes through to the living room and sits down with one hand over her eyes, crying. I try to sit on her lap on the couch, but she stands up.

'Thera, why did you cut your hair?'

'I don't know, I just wanted to.'

'Go to your room.'

'What? Why?'

'Just please— Oh, fine!' she says angrily. 'I'll go to *my* room.' She runs upstairs and shuts her bedroom door. She doesn't come down for teatime.

'Maybe she's ill,' I say when Dad calls her and she doesn't come down.

Dad huffs and says, 'She's not ill.'

He goes up and they yell at each other. I'm starting to get worried about them. Poppy's and Hattie's parents don't live together any more; they haven't for a few years. Mrs A said it's like an epidemic with this generation. (Obviously I asked Grandad what that meant.)

I protest against Dad shouting by eating my sausage, beans and mash on my bed instead of with him at the table, so Dad eats alone because Sam is still at Barry's. It's one of my favourite meals and I know Dad has made it to be nice to me, and this makes me cry because he wants to be friends again but I can't quite. He's just like the other men in the pub and the man who killed Billie. They're scary and big and they keep reaching for me. Hands in the pub on my back, Mr Kent's hand on my neck, that man in the shop in town when I was asking for the knife, that man feeding the birds on Cleethorpes on Saturday when Nan and me were out. 'My little love', he called me, and then he took my hand. I felt bad, but I pulled it away and wiped it on my jeans. I just wish they would all go away and Billie would be back and things would be simpler.

I eat my tea for sustenance's sake and do my workout again. I try on my outfit I bought on my shopping mission. I paint my nails pink and wait for them to dry. I bodge them and have to do them again, but this time I do it very carefully. I put my lip gloss on. I look pretty now. Nowhere near as pretty as Billie, but maybe Nathan would properly want to rape/have sex with me like this.

I have been very scientific so far about mine and Nathan's experiments. I lie back on my bed, feeling warm and funny. I liked when he kissed me on the cheek, and I liked how hard his chest felt against mine. He's a bit older and a bit more grown-up, maybe. It was weird seeing his thingy, but it didn't look horrible. I mean, I guess I'm supposed to like it, because I'm a girl, and I'm not gay. At least I don't think so, because I fancy Nathan, and Edward Furlong, and Leo, and Zack, and I think the middle Hanson brother is okay. I do like Tia from *Sister, Sister*, but I think that's because I want to be her.

I'll be sad if Nathan has fallen out with me, or told on

me to his mum. I hope she doesn't know about my whole plan. No, because I didn't tell Nathan the whole thing, did I? It would be so poopsticks if I never saw Nathan again. I mean, obviously I would see him at the bus stop, but if we weren't friends that would be rubbish. That would mean I didn't have any friends, apart from Sam. Nathan is bigger than Sam. He'd be a better fighter if it came to him standing by my side in battle, being Lancelot to my King Arthur or whatever (obviously I wouldn't be Guinevere, because princesses are saps). Has Nathan fallen out of love with me? Am I still in love with him? Were we in love at all?

I climb under the bedcovers and stroke my hand all over my chest and my crotch and my legs, imagining it's Nathan. Then I bang hard against the bed like he did to me, and then I make a little mouth with my thumb and my pointing finger, and I kiss it. It's so nice imagining him kissing me. I touch my boobs that he said were almost, and think how sweet he was to say that. I get lip gloss stickiness all over my hand, and rub on my knickers between my legs because it feels nice, and fall asleep in my new dress under my Care Bears duvet cover. It's a Tuesday tomorrow. Mum and Dad both have to work, Sam will be at another friend's house (Mum's got him booked practically all week), and I'll be home alone again. It's time. I'm not nervous. I'm ready.

When you fall in love all at once, by the time you find out what the consequences of being swept up are, you're already drowning. They are the only one holding you up. Your whole version of the world belongs to them. There is no way to live without them.

We moved into a flat together and got engaged. It was very quick, but everything had been. I was Catholic, and I wanted to wait until our wedding night to make love. That might sound old-fashioned, but I was nineteen and a virgin, and I thought, why not? We're getting married in three months. Truth be told, I was still scared. We had done so much already. He liked to play a lot of games. He liked me to dress up like a schoolgirl. He liked to pretend to snatch me and take me against my will into our bedroom, where he would force himself inside my mouth and call me names. I wouldn't have done it with anyone else, but with him I felt safe. I knew how much he loved me. And I may have been naive, but I wasn't unaware of the fact that men were supposed to respect you, and he did, despite his games. He was marrying me, wasn't he?

And he depended on me. We depended on each other. He did everything I wanted him to do, decorating the flat, buying me gifts, taking me lovely places. He always paid, and I always did what I could to make him happy. I did the sexual things he wanted, and I liked them. They made me feel powerful, to be so wanted by a big, attractive man everyone was drawn to – men and women. I liked that he could overpower me. He liked to pretend to treat me unkindly. Afterwards he would whisper the sweetest things. We would do everything together, always.

Except . . . he went out at night without me, looking for women. This began shortly before we were married. I thought, well, he's cheating on me. He wants someone with bigger breasts. He wants someone really sexy. I looked young. I was young, but I looked a lot younger. I looked childish and stupid. I hated my hair. I hated my body. It didn't do it for him.

But I couldn't say anything. Because when I woke up in the morning, he was the person I told about my dreams. We ate breakfast together and he drove me to college. I could have got the bus, but I had become unused to going anywhere on my own. He would always tell me how dangerous it was, how the bus wasn't the place for a little girl like me. How I needed him to protect me. We went to the same classes. He had persuaded me to change subjects, so I was studying what he wanted to study. He talked about kids. I saw my future in him. We took notes together, sat together. He didn't like me talking to anyone else, and I didn't care one bit; I liked talking to him. We ate lunch together, playing footsie under the table. We felt sorry for people who were alone. I didn't have any friends because he wanted to be with me all the time, but he didn't have any friends either so I thought that was fair. I especially wasn't allowed to talk to men who I wasn't related to. He thought they wanted me. They didn't, but I liked that he thought that, so I didn't complain. We drove home together, and I cooked because he loved me to cook for him, and afterwards we might play a game. We would pretend we were kids doing our homework, and he was a little boy curious about what was in his trousers. It was naughty. I knew other people who were turned on by naughty things, and now I was one of them. A grown-up. Desired. I had a great sex life, even before we had sex.

The first time was before our wedding night, although that wasn't the plan and it didn't happen at all like I imagined. He was excited, holding me down on our bed. He said how small and precious I was. He held my wrists and asked me to struggle. We did this frequently. I didn't think he was going to put it in. He ripped off my knickers and when I cried out and tried to cover myself with my hands – he hadn't seen that part yet – he let out a howl I hadn't heard before and thrust savagely inside me. It felt like he was punching me with it. It felt like a rounders bat. It was painful, and I begged him to stop the whole time, but it was over so quickly and he was in another place entirely, inside his mind. He didn't hear me before he had finished inside me. I cried. He said he was sorry. He loved me so much, he desired me so much, he couldn't help himself.

I knew he loved me, because once, at a party, a guy from the chemistry department looked at me, and he beat him until his face was a swollen, red bruise.

On Tuesday morning, I wake up at six thirty. My tummy is very tense. I prod it. My muscles are getting harder and bigger, I think, with all my exercising. I spring out of bed and open the curtains to see the sun already pretty high in the sky. I haven't noticed it that much over the last month, with everything going on. Usually I love summer. I lie down on my fluffy carpet and do my one hundred and fifty crunches, then my press-ups, and then my star jumps (it's okay because it's only the kitchen below my room), and then I use my books to do some bicep curls. 'All the better to punch your face in with,' I say to myself. Lastly I practise attack moves in the mirror. 'I will not be afraid, I will not be afraid, I will not be afraid,' I whisper as I do them. I make a fist in the mirror like Billie and me made, even though she's not here now. I feel sad about that. I would have thought she'd be with me this morning in case I am going to my doom. But maybe Billie's mum is upset and needs her, and so Billie's staying with her. I understand.

I practise things that I could say to the pervert. I put my hands on my hips and wink, sexily. I drop my knee and giggle prettily, batting my eyelashes. It's probably not as good as Hattie would do it, but it's not bad. It would be better if I could use Hattie for bait, but she won't do it.

I asked her before I thought I could do it myself, before school ended. The dead girls were with me, although Hattie didn't know. They followed me as dogs all the way from the house. I don't like them as dogs – they're scary, with their big teeth and their drooling. I felt their hot breath on my hands. When we found Hattie, they turned into girls again. Hattie still wasn't talking to me, so I had to basically corner her.

She accused me of threatening her again. Well, she said, 'What are you doing holding that knife?'

And I said, 'Woops! I was just polishing it to make sure it was sharp', and I put it back in my pocket. I had been carrying it around hidden in the palm of my hand in case I was attacked walking alone through the village. I thought about putting it away when I met Hattie, but . . . I didn't. 'It's just a Swiss army knife,' I said, shrugging nonchalantly. I think she got the message, which was 'Don't mess with me'. 'Dad got it me for camping. It's barely lethal.'

'You're insane,' she said. She was on her way to Poppy's when I found her, and now she was leaning against the red phone box near her house. She kept looking towards home, like she wanted to escape.

'You couldn't spell to save your dog's life,' I said grumpily. It was the worst insult I could think of in the moment.

'Huh? Are you threatening my dog now?'

'No, stupid! I'm trying to talk to you. Don't you care about Billie dying? Don't you want her killer to be found?'

'What's that got to do with you?'

'I have a plan to catch him.'

'The police are after him, you nutter. You're just eleven, and a girl. You can't do anything.'

'You know what?' I folded my arms and looked her up and down, with lots of judgement. 'You've always agreed that girls can do anything and we're better than boys. I guess you don't think that any more, huh?'

She rolled her eyes, but I could tell I had made her think.

'The Spice Girls would be on my side in this argument,' I pointed out.

'Urgh. Fine. Go on.'

Hattie's obviously been brainwashed by Mrs A. Mrs A keeps saying we can't do anything to stop the man. Mrs A has no girl power. She's weak.

I looked both ways and lowered my voice. 'So you can't tell anyone about this, but my plan is to catch the killer using bait.'

'Okaaaaay . . .' She frowned.

'I've been training physically, and I think, with the element of surprise, I'm tough enough to take him. I will also be carrying weapons.'

'*Weapons?*' Hattie said loudly.

'Shush! Yes. Brick rubble in a sock, a knife, and stuff to tie him up with. Then, when we get him where we want him—'

'Who's we? You and Nathan "dirt on his face" Nolan?'

'No.' I paused uncomfortably, which was a big mistake because it's like an antelope pausing to check if a lion is watching when you're with Hattie.

'Oh, didn't he want to go out with you? Ha! Thera "weirdo" Wilde is even too crazy for a Gypsy like Nathan!'

'Stop saying people's names with things in between them!'

'Whatever, Thera "can't get a boyfriend" Wilde! Haha!'

'Shut up! Listen to my plan!'

Hattie was laughing loudly.

'What if the killer is just around the corner, and you're alerting him to our plan?'

'What is this "ours" thing? You didn't mean you and me when you said "we", did you?'

'Yes, actually, I did.'

'I'm not helping.'

'What a great friend you are. I bet if Billie was here now she would be so pleased,' I said. Even the drool around my molars tasted sarcastic.

'Urgh! She's dead anyway, she doesn't care,' Hattie said, but she looked down straight after this, and I knew she was ashamed.

'You wouldn't be in danger.'

'What do you mean?'

'I mean I'd keep you safe.'

She squinted at me. 'Huh?'

'I'd be really near you, in hiding, watching you the whole time. I wouldn't get distracted. And I'd have all the weapons. When he pounced on you, I'd just run over and bash him in the head really hard with the brick rubble in the sock, and it would knock him out.'

Hattie's eyes widened at the geniusness of my plan. Or so I thought. '*What?*'

'I know! And then, when he's unconscious, that's when we tie him—'

'What are you talking about?'

'We'll find out the truth of what happened to Billie by—'

'Oh my god!'

'I know! It's so clever! And afterwards, vengeance shall be—'

'STOP TALKING, YOU PSYCHO!' Hattie shouted at me.

I stopped in surprise. 'Why?'

'You led Billie to her death and now you want to get me killed too!'

'No!' I said, horrified. 'That's not true! I'll be right there to protect you!'

Hattie took a deep breath, shaking her head. 'You are *crazy*!' She started to walk off, towards her house.

'No, I'm not. Hattie, this is a great plan.' I tried to appease her. 'You'd be much better bait than me, you're so pretty.'

'Yeah, well, the guy who killed Billie likes kids, and I'm not a kid any more, so if you want someone to be bait, *you* should do it, you weirdo.'

'What? Why are you not a kid any more?'

She turned to me and I almost ran into her. She looked down at me. It was like she was suddenly taller. 'I got my period.'

I hesitated. 'Whoa. What was it like?'

Her face screwed up and she looked at me like I was dog poo on the pavement, a classic Hattie look. She started to walk towards me, snapping and looking down at me until she was actually pushing me backwards. 'It was horrible. There was blood everywhere. It looked like my knickers had been murdered.' She stopped. 'But you can't *ask* women that, you *child*.'

'I'm not a child,' I mumbled.

'Don't you want to be? Then you can be bait,' she said, turning away and sashaying back to her house, her bum swinging her skirt from side to side. She has hips now. I don't have hips.

Anyway. That was before I realized men thought I was pretty. Now I know I'm okay doing this alone.

Mum pops her head in while I am dancing in front of the mirror, doing high kicks and imagining the pervert going flying. 'Hello, monkey.'

'Hi, Mummy!' I shout, hopping over to her.

'You're in a very good mood today!' she says happily.

'Yes, yes, yes.' I jump around her. I do feel good today. I think I feel powerful because I'm finally actually *doing* something about Billie's killer. I jump up and she catches me.

'Oof! You're a lump!' she says, and holds me on her hip, even though I am almost as tall as she is.

'Do you still hate my hair?' I ask nervously.

'No, I don't hate it.' She sighs, smelling my head. 'I just always loved your long hair.'

Quietly, I say, 'Yeah, but it's my hair, not yours.'

'I know.' She pops me down on the floor and flops on my bed, even though she is in her work suit, with her tight skirt and square heels.

'Are you tired, Ma? You look tired.'

'Why, thank you.' She is being sarcastic.

'You still look beautiful.'

'Oh, good,' she says. I lie next to her on the bed and cuddle into her armpit, smelling her Mum smell: soap, flowery things and also the sharp, alkaline scent of her deodorant. 'How are you getting along, treasure?'

'Fine.'

'Really?' She strokes my hair. 'What are you going to do today?'

'Play, probably.'

'That sounds nice. Don't leave the house and garden, and if a man comes to the door, whoever it is, scream loudly and call the police immediately.'

'I will. Bleurgh, men.'

'Thera, I'm being serious.'

'I know. So am I!'

'Thera,' a voice says from the door. It's Dad. I sit up. He's holding the handle of the axe.

'What is it?' asks my mum.

'Thee, did you break my axe?' He shakes the wood at me, shoving it under my nose. It smells like damp. I look away from him, embarrassed.

'Answer me, for god's sake!' he shouts. 'There are chopping marks all over the side of the bloody shed. What were you doing with my axe?'

'Nothing!' I say tearfully, folding my arms. 'Stop shouting and get out of my room!'

'Thera!' Mum says sharply, sitting up on the bed.

Dad grabs my arm, and I try to push him off me, but

he smacks my bottom and pushes me so I sit down next to Mum.

'Thera, were you playing with the axe?' Mum asks.

'No, I wasn't *playing* with it!' I shout. 'I was just trying to get used to attacking with it so if the killer attacks me I can get him back!'

'Christ alive!' Dad shouts. 'You could have killed yourself! What the bloody hell did you think you were doing?'

I burst into tears.

'Thera, that was very silly,' Mum says.

I feel angry at myself for crying in front of Mum and Dad and for being weak on the day when I'm supposed to be strong for Billie. It makes me cry harder. I don't know what's come over me. I feel suddenly knackered. All the dead girls, apart from Billie, appear. They gather behind Mum and Dad in a line. I close my eyes because I don't want to look at them. Ellie's voice sounds in my head. 'You promised you'd help us, Thera,' she says.

'You are grounded – do you hear me, Thee?' Dad says. 'You are not allowed out of this house. And I'm going to call Nan so she can babysit you.'

'Why do I need Nan here? I'm eleven!' I say, thinking about the plan.

'Because you can't be trusted!' Dad yells at me. 'I'm calling her now.' Mum walks out of the room, leaving me with him. I cower towards the back of the bed in case he really is the killer, and then I cry harder because I don't want Daddy to be the killer – he's my daddy. 'Calm down, Thee, stop crying. You could have really hurt yourself.

Stay in this room and think about how silly you're being.'
He walks out of the room and slams the door.

I do think about how silly I'm being. Silly for crying
when Billie is dead and way worse off than me, silly for
thinking we lived in a safe place and bad things only happened to other people, silly for ever thinking Dad and
Mum were my friends, silly for ever trusting anyone. I
should have been more careful to hide all evidence of the
plan. I lie in the bed snuffling. I can hear Dad crashing about
in the kitchen. I hear Mummy leave for work. Finally I hear
Nanny come in and Dad leave.

I climb out of bed, still shaking and sniffing, and I do
what I have to do. I put on the new Wonderbra and the
pretty dress, and my black canvas platforms and a nice
pair of pink knickers. I put lip gloss on my lips, and eye
shadow in purple on my eyes. I take my little velvet backpack and in it I put the mini tape recorder I stole from
Mum, the mini tapes I bought in town, and the knife. I
add four sealed freezer bags, for evidence. I am about to
put my Nano Pet in my bag, when I remember it beeps. I'm
uncomfortable about leaving the new one, Lottie. She's
only a baby. I can't risk being caught, though, so I leave her
in Sam's room so he'll know to take care of her if something happens to me, and then I open my window and
shimmy down the drainpipe to the ground below.

I let go of the drainpipe, land in the garden and immediately drop to my knees. Crawling might mess up my
dress, so I pull it up and hold it in one hand, and crawl
with just two legs and one hand underneath all the windows until I am around the house. When I reach the road,

I stand up and run. The platforms are really hard to run in, though, and my toes keep shoving into the toe bit of the shoe. I guess it must be because my feet are on a slant because the platform is slightly bigger at the back? I wish I'd worn trainers, even though the pervert might not like me as much.

I get to the copse about twelve o'clock, according to my Action Man watch. I figure the pervert might be wandering about in the fields, since that's where he found Billie, so I do a recce back and forth across most of the big fields, tramping down the wheat a lot. I have to be careful the police don't see me, because there are still some hanging out around the top road, so whenever one looks my way I lie down flat on the crop. I lie down flat a lot, because as well as hiding from the police it's hard to walk on the wheat in platforms and I keep falling over. Probably the cops can see the zigzag lines and crop circles but they don't know the fields like Billie, Sam and me, so hopefully they will think I'm a big rabbit. There are two policemen doing the walking about this time. That's all they do, they just walk about. Their car is stopped on the top road, and they are drinking from a flask a bit, and talking and walking up and down looking at everything. I tut at them. What a fat lot of good they are. They didn't think of the bait idea.

The night Billie went missing was the first time the police came to talk to me. It was two men about Dad's age, but I didn't realize then that men were so bad, so I didn't mind. I came down in my 'jamas to talk to them, and I sat at the kitchen table while the blonder one held my diary. He had stubble all over his face and I was staring at it.

'Feel it,' he said, so I did, and I laughed. He seemed to be in charge. He went over how Billie and me went our separate ways home. 'Was there anything out of the ordinary?' he said.

'Nope.' I shook my head. 'I'm sure she's just out exploring and has lost track of time.' I felt a need to cover for her, so she wouldn't get told off. The police didn't seem that worried. I forgot to mention the walker and the predictor, which Georgie the policewoman asked me about a few days later, but they had both seemed pretty ordinary at the time. I didn't know then that the walker might be the killer, or even that Billie was dead. Billie always made predictors, and sometimes we tailed people if we thought they were up to no good. They must have found out about them afterwards, from reading my diary. I looked at it. 'Is it okay if we borrow this diary, Thera?' the blonde policeman said. 'It would really help us out.'

'Of course. We always cooperate with the police,' I replied, meaning Billie, Sam, Mum, Dad and me. And probably I also meant Billie's mum and dad, and the people in my village, like Mrs Stephenson the dinner lady and Mrs Underwood the shopkeeper. I thought of the village as 'us' and the rest of the world as 'them' before Billie got killed. Now I know a killer lurks amongst us, I'm not so sure about my village.

The policeman laughed and I still don't know why.

'If you need extra help, you just give me a call,' I said.

'Thanks, Thera, I will,' he said sincerely.

'You could hire me if you needed to.'

'We'll certainly think about that.' He smiled. I imagined it. It would have been so great if they had hired me. For years, I have thought a secret government branch might take me out of school and train me to become a spy, because I'm the smartest in my class by miles, and I win all the races too. They could train me in martial arts and boxing, and give me a licence to kill. I'd only kill bad guys, though. I'm seriously surprised they haven't come to me for help. The bait idea seems almost *too* easy and clever. The fact that they haven't thought of it makes me worry the police are total ninnies and as bad as everyone is saying.

Back in our kitchen, on the night Billie went missing, I added, 'Don't worry. She'll turn up. She won't have got far yet. The trains don't run all night.' I figured, if she was running away, she could make it to the station on foot by dawn, and then take the earliest train to London. I was wrong, obviously. She only made it to the wood. When I was talking to the policeman, she was probably already dead.

When I get to the copse, there is a policeman stood next to the gate. He smiles at me, and I smile back at him, then slink a little away and sit on the fence. I pout my lips, and reapply my lip gloss, and then sit with my legs showing and the top of my boobs visible above the neckline of my dress. I've only been there five minutes when the police-man calls over to me. 'Do you need some help, miss?'

I turn around and shake my head at him. 'No. I want to be alone.'

He stops walking towards me and holds up his hand in a wave to say 'Okay'. I guess even he could be the killer. Every so often while I sit on the fence, I think I hear him close by, and then I jump in fright and whirl around, but every time he's still there, stood at the entrance, his hands clasped together.

It's half past one now. Nathan Nolan is watching me from the hedge. I don't think the policeman can see him, but I recognize him. I won't make the first move, since he shoved me and ran away from me last time I saw him. I want to, because I want him to love me again and I think he's being really stupid, but I can't. My pride won't let me. I hope I'm not cutting off my nose to spite my face. I don't know exactly what that means, but that's why I'm so worried about doing it.

I adjust my Wonderbra to make my boobs pop up more. They are sadly lacking a line between them – cleavage, it's called, or, as Grandad says, décolletage – unless I straighten my arms, and push them together with my biceps. I hold them like that for a bit, but my muscles start to tremble, so I stop and sigh. Hmm. No perverts here today, I guess.

I wait another million years, until it's two o'clock, then I decide to try my luck hanging around the village, and I set off towards the centre. There will be plenty more possible perverts in the village, because of the pub and the workmen who are fixing the telegraph wires today and all the men you usually see loitering around the . . . around the . . . I squint into the distance, and as I approach the green triangle I slow down, feeling pinpricks of sweat burst out from under my armpits. I stop in the middle of the road, my throat tensed, my body frozen. I feel like screaming, but all I do is stand there and watch, my shoulders trembling, my fists clenched in fear and determination.

I stand there, and I watch him.

The walker.

The walker is sat on the bench in the middle of the green grass triangle. This time he is eating an apple. Not a sandwich. He stretches his jaw like those extinct dogs Grandad told me about that can stretch their jaws to ninety degrees and then CLAMP down on their victims. Fear creeps all through my body, making me cold even though it's hot. I look back and forth, but for the first time, it seems, in *ages*, there isn't a policeman around. Which . . . I guess is good. For my plan. I'm alone with the walker.

I am frozen like those kids should have been in front of the T-rex in *Jurassic Park*. It seems absolutely crazy to me now that they wouldn't be able to stay still, because I'm frozen by animal instinct in front of this predator, just like they should have been. I wish I could run. But a part of me knows that if I ran he could run faster than me, catch me, rape me and kill me. The idea of me attacking him works only if he doesn't see it coming. I take a deep breath. For the first time, I wish the ghost-girl dogs were here with me. So they could tear him apart.

He continues to eat the apple. Because I am so focused on him, even though he is still maybe thirty feet away, I can hear him munching. CRUNCH. It sounds like the bones of small animals snapping, like when you step on a snail and break its shell.

I swallow, and I wonder if he can hear me. But he doesn't move. A predator doesn't need to hear every little sound around him. He can just wait until someone gets really close and then snatch them. I stand there for ages. No cars drive by. Sweat is making my arms stick to my ribcage at the armpit. I feel like I could melt into a puddle of tears and being scared and shaking and sweating.

No, I remind myself. *I'm* supposed to be the predator here! I'm the one out to catch him. That's the thing. He doesn't know. But I know. I'm here to get him. For the dead girls. For little Ellie. For Billie.

The air is thick and heavy with heat and silence. I draw myself up so I'm the tallest I look. I pull my shoulders back so my boobs are pushed out. I straighten my dress. I feel the zip on my bag, where my pocketknife is hidden. I smoosh my lips together to make sure my lip gloss is good, and then I walk towards him slowly through the humid air. I walk towards the man who killed my best friend, who lay on top of her, and made her dead. He looks up. I smile at him. 'Is this seat taken?'

He laughs. 'No. Go ahead.'

I sit down. He keeps looking at me. Good. The make-up and clothes are working. I wink at him and he smiles.

'Haven't we met before?'

'Yes, I saw you here.'

'Yeah, you were with your friends!'

'Mm, yes, I was with my friends,' I say in a sophisticated

way, like Mm, yes, we were having a conference. 'And you were walking,' I add.

'Oh yes,' he says cheerfully. 'I love to get out on the weekend. Day off work today so I thought I'd take the opportunity. My wife doesn't like me walking, so I have to do it when I have alone time.'

'Why doesn't she like you walking?'

He laughs. 'She likes to spend all our time together, but she doesn't like walking and I do. She's jealous of the time I give to my mistress.' He grins. 'Walking, I mean. That's a saying, like football is my mistress, or beer is my mistress, or walking—'

'Yeah, I get it,' I say.

'I'm sure you do – you seem smart.' He takes a bite of his apple.

He's quiet for a bit, and I think of what ladies say to men. I turn to him, smile, and say, in a pleasing, high voice. 'Do you like my dress?'

'Yes, it's very pretty,' he nods. 'Is it a new dress?'

'Yes, it is. Do I look fat at all?'

'No, not at all, you look lovely! You shouldn't worry about things like that at your age. You're perfect just as you are.'

I beam. Excellent. Now I draw attention to my lips. 'I'm wearing lip gloss.'

'So you are. Girls are wearing make-up younger and younger these days, but it's not always a bad thing. These days! Listen to me, I sound like an old man. I'm only twenty-nine.'

'How do you know girls are wearing make-up younger

and younger these days?' My heart is starting to pound really quick.

He munches on his apple and shakes his head, looking at a bird in the sky. He seems quite happy. I had expected a pervert would be mean and grumpy.

I swallow, steeling myself for the inevitable attack. Now I'm wearing a Wonderbra, my almost-boobies rise up and down with every slow, deep breath. I'm trying to make my breathing slow and calm, because I feel like breathing either fast and scared or not at all. He finishes his bite of apple and swallows.

'I have some nieces. I think I showed your friend their pictures.' He chomps on the apple again, juice on his lips. He's actually really good-looking. He has big, shiny lips, good cheekbones, beautiful eyes and soft-looking hair. He fishes in the pocket of his jeans with his hand and pulls out the leather wallet he must have shown Billie last time. 'See?' he says, through apple. He flips through them quickly. 'This is Kerry. She's clever. And this is my youngest. Isn't she adorable?' I nod, barely seeing. Instead I'm looking up at him. This is my big move. He holds the photos in front of me and I look up to his eyes. I want to make him totally fall in love with me. Or lust. Whatever it needs to be.

'Are you alright, sweetheart?' he says, frowning. 'What was your name?'

'Thera. Thera Wilde.'

'Thera? What a lovely name. That sounds familiar, actually.' He puts the wallet back. 'Where could I have heard that before?'

'You may know me . . .' I smile innocently. 'Because my friend who spoke to you the other week was Billie Brooke, and she was killed that night.'

He turns back to me at once, his mouth open. He actually looks really distraught. 'Oh my god! Your friend who was with you? She was the girl who . . .?'

'Um, yes,' I say uncertainly.

'Jesus Christ!' His eyes search across my face. 'I didn't think – it never occurred to me – I'm so sorry, poppet. That's horrible.' He reaches his hand out to me and I take a sharp breath in. Here it comes.

But he retracts it again, like he's afraid to touch me. He scratches his head. 'That's awful. We went off to see my parents that weekend, after my walk. They live in Shropshire. We got back late Sunday. I only saw the news Monday morning. I just didn't think. That's just . . . Her poor parents.'

'Um, yeah,' I say, annoyed. This isn't helping the seduction. He isn't looking at me any more. But he's also behaving really surprised, like he didn't know it was Billie that was killed at all. So . . . maybe . . . he isn't the killer? He doesn't really have the aura of a killer. He seems just a nice, normal guy. My spider sense isn't tingling a *murderer* warning at all, and I don't feel any ghostly energy about him that might mean he has recently been associated with death. Urgh, that's so annoying, when I spent all this time and effort seducing him. (On the other hand, if I didn't hand Billie to her killer, this is actually awesome news.)

'Christ,' the man says, again, just like Dad. 'And now

I'm swearing in front of a little eleven-year-old! You must think I'm awful. Forget about me, though – are you okay? Of course you're not. How are you feeling, sweetheart?'

'Um . . .' I look at him. If he isn't the killer he's just being nice, and basically no one has just straight-out asked me how I'm feeling in ages, probably because they don't want to hear the answer, and they all hate me for getting Billie killed. I guess as well, if he is the killer, this still counts as seducing him, so I'll answer. 'I feel okay. I mean, I feel not that great, obviously. I mean, I feel bad most of the time.'

'Yeah? I'm so sorry, kiddo. You poor little thing.'

My shoulders droop. I'm not even pretending to be bait now. Sometimes it's hard when people are nice to me because if I'm sad, it makes me even sadder. I start talking, and my voice gets smaller and smaller with every word until it's not much of a voice at all, but basically a wisp of a whisper. 'Yeah, life is pretty rubbish. I miss Billie . . .' Accidentally, a tear slips out of my eye. I wipe it quickly away. 'I feel like it's my fault she's dead.'

'No! Of course not. Why do you feel like that?'

'Well . . . I left her in the field.'

'Why did you leave her in a field?'

'That's how we always walk home,' I say. 'She's never been killed before. Well' – I roll my eyes at myself – 'duh.'

'That's not your fault, kiddo. No one could have predicted that.'

'Also . . .' I hesitate.

'Also what?'

'Well . . . they think the killer is you. 'Cause I wrote

about meeting you in my diary. So they thought I led Billie to her death, because I dared her to go up to you.'

'Oh my god!' he exclaims. 'You thought—? Do the police think—?' He bites his lip, shakes his head and puts his arm around me and rubs my shoulder. 'I'll go and talk to the police.'

I sniff. He smells pretty good. 'Why?'

'We don't want them to waste their time looking for me and not catching the real killer, do we? I'll just go to the station and talk to them; don't worry, you won't get in trouble. They can tell when people haven't been involved. They'll swab the inside of my cheek for DNA.'

'I know how the police eliminate suspects,' I say, slightly affronted by him explaining this to me like I don't know anything. 'I've watched *Poirot*.'

He nods. 'Such a smart girl.'

I sigh, deflated. 'So you're not the killer?'

'You sound disappointed!' he says, and smiles affectionately.

'Well, if you look at it from my point of view, it would have been easier if you were.'

He laughs. 'What do you mean?'

'Now I have to go and find a whole new prime suspect.'

He looks behind us, up the lane where I came from. 'Sweetie, if you thought I was the killer, why did you come and sit next to me?'

'I'm trying to catch him.' I gesture to my outfit.

He looks down at my legs, then up to my face again, and shakes his head. 'Oh, lovely, you don't want to be doing that. That's very brave of you but . . .' He looks sad suddenly. 'You don't want to tempt fate like that. You don't know what could happen when he's . . . desperate.'

'Desperate?'

He shakes his head and sighs, then tousles my hair. 'I think we should get you home. Where do you live?'

'I'm not going home. I have work to do.'

'Darling—' he begins, putting his arm around me again.

I leap up off the bench. 'Get off! What is this obsession people have with touching me?'

'I'm sorry,' he says gently, holding both his hands up. 'It's okay, kiddo, it's okay. I would never hurt you. I promise, I would never hurt a little thing like you.'

I believe him.

Maybe it's because I was so tense, ready for a fight, or so scared when I saw the killer, or so sad when he asked me how I was, but I can't help it. I start to cry. 'I hate it. I hate you all. You men. It's so confusing. First you're nice and then you're mean. A man killed Billie and now he's going to kill us all.' I put my hands up to my face. I don't want to be here. I want to be far away. I want to be dead and not have a body so no one can ever touch me again without my permission, ever, ever, EVER. I am crying really loud now, and I feel his hands on me again, but this time it's really soft.

'Shh,' he says. 'It's okay, kiddo. It's alright. Come here, sweetheart.' He pats my back, and I lean on his chest. He feels like my dad, but not like my dad. He feels warm and his chest is hard, like Nathan's. He has those hard man-boobs, not fatty but muscular. He wraps his arms around me and pats my back, and I wrap my arms around him.

'I'm sorry,' I mumble into his T-shirt, although I'm not. Well, I am, but I don't know what I'm sorry for. I'm sorry for existing in front of him, for crying, for yelling. I'm sorry I got Billie killed. I'm sorry I haven't found the killer, that the dead girls are counting on me and instead I am crying like a weak person on the man who was my prime suspect until five minutes ago.

'Don't be sorry,' he says into my hair. 'Don't be sorry, darling.' Slowly he pulls away from me and looks down. 'There.' He wipes a tear tenderly away from underneath my eye. 'There, there.'

I sniff, but the tears have almost stopped. I wipe the rest away. There is a butterfly of wet on his shirt, made by my tears. He looks at it when he sees me looking, pulls it away from his muscular chest and smiles. His hands are gently resting on my shoulders. 'Alright, then. Let's get you home.'

I look down at my feet in my platforms. I want to go home. I suddenly feel really tired and sad. But if I go home now, and the walker comes with me and tells Mum and Dad or Nan what I've been up to, I'll be grounded forever.

'I can't go home,' I say.

He strokes my face. 'Come with me now.'

The walker has turned out to be really nice, but I have to find the killer. I can't let the girls down. I summon all my strength. It comes up from my feet, up my legs, under my skirt, up through my stomach, and fills my whole body, right out to my fingertips, until I shout, 'NO!', shove him away, and run.

I race through the village at top speed. I can hear the walker calling behind me. 'Thera! Stop! Thera, sweetheart!'

I keep going as fast as my legs can in these stupid shoes with the squishy platforms, with my toes squidged uncomfortably in the toe parts, and my heels rocking about on the plastic. I run around the corner with the bridge over the river, and suddenly there is a group of men in orange suits and hardhats working on the road. I am still crying and red-faced and my hair's all coming undone, and the road workers try to stop me, one after the other, these huge, scary men, reaching for me and shouting after me.

'Hey!'

'Are you alright?'

'Stop!'

One grabs my arm, and I scream. 'STRANGER DANGER! STRANGER DANGER!'

'What the—?' the road worker says, but I'm miles away from him already, my feet slapping the pavement.

I run onto the road leading to my primary school, but the bend of the corner is really tight, and as I turn I feel the soft platform heel of my sandals give. I stagger, spreading out my arms, and then crumple into a pile on the pavement. 'Ow!' I moan, and then immediately shut up. A man and a woman are talking by a big jeep. I don't want them to see me, so I try to stand, but my ankle really hurts, and instead I crawl into the hedge and tuck my legs right up to my chest.

I don't have my binoculars with me, but I read in a Famous Five book that if you make binoculars with your hands, it works almost as well. I make binoculars and squint at the man and the lady. I knew it. It's lame Mrs A and creepy Mr Kent.

I decide to get a little closer to hear what they are saying. The undergrowth continues on the other side of the small road, so, very slowly, like in Grandmother's Foot-steps, I cross the tarmac. If one of them turns they'll see me, but I also know if I move too fast I'll catch their eyes, so I take one tiny step at a time and steal across to the side of the road Mrs Adamson is on. There I slink into the undergrowth, and then I climb through the fence into the Nelsons' garden. They have loads of evergreen trees, so I can't be seen here, and I can get really close to Mr Kent and Mrs Adamson. I sneak right up to the end of the garden, take off my rucksack and peer through the fence, listening intently.

'What do you think of me?' Mrs Adamson is saying.

'. . . just a strange thing to say,' Mr Kent replies.

'I don't know,' she says, and lowers her head. She starts to speak in a sad, quiet tone. I can't hear most of what she says now, just the occasional word. 'Muh-muh-muh stressed, muh-muh some time off.'

'Summer holidays,' Mr Kent says, like he's agreeing

with her. 'Training finished now. Something something good for everyone.'

They must have been doing teacher training at school. Sometimes they do that in term time and we get days off.

'Muh-muh not sure,' Mrs Adamson says. 'Muh-muh-muh career muh better somewhere else.'

'You're considering something-y leaving? You seemed very settled here.'

'Oh well, muh says a change of scenery might be muh for us.'

'I thought you were thinking about children?'

Children? Is Mrs A going to have a baby? I try to listen harder, but that's a weird feeling because when I concentrate too hard on listening, my ear feels itchy. The itchiness makes it even *more* difficult to follow conversations, because I'm just thinking about how much I want to scratch it. The doctor told me you're not supposed to put anything smaller than your fist in your ear. A finger is part of a fist so I guess that's okay. I scratch some earwax out of my ear, then listen again.

'*I* am!' she suddenly exclaims. I raise my eyebrows. I heard that. 'Muh-muh not helping me build a stable muh-muh need stability muh-muh considering moving nearer to his parents.'

Then Mr Kent gets a bit grumbly too. 'Oh, well, muh-muh-muh women muh-muh time muh-muh important.

Mrs A puts her hand on the jeep door. 'Muh-muh lift?' she says.

'No, I think I'll walk home,' Mr Kent says. 'Don't want to muh-muh jealous.'

They laugh, and then Mrs A wipes at her face like she is wiping away a tear. 'He's like that,' Mrs A says mysteriously.

I hear stompy footsteps, so I shrink back. Mr Kent's legs pass me. He's so big, even bigger than Dad. His smell is really strong too, men's-deodorant-type smell and bad breath. I think about his eyes on me in the cinema and shiver.

I did wonder if they were in league. That would give him access to the stuff in her car, and even more access to Billie, because Billie and Mrs A always got on. When I hear the car engine start, I jump, even though I'm sat on my bum. I curl up and watch Mrs A's jeep drive past. The police said they were looking for a jeep, on telly ages ago. Lots of people have jeeps around my village because it's the countryside. Farmer Rawley has a Land Rover, which looks like a jeep. There are always a few jeeps and Land Rovers in the pub car park. Creepy Mr Kent doesn't have a jeep, but he could have just used Mrs A's. She invited him in it just now!

Mr Kent might have borrowed her jeep, and then he might have driven it to the woods. He could say to Billie, 'Come with me, Billie', and she would have to, because he is older than us and in charge of us. He could lead her to the copse and do perverted things to her. Of course, she would know him. She would be able to tell the police what happened, so instead of letting her go he would kill her, and drive away from the crime in the knowledge that no one would be able to find out, cunningly disguised in Mrs Adamson's jeep.

I look at my watch. The time is half past four. Mum and Dad will both be home in about half an hour. I think for a moment, but I know what I have to do. I hope he hasn't had too much of a head start. Mr Kent lives up the lane, in the next village. I leap over the fence – my ankle still hurts, so I take my shoes off – and I start to limp-run to catch him up. It's not until later that I realize I left my rucksack in the Nelsons' garden.

The village is emptier now. The road workers have disappeared – maybe they're taking a break – and so has the walker. I've put my shoes back on and been trailing Mr Kent through the village, back to near my part of it. He is only a little way ahead of me now, so I am just dawdling, when a car pulls up next to me and stops with its engine still running. 'Hello, Thera,' someone says. I look up.

'Oh! Hi, Mr Brooke!'

'Hi! How are you doing?'

'I'm good. I'm just . . . walking.'

'Do you want driving home at all? It's so nice to see you. It's been . . .' He trails off.

'About three weeks, yeah,' I say.

Billie's dad has a shaved head, and is very big and pale, and a lot older than Dad. 'It would be nice to have a chat. I'm sorry about what Rebecca said when we were in the woods. She's just upset.'

I wriggle uncomfortably. 'Yeah, that's understandable.'

'Do you want to get in?' He gestures to the passenger seat.

'Um . . .' I look down the road. I think about lying, because I would to all other adults, but I take a chance on Mr Brooke, because he has the same priorities I do. I bet he's out looking for Billie's killer too. 'I can't right now, I'm trailing someone.'

'Oh, okay.'

I tap my nose. 'Got a lead.'

'Right.'

'I'll see you another time,' I say conspiratorially (Grandad word).

'That will be nice,' he says, and he smiles at me. I start to walk off after Mr Kent. I look back. Mr Brooke is still watching me with the window down. He waves. I wave back and carry on down the lane. I get a way up, then happen to trip over something in my stupid shoes, which makes me look behind me. That's funny. Mr Brooke has moved his car closer now. He's still watching me with his window down. He waves again. I frown and wave back. I turn around and keep walking, up and over the hill. Across the field, the police car on the top is moving towards the road. I keep an eye on them, and see them turn my way. I hop off the road and hide in the bushes, squatting down, waiting for them to go past. Mr Kent is just reaching the crest of the next hill, on the road.

For a minute nothing happens, but then I hear a car engine. The pitch sounds like it's getting slower, and it begins to rumble, and then it stops close by.

I squat down even lower. I hear footsteps through the grass. I look down. A trick of hiding is that, if I can't see them, they can't see me. Although thinking about it now . . . is that right? I've always assumed—

'Gah!'

A big black boot is right in front of me.

'Thera Wilde?'

I look up. It's a police officer. I frown. 'Poopsticks.'

'We'll be escorting you home today, young madam,' he says. He looks almost like the blonde policeman who interviewed me the night Billie went missing, but he's a bit lankier and has light-brown hair. I stand up and the policeman picks a leaf out of my hair. 'If that's alright with you.'

'I guess it'll bloody have to be, won't it?' I say, swearing 'cause I'm annoyed. I clap my hand over my mouth immediately afterwards. Grr. That stupid walker must have called them, sticking his nose where it doesn't belong. As I walk over to the police car and get in the back seat, flanked by the two officers so I can't escape, I look down the lane. Mr Kent has disappeared. He isn't on the road. I wonder where he went. Then I look up the lane, towards the village. Mr Brooke's car isn't there any more.

The police drop me home. The tallest man walks me to the door, his hand on the back of my neck, pushing me forward. I get the impression that, if I try to run, he will clamp his hand around my neck and threaten to break it. When we get to the door, he reaches over me and knocks.

Dad opens the door.

'It's your most annoying child,' I say. 'Feel free to shout at me.'

'Thank you, officer,' Dad says calmly, and they shake hands.

The officer pushes me a bit and I walk inside, then he leaves, and Dad shuts the door. We regard each other. I flick my eyes in the direction of the front door then back to Dad, and fold my arms. 'Collusion. That's another word Grandad taught me.'

'I'm going to ban that mad old man from teaching you these words.'

'I bet you would.'

'That's it, Thee,' he smiles. 'No more long words! Problem solved.'

'Nazi,' I say, and his smile goes.

'Come in the kitchen,' he says.

I follow him in and my guard is up immediately, but I

try not to show it. Mum is sat there, with Billie's dad. I thought there was something funny about him trailing me. I remember how kids have better intuition than adults and I squint to see blood on his aura, which is this blurry colour that goes around everyone like an outline and if you're sad it's blue, and if you're jealous it's green, and if it's red you're in love or you've just murdered somebody. Or both. I read about it in the Ouija book. It talks about changes to the aura when you are being haunted by a ghost because you did something bad to them. I was thinking about it when I was with the walker, but I couldn't see anything weird about his aura. It was a nice blue colour. If the walker isn't the murderer, someone else must be. And if there's blood on Mr Brooke's aura, I tell myself, then he's killed Billie and I have to scream and run.

But I can't see any fresh blood on his aura. I can smell death, though. Lots of it. He stands up slowly. It's like I can see it above him, a big, heavy, dark-grey cloud.

'Hello, Thera.' Billie's dad's voice is always really soft. 'It was nice to see you today.'

'Um, you too,' I say.

'You can come and visit us any time you like,' he says. 'You can play in Billie's room.' His voice catches like he was going to say something more but decided not to, and he looks down into a plastic bag that he has. Both the handles are wrapped around his big hands, and he pulls it up onto the table and pulls the handles apart.

He rubs his eyes and Mum says, 'Oh, Paul', and puts her hand on his back for a moment.

'I thought . . . Billie's mum and I thought you might like

302

some things of Billie's. Some things you two used to play with.' He pulls out Billie's neon-yellow art pencil case with all her felt-tips, and puts it on the table.

'Cool. Thanks.' I look at Mum and Dad and they both nod.

Billie's dad takes out more things and puts them on the table. Her OshKosh coat, which is really cool and comes from America, in Florida, where Billie went on holiday last year. The board game Dream Phone, which she got for her birthday in May. Our friendship bracelet kit, which we bought together. I don't point out that it's half mine anyway.

'Her Sylvanian Families? Are you sure? Billie really liked these.'

'I think she would want them to have a nice home with you, don't you think? We don't have any other children. They'll just get dusty. I think Billie would hate that. She didn't like them to be alone even for a few days when we went on holiday.'

'Okay,' I say. 'I'll play with them and keep them not dusty. They do get lonely.'

Billie's dad nods. He pulls out the book I lent Billie, *Mystery Stories* by Enid Blyton, and *Double Act* by Jacqueline Wilson too.

'That's the book that inspired us to write diaries!' I exclaim.

'Billie wrote in her diary every night the last week,' Billie's dad says, but he says it weird, like he's not talking to me any more. 'She really enjoyed that.' He pauses. 'You were such a good friend to Billie, Thera. I will always be grateful she had you. I was always proud of how honest and straightforward Billie was. She wasn't mean and she didn't . . . grow up too fast. You were the same. Just two little girls, always having fun. You had so much fun together. She was always so happy. Whenever you were round, you two giggled constantly in Billie's room. We could tell when Billie was coming home from yours because we could hear you both laughing out on the fields. Thank you for making my daughter's life such a happy one.'

When he says all this, his voice is a tiny bit higher than before, and he doesn't look at me, just looks in the bag, as if there is more in it. But there isn't. It's empty. I can tell.

Turns out Billie's dad called the police. He had the number of the local ones, so the car on the top came straight to me. Seems like everyone wants to get in the way of my mission, including Mr Brooke. After he gives me all Billie's stuff, Mr Brooke leaves with the empty bag. Mum shuts the door and then there is a big silence.

She walks through to the living room and sits down on the sofa. Dad gestures for us to follow her, so we do, and Dad sits in the armchair across from me. I keep looking at Mum. Her face is stony.

'Thera, I know your father and I have been arguing a lot. We haven't kept an eye on you well enough, and that's our fault. Mr Brooke said you were following your head-teacher.'

I open my mouth to speak, but Mum holds up her hand.

'Let me finish. The police told us they saw you earlier today by the woods, where we have expressly forbidden you to go. Things have to change,' Mum says, like she's tired. 'You are forbidden to wear make-up and dress like that, and you can give me that dress because I'm taking it back to wherever you got it from. You are forbidden to leave the house without an adult with you. There will be no more talk of murder in front of Sam. This is not a topic for little girls.'

'That's funny. I thought it was a topic exclusively for little girls.'

'Don't answer back to your mother,' Dad says immediately.

Mum raises her eyebrows. I fold my arms. 'If you want to talk to us about Billie, you can ask and we can go into your room. You are absolutely forbidden to try and find Billie's killer. Do you understand? You are' – Mum swallows, like she can't get the words out – 'risking your life following strange men. We did not spend all our time and energy loving you, and caring for you, and making you eat your greens and read books and go to bed on time, to lose you to someone—' Mummy doesn't finish her sentence. Instead she wipes tears from her cheeks. 'If you break any of these rules, we will be really, really angry, Thera. Do you understand?'

I look at Dad, then back at Mum, and nod. 'I'm sorry I made you upset, Mum.'

'You'll be a good girl, now, won't you, Thera?' Mum says, and I run into her arms for a cuddle. 'Thera?' she says when I don't reply. 'You will, won't you?'

I look into her big blue eyes. I love my mummy so much. I lower my head, and hope the dead girls aren't nearby and don't leave before I can explain myself. 'Yes, I'll be a good girl,' I whisper in her ear.

Mum looks at Dad. He nods and stands up.

'There's something else we have to talk to you about, Thera. Sit down.'

'What is it?'

'You've probably been wondering why we have been arguing so much.'

'Erm. Well, not really. I've been thinking about Billie.'

Mum and Dad exchange a look.

'Even so,' Dad says. 'It's not good that we argue, is it? Because it upsets you and Sam.'

I don't reply. My body is suddenly tense all over.

'Don't you think, Thera?' Mum asks as if she wants me to agree.

I shrug. I feel like I'm being tricked but I don't see why they are tricking me. 'Yeah, I guess.'

'We don't want to fight,' Dad says. 'Mummy and I want to be friends. And we think . . .' He gives Mum another glance. 'In order to do that, we should live apart.'

I frown in surprise. 'What?'

'You and Mummy and Sam will live here, and I'm going to rent another house in Eastcastle, and you and Sam will live with Mum in the week, then come and stay with me on Saturday night and Sunday.'

I blink at them. '*What?* That's a stupid idea! Why on earth wouldn't you want to live with us?'

'Thera,' Dad says as if he's trying to be patient. 'Your Mum and I are getting a divorce. You're going to have to be a grown-up about this—' he starts to say, but I leap off the chair and my voice explodes into the room.

'What the hell?'

'Thera! Language!' Mum says.

'Are you kidding me? This is literally the stupidest thing I've ever heard ever. You two are horrible liars, and this whole time you've been lying to me! Why do I ever trust you at all?'

'That's enough!' Dad says. 'Calm down, we're trying to talk to you like an adult.'

'Why? You don't bloody talk like an adult, you talk like a lying idiot, and you don't want me to know the truth about anything, not Billie, and not why you're arguing, and not rape or men being violent and bad or anything!'

'Enough!' Dad roars. 'How dare you shout at me like this?'

'You're shouting at me!' I roar back. 'You're such a hypocrite!'

'This is a very difficult situation, Thera, but this is no time for dramatics,' Mum says.

'How could you?' I ask her.

'Sweetheart, we don't want to get divorced.'

'Then don't.'

'But we don't want this house to have an atmosphere of arguments and have everybody upset all the time. We don't want shouting. We need you to try to understand and be strong, for us and for Sam.'

'Looks like I'm the only person who has to be strong for anyone around here.'

'What?' Dad says.

I shrug.

'Thera,' Mum says, 'enough of this attitude. And I've had enough of you being angry with Dad in general. What's got into you?'

'But you're angry with Dad in general too!'

'So it makes sense we live separately, doesn't it?'

I frown. She's tricked me again. There is an awful lot of tricking me this afternoon.

'You promised me you would be a good girl,' Mum says. 'Go to your room, and when you come down tomorrow I want to see a changed young lady, or we'll send you to stay at Nan and Grandad's for the rest of the summer.'

'And if I don't change?' I say quietly. 'Will you send me away after that, to boarding school?'

'We're not millionaires and this isn't an opportunity for you to play Malory Towers,' Mum says. She always knows what I'm thinking. 'Go to bed.'

'I'm hungry.'

'I'll bring you supper,' says Dad. 'Since you missed tea.'

I don't want to, but I nod at him. 'Thanks.'

I go quietly upstairs and fall asleep in all my clothes.

When I wake up, the glow-in-the-dark strips on the hands of my alarm clock say it's ten thirty at night, and my supper is next to me, cold. I eat the cheese on toast and drink the milk anyway. How come the cheese is cold but the milk is lukewarm? How does that happen?

I can't sleep. I lie in bed thinking about Nathan, because normally it makes me feel nice. But it doesn't make me feel nice tonight, because his mum won't let him see me, and maybe he doesn't want to see me. I really like him. I didn't realize it at the time, but I think I was in love with him too. I can't think about him. It's too painful.

For a while I kiss an imaginary boyfriend who looks like Nathan. But then I realize he's probably a dead person, like the dead girls, and I feel bad but I tell him I can't hang out any more because I am upset he is dead. He goes away and I cry because I don't want him to be offended. I'm just tired of thinking about dead people all the time, and we could never be forever because the dead boy will always be his age and beautiful, and I'll get old and uglier and uglier. I mean, for a while my boobs will get bigger and I'll be more beautiful, but then soon enough I'll be old, forty, grey-haired and middle-aged. He'll just be a little boy. And then will that make me a pervert? I don't want to be a pervert. I cry harder into the pillow.

All the options for my life are horrible. To go on without Billie? Without my bestest, truest, forever friend? To go on without Nathan? What if I never fall in love again? What if I never find someone as heavenly beautiful, with those soft, guarded eyes and shiny brown hair? The way he kissed me so softly on the cheek, and the way he was in his bed. Even though it hurt, I liked hugging him. Life is awful. Will I always be alone? But then I feel doubly bad because Billie is dead and I'm still alive and I ought to be grateful. But I miss her so much and I haven't seen her for ages. She hasn't even shown up today, after everything I did to try to snare the killer. Maybe I'm going in totally the wrong direction. Maybe she's disappointed in me. I'm holding tears in but that just makes them run down inside my nose. I sniff, and wipe the snotty tears away with the edge of the duvet.

I guess this is why weak people talk to god.

After a while of trying to get to sleep, I think I feel the dead girls. Even though they still freak me out, I steal myself, open my eyes and sit up quickly. But instead it's Hattie, standing at the end of my bed, looking moody as usual. Sometimes I imagine Hattie talking to me. She's one of the evil voices in my head, as opposed to Billie's good one. Well, Mum says I imagine her, but I think Hattie probably astral-projects herself into my room, just so she can annoy me even when we're not at school. She is hovering above my bed.

'Urgh, what are *you* doing here?' I say witheringly.

'Hello, killer,' she says snottily.

'I'm not a killer, Hattie, stupid bumface, I'm the hero!'

'You basically did nothing today; you just ran around like an idiot crying. No wonder Nathan wouldn't go out with you.'

My bottom lip juts out without me wanting it too. 'I didn't catch the man.'

'Well, you're not pretty – of course you didn't.'

'Well, if *you* had been bait, maybe it would have worked out.'

'Probably. But I can't be any more; I'm too grown-up for a kiddy-fiddler.' I heard the word 'kiddy-fiddler' from Sam. He said that's what Barry's dad calls the pervert. 'Although . . .' says Hattie. She raises an eyebrow.

'What?' I say, even though it's annoying because I know that's what she wants me to ask. She's just being dramatic.

'Now I'm haunting you . . .'

'You're not haunting me, you're astral-projecting.'

'Am I? Or can you see me because I'm the next dead girl? Or maybe I'm already dead?'

'Shut up!' I yell. I put my hands over my ears. 'Shut up, shut up, shut up!'

Suddenly Hattie is gone, in a puff of nothing. I'm staring straight into five translucent faces, because the dead girls are stood at the end of my bed. They make me feel crazy because sometimes they just sit and stare at me, willing me to do things for them that I can't do. Even Billie is driving me crazy, just waving and making faces and not saying a word.

'Why are you haunting me?' I whisper-howl. 'I'm sorry. I'm so sorry, but I can't save you. I'm just eleven! I can't do anything for you!'

They don't move. They just smile.

'Why won't you talk to me?' I cry. 'I tried! I promise I tried.'

They still don't talk, but I look down the line of them, five girls. Billie is on the left, wearing the backpack she set off home with, then there's Haadiya with her long, dark hair in a plait. After Haadiya is little Ellie, holding her pony, and then Jenny Ann Welder, aka the girl with strawberry-blonde hair, and then the older girl in her school uniform. I squint at her. She looks smart, with her hair brushed and some make-up on her eyes, stood at the end of my bed. But if she wasn't wearing that uniform, and her hair was slightly messed up . . . I remember seeing someone who looked really like her recently. Just a glimpse. I open my mouth slowly, looking at her, and think myself back to the bench on the green triangle. I wasn't really paying attention to the walker's wallet as he pulled out a little plastic folder the size of a playing card and flipped through the pictures . . . but if I look back, I see, in my peripheral vision, a photograph that looks exactly like her, wearing a strappy top. He called her Kerry. And then in my mind's eye he turns the page and there is another photo, of a pale little girl with bleary eyes, propped up on a pillow. It's Ellie.

There was a discrepancy between our roles, like there was between my mother and Dad. With us, it was less defined by who cooked and who cleaned, and more by what happened outside the house.

After we married, I still wasn't allowed to spend time with other male students. It became an issue with one of my professors – my personal adviser on my dissertation. I had to switch, to a woman. They asked why. I pretended I had been raped. I don't know why I said that. It just came out of my mouth.

Conversely, while I'd thought he might stop seeing other women after we were married, he didn't. He still went out some nights and didn't come back until three or four o'clock in the morning. He would make comments about being out with mates, even though I didn't ask. In fact, I didn't say anything to him about those nights, about the smell of sex on him. I was terrified of losing him, but I also felt oddly apathetic at the thought of any action on my part. What would it accomplish? I didn't want him to leave me, and I was sure he wouldn't change. Perhaps he would start lying to me outwardly, slipping away in secret, telling me I was being controlling.

There were times he would become angry. He failed the

exams at university. He couldn't get qualified. He became unhappy, frustrated. Once, when I asked him what he was going to do instead, he slammed his hand down on my hand on the table. I screamed, and he shouted at me for the noise I was making. The sex we had afterwards was frightening. He threw me on the ground in a ball. He tore my skirt in two. Afterwards he was sweet to me. I had bruises all the way down the left side of my body. He said he didn't know his strength, as if he were proud. I believed him, because everything good that had ever happened to me had happened because of him. Not to believe him would be to end my own happiness, to risk everything that gave my life meaning and colour.

I think he knew I knew about the other women. He didn't hide it. He kept a packet of condoms in his coat pocket that would diminish then be replaced. One day I read in the paper that there had been a series of assaults on women on our campus. I worried for him, I thought he might see something and get involved, try to stop it happening and be hurt. But then I realized, one night while he was gripping my neck. I asked him to stop. It was too hard. He said of course he'd stop; I was his wife. With that comment I understood he made a differentiation between me and other women. With other women he wouldn't stop when asked. I knew his sexual appetites were voracious; his approach to relationships was adoring, but controlling. He liked to flirt and make a woman want him, then take her harder than she had planned. One day I was doing his laundry and I found blood on his jeans, around the zip. I knew he didn't have a cut on him. I had given him the sex he had demanded that morning. I saw the blood and ran through to the kitchen, vomited in the sink. The assaults. It was him. I cried, thinking about my perfect life, my perfect marriage; how hard life was before and how relieved I had been to find him, how relieved I still was not to be alone; how much he loved me and how sweet he could be. How, if I told anyone, I would have to give that up.

He didn't choose to be turned on by these things, he just was. And then something happened that crossed a line, for both of us.

In the morning, I get up and put on clothes that don't make me look pretty. Inoffensive tomboy clothes, like my big baggy T-shirt with Garfield on it and my long shorts. I put my hair in a ponytail, brush my teeth and wash all the make-up off my face. It doesn't all go, but it basically does. I haven't slept much, so I'm yawning my head off. I've been thinking about the walker all night. Something just isn't fitting right about him and the way he talked to me. He must be the killer, because of the photographs, but I didn't get a killer vibe from him somehow. It seemed like he cared about me. I think he wanted to cuddle me, not kill me. I can't put my finger on it exactly, but I've always had good intuition. I knew where to find Billie, didn't I? Grandad says some people, particularly children, have great intuition, and those people also tend to be able to hear spirits and see auras and all sorts of things. The Ouija book says the same thing. I should trust my instincts. They've got me this far. Aren't I the one the dead girls talk to?

I'm just walking out of my bedroom and towards the top of the stairs, when I stop. A shiver goes through me. I reach out and steady my hand on the banister. The cold air that comes with the dead girls is around me, but when

I look they aren't there. I frown. A thought is moving like fog through my mind, and suddenly it solidifies, becoming clear. What if the walker *is* the pervert, but *not* the killer?

I hear a knock at the front door. I frown and listen. It's only eight, so Mum is still here. I hear her clompy steps reach the door, and the click of the latch.

'Hello, Nathan! What a nice surprise.'

'Um, hi, Mrs Wilde. I've brought Thera's bag back. She dropped it the other day.'

'That's very kind of you, Nathan. Would you like to speak to her? I think she's up.'

'Nah, I'm fine,' Nathan says quickly. 'I have to go and do some chores for my dad.'

'Oh, is your dad home?'

There is a pause. 'Kind of.'

'Are you sure you don't want to stay?'

'Can't,' Nathan says shortly. 'Bye.'

The door closes. The cold air has gone. Then Mum calls up the stairs, interrupting my thoughts. 'Thera, are you coming downstairs? We've got a big day ahead.'

I start down the stairs. 'We do?'

'Yes, we're going to see a nice lady today.' She goes into the kitchen and I hear her bashing crockery about, doing the washing-up. 'You can talk to her about Billie, and everything you've been feeling,' she calls back through. 'Isn't that a good idea? It's okay to tell her anything that's on your mind. Oh! And Nathan Nolan just dropped off your rucksack. It's a good job you didn't lose that!'

'Huh.' Nathan still didn't want to see me. And there was that cold air when he came to the door . . . Hang on a minute . . . I think back to mine and Nathan's conversations about the killer and I realize something: he doesn't have an alibi.

'Ooh, it's a lovely sunny day!' Mum calls. 'Better get some nice sundresses on to go and see the lady!' I roll my eyes. Mum is being fake cheery to lure me into a false sense of security. This so-called 'lady' she is talking about clearly sounds like some sort of psychiatrist, to check I'm not going crazy with grief. But I'm not crazy at all. In fact, this morning I have a new sense of purpose and clarity. I have never been more productive than lately, figuring out what happened to Billie and tracking down her killer. I've never been so connected to the world, feeling instincts and changes in the air, and interacting with the dead girls even though they scare me. I'm doing something useful. I'm logically following the trail to its conclusion. And now, just this morning, I have a new theory. I feel, for the first time in a while, strong.

Mum thinks she can trick me, that I'll just go along with her fake cheeriness and forget about Billie and be fine with Dad moving out and be as stupid and quiet and obedient as they want me to be. They think so little of me. But I can trick them too.

My trick will be to lull them into a false sense of security before my next act of bravery and cunning.

So for a week I play at being good. The lady Mum was talking about taking me to see turns out to be a grief counsellor, and so I go to see her to talk about Billie. I make up a bunch of stuff about imagining Billie up in heaven and wondering if she misses me and her parents, which is all lies, because I know she's here, haunting us. The lady recommends that I go on some pills to stop me being depressed. I have to take them every day for a few months, which I do for the first few days. They make me feel woozy and lazy, which won't help my plan, so I start to keep them next to my teeth when Mum gives them to me, instead of swallowing them down with water. Later I spit them out.

I'm bored, obviously, because I'm pretending to be a stupid, weak girl who isn't strong or tough, but I try to have patience. I'm waiting for Mum and Dad to trust me again and unground me. Sometimes I sit and read in the garden. The dead girls stand around me and stare at me. They make the air so cold I tremble constantly and Mum asks what's wrong. I tell the dead girls the time is coming, and not to worry. They don't say anything in reply, but sometimes they enter my body and hands, and make me write terrible stories of things that happened to them in the margins of my books. I promise them I won't forget all of them, everything that happened. I promise them that I will be their champion.

Mum takes me to see a summer-school teacher, who is really nice. I spend all Saturday and Sunday in her class, and I get to write and bind a book about the Greek myth of Medusa, design my own city and draw the map with all the sewerage and public services like trams and other intricate things on it, learn some Chinese, and dissect a sheep's heart (good practice). It's better than normal school, because we do more work and more creative things. I like learning, but school makes it so boring. I also raise two Nano Pets through infancy to two and a half, and then they die. I think that's pretty good. They were called Aisha and Benji. Then I have another one called Frogs, but he over-eats and dies of being fat. (That was depressing.) Sam and me make our packing lists, to decide what toys we will take on the plane to Majorca for holidays. Just Mum is coming now that they are getting divorced, which is rubbish because it's Dad who likes to do fun stuff like jumping over waves or lining up all our toys beneath a balcony and bombing them with tissue balls soaked in water. I shut Sam in the big leather suitcase and take him on the bed, which is an aeroplane, and we play going on holiday, but Mum runs in and opens the case, shouting about the lack of oxygen. Sam yells, 'Close the lid!' but Mum says he'll suffocate. I tried to stay calm with her, but she is being hysterical. I say, 'Mum, obviously if Sam is suffocating, he'll tell me and I'll unlock it again.'

'Yeah,' Sam says. 'It's perfectly safe.' He trusts me. He should. I'd die for him just like I would for Billie.

At three in the morning one night, I'm doing the automatic writing when Billie finally writes to me. The mere fact it is Billie means I know I am on the right track: she is talking to me because she has faith in my new plan. But the words she writes make me certain I know how she died:

> I THOUGHT (S)HE LIKED ME
> BUT IT WASN'T TRUE

I write brackets around the 's' on my drawing pad after the session is over. Maybe 's' is the automatic-writing equivalent of a typo.

Her statement isn't about the walker. I know that as soon as I take my pencil off the paper and read back what I've written. The walker is the pervert, but even though she could have told someone what he did and he could have gone to prison, he couldn't've killed Billie. He liked her too much. It *was* true, in fact, that the walker liked her, even though he showed it in a weird way. I could feel that he liked little girls too much to kill them from the way he interacted with me. I knew it instinctively.

But after the walker went away, Billie was alone, possibly disoriented, in pain. Someone she trusted found her in the woods. Someone who she thought might like her (for example, a boy who fancies girls), but who turned out not to at all. And for some reason I don't know yet, he strangled her to death.

Think about it: how come Nathan was so certain I didn't kill Billie? How did he know for sure the killer was a man? How did he know his dad hadn't murdered her? He acts weird, his home is strange, and the vibe I get from him isn't normal. He keeps saying he is bad. When he talks to me he often blushes, and he seems like he has something to hide. And then there is what his mother said the last time I saw her at her caravan: 'Don't want to end up like her, do you?' She wasn't threatening me. She was warning me.

I'm now convinced: the killer is Nathan Nolan.

Shortly after Billie automatic-writes to me, and a few days before we go on holiday, Mum finally lifts the grounding. I ask to go to the shop, so I can track down Nathan.

I am worried she will say no, but because there are still police around, Mum lets me go. She says they'll watch me the entire time. The first thing I do is buy a 10p bag of sweets, so I can show her the bag when I get home to prove I went to the shop. Then I head for the caravan park. I'm looking, as I walk along the pavement, for a big branch that might have fallen off a tree, as all my weapons have been confiscated. I am poking the hedgerows and sucking on a cola bottle when I become aware of a footfall in time with mine. It's a little heavier, and just behind me. I walk for a bit, then I whirl around, my fists ready.

Nathan jumps back. 'Don't! It's just me!'

I keep my fists up to protect myself. 'Hello, "Just Me". What are you doing following me?'

'N-nothing,' he stutters.

'Oh,' I say coldly. 'Okay, then.' I turn and keep walking. This is called playing chicken. I make an effort to keep my breathing steady, but I am listening intently for the sound of a weapon swooshing through the air towards my head, and I keep my eyeballs swivelled to the side so I can make sure he isn't right behind me (without looking like that's what I'm doing).

'Hey,' Nathan says. 'Hey! Wait up! Thera! I'm sorry 'bout my mum the other week. She wouldn't let me out the bedroom. I was grounded. She doesn't like trouble. She said with the police around, if I messed about with you I'd be banged up.'

'She hit me with a wooden spoon,' I murmur drily.

'She doesn't mean anything by it.'

'I guess you think hitting people with a wooden spoon is okay. I guess your dad does worse. And what about you, Nathan?'

He stops walking. I keep going for a few paces, then turn around. His expression is troubled. His shoulders are rounded and he chews his lip. He can't look at me.

'Were you following me the other day?' I say.

'Um,' he says, almost in a whisper. 'When you were dressed in a pretty dress and stuff?'

'Yeah.'

'No.'

'How did you find my bag?'

'What bag?'

'The bag you brought to my house, dummy.'

'Oh . . . I only wanted to play with you. That's why I was following you. I want us to be friends.' He hesitates. 'Maybe I could be your best friend. Your new one.'

'Is that why you did it?'

'Why . . .' Nathan scratches the skin on the back of his hand like he's nervous. 'Why I did what?'

'Look at me,' I command. He looks up slowly. 'I

thought you were going to say you were finally going to stop being a wuss and help me with my plan. But you're not going to, are you? Because you're afraid of what I'd find.' I take a step towards him. I lower my head, like a hunting polar bear on the programmes Dad watches. It's a universal sign of threatening, and Nathan looks appropriately worried.

'I will,' he says quickly. 'I will if that's what I have to do to be your friend.'

'Forget it. I don't need anyone to help me any more.' I wonder about accusing him now, but then decide against it. I want to get him talking, find out why he did it before I enact the revenge Billie and the dead girls need to rest in peace. 'You thought it was stupid anyway,' I add, pretending I'm a little sad.

'It wasn't stupid,' Nathan says quietly.

'You haven't spoken to me in ages, and you told your mum about what we did. Why would you want to be friends?'

'Because I . . .' His voice is sad and awkward. 'I like you. And I owe you, for telling on you.'

I toss my head and scoff scornfully. 'If you do want to do stuff with me just because you owe me, then I don't want it. Any of it.'

He stands there in silence for a bit, and then he says, 'I really am sorry about my mum. She made me tell her, 'cause she saw I was . . .'

'Crying like a baby?'

'Crying,' he says.

'Did you tell her I was "leading you astray"?' I say,

quoting her. I start walking away from him. I'm going to take him somewhere I know the police won't be watching.

'No,' Nathan says, following me, as I knew he would. 'She made that up. She's just pissed off these days. Dad keeps calling her and coming round and . . . she's angry with me too. I'm bad.'

'How are you bad?' I snap impatiently, turning around to glare at him. 'Why do you keep saying that? What did you do?'

He stops abruptly, surprised. His lips are parted and his hair is tousled. He has a red mark on his cheekbone. Despite what I know I have to do for Billie, I find myself studying him in a fancying way. His neck is lovely, dipping into his T-shirt. His arms are golden-brown, and I know his skin is soft. I know his chest is hard beneath that dirty fake Adidas logo. His combat trousers are baggy, but I know his legs are nice, like a footballer's. Suddenly, stupidly, because I'm sure he's the killer and I know I'm risking the whole plan by getting close, I walk towards him. He pulls back a little, but I grab his T-shirt and plant my lips on his.

I kiss Nathan Nolan. As I lean in, his lips part. I touch my lips on his like he did on my cheek on the first day we hung out, very gently. We kiss once, twice, three, four and then five times. They are very soft kisses. Nathan leans in again and I pout my lips, but then he goes past them and he puts his lips on my neck, and I feel his cold nose on my shoulder, and he hugs me. I put my arms around him and he hugs me tighter, and then so tightly I panic for a second that this is how he suffocated Billie, and I go, 'Nathan, I can't breathe.'

He pulls away quickly and looks down. 'Sorry.'

I frown and try to peek under his floppy hair. 'So, um . . .' I begin. I am about to ask him what he did to her.

But then he interrupts me. 'Meet me tomorrow at two.' Nathan sniffs, once, sort of firmly, and then he looks up. 'At the caravan park.'

'Why? You're leaving now?' I say quickly. Damn it. I shouldn't have kissed him. I lost control of the situation.

'Yeah. I'm going to tell you . . . I'm going to show you . . . why I'm bad.' He looks suddenly resolute, but nervous at the same time.

'Okay,' I say, nodding. Now I'll find out what happened to Billie. 'I'll be there.'

'Don't come up to my caravan. Wait at the entrance to the field. Don't let my mum see you.'

'Okay.'

'Come on, I'll walk you home.'

'I don't need anyone to walk me home. Go on, you head off.'

He hesitates, then starts to walk away in the opposite direction.

I set off. All the way home I see no one. Not even a police officer. Just Nathan Nolan, about fifty feet behind me, sticking to the shadows, following me every step of the way.

The next day, when I get to the caravan park, Nathan is waiting for me. He looks at me miserably, as if he wishes I hadn't shown up, and then he turns and starts walking. 'Come on,' he says. 'You deserve to know.'

He walks with his hands in his pockets. He is wearing those sports trousers in that silky material with the poppers down the sides, and a dark-blue T-shirt. We walk in single file, Nathan in front, and don't speak for a while. I'm still on alert for what he might do to me, and for what I have to do later, but he doesn't seem like he's going to attack me. It's a hot day, and as we walk we see a heat haze constantly ahead of us, now in the crops, now along a muddy road. Suddenly we are on a little raised footpath, coming up on the other side of the wheat field where I last saw Billie.

'I bumped into Billie here,' Nathan says, gesturing casually. 'I was on this track between the two wheat fields. I was going to the woods and she jumped out at me and said 'Boo!' It frightened the life out of me, but she laughed her head off. I kind of didn't know what to say. She kept laughing like a maniac. Billie was always really loud and funny, but I liked you better.'

'Billie was perfect,' I say firmly, although this is nice to hear.

'You would say that, though, wouldn't you?' Nathan points out. 'She was your best friend.'

'*Is* my best friend.'

'Oh.' Nathan looks disappointed, then turns away from me and starts walking again, towards the copse. 'She asked me where I was going, and I said to the den. I know you guys thought nobody knew about it, but it's just behind my home and I kept seeing you all going in there, so I went in and found it. That day Mum was being a . . . well, anyway, I went for a walk in the village. I like to pet Mr Childer's dog. She's called Sally. She likes me. She always wags her tail when I'm coming. After I played with her for a while I was tired, but I didn't want to go home, so I decided to go to the den.' He is picking the dirt out of his nails, tramping along and not looking at me. 'So Billie said cool, and she would come with me. I said something like she'd better go home before dark and she was like, "There's half an hour before sundown, poophead!" And there was, and she had already started walking towards the den anyway, so I just went along with it. She was pretty pushy, Billie, wasn't she? You couldn't really say no. She would just bounce along, doing what she wanted.'

'I guess so,' I say, unsure, because I'm not certain he means this in a good way.

'So we walked towards the trees along the path here, like we're doing. I don't think I said much. Billie was talk-ing lots. There were headlights. They were driving past in a big car as we went in the copse, so Billie yelled, "Duck and cover!" and ran into the copse. I ran after her because she was a girl and the woods were dark, and anyway it was fun. Most of the caravan kids are older than me and we don't hang out much. They just smoke up and talk crap anyway, they don't do anything fun. And at school . . .'

I hate smoking. Yuck.

Nathan snaps a stalk of corn and swipes the floor in front of us with it, back and forth. '. . . at school, some of the girls talk to me, but mostly people avoid the Gypsies and snotty kids and they say all the time the things I have are dirty and broken and they say I don't do my home-work and I'm not organized and I'm . . . I'm . . .' We've reached the entrance to the copse. He looks at me. We turn to the trees together and walk in between them, through the gate. The policeman isn't here any more. Must be long enough after she's dead that all the evidence is gone.

Nathan is silent in the woods.

I ask him, 'What did you do when you got in here?' but he doesn't say anything, just gestures to the entrance to the den, and I crawl through it. He crawls through after me and stands up. Like Hattie, it seems like he has become an adult over the summer. He feels tall, but also his face is heavier and there are shadows under his eyes. He looks into the middle of the den, right where I found Billie.

'We crawled really fast into the den. When we were here, Billie was laughing loads. I can't remember what she was saying. She danced about and threw herself down on the ground. Here.' He points to the centre of the den. 'She kind of patted the ground like she wanted me to come next to her, so I sat down next to her and she sat up and was like, "What are we going to do here? Aloooooone?" like it was spooky, but also like . . . flirty. I dunno. I shrugged. She shrugged. She said . . .' He stops and he licks his lips. His cheeks are pink. 'She said did I want to kiss? She laughed, like it was a big joke. I don't know if she was really serious or not.' He turns to me. 'I told her, "I don't know. I like someone else." I meant you, but I didn't say.' His face crinkles up, like he's confused or upset. He sits down on the ground, and looks at where he said Billie was sat. 'I didn't tell her I liked you more, because I thought then she wouldn't kiss me. And I'd . . .' He blushes and looks up at me. 'I'd never been kissed before by someone I liked. Just Hattie's sister, and that was because everyone was shit to me about living in the caravan park, and she bossed me into kissing her, and I thought it would make me more popular, and she said if I didn't things would be worse. So I wanted to kiss Billie. I thought it would be more . . . nicer.' He looks down again and his hair covers his face. 'She was like, "Okay, let's just kiss for practice." I don't think she fancied me or anything. She wasn't being serious. She said something about finding her Prince Charming one day and she wanted to know how to kiss and he wouldn't be a snot-nosed badger. I don't know why she said that.'

I laugh. 'I do.'

'Why?' he asks.

I hesitate. 'Friendship secret,' I say. 'What did you say after?'

'Well, she said I could practise on her so I wouldn't mess up with whoever I liked. It was just swapping practice. She said you and her kiss your hands. I said, "I dunno, do you want your first kiss to be with me?" and she was like, "Practice kisses don't count! Silly bum", and then she laughed more. She was making a racket. Neither of us noticed . . . Anyway' – he scratches his head – 'I closed my eyes and I imagined you. I pouted my lips, like you're supposed to do. I felt her lips mush against mine for two seconds, and then she took them off and we both took a breath. I opened my eyes. "What do you think?" I said, and she said, "Well, it was okay." She said maybe it was better when you fancied the person.

'I nodded. I said I was imagining who I fancied. She said something like, "Okay, do it again and I'll imagine Leo." So I closed my eyes and pouted again, and she kissed me. She went "Hmm" so I said, "Was that okay?" And she said I wasn't bad and that imagining Leo definitely helped. Then I was like . . . I was like, "Do you want me to tell you who I fancy?" She said something weird like, "Wait a minute, lie down here next to me, I always imagine Leo in the back of that steamed-up car" and I was like, "What steamed-up car?" and she said, "In *Titanic*" and I said, "I haven't seen it" and she yelled, "You haven't seen *Titanic*?" and I said, "I don't think I should lie down with you anyway", and she asked why not and I said, "Because."'

'Because what?'

Nathan is still sat on the dirt, with his knees up to his chest and his arms around them. He puts his chin down on his knees. 'Well.'

'Well what? What did you say?'

'I didn't. I didn't say anything, 'cause. Well, there was this man in the den suddenly. I didn't see where he came from, but he must have climbed through the back of the den from the field behind the fence. He was just there. We didn't hear anything 'cause Billie's voice is so loud. Was. So loud.' Nathan is staring into the air in front of him, like he is seeing the whole thing playing out in miniature before his eyes. 'The man said, "I'll lie down next to you" and then laughed, like it was a big joke. He seemed friendly when he said it. Lots of blokes say stuff like that and it's just a joke. My football teacher and my dad. Dad's a twat, but when he says stuff like that to girls in pubs he doesn't really mean it, he's just joking. Billie laughed too, and then so did I. Then the man looked at me and he said, "What's a pikey like you doing with a beautiful young girl like this in the woods?" I stopped laughing then. I said, "Nothing." He was like, "Yeah, sure, nothing. Liars, thieves and scum, pikeys are." Then he went on, kept calling me a pikey.'

'What's a pikey?' I ask.

Nathan looks at me witheringly. 'Like a traveller. He said I was a Romany Gypsy, and I said I'm not, I'm Irish, and he laughed and said, "That's even worse!" and then he said to Billie, "What's the difference between an Irish wedding and an Irish funeral? There's one less drunk." Billie laughed. The man still sounded like he was really nice and cheerful, but I realised he wasn't. I know blokes like that. My dad's like that. Really nice and then bam! He just gets mad or drunk and smacks other people about. Doesn't matter if they're men or women. Doesn't like his fucking pride dented. Something makes him angry and then he totally turns . . .' Nathan's thoughts seem to drift. He shakes his head. 'Anyway, I was annoyed Billie laughed. I said, "Do you know him?" and she said, "Yeah, he's—" Then the man interrupted her and said, "Hey, Billie, did you hear the joke about the Irishman who was found dead on the roadside in the middle of summer?" Billie said no. "His friend told him that, in the heat, you should just imagine you're cold." He turned to me and was like, "D'you know what he died of?" I didn't say anything, but then he grinned and said, "Ask me, mick, or you'll be for it", so I said, "No, what?" and he said, "He died of frostbite." Billie laughed again. Then he said, "What's the difference between a smart Irishman and a unicorn? Nothing, they're both fictional characters!" I've heard them all before, they're all stupid jokes, but Billie was howling by then and I stood up. He came at me quickly and was like, "Now don't try anything, you, I know what you lot are like, causing trouble. Get out of here. God knows what you're doing with her, but I won't call the police if you go now!"' Nathan does an impression of him. He makes him sound like he's pretending to be nice, like he's being responsible and making a bad boy go away.

'What did you do?'

'Well, I was annoyed at Billie for laughing, and she said she knew him . . . and I didn't want to get in trouble with the police. I used to live at this other park. They came round all the time, telling us off. I was never doing anything, just hanging about. Once me and some of my mates climbed over a school gate and sat on the picnic benches drinking cans and talking at two in the morning. The police got called and we got done for trespassing and they took us home in their squad car. Dad lashed the shit out of me for that.'

My eyes widen. Nathan notices and looks away.

'Anyway. The man changed then. He smiled at me. He said it was okay to have urges, but I didn't want to get into trouble, did I? So I said, "No." He said he wanted to talk to Billie. He said he knew her, that he had a secret to tell her, from some lady. Mrs something. Adams?'

'Mrs Adamson?' I frown. 'She's our teacher.'

'I dunno. Maybe he said her name then to get Billie on his side or something? She was fine with it. She said bye. She was still laughing when I crawled out the den. I walked a way through the wood, but then . . . I saw the car lights near the gate. The engine was running. I felt funny. I was a boy, and older, and I should have been watching out for her. I dunno. I went back and I crawled through the entrance to the den again, but when I got to the end I looked up and I saw him on top of her.' Nathan's voice lowers to a whisper. 'I just watched,' he says. 'I froze. At first I didn't know what was happening. It wasn't for long. He was moving back and forth. I felt funny. Not quite like I did with you, but, like, interested or something. Felt . . . felt it stirring in my boxers. And then she started screaming. He'd taken his hand off her mouth. The sound was so horrible. I was scared he'd kill me too. He was big, like my old man. And my old man is horrible. He really hurts you when . . . he can really hurt people when he wants to. So I crawled out backwards as quietly as I could. When I got out the thicket, I ran. I heard the screaming stop, so I guessed he killed her. Then I heard him running after me.'

'Did you go for help?'

'The man knew what I looked like. He could tell the police I did it or come after me and kill me. He still could. Besides, Mum hates the police. She'd be really angry at me if I got involved with them. And she was dead anyway, so . . . I didn't think I could help,' he adds sadly.

'Was there anyone in the car? If the engine was running?' My mind was racing.

'Yeah it was weird. I think there was. I didn't see them properly, but I could make out a shape.'

'Wait, Nathan,' I touch his shoulder. 'You think there was definitely a second person in the car.'

'Yeah. I mean, I think so.'

I was right. The walker isn't the killer. But if it isn't Nathan . . . I have to make sure he's telling the truth. I decide to ask him lots of questions, quickly and loudly, to see if he sticks to his story and make sure he's not just making it all up. 'Where did you go after?'

'I kept running.'

'How far did you run?'

'I got to the church before I realized he wasn't chasing me any—'

'And then what did you do?'

'I waited for a while, then I went back. The car was gone, but she wasn't.'

'She? Who?'

Nathan looks confused. 'Billie. She was lying there, in the middle of the den, really still.'

'In the *middle*?'

'Yeah.'

'That's not where I found her. She was in a sheet in the ditch.'

'No, no – not when I was there.'

'Well, how did that happen to her, Nathan?'

'I – I don't know. I mean, I brought the sheet from the caravan. I snuck in and took it while Mum was in her room, but I didn't put it in the ditch. I just put it over her. So she wasn't . . . cold.' He sobs once, and then pushes his fists against his eyes, almost violently.

'Cold? She was dead, Nathan. Of course she was cold,' I say impatiently. 'So how did she get in the ditch? How did she get the DNA burnt off her?'

'I don't know, I said! Someone must have come back and done that stuff to her.' He cries more. 'I didn't do anything to her, I swear!'

I stop interrogating him. I've broken him and he hasn't confessed to anything, so he must be telling the truth. Then, somewhere in my mind, a little alarm is going off. 'Someone?' I repeat. 'Someone must have come back?'

'Yeah. When I found her . . . I touched her and she didn't move, so I flipped out and ran away. I came back with the sheet. I was scared, though, that the killer would come back. I thought I heard a car door. It was really late. So I ran home through the back way of the den. I got all scratched up and fell in the ditch. I thought Mum would be mad when I got back home, but she was already asleep. So I just' – Nathan shrugs – 'brushed my teeth and got into bed.'

'You brushed your teeth,' I repeat softly.

'Yeah,' he murmurs.

I walk over to him and sit down on the soil and leaves, the other side of him from where Billie sat.

Nathan hangs his head. 'I could have saved her. She only came to the woods 'cause of me. I should have said something when I came back to check on her. I think about it every night and I can't get to sleep. I imagine running in the den and jumping on him. You would have done. But instead I just . . . watched. I felt weird, like kind of . . .' There are tears in his eyelashes. 'Kind of hot and bothered. You know. It made me feel funny like . . . because it was sex . . . I don't know.' His cheeks are blood-red and he is crying. 'All I know is I'm a bad person. I'm, like, perverted and sick, like him.'

I frown. 'Like who? The man in the woods?'

'Like him . . . and like my dad. Like those fucking twats, all my dad's fucking friends. It's my fault she's dead.' Nathan sobs into his hands. 'And that's why I'm bad and how I know it's not your fault. It's my fault.'

'No, Nathan,' I say after a minute. 'It's mine. She was my best friend. I'm a month older than her. She was my responsibility.'

'It's not your fault,' he moans, burying his head into his knees.

'I shouldn't have left her,' I say, and put my hand on his shoulder. 'And the thing is . . . I can't live without her. Not really. But I might just be able to if I know her killer got what was coming to' – I frown – 'him.' I sit up suddenly. 'Nathan! That's it!'

'What?'

'It all makes sense.'

'What does? What are you talking about? Thera?'

I turn to him, almost grinning. 'I've figured it out.' I scramble to my feet and Nathan follows suit. 'I've figured out who the killer is. Billie's last message to me. I thought it was a mistake, but it wasn't.'

'What did she say?' he asks.

'She said: "I thought she liked me but it wasn't true."'

'But that doesn't make any sense.'

'Not if the killer's a man.' I dive into the tunnel and crawl out of the den, then pace towards the gate to the woods. I can vaguely hear Nathan behind me, but I'm almost unaware of him. I can feel in every bone in my body that I'm right; that I know who the real murderer is.

'Thera, wait up! Don't you think the killer's a man?'

I turn my head just a little, to talk behind me to Nathan as he catches me up. '"I know I couldn't live without him."'

'You couldn't live without him who? What?'

'It's what Mrs Adamson said to me. That she couldn't live without her husband. And she's got all this crap in her car, Nathan, rope and matches and stuff. And the walker, I've met him. But when I talked to him, I didn't feel like he was going to kill me. I could tell from his aura, from my instinctive reaction to him, that he wasn't a real threat, that he was kind of wet, even. But Mrs Adamson has always seemed off to me. Sometimes she's mean, sometimes she says weird things. What if she was jealous of the walker's affection for Billie? What if she thought she would lose him? What if she even saw him with Billie in the woods? Mrs A can't live without her husband. Could that drive someone to murder?' I stop pacing at the top of the hill after we've walked through a fallow field. I am panting, but I'm elated. I cast my eyes over the heavens. They are clear and blue. I nod. Everything feels right. 'And then the walker has pictures of two of the dead girls, at least. I think not only was he a pervert with them all, but they also all have the same killer.'

'What dead girls? And who did you say Mrs Adamson was?'

I whirl around and grab him by both arms. 'You're right, Nathan. The biggest fault isn't ours.' He looks up at me all miserable, and to make him feel better I push my lips against his softly. When I take my lips away, he opens his mouth and looks all starry-eyed. 'You're not a bad person. Listen, the car – was it a big one, like a jeep?'

'Yeah.'

'Do you ever see it? Driving through the village or anything?'

He licks his lips and swallows.

'What?'

'I can recognize it,' he whispers. 'The jeep. The number plate has an L in it. It has this scratch on the side. Sometimes I see it around the village.'

'Really?' I say, excited. 'And who is driving it?'

'The walker, I guess.'

'You guess? Don't you know?'

'Well . . .' He looks embarrassed. 'I always run away. I don't want him to see me.'

I nod. 'Excellent. This is excellent.'

Nathan grimaces at me warily. 'What are you gonna do?'

I feel the wind lift the wisps of hair around my face and I close my eyes and then open them again, looking around at my land, my village, my territory. 'In some way I've known what I had to do ever since I found Billie.' I look back at his lovely face. How could I ever have thought he was the killer? 'It's time to put the blame where it belongs.'

'You don't know who the blame belongs to,' Nathan says. 'You don't know who the killer is.'

'You're wrong, Nathan,' I tell him. 'I do.' I let go of his arms. 'Come and get me the next time you see the jeep. Come as fast as you can. I have to get to it before it leaves.'

I turn away from him and set off for home, running down the hill, my hair streaming out behind me like the flag of a victor.

I don't know where Mrs A lives – only that she lives outside the village – so I have to wait for the signal from Nathan, but as it turns out it doesn't take long. He's been looking out for the jeep, and shortly after we meet, before we go on holiday even, it comes to the woods and he runs over to my house. I almost miss him, because he is a bit of a scaredy-cat about throwing rocks at my window, even after I convinced him it was okay. He throws pebbles instead, and I don't hear them because I'm listening to an All Saints CD and doing automatic writing. Sam sees Nathan through the window downstairs and runs up to my room, yelling, 'Nathan Nolan's outside! He's outside!'

'Shh!' I hiss. My hand is scrawling fast on the paper. I'm writing down everything that happened to Kerry. When I take my hand away I get a burning sensation. 'Shit!' I say, and Sam gasps. 'Sorry for swearing,' I tell him. 'It's hanging around with Nathan. Go – go and tell him I'm coming!'

I apologize to Kerry's ghost quickly, grab the bag I have pre-packed and hidden under my bed, and run downstairs. 'He says to meet him behind the hedge on the top road in the fields,' Sam whispers loudly.

'Shh!' I tell him, then: 'Nan! I'm just going out for a bit!'

'Young madam, why are you yelling? I'm in here!'

'Oh. Sorry, Nan.' I stick my head in the kitchen. Nan is making sandwiches. 'I'm just going out for a walk.' I don't say with Nathan, because if something bad happens I don't want him to be blamed.

'Where are you walking?'

'Through the village.'

'You're not allowed on the fields.'

'I know, I promised Mum I wouldn't go there any more.' Nan looks at me suspiciously. 'I'm being good now, Nan,' I say. 'What do I have to say to convince you?'

'Hmm,' she says. 'Well, alright. Do you want some sandwiches?'

'I've got to go.'

'I've already made them. They're tuna.'

'Okay, sure – eight, please.' Four for me and four for Nathan. Nan wraps them in tinfoil and I take them with me and run out the door, stuffing two in my mouth. As soon as I'm outside I pelt as fast as I can down the close and into the nearest field. (I lied – it's called doing something bad for the greater good.) I run through the barley towards the top road. I can see Nathan at the hedge, near the entrance to Rawley Farm. When I reach him, I motion to him to crouch down.

'Stealth mode,' I say.

'What?'

'Get down and be quiet!'

We duck behind the hedge. I open my bag and start to change. Nathan stares at me as I take off my top. 'Erm, what are you doing?'

'I'm bait, remember?' I say.

'No. I don't remember you saying that,' Nathan replies, a little distressed.

I pull on a vest top that clings to me and makes my almost-boobs look the most like boobs they can. It's white, the colour of purity, which, as we have ascertained, is what perverts like. I pass Nathan my jeans and T-shirt and he holds them and watches me change with a confused expression. My hair is in pigtail plaits, with purple hair bobbles and butterfly clips. On my bottom I pull on a blue tartan skirt and pink knickers. I'm wearing my trainers with purple elastic laces and socks, for running fast. It all seems to work because when Nathan sees my knickers he says, 'Wer-er-er, um, are you sure about this?'

'Totally,' I say. I look through the gap. The jeep is there, with the engine switched off.

'I think he's down at the farm shop.' The farm shop is just inside the farm gates. Farmer Rawley sells vegetables, flowers and eggs there. It's just an honesty till: you put money in a cardboard box and take what you want. Before Billie was killed, sometimes Mum used to send us there to buy tomatoes and stuff. 'Do you want me to call the police?' Nathan says. 'From the phone box?' About half a mile to our right is the red phone box where I reported finding Billie.

'No,' I whisper. 'Don't you dare.' I look at him. 'Promise me.'

'Okay.'

'I said promise.'

'Why, though? If you know it's him, why?'

'Nathan. If you have to ask why . . .' I breathe. 'You don't love me.'

He bites his lip slowly and then he makes the sign across his chest. 'Cross my heart and hope to die.'

I beam. He loves me. 'The police can't handle this,' I say. 'They haven't even found him so far. Anyway, they won't do what the dead girls want. He's toast.'

Nathan gulps. 'Okay, well, do whatever you're going to do quickly. I can hear footsteps.'

'Okay. Perfect.'

'Perfect for what?'

'My purposes.' I hand Nathan his sandwiches. 'Here, take these. For lunch.' I stand up and start to push through the hedge.

Nathan catches hold of my arm. 'Thera . . .'

I look at his hand. 'Don't you dare stop me, Nathan Nolan.'

He lets go of me. 'I wish I could.'

'I'm in charge of my own destiny. You can't tell me what to do.'

'I know.' He tenses his fingers around the tinfoil parcel.

'Don't squash those,' I say. 'My nan made them.'

'What are they?'

'Tuna.'

'Thanks very much,' he says weirdly, like he's half grateful, half offended, and maybe a bit sarcastic.

I look over to the copse.

'Thera?' Nathan murmurs nervously. 'What happens if, you know . . . if you don't make it back?'

I look back to him. 'Don't you trust me?' I smile. 'Goodbye, Nathan.'

He doesn't reply, just breathes and blinks at me, so I leave, pushing through the hedge, keeping low and running over to the jeep. I imagine Nathan saying something romantic like, 'Goodbye, Thera. I'll never forget you' or, 'I know you'll make it, Thera, you're a survivor' or, 'I'll wait for you forever, no matter what happens', but then I'm near the jeep and I have to concentrate.

I squat behind the jeep. I look underneath it. I can't see anyone. I run round to the back and try the big back door with the tyre on it. Luckily it opens, and I climb into Mrs Adamson's boot. There's a dog bed right in front of me, and I climb over the spade, the cleaning stuff and the rope, climb in the dog bed and pull the blanket over my head. I fit right inside it. It stinks.

In one of the Mystery Kids books that me and Billie like best, the hero, Holly, gets stuck in a villain's car. To figure out where it's going, she uses counting and her senses. I always thought this idea was great and would probably come in handy so I plan to use it today, although the stench in the jeep is horrible and I can't really smell anything outside the boot. As Holly went through the streets of London, she could smell fish and chips and things like that. The jeep surprisingly doesn't smell like dog, what with the dog bed in it; it smells like rotting stuff, like when the bin gets old. The idea is, you count in seconds after you leave or make a turn, so you remember your way, like: 'Seven, right, five, left, three, bridge, six, smells like pigs, must be near a pig field.' I guess I don't have to count, though, until I reach the road, 'cause I'll be able to tell when we're going through the fields because it's so bumpy.

When the jeep starts, I feel it rumble off across the track in the fields, and then the engine vrooms a little bit as we go up the hill and reach the top road. Then we pootle quietly down the gentle slope until we reach the lane, which is actually a real road, but pretty thin and with bad tarmac. It's the one I followed Mr Kent home on. But when we get on the lane, the jeep takes a left, away from his house. I start counting. I'm not wearing a seatbelt, obviously, and I bounce up and down with the bumps and cracks in the road surface.

'One, two, three, four, five, six, seven, eight,' I mouth. We are at the green grass triangle. We go right, towards the school. 'One, two, three, four, five, six, seven, eight, nine, ten, eleven.' I can tell by the swerving that we are going through the centre of the village. We are past the school now, and we continue down the long straight. We are travelling relatively fast, as if we are going to leave the village. I can tell when we hit the forty-mile-an-hour signs, because the jeep speeds up. We are on the road to Eastcastle, where the big school is. I keep counting and it helps me keep track of where we are. We go over a little humpback bridge and I hear the river, and then more noise. The driver of the jeep has the windows down and I hear kids talking, so I guess we are nearing the new estates on the edge of Eastcastle.

The problem is, in the book that this was in, *The Mystery Kids: Funny Money*, when Holly got stuck in the bad guy's car and had to do the counting trick, she only ever counted small numbers because the roads were all short and the villain was only driving around the corner. On this current road, from the village into town, I am on number three hundred and eighty-nine.

Just then, we turn left. I can't think which road we are going down, but then we curve left again and it's quite windy, so I guess we have actually driven onto one of the new estates. I've never been on them before, so I don't know which.

I zip open my bag for a second to check my weapons. Everything is there. I'm ready to pay them back for what they did. I can smell Mrs A's perfume. She's driving. I *was* right! I think gleefully, then, because I think it's important that I know where we are, I risk popping my head up just a tiny bit and looking out the window at the back. New houses are pretty blank-looking. I never thought about it before, but they do look like the kind of places where psychos would live. They don't have any ivy growing up them, or any flowers in the garden. All the grass is that green like when it's late at night and the telly stops, and the colour chart with the girls and the puppet comes up and the green there is weirdly bright. (I've seen it once, at Nan and Grandad's, when I woke up in the middle of the night and decided to be naughty and sneak down for a glass of milk.) All the bricks in the houses here are orange. They ought to be dark-red or brown, like our house. 'Hmm,' I say to myself, before I remember I have to be in cog knee toe.

I slip back down into the doggie bed, but then we turn a tight corner and the bed slides over to the right of the jeep and I bash my head. I almost swear out loud. The jeep comes to a stop and the engine turns off. I hear the driver fiddling about with something for a minute, then there is a silence. I hold my breath. I hear the click of the door opening, and then two shoes on the drive. The door slams shut. There is another pause. I hear walking footsteps. I can't tell where they are walking towards. There is yet another silence. But then a house door closes and I know I'm safe. 'Phew!' I whisper.

I climb out of the doggie bed and unlock the back door from inside – easy peasy. I jump down and quietly shut the door behind me. A big hand reaches around my front, near my tummy. I look down at it, frowning, and then my eyes get big as a second hand reaches around my front at my face level. I try to scream, but the first hand grabs me and lifts me up, and the second hand clamps down over my mouth. The fingers spread out. His thumb presses into my right cheekbone. His pointing finger is over my left cheekbone. His palm is pressed down hard on my lips. He lifts me up like baggage and walks me into the house. The front door is open. Mrs A must have opened it, faked closing it so I would hear the sound, and then opened it again and got the walker to come out to get me. I should have noticed.

It's weird seeing inside people's houses when you've met them a few times. You realize you have kind of already imagined what their house would be like, and then it isn't like that and you are surprised. It's funny how we judge people without even really thinking about it. I wonder how people judge me. Do they know immediately that I am brave? Do they look at me and think, 'That girl will die at the hands of a man twenty years older than her because of her own bravery and (maybe) foolishness'? Well, they're wrong.

The walker's wallpaper has little flowers. I can tell, even though he has gagged me because I bit his hand, and is now carrying me upside down in a fireman's lift through the corridor at the entrance to the house. There is a light-pink coat hung up in the hall. I'm hitting him but he doesn't seem to feel it at all, like he's a monster or a robot or something. Like the Terminator. Why do I always think of that movie? Oh yeah, Edward Furlong.

The walker's house has ornaments. Little Siamese porcelain cats, white with brown tips of their tails and ears. It has lots of mirrors. They are shaped like ovals, like ponds, to look in. When he throws me down on the couch, I notice it's beige with beige throws. It's exactly what I would have imagined Mrs A's house to look like. The cushions are the shade of Mum's blusher and they feel like they have feathers in them. It's quite soft. I could go to sleep here. It won't be the worst place to die. But I won't die here. I'll die there, by the fireplace, having my brains bashed in by the poker. The photographs on top will watch me. The happy faces, the walker and his wife. I smile, looking at them. I knew it. I'll be dead soon, but I was right.

When I'm dead I'll join Billie, Ellie, Jenny and the rest of the dead girls. We'll fly around the country avenging the deaths of little children. We'll live in the cloud kingdom, but we'll make day trips to earth.

He moves me around a few times on the sofa, picking me up and putting me back down, making my head comfortable, tucking the cushion underneath it. They have bare walls. No bookshelves. At Grandad's, every wall is a bookshelf. The walker is a heathen. What was that other word Grandad used? It meant someone without culture . . . 'Neanderthal'? No. 'Neophyte'? No . . . I'll think about it. It'll come back to me.

'I'm sorry I had to gag you, my little sweetheart,' the walker says. 'We just have to find out what you were doing in my wife's car, don't we?'

I smile as best as I can with this gag in my mouth, and nod. Now I am here, it's not like I don't feel any fear, but it's as if the fear isn't really getting to me. The top five per cent of me, somewhere around my skin, is aware of terror, but I – my real, thinking me – am somewhere inside my body, and I'm not afraid. Is this how everyone feels when they are in the vicinity of a killer? Is this how Billie felt? As the walker is adjusting me, he brushes his hand against my almost-boob area, and I hear him suck in a little breath quickly. He is saying something, but I haven't been hearing him at all. I've been listening and watching out for Mrs A, but she hasn't reappeared yet. There are just signs of her, everywhere, like the magazines on the coffee table: *Beauty Essentials* and *Good Housekeeping*.

'What are you doing here, then, kiddo?' he is saying while I bat at him and he struggles to tie up my hands. I wish I didn't bite my nails. I might have been able to scratch my way to freedom. 'What were you looking for in the car? Or did you just want to get closer to me?'

It's so easy for him to hold me down. It feels like it doesn't take him any effort at all. Maybe it's not that girls are pretty and that's why people kill them. It's that girls are small and it's fun to kill small things. Like squashing a bug. Like throwing stones at pigeons. It must be fun to be big, and to watch something you squeeze snap. I can never get anything I strangle to do that. Not Sam, not that bloody cat that scratched my arms, not that kid at the new summer-school classes who let me practise on him.

When I'm safely tied up, the walker sits down next to me and puts his arm around me, like we're a couple. He puts his hand on my thigh. He speaks softly now. 'Did you come back to see me, Thera? It's okay. I feel it too, this . . . connection between us.'

'Piz tek is gug aff,' I say.

'There's nothing more beautiful than a girl like you,' he murmurs. 'Vulnerable and sweet. So clever too, tracking me down. It makes me think we can talk honestly to each other.'

I try to speak more clearly. 'Please take this *gag off*.'

'But' – he hesitates – 'if I take the gag off, you'll scream.'

'I romise I on't.'

'What, darling?' He comes close to me. He is breathing heavily. It's hot and smells like mint and meat. Not like Nathan's. More like Dad's.

'I *promise* I *won't*. You can kill me,' I say, 'and I won't yell. I just want to talk to you.'

He looks really sad suddenly. 'I wouldn't kill you, kiddo.'

'Well,' I say, but there is a lot of spit in my mouth. 'I oh aht, but still.'

'Huh?'

'I *know* that, but *still*.' I roll my eyes, getting impatient. '*Urgh*, take this bloody thing off me!' I accidentally swear, but it comes out like 'ruddy' anyway, which is not a swear word, so it's fine.

He strokes the hair on the back of my head. 'Are you sure you won't scream?' he murmurs.

I nod. He takes the gag off and I swallow all the drool I made talking through it.

'Is that better?'

'Yes,' I say. 'Thank you.'

'Good girl,' he says.

Here we go, then. I know this game. I'm an excellent player. I played it all last week to trick Mum and Dad. This is the good-girl game. I play it with Mr Kent and other adults for parts of almost every day. I talk in a high voice, and do what they say. I smile my small, neat, I'm-a-good-girl smile, and try to look innocent. This is how I tricked Mum and Dad into relaxing, into me not being grounded. This is how I will trick the walker, and get him to let his guard down, so I can bypass him to get to Mrs A and exact Billie's revenge.

'That's much more comfortable,' I say.

He chuckles. 'I'm glad.' Then he frowns. 'I have to talk to you about something serious, though, Thera. I didn't kill Billie. I would never do that. I really want you to believe me—'

'I do,' I say. 'I know you couldn't kill Billie. You loved her too much. You just wanted to cuddle her.'

'That's right! I knew you would understand.' He gulps, and I hear it louder because of where my ear is. 'Did you really come to my house to see me, sweetheart?'

'Yes. I climbed in her car to get to your house.'

'How did you know Eve was my wife?'

'You mentioned her to my friend Nathan,' I say. I don't say what really happened, which is that my dead best friend dobbed her in. 'And then it clicked. I'm glad. I wanted to see you again. We have a connection.'

'That Gyppo? I'll have to sort him out, Thera, I can't have him telling lies about me to the police. Don't you lie to me either, okay, Thera? You mean it, right? You feel something between us too? Maybe not like what Billie and I had but . . . something.'

'Maybe because of Billie?' I suggest. 'We were both close to her. Maybe we're cosmically entwined.'

The walker chuckles quietly. 'Do you really fancy me, then? I wanna hear you say it.'

'Yes,' I say. 'I like your eyes, and your hair, and how big you feel with your arms around me.'

'Yeah? Go on.'

'And I like . . . how cuddly you are, and the sound of your voice when it's close to me, and . . .' I think about what women like. 'Your lips. And your bum.'

He laughs. 'Yeah?' He glances in the direction of the stairs. I wrinkle my nose, feeling grossed out, but I bury my face in his neck to hide it.

'Oh, Thera,' he moans. He leans back. 'We have to slow this down. I'm going to make us some tea,' he says. 'Or a warm glass of milk, to help us chill out? Have you ever had rum?'

'I'll have some tea, thank you.'

'What about the rum?'

I don't know what rum is. 'That sounds great, thank you.'

'Just before I go . . .' He nips back across the room to me. 'Stay still.' He gets a camera out of the sideboard and takes a photograph of me. It's not a dirty photo, it's just of my face.

'Cheeeeese,' I say. He looks a little unnerved, but when I smile at him he grins back, then goes to put the kettle on. I smile at him vaguely the whole time. How you win the good-girl game is you stay you inside: tough, brave, strong, wild and full of hate. Outside you nod and say thank you for things you didn't want anyway.

The kitchen is through a big double-door space without any doors in it, so he can see everything I'm doing. He stretches and rubs his hands on his chest under his T-shirt. 'Do you want me to take my top off, Thera?'

'Sure,' I say. That'll make things easier. A clearer target.

The walker takes his top off. He strokes his naked chest and beams at the kettle, his mouth wide open and his teeth showing and everything. He's a bloody loony. While he makes the tea, I kind of scope out the room. There are two doors, a front one and a back one, which is a sliding glass door. There is a set of windows at the front of the house where I might have been able to get out if we were in an older house, but this is a new one, and they are thick. I bet even if I did scream, I would barely be heard. I could run upstairs. But really I'm just not fussed about escape, because escape wasn't what I came here to do. My bag is lying by the front door, where he hit me after I bit him. He apologized right after but it doesn't mean anything if a psycho apologizes to you. It's like a bull apologizing for charging at you – they have no moral compass, they just act without thinking.

I need the bag to be in the living room, ideally, but I can't attract his attention to it, because then he will look in there and probably throw away everything I need. Hmm. I need a distraction. That's what happens in the films. Before you are killed, just in time, there is a sound, and the killer looks away. Only no one knows where I am to come and distract him. The kettle clicks off. He is whistling while he makes the tea. He pours the hot water into the teapot, still grinning, and looks towards me and winks like we're sharing a big joke.

I grin back and pretend he's a big ball of fluffy pink

candyfloss. I say things to him in my head, like, 'Hi, loony tunes! How's the weather where you are, bumhead?' It makes the slightly sick feeling I had just now – thinking about how this idiot is going to rape me, and I'm probably going to have to let him – go away. I tuck my legs under myself on the couch so I'm sitting up. He brings the teapot and cups over carefully, and puts them on the table beside me. He pours me a cup of tea and feeds it to me like I'm a baby. I sip sweetly. 'Thank you. What was your name?'

'Nick. Call me Nick'. He sips his tea. 'Would you like some more?'

'Sure.'

He feeds me from my cup again. 'Do you like it?'

'Yes. It's nice.'

'PG Tips.'

Only a psycho would prefer PG Tips to Tetley's. I smile politely.

'Oh, Christ, Thera,' he says, and puts his chin down on his chest. 'Christ.' He runs his hands through his hair. 'Fucking Christ.'

'Don't swear,' I say without thinking.

He looks up. His face is all red. 'I know, I know, but I just . . . come here,' he says, and he takes my waist in both hands and pulls me down so I'm lying on the couch again, but this time he climbs on top of me and stretches his legs out. His fingers stroke the hair at my temple, one by one. I have a sensation, an idea that I will in fact not be able to overpower the real killer; that everything that came to Billie will come to me, including death, like a warm blanket, like a black cloud, like a ticket to Billie and the dead girls, and I'll haunt another living girl with them, until she dies or triumphs, and maybe we'll do it, over and over, until time ends, and everyone who loved us and missed us and longed to touch us again is dead. A cold stillness seems to take over my heart. I can't even tell if I'm breathing.

Suddenly there are footsteps on the stairs, and a pause in the hall, then more steps along the carpeted corridor, followed by the unmistakable sound of my rucksack hitting the floor nearby, just like it does at home every day at three forty when I came in from school. I tilt my head back, looking upwards and then behind me, from my position on the couch. There she is.

'Hi, Mrs A,' I say.

She looks annoyed.

We went on holiday. I think he wanted to get away from his disappointment at failing the degree I had passed. He booked it on a whim, I didn't know. He didn't have the money, because I had been able to get a job and he hadn't, so he used mine. We went to Disney World in Florida. It was a childhood dream of mine. He liked me dressing up in Minnie's clothes, acting the kid. One day he went out in the hire car for a drive. I knew something was wrong, because we did everything together. The only times during the holiday we were apart were when he would say I'm going for a walk, and I'd say can I come with you? and he'd say I just want some time to myself. Those were the times he would go to see the women.

So I thought he was going to find a woman. An American woman, with a crass accent and big, fake boobs. I went out shopping, angry at him. I bought make-up and underwear, I plaited my hair on either side, which I knew he liked, to make him want me. When I got back to the holiday home he was there. He met me in the living room. He seemed nervous. And then he told me he had brought a girl home. She was up in his room. A little girl. What do you mean? How little? I asked. Little, he said.

I walked up the stairs with him, quietly. She was

half-dead on the bed. He had given her some drugs he got from the pharmacy, American ones you can't get over the counter in the UK. Her mouth was open, and her jaw-length baby-blonde hair was messed up and sweaty. She was wearing a pink-and-purple top and flowered leggings. There was a pony doll on the bed. He put it in her hands and stroked her hair. He sat down next to her and started crying. I don't know what to do, he said. She won't wake up. The police will arrest me, and maybe I'll get the death penalty. I'm so scared.

It was the first time I had seen him so vulnerable. I was horrified, but I was also touched he had come to me. For the first time, I realized I had some power in our relationship. You've no idea what a revelation that was for me, to know he had that admiration, that respect for me; to know that he needed me. I saw how I could be close to him, how I could still be that special girl, more special than all the others, the girl I had seen in his eyes in that room at university when I was young. I said, I'll take care of it, and he looked at me so gratefully I felt like a queen deigning to do a favour for a subject. I folded her up into a large shopping bag and dropped her off a bridge late at night.

It has been almost two months since I found Billie. Weeks of trying to piece together what happened, of the girls hounding me for answers that seemed so obscure and out of my reach.

What little evidence there is about Billie's death has amounted to the murderer having a jeep, and being a man, a fact that, of course, threw me off the scent of the true killer. To be fair, I did note that Mrs Adamson had a jeep filled with items used at the crime scene . . . but what would a woman want with a little girl? I dismissed her as a suspect and turned my attentions to making sure Dad couldn't be the killer, wondering about Mr Kent, trying to bait the walker and, just briefly, suspecting and planning to kill Nathan.

When I managed to find Nick in the village, his aura, the feeling I got from him, confused me. He was sweeter to me than most adults. How could I imagine him killing me when he so obviously wanted to make everything okay? Later, after I realized he had shown me photographs of the dead girls, I had to admit he must be the killer. And yet . . . it didn't feel right, in my gut.

A gut feeling is a difficult thing to explain. It's not based in logic, although it's influenced by facts you pick up, here and there, and your experience of people in general. Mostly, however, it's intuition. Imagination, even. I have always had a big imagination. I had imaginary friends and I could always make up stories about people, with fantastical but convincing ideas embedded in them. But Nick? Nick didn't have the character of a killer. I couldn't extrapolate the story of a murder from his soft eyes and gentle hands.

And then Nathan told me what Nick said to him and Billie, about 'Mrs Adams'. Mrs Adamson, my teacher. It was too close to her name to be a coincidence. Perhaps, knowing what was in her boot, I would have figured it out sooner or later. But Billie's message made everything click into place. Mrs A is selfish, strange and oddly jealous. She looks out for herself and seems to blame everyone else for her own problems. And she said she would do anything to be with her husband. Maybe she can justify killing if she feels it necessary. The only thing I can't figure out was why she was always nice to Billie. She even said maybe Billie could visit her house, quite recently. At the time, we thought it was cool that a teacher would ask Billie over. I wasn't sure why, but I thought I was right about the rest of it, and I figured I could get in their house and ask.

Luckily, it doesn't take long to find out. When Nick looks up at her, Mrs A rearranges her face from annoyed to hurt. 'Sweetheart, I've only been up there five minutes.'

Nick gets off me and sits up next to me. 'I know. I'm sorry. The feeling is so strong.'

'But you said you liked *Billie*. I thought after her this might all stop. You *said* you'd try, Nick, you *said*.' She is on the edge of tears. I raise my eyebrows, listening. She looks over at me and I look away, pretending to be upset.

'I said that when we . . .' Nick looks at me and tousles my hair. '. . . we thought Billie would become my friend, for the long term.'

'But, Nick—'

'You're the one who decided that couldn't happen, Eve.'

'She *could* have been your friend if you hadn't gone too far that first time. If you had just talked to her, and not done what you did, she would have become your friend and then eventually you could . . .' She wipes her tears away. 'Oh my god, how are we having this conversation? Why is this my marriage? This is so unfair!'

'It's your choice to be in it,' I say.

'You—!' Mrs A – Eve – turns on me, but then she stops. She wants to explode at me, scream, call me names. But Nick is here. And in front of him she has to perform the good-girl act too. Only, for her, it's become the good-wife act. She has been playing it all her life, just going along with what he says, letting him have what he wants. Suddenly all this knowledge is arriving in my head like a series of big obvious signs. I feel like I am expanding to take in the whole universe. I understand everything.

And just like that, the dead girls are inside me.

I am having an out-of-body experience. I am on the ceiling, looking down at myself. I am in the woods as Billie, with Nick moving inside me. I am Ellie, in Florida, meeting Nick in a mall. I am Kerry, and Nick is stroking my hair. But I am other girls too, girls I haven't met yet. I am on a farm somewhere in Scandinavia, running around a wooden building away from someone, when I trip and fall on a piece of farming machinery and my foot is bleeding. I am in a desert and a man wrapped in towels is dragging me through the streets. I am somewhere hot and tropical and a man who speaks with an American accent is giving me money and my arms are brown. I'm in Nigeria, and men are coming at me and my sisters with guns. I'm in Washington, DC, under a bridge, choking on water. I'm in Germany, trapped in a cellar. I'm in Iraq, carrying a baby I resent because it's his. I'm back in England, wearing old-fashioned clothes and bleeding from the temple.

I am drowning in a lake. I am locked in a fridge on a dump and no one can hear me screaming. I am Billie, being strangled. I want to stay with her but quickly I move, assimilating the next ghost. I am small, under rubble. I am buried underground and when I breathe the dirt gets in my throat. I am fighting back, I am being stabbed with a knife in my belly, I am writhing my way out of ropes but I'm too late, I'm struggling, I'm scratching, I'm getting his skin under my fingernails.

I hear my breathing loud because it is joined by other breaths, and then suddenly they are all extinguished, yet still I know they are with me. I can feel their strength in my body.

The Scandinavian is strong and tall. Kerry is here; she is smart. Between them, the girls can speak 137 languages and I feel as if I could open my mouth and any one of them could come out. In there somewhere is a boxer. She's been doing it since she was four. When she died he tricked her, but together we will see them coming this time. We have eyes that see from every angle of my skull. Alexandra is a gymnast. Phoebe can drive, she learnt with her dad, he owns a race track in a paddock; it's muddy and fun. They each died alone, but together we have a chance. On our own, we are small, vulnerable, naive, slower, weaker, younger, helpless; but together, with so many voices and minds and skills and the years of many lives in one body, we have power; we can overcome Nick, rape, pain, even death.

Together, we are eternal. Nick is just one man. And Eve is just one woman.

When I get a hold of myself, I am on a double bed upstairs. It's like my eyeballs have been looking straight back into my head, but they shift a bit down so they are back in the right place, between my eyelids. I can see the ceiling. My breathing is steady, but I can hear it loud in my ears. It's the breathing of a hundred or more girls, maybe a thousand. My eyeballs ache. My ears hum. I can't move. I look left and right. 'Nick?'

'Shh, it's alright, sweetie,' Nick says. 'Just getting ready.' I hear sounds of splashing. 'Washing up. I want to be clean for you. You're so pure and clean, baby.'

My eyes roll around in my head and the words of an argument come back to me, as if from far away, down a long corridor in an echoey building, although I must have heard it downstairs, just moments ago.

'I need this. You know that. What I want doesn't hurt anyone. They love me too.'

'You'll be locked up if anyone finds out, and *every time you do it* is another chance of you getting caught.'

'I know, baby, I'm sorry. But I don't deserve to get locked up, and you knew I fell in love easily with young, beautiful women when you married me, because I fell in love with you, didn't I?'

My eyebrows rise, remembering the words that filtered through my ears when I was absorbing the power of the dead girls. Nick tricked her too. Eve was one of them. Kind of. But I don't feel sorry for her.

'And I'm not the one who thinks we need to do away with the evidence,' says Nick. 'That's what they would really lock me up for.'

'What do you mean?' Mrs A whines.

'Well,' Nick says softly, 'it's not like I'd let you go to prison, would I? You wouldn't last a day. I'd tell the police I killed the girls.'

Sniff, sniff. 'Would you really go to prison for me?' This is whimpered so pathetically by Mrs A that I want to pretend to be sick to make a point.

'Of course I would. I'd do anything for you, just like you do for me. I just need you to be respectful of my needs. I don't think you're being fair by crying.'

'Shh. Shh.' She nods and wipes tears from her eyes. 'I don't want to talk about it any more.'

'Okay.' Nick murmurs this soothingly. 'Okay, baby.'

I can just see them through a blur of light and colours and scenes from the girls' lives. Mrs A is clinging onto Nick like she is *actually* a baby and he is her mum. She looks at me with her lips all trembly and then buries her face in his shoulder. 'Nick,' she says. 'Nick, I can't lose you.'

'I know. I know you can't.'

'I get so scared.'

'It's okay. I'm here.'

Mrs A looks back towards me. 'I have to take her away, Nick.'

'No!' He sighs. 'She's here now. She could become my friend. Like I wanted Billie to be. If I just have one, that I can be with when I need, then there wouldn't need to be this . . . these sad occurrences.'

'When they die,' I whisper. We whisper, me and Billie and the rest. Nick looks at me as if we understand each other. We nod my head at him, as if we did.

'But the police are already on high alert!' Mrs A screams. 'As soon as they hear she's gone missing, they'll be blocking all roads to the area. They'll be searching every piece of woodland. This isn't a good idea. I have to . . .' She looks at me. 'To take her home.'

'Stop being loud!' Nick snaps. 'I'll be quick,' he says, and then he stands up and lets go of her.

'No, Nick!' she cries, and tries to grab hold of him. He slaps her away, hard on her face, and points a finger at her.

'Hey! Be good,' he says sharply.

She goes quiet and looks at me resentfully.

Nick turns to me. 'How about it, kiddo?'

'I don't really know what you're asking me,' I reply calmly.

'It's too dangerous. They'll come for you,' Mrs A whispers.

'Stop being a silly bitch, Eve,' Nick says.

I'm no fool. When he held out his hand for me, I stood up. The energy and anger and intelligence of all those girls pushed against my skin. My legs felt supercharged. I stumbled towards him. 'Oops, too much rum,' he laughed. But it wasn't the rum. It was the ghost girls crashing through my blood. I went with him, instead of staying there with Eve. My bag was beside her. I realized I wasn't going to die. Death was near, but not mine. I was going to finish what I came here to do. I'd be coming back for that bag in a minute.

I suddenly move from the memory of their argument to the present, on the double bed. The girls are inside me still. I hear them all breathing, even though this is something they don't do any more. Nick sits down on the side of the bed. He places his hand on my stomach. It's so large it covers it. He pats me gently. 'Well,' he says, smiling knowingly. 'Thera.'

He leans towards me.

When I come back downstairs, Mrs A is sat on the floor, her knees tucked up to her chest and her neck bent over them.

'He said he didn't want to be my permanent friend.'

'What?' she says, surprised.

'He said I did the wrong thing and to take me home right now.'

I pick up my rucksack and walk past her without further comment. It's like I'm made of supernatural steel. The ghost spirits run through me. They carry me along. We move together, we talk together. Mrs A is frowning, but when I walk out the door she grabs her keys and runs after me so I won't tell anyone. I open the car door, which is unlocked, and sit in the passenger seat. I put my ruck-sack on my lap and make sure to open it slightly before she gets in. She starts the engine. 'He said that?'

'He said I hurt his thingy,' I say, and turn to look out my window. 'He told me to fuck off. He said I wasn't worth the trouble.'

I'm not looking at her, but with my ghost powers I can feel her satisfaction. We back out of the drive, with her arm on the back of my seat. She looks at me and smiles, in a fake way. 'Not long 'til you're home now, Thera,' she says.

I smile back. 'That's right. Not long.'

We sit in silence for a little while, but my head is full of voices.

'*I died when I was nine.*'

'*He gave me a Barbie and told me to come with him.*'

'*We saw him in the sandpit.*'

'*I lost my life for a shrimp sweetie. I loved them. Now I don't taste. I don't touch. I just feel everything in my heart, so loudly that if I could scream it would kill a man.*'

'*This is it.*'

'*This is it.*'

'*This is it!*' The last one is Billie's voice.

Mrs Adamson heads out of town.

'You know, you and me have actually got a lot in common, Thera,' she says quietly, but sort of meanly, once we're in the countryside. I look over at her. There is make-up all down her cheeks from crying. I don't think we have a lot in common. I'm too brave not to have run away from a marriage with Nick. I'm too independent to need someone else just to exist. I wouldn't hate another girl like Mrs A hates the girls Nick likes – hates them enough to insist on killing them, and to be able to do it herself. That's not girl power. I look at my wrist and touch the two bracelets on it. Mine and Billie's. I found hers on Nick's bedside table while we were up in his room. But I know how she died. Mrs A killed her and she told Nick it was out of fear that Billie would tell and he would go to prison, but it wasn't. It was out of jealousy.

'We do?' I answer politely.

'Yes. We're both second place.'

'Oh.'

'Second place for Nick,' she mutters angrily. 'He wanted *you* before me.' She says this like this is preposterous and I'm disgusting. 'But he wanted Billie before you. We both cared about Billie. She betrayed us both.'

'No, she didn't,' I say, with Billie's voice in my head, her smile in my mouth. 'She didn't betray me.'

'She was there with that little traveller boy from the village, wasn't she? The one Nick says he's seen around you.'

'She didn't know he liked me.'

'They were kissing. Nick told me.'

'We were practising,' Billie says in my head. 'I wouldn't have kissed him if I'd known you liked him.'

'I know,' I tell her silently.

'They were practising,' I say out loud, and curl the fingers of my right hand into the hole in the zip of my bag.

'We both wanted the best for Billie,' Mrs Adamson continues, not paying attention to me. She sounds so sorry for herself. 'I know how you feel about her death, in a way. Because of how Nick treats me. Left behind . . . discarded.'

'You don't know anything about me,' I say. 'And Billie didn't leave me.'

'I know,' she turns to me. 'Nick killed her. He's a really bad man, Thera. You young girls ought to steer clear of him.'

'Mm-hmm,' I grin, and all the dead girls grin with me. 'Well, we will now.'

There's a bit of a silence as she turns onto the road to Otter's Plantation, the forestry commission land. It's full of pine trees, tall and dark, in long rows. The sun comes through them in shafts. The tarmac gets bumpy and full of potholes on the smaller road. 'This isn't the way to my house,' I tell the girls silently.

'We know,' they whisper back in unison.

'You're so lucky you're young,' Mrs Adamson says to me, as if she has been thinking about this for a while.

'I suppose,' I reply. We're on the track that leads to the World War Two bunkers. They are made of thick cement, and are deep and creepy. The heavy metal doors don't have locks any more, but they are so thick you can't hear through them, not even if a person in the bunker cried out in pain. 'Excellent,' I whisper. The dead girls curl my lips back in a grin. 'Stop it,' I whisper to them. 'I have to look little and frightened. Like a victim.'

They laugh, and it echoes around my skull and in the hollow cavity of my chest.

'What?'

'Yeah, we get holidays and pocket money,' I say encouragingly. 'Those are nice things about being young.'

'Hmm. I didn't mean like that.'

'And sweeties.'

'Now, that *is* a point!' she agrees. 'I always have to watch my weight, but you eat whatever you want!'

'Yeah.' It's really difficult to hear her. It's like I'm in the haunting realm, the spirit world, and she is on earth. There are so many girls whispering excitedly in my body. They are all inside me, laying their bets on me to get them to heaven. I won't let them down.

'And you're not grateful at all, are you?'

'Huh?'

'You're not! You don't know how lucky you are.'

'Well . . .' I think about this, try to concentrate. 'I wish I had more say over stuff. Like—'

'You're just ungrateful,' she complains.

I shrug, not caring now. I'm tired of making small talk. I can't wait for what's coming. The energy is surging around my body, making my legs and hands shake and jitter. My fingers grasp the end of a sock. 'Whatever.'

'To be young and pretty and not have any hard choices to make or compromises or men that . . .' Her lips tremble again. 'He loves me, I know. He can't help it. I've seen him try. But you're his type, aren't you?'

The dead girls are thundering in my head behind Mrs A's boring drone. She looks at me as if she expects me to reply, and I stare at her for a second and then say, 'Who? Nick?'

'Mr Adamson. My husband,' she says, like I'm stupid.

'So . . . Nick?'

'Yes! Nick. But don't call him that.'

She's so ridiculously jealous. Why? He's good-looking, but he's totally insane. Was. Totally insane. 'Did you know he killed Billie?' I ask innocently, half expecting her to confess to Billie's murder now.

She looks away. 'Only after the fact, of course.'

I grin while she can't see. So she isn't going to own up to it. She would let him take the rap. 'So you didn't suspect anything while it was happening?'

'No, no.'

'Even though you were parked in a jeep outside the woods?'

'You heard us talking, Thera – I just thought he was going to spend some time with her.'

What an idiot. It's like she thinks I wasn't listening earlier when they talked about him going to prison for her. 'So what's his type?'

'Young girls, petite, blonde.' She is getting angrier. That's good.

'Not you, then?' I say, winding her up.

'Of course me!' she squeaks. 'I'm still young. And he like red hair better than blonde, anyway. It's just too rare to be his "type".'

'Well, you dye it.'

'What?'

'You're not natural ginger, are you? Bet you're grey underneath.'

'What are you doing? Stop saying things like that.'

I look into the dark of the woods. 'Are you taking me home, then? Like he said?'

She looks at me and seems to catch herself. 'Of course. This is a shortcut.'

'Cool,' I say. 'It's funny you didn't suspect that he would kill her.'

'Yes,' she says quickly, her nicest voice. It's still obviously fake. 'Yes, I suppose it was funny I didn't suspect anything.' She looks into the distance again, ahead of us. She has turned onto the track into the woods now. 'He would often talk about their skin, how their skin was so different from older women's.'

'Really?'

'But his favourite thing was that they were so timid,' she whispers to herself. 'They made him feel like a god, but like an adoring, worshipping . . .' She shudders.

We – the dead girls and me – all play the good-girl game, and we turn my head to her sweetly, batting my eyelashes. 'Did they make you feel like a god too?'

'What?' she laughs nervously. 'What a thing to ask! Haven't we cleared this up already? Nick's the murderer. I'm just an innocent bystander.'

'I know. I didn't mean it like that.'

'Good.' She frowns. 'That's settled, then.'

'Why are we in the woods?'

'It's quicker this way. It's a detour. I wanted to show you something.' She slows the car down so we can park. We take my hand slowly out of the side of my bag. 'It'll be a little secret, between you and me. It's just ahead, beyond those trees.'

I laugh. That's where the bunkers are.

She looks at me. Maybe something dawns there, and maybe it doesn't.

'You must think I'm bloody stupid,' I say, and the ghost girls' voices are in my voice, and it howls and haunts and sounds like the scraping of skin off flesh, off bone. And then we whack her on the head as hard as we can with the brick-in-the-sock.

When I came up from the bunker it was about six in the evening; bright and pleasant. I squinted down the path through the trees, my hand shading my eyes, but there was no one in sight. There were usually some walkers around and I was kind of relying on one for a lift. I wouldn't have taken one from a man, because even though Nick wasn't a killer, his weird perverted urges were still the catalyst for everything that happened to Billie, but there are usually families and people with dogs wandering around at tea-time. I walked all the way around the bunker and called out. The sound of my voice rose above the trees, sounding lonely and like it was spreading wide above them, filling the sky and scaring the birds. Some of them took off from the treetops. I decided everyone was probably eating tea at home. Hopefully I could get a lift on the road. There was no one at all in the forest as I walked back to the track; no cars as I passed through the car park, except Eve's jeep, crashed into a tree, the driver's-side door still open. I closed it, so no dogs or people could jump in there and disturb the evidence.

I felt exhausted, depleted, as if the dead girls had taken something of me with them when they went, and now there was nothing left inside me. It was silent in my head, and I couldn't decide, as I walked through the rows of pines with their nice winter smell, if the silence was peaceful or cold or good or evil. It was weird to think the atmosphere of the forest could be changed by something people had done, especially by something I had done, but I think that was what had happened. The trees whispered to each other and looked at me funny. I waved back at them tiredly, my arms heavy.

It took me just over an hour to walk the three miles back to Eastcastle. First I took the small road down through farmland, and then I joined the Viking Way, a footpath with birches and brambles either side making it like a tunnel running parallel to the road. I came back onto the main road half a mile out of town. By this time, I was almost falling asleep, even though I was walking. I tried to hitch a lift into town and stuck my hand out with my thumb up, like people do in films, but it didn't work and I gave up. A girl a few years older than me even sped up when she caught my eye. Luckily Eastcastle is in a valley, so I let my feet fall in front of each other and momentum carried me down the hill.

My eyes were closing and opening in starts and fits, and I tried to imagine Billie walking beside me along the road, but I couldn't make her be there. I tried to conjure the other dead girls, but they wouldn't come either. The atmosphere wasn't ghostly any more. It just felt done: an atmosphere of something having ended, a bit like my last day in primary school.

I guess the dead girls had gone to the cloud kingdom, satisfied with what we had done. I let the rest of them go in my mind, but I tried over and over again to get Billie to be walking beside me. I wanted to say a last goodbye, to tell her she'd always be my best, true, forever friend, even though she wasn't alive any more. I could see totally well in my mind's eye the way she crinkled up her nose when she laughed, as if our jokes were always gross. (A lot of the time they were.) I could hear the sound of her voice but I couldn't make her appear and I couldn't make her talk. That is why, I realized, Billie was Billie and I was me. Billie always made up what she said, the stupid limericks and jokes she would tell, the funny impressions and her gurgly laugh. I couldn't do it. Billie was capable of being Billie, and I'm capable of being me. Billie wasn't there to be her anymore, to make up those limericks and sing silly songs. She wasn't anywhere. She wasn't with her parents, or haunting the woods, or waiting for me in my room with other dead girls. Now I had enacted vengeance, she was gone, her spirit at rest. I guess that's for the best. Maybe, on some level, I thought finding her killer and bringing her to justice would bring Billie back to me, but it hadn't. Even though she was better off in heaven, I felt alone, and broken, without my friend. I realized I would never see her again. A part of me would always be gone. The part of my heart that was Billie's.

On the last steep slope into town, I start to cry.

Either side of the road are houses, and I pass a few people, but they don't look at me. They are busy doing other things, getting shopping out of their cars, gardening and calling 'Don't run!' at their kids.

I take a cut-through that leads to the swimming pool and walk over a playing field to the police station. It is teatime, and as I walk past the last houses before the station I look in the windows and see lights on and people sitting down to eat, carrying casserole dishes and salad bowls in from their kitchens. I wipe my face on my arm before I go into the station, getting rust-coloured tears on my skin, and then walk up the steps, under the blue-and-white police sign.

I push open the door, leaving a smear of blood on the white paint. I blink and stop just inside the doorway, my eyes adjusting to the light, and see the lady detective, Georgie, leant over the shoulder of a man at the reception desk. They are both looking at something on the desk that I can't see. She looks up, drops her pen to the floor and shouts, 'Thera!'

'Oh good,' I say tiredly. 'You're here.'

She flies around the corner of the big built-in desk and runs to me, which is weird because the room is small and I am not far away. As she approaches me she bends over to my height and grabs my arms, then my face, looking into my eyes. 'Are you alright?' she shouts. 'Who did this to you?'

'No one,' I say. 'What?'

'Call an ambulance!' Georgie turns and shouts to the man at the desk. 'Now!' Other police officers are running out from the back, where the little cells and the interrogation room are. She looks at me again and pulls up my T-shirt. 'Where are you hurt, Thera? Where are you bleeding?'

'It's not my blood.'

She frowns. 'What happened? Did someone hurt one of your friends?'

'No . . .' I sigh, suddenly tired. I feel faint. Maybe my blood sugar is low. I saw a diabetic on the telly once. 'Can I have a biscuit?'

'Thera, sweetheart.' Georgie looks back and forth into my eyes. She even puts her fingers on them and holds the lids open. 'Did anybody give you anything strange to eat or drink today?'

'No,' I say, forgetting about the tea Nick gave me because I'm so tired.

'You're not hurt?'

'No, course not.'

'*Was* one of your friends hurt?'

'No.'

The police people continue to run around us, out the door, and to call to each other loudly. A man officer runs towards me with a towel and puts it around me. I wonder for a moment if I am shaking, but I don't feel much. He rubs my arms with the towel, but Georgie takes it at both sides, tugging it round me, and wipes at my face, pushing my hair back from my forehead.

'Thera,' she whispers almost nervously.

'Yes?'

Georgie hesitates, studies me all over, up and down, with her eyes. 'You're covered in blood.'

I look down, pinching my T-shirt between my hands. It is red, a darkness that has soaked down into my skirt and dried on the walk back, becoming an itchy crust that sticks to my skin. I look at my hands and start to pick it out of the beds of my fingernails.

Georgie stands up. 'I'm taking her to an interview room,' she tells the young policeman. 'Get Chief Inspector Macintyre.'

'It's . . . He's at home today.'

'Yes, I know!' she snaps. 'Just do it, will you?'

Georgie has her hand on the back of my neck, like when Felix, our school cat, had kittens, and picked them up in her mouth by their scruffs. (People touching me again. I really can't stand it any more.) She steers me past the desk and down a corridor into a little room. Everywhere looks old-fashioned, and the ceilings are high and arched and have cream-painted bricks. The little room has blue soundproofing fabric on the walls, and not much in it but a table, two chairs, and a jumble of different cassette players stacked on top of one another in a corner. She plonks me firmly down on one of the chairs. I try to shuffle it closer to the table, but it is bolted to the floor, so I lean forward to rest my arms on the table, then lay the side of my head on them, turned towards Georgie. I can barely keep my eyes open.

'Can I have a biscuit?' I say. 'And some tea?'

She blinks at me as if considering something, then rubs her eyes in a troubled way. 'Did anyone force anything in your mouth? Because if they did . . . before you drink we should swab—'

'No, nobody did. Please, Georgie, I'm really thirsty.'

'I'll get you some tea,' she says, turning.

I relax, then I remember. 'Oh! Georgie!'

'Yes?'

'This is for you.' I hand her the audio recorder, which I have been carrying in my left hand since the bunker. I realize now my hand is cramping badly. It shakes as I hold out the bloody machine.

'One second,' Georgie says, and runs from the room. She comes back holding plastic gloves and a clear plastic bag. She pulls the gloves on delicately and takes the recorder from me. 'What is it?' she asks.

I am distracted, massaging my painful hand. 'Um, the confession.'

She looks down at it and slips it into the bag. 'Hmm.' She turns and marches out of the room. 'I'll get your tea,' she says at the door. 'Wait here.'

I don't see her come back. Instead, I wake up with my cheek pressed against the table, and a Family Circle box and a cup of tea next to my head. My throat is dry, and I reach immediately for the tea and swallow. It is almost cold. Still, I open the biscuits, take out one with jam and cream in, and hold it in the tea, to make it soggy. I chomp it down, and pick up a custard cream. When I have worked my way through five or six biscuits, I start to get curious about why I am alone. It seems like I might have been asleep for a while. I can see through a tiny window in the door that the corridor is darker than before. I stand up and walk to the door, but it is locked. I knock on the glass, quietly at first, and then louder, until Georgie rounds the corner. At first, she doesn't see me – she has her head down – but then she looks up. I wave and point to the door, mouthing, 'Can you let me out?'

She starts to walk towards the door, but then an older police officer, a man, the one I saw with her in the woods when Billie was found, appears and takes hold of her arm. He steps in front of her and they argue briefly, but the door must be soundproof because I can't hear a thing. Just then he seems to call for someone, and a woman in green ambulance clothes walks around the corner. She looks like the people who took Billie's body away. The policeman walks towards the door, taking some keys off Georgie. He unlocks it and walks towards me, into the room, so I have to back up for everyone to enter.

'Hiya,' I say. 'I'm tired. Can I go home now?'

'You'll have to wait,' he replies with a Scottish accent. 'This lady is going to take some swabs of the blood on you.'

'For evidence?' I nod. 'Sure. But if I have to stay for a bit, can I have some warmer tea?'

'Waters,' the man says, and Georgie picks up my mug and hurries out.

The woman squats by me. 'This won't hurt. Open your mouth, please.' She sticks in a swab and rubs the inside of my cheek, then uses tweezers to scrape a bit of blood out of my nails and into a tiny clear pot. 'Hold out your hands, dear.' She looks me all over and pulls a bit of ginger hair off my sleeve. It's caked in the crusty blood. She puts it in another pot, then gives me a clean T-shirt that belongs to the police, so I put that on and they take away my old one, for evidence. Finally she nods at the man and leaves the room.

He kind of harrumphs. 'Sit down.'

I sit in my chair again, and he sits in the one across the table and leans in to me, frowning. It feels weirdly threatening. But then I realize I am probably just feeling weird because I am still thinking that, being a man, he might kill or touch me, and obviously now I know the pervert and killer have been taken care of, it's okay. I relax.

'I am Chief Inspector Macintyre.'

I nod. 'I've seen you around.'

'Well, yes.'

We sit in silence for a moment.

'Waiting for Waters to come back,' he says awkwardly, staring at me.

I eat another biscuit and Georgie arrives a few minutes later, holding my tea.

'Thanks,' I say, and take it hungrily, dipping a Bourbon into it.

'Thera,' says Chief Inspector Macintyre. 'I just want to let you know your parents are here.'

'They are?'

'Yes.'

'Where?'

'In the – in reception,' says Georgie.

Macintyre glares at her and then turns to me. 'I want to interview you this afternoon . . . as a suspect for the murder of Eve Adamson. Detective Waters is present, as a suitable second party is required to be in the case of minors, but would you like one of your parents here while we talk?'

I think about this, and shake my head. 'Probably not. They'd be annoyed at me.'

'Why do you think they would be annoyed at you?'

'They thought I was being good and not thinking about the murderer, but I wasn't. I was just acting good. I'm a good actress. I was tricking them so they would unground me and then I could go out whenever I wanted and find the killer.'

Macintyre draws back, still eyeing me weirdly. He scratches his stubbly chin and flips open a notebook. 'We're going to record this interview, Thera. Do you understand?'

'Sure,' I say. 'I'm really smart. I know how police interviews work.'

He nods to Georgie, who presses a button on a big machine on the desk.

'I have lots of questions for you,' Macintyre says.

'About what?'

He looks stern and I don't know why, but I do know I am getting tired of people looking stern at me. What do they want from me? I've caught the killer. I handed her to them on a plate. They hadn't done a bloody thing and I managed it all! 'About what happened on the tape.'

I fold my arms, just like him, and look stern back. 'What about the tape?'

TRANSCRIPT: AUDIO CASSETTE TAPE
Recorded Tuesday 17 August 1999
Recorded by: Thera Wilde
(age 11, D.O.B. 1 April 1988)

Two voices on tape:
Thera Wilde (age 11, D.O.B. 1 April 1988) [TW]
Eve Adamson (age 28, D.O.B. 23 January 1971) [EA]

Tape on, approximately 16.30 hours.

Sound: heavy breathing
Sound: zip
Sound: metallic clattering sound

TW: Wake up, Mrs A! Wakey, wakey! I didn't know you were called Eve.

EA: Oh my god, what? Oh, my head.

TW: Can you sit up, please? I need to talk to you about something.

EA: What's happening? What the fuck is this?

TW: Don't swear at me. I'm giving you a chance. To tell me your side of the story.

EA: Where's Nick? [*screaming*] NICK! NICK!

TW: Stop shouting. No one is going to hear you, are they? You brought me to a deserted bunker.

EA: I didn't bring you here! You dragged me here! Oh, my whole body is sore.

TW: [*sighs*] Urgh, stop moaning. We're bored of you.

EA: We?

TW: Er, I. I'm bored of you.

Clanging of metal.

EA: [*panic*] What are you doing? What's that?

TW: I know you killed Billie. I want to know why.

EA: No, I didn't! No, I didn't! It was Nick. He's sick. It's not his fault. He goes crazy if he doesn't do it!

TW: Do what?

EA: You know.

TW: Why don't you tell me?

EA: You know already! Pretending to be innocent. Flirting with him. I knew your game, you little—

TW: Little what?

Beat of silence.

TW: Were you about to use bad language again?

EA: You led him on. Where is he?

TW: At your home.

EA: He'll be after you! He'll be coming to find me. I always go home right after. I always go straight back to him.

TW: Right after what?

EA: What?

TW: You said you always go home right after. Right after what?

EA: Nothing. After nothing. After he gets with the girls.

TW: [*laughs*] You mean after you kill them and clean up after him?

EA: No! No I didn't say that. Don't be silly, Thera.

TW: For a teacher, you're really pretty stupid.

EA: It's him! I have nothing to do with it!

TW: Well, if you're not going to say what you did, I will. He went into the woods with Billie, and you waited in the car, like a getaway driver.

EA: I'm his [*shouts*] WIFE. I wouldn't wait in the car while he—

TW: [*interrupts*] Nick raped Billie. He wasn't meant to, just then – he was meant to wait, so she could become a regular girlfriend for him, but he couldn't. You got curious – no, jealous – and so you walked into the woods. You were probably muttering to yourself 'what's taking so long', when really you knew anyway. Then she was scream-ing, and you ran in and said stop it, now we'll have to kill her because otherwise she'll tell on you. And your pervy husband said no, I want to keep going.

EA: Shut up, you little witch, shut [*shouts*] UP!

TW: I will if you tell me what really happened.

EA: Just shut your fucking mouth. [*emphasis*] Shut your fuck-ing mouth!

TW: I bet Nick fancied Billie way, way, way more than he fan-cied you. And he likes me better too. If you weren't around, he'd be with one of us. A girl. Not a woman.

EA: No! No, he wouldn't, that's a lie! You're a liar!

TW: I'm eleven. Why do you care what I think? Oh yeah, because your husband's a perv for eleven-year-old girls.

EA: [*shouts*] NO. Fuck you, you little slut! I'm going to fucking kill you, you stupid bitch, you horrible, disgusting piece of [*squeals*] AH!

TW: I said stop swearing.

EA: [*unclear*]

TW: So you're going to kill me, are you? Like you killed Billie after you saw Nick loved her more than he loved you?

EA: No, no that's not what happened. I saw that little boy run out of the woods and I went in to tell him! I knew the boy would tell on him. I didn't want the police to take him away. You understand, Thera. He's my husband.

TW: That little boy is my friend Nathan, and he's actually almost as tall as you. Nathan's the one who told me your jeep was at the woods today. So you were right. He did tell on you. To me.

EA: Well, I probably should have done something about him, then, shouldn't I? [*mutters*] I might when I get out of here.

TW: [*murmurs*] You're not getting out of here.

EA: What?

TW: So you're confessing? You killed Billie?

EA: Why would I confess about something like that to you?

TW: Why not? Get it off your chest.

EA: You'll tell someone.

TW: I won't let you go until you confess. And then I will.

EA: Why . . . why would you do that? Let me go?

TW: I only want to know why you did it. I'm so sad about it. But you have to promise you won't hurt me when I let you go.

EA: Promise?

TW: Yes. You have to cross your heart and hope to die.

EA: Okay.

TW: Okay? You promise?

EA: Yes. I promise.

TW: So . . . you killed Billie.

EA: [*whispers*] Yes. I killed her. Is that what you wanted to know, Thera? [*calm*] I wrung her neck, and then I drove Nick home, and then I came straight back and dressed her, burnt her to get the DNA off her, cleared up his mess, his

. . . condom. He didn't even use them in the beginning. I made him start, so he wouldn't leave DNA evidence. I do everything that needs to be done but that he won't do. [*cries*] Do you know how hard that is for me?

TW: Did she say anything? A funny comeback or last words?

EA: No. She was out of it already. He gave her a pill, I think.

TW: That's how Billie died? That seems so . . . so lame. Her whole life just gone. Just like that?

EA: Why do you care so much? [*sniffing*] She was your rival. You looked exactly the same, you did everything together, but she was prettier and more popular. Now you have no competition.

TW: Billie was my friend.

EA: Puh.

TW: She was my friend.

Beat of silence.

TW: You don't have any friends at all, do you?

EA: I have Nick. He's all I need. We have been in love since the moment we met.

Beat of silence.

TW: Why did you go back to the woods today? Are you sad about Billie? Or do you just feel sorry for yourself because your hubby likes kids?

EA: [*sighs*] He doesn't like them more than me. He just has a compulsion. He has to have them occasionally. That's not my fault, is it?

TW: Why do you kill them?

Beat of silence.

TW: Go on. It's only me here. I just want to know.

EA: Because if I don't, they'll tell, and I'll lose him.

Beat of silence.

EA: Is that it?

TW: Is there anything else?

Beat of silence.

EA: Yes, actually. You're looking at me like I'm so terrible. You think I'm so different from you, that you couldn't be me. But I'm going to tell you why it isn't my fault. I'm going to tell you a story . . . about a little girl just like you.

EA: I folded her up into a large shopping bag and dropped her off a bridge late at night. I felt almost . . . that I'd got away with it . . . [*whispers*] powerful, and excited.

TW: Excited?

EA: No, no, that's wrong. But it felt strangely empowering, to have such affect on a life that you could end it, to know I was in control of something, when I felt under Nick's control in so many ways. When we got back to England, we talked about the little girl, and we agreed no more small children. I knew about men. Full of sexual perversions. Nick wasn't like the others, he really wasn't. He didn't force anyone. He liked to make them feel good, feel beautiful, understand their sexuality when it was just becoming real to them. They always wanted him. Always.

TW: What about Ellie?

EA: Who?

TW: The little girl.

EA: I didn't tell you her name.

TW: Wasn't it Ellie?

EA: I . . . I don't know. I don't know what it was. Stop interrupting me, I'm trying to explain something to you. Nick has always been strong and powerful and handsome. Why wouldn't everyone want him? Want to drown in him? To do him every favour, sexual and otherwise; to do everything he asks? After I helped him out with the little girl, he worshipped me even more, bought me more beautiful things, I felt that he loved me completely and would never leave me. I felt secure for the first time in my life. We had a bond that couldn't be broken. We would die without each other. He kept seeing girls, but not *little* girls. Only girls that wanted him and knew what they were doing. That had . . . gone through puberty. Become adults. We had conversations when we agreed on these rules. They were difficult at first but I saw he couldn't help how he felt. He loved them too much. And he didn't plan anything, he just got swept up in things. When he saw Billie in the village, he called me and said you need to come with the jeep, I think it's going to happen again, and it needs to happen now. I'd been . . . preparing Billie. We thought if he just had one girl, if he could keep things reasonable . . . someone who had gone through puberty, who would touch him of her own free will, and if he didn't go too far with her, didn't hurt her, then we wouldn't have to go to the trouble of . . . disposing of her. We went looking for her and saw her on the fields. He was going crazy just wanting to talk to her. I said that's it, you just talk. No more. We need to take it slowly this time. You need to take it slowly. We had been discussing for a while about how to approach her, how to be intimate without risking too much. Possibly I would invite her over, or find her in the village and drive her home on the promise of . . . cake or . . . Well, ultimately, it didn't work. When he saw her that day he had to have her. I knew I had to be there, in case . . . to clean up the mess. Believe me, Thera, he doesn't want to be like this. He doesn't plan it, he can't control it, it just happens, quickly, before he's realized what he's doing. He can't help himself. It's a disease. You can't blame someone who has a disease.

TW: It was like he couldn't help himself.

EA: Exactly. Thera, you don't know what it's like to be so lonely and overlooked – you're bright, you're popular – and then to have someone come into your life and love you. Nick is a good man. He doesn't deserve prison. It's not his fault. If you had been there, if you could see him, you would understand. How distraught he was afterwards. I couldn't let him be taken away. After the little girl in Florida, I gave him permission to bring the next girl home while I was away visiting my parents. She liked him, so she was into the things he wanted to do. They stopped doing things when she started to get upset that he sometimes hurt her. I told him to be more careful; we didn't want a repeat of the Florida episode. But then the next one was a girl from the school where he was working as a teaching assistant, on a temporary contract. He had to leave work and he had this compulsion to have her. At first, she came home with him because she liked him. They all did. But then he drugged her. I was away again; I wasn't there to stop him. When I got back, I said what was he trying to do, the police were going to come. She was hurt, she was crying. Being in that much pain, it was a mercy to end her life, just like when I found the little girl, half-dead; like when I found Billie. I had him blindfold the girl from his school, and then I stopped her breathing. [*tuts*] Our whole room was . . . in disarray. Her clothes were everywhere . . . They looked like they had been having a party there.

TW: You didn't like him being there with her.

EA: Well, she knew he was married! These girls know. He wears a ring on his finger. They know what they're getting into. But they'll go and tell on him afterwards anyway, won't they? As if they aren't to blame at all. As if they didn't want to fuck him.

TW: You wanted him to stay with you.

EA: Fucking a girl under sixteen is an automatic prison sentence. I couldn't let that happen. He was so happy, so grateful again when the next girl died. It gave me a power I . . .

TW: And there were others?

EA: A few. A homeless girl and . . . a few.

TW: And then Billie.

EA: Yes. But Billie was meant to be different. He was meant to take his time, gain her trust. Except he couldn't wait. Didn't wait. She was near the end when I found her. I just made it quick. Nick has his flaws but he tries not to go through with it, he really does. I'm the only one who understands because I've been there with him through everything. I've always been completely dependent upon him, but when I cleared up his mess those times, I saw how he is dependent upon me too. He needs me.

TW: To kill the girls.

EA: No, no. No, Thera. He needs me because he loves me. We're in love. We can't live without each other. Love sweeps you up into situations you can't control, and you have to make the best choice you can at the time. It begs to survive, deep inside you. You know to keep it alive you'll do anything. You're like a slave to love. A slave to each other. So you see why I had to do it. It's not my fault. I'm a victim too.

EA: Are you going to let me go now, Thera?

TW: Why?

EA: Why what?

TW: Why would I do that?

EA: Because you see now why I did what I did. It's not fair for any of us. I'm just like you. I've always thought we had a lot in common, Thera, always. And I'm going to tell Nick off this time, I really am. What he did to you was terrible.

TW: How do you know? You were downstairs.

EA: I just do. It's very painful.

TW: Well, it wasn't that terrible. Certainly it's not best for me that I die after it.

EA: That's not what I meant.

TW: Anyway, I've done it before.

EA: What?

TW: Yeah, with Nathan Nolan. So don't act like a know-it-all.

EA: Goodness, I—

TW: What about Jenny Ann Welder?

EA: What?

TW: Didn't Nick kill her?

EA: Erm . . . Why are you asking about her? She was in Scotland. We don't live in Scotland.

TW: I got the impression he might have killed her.

EA: From who?

TW: Um. No one. Did he?

EA: Who have you been talking to?

TW: Did he kill her?

EA: I . . . don't know, Thera, I don't . . . follow him around everywhere.

TW: Have you been to Scotland recently?

Beat of silence.

EA: We went there on a short holiday in March. I suppose . . . Gosh, I suppose he *could* have killed her.

TW: It's so weird that you never suspected anything.

EA: Well, that's all finished now. Nick. The girls.

TW: Oh, really? How are you going to end it?

EA: I'm going to go to the police. And tell them about Nick. Then he'll stop. It's gone on too long.

TW: He's already been stopped.

EA: Pardon?

TW: I said he's already been stopped. He won't ever hurt another little girl again. And, as a bonus, I think he will be a deterrent for paedophiles and pervs everywhere. Hopefully it'll be in all the newspapers.

EA: What? Why would he be a deterrent?

TW: Because I killed him.

EA: No, you didn't.

TW: Yes, I did. He's dead.

EA: No, he isn't.

TW: We left and he didn't even say goodbye, did he? He was upstairs, on the bed, bleeding from his head. The base of your lamp made a good weapon. I think it was, like, marble, right?

EA: You're lying.

TW: No, I'm not. He crawled on top of me. I got the lamp and swung it at his head. It was one thud. Then we switched places, and I bounced on top of him hitting him with the lamp over and over again.

EA: No. No. He's too strong! You're tiny!

TW: I overpowered him.

EA: You couldn't do that alone!

TW: Oh, I wasn't alone.

EA: You weren't?

TW: Nope.

EA: Who else was there? I didn't see anyone.

TW: [*calmly*] You've met two of them, apparently.

EA: [*louder*] I've met them? Is it your school friends? Is there another one of you little sickos somewhere in the woods?

TW: In fact, there's quite a few of us little sickos here, Eve. And you know what? We're all mad at you.

Screaming.

Banging.

Wet sounds.

Light footsteps coming closer [to the tape recorder]. A noise as it is picked up.

Tape ends.

Shortly after they play the tape for us to listen to, they bring Billie's bag and her diary and Nano Pet into the room, and I have to identify them as the things she had on her that day. Nick had them in a cupboard, along with keepsakes from the other girls, including Ellie's My Little Pony and the older girl's school tie. They tell me they've found him, on the bed in his and Mrs A's house. The whole interview is much more exciting than the one on the night Billie went missing. I feel finally like I'm being helpful, and adults are taking me seriously. We really get into the nitty-gritty of things.

I tell them how I realized Mrs Adamson had been involved (minus Billie's message). I tell them how I had made a plan. When Nathan saw the jeep, he would run immediately over to my house and I would run back with him and get in the jeep. I didn't tell Nathan this part of the plan. I remember tucking myself down as the jeep drove away, a final vision of him running out into the road, calling my name. I knew he wouldn't agree to the whole thing. To avenging Billie's death by killing her killer. If the plan didn't work the first time, I was willing to wait and keep trying. If it had been in term time, I would have been able to climb in Mrs A's car and go home with her from school, but without Nathan I couldn't have found her. It wasn't term time any more, and I didn't know where she lived, and I didn't know how to differentiate her jeep from all the other bloody jeeps that drive around the village all the time.

My plan was to get to their house in the jeep, tie them both up and get them to confess to Billie's rape and murder, and then kill them and tape the entire thing. In the event, I was alone with him upstairs and I didn't want him to rape me, so I had to kill him then, and quickly, so Eve didn't hear anything. That was why I hit him so hard the first time with the lamp. After that he was pretty much dead, I think. On the way, anyway. Like what Mrs A said about Ellie. Then we went to the woods, and I thought that was perfect because I would have plenty of time to talk to her and no one would disturb us. Which maybe is what she wanted from me, although I expect she would have preferred me just to listen to her go on and on.

After I have finished explaining all of this, Macintyre gives me a cold stare and says, 'We played a little of your tape for your parents.'

'You probably shouldn't play the whole thing for them.'

'Quite,' he says.

I laugh and take a sip of my tea. I feel better now I have had some sleep, and seeing their faces look so amazed at what I have been able to accomplish has cheered me up. I enjoyed getting the confession out of Eve, but I'm relieved that it's over. In fact, the sense of relief is making me feel light-headed. Kind of euphoric – Grandad word! – and powerful. Which, weirdly, is what Eve said she felt like after killing the girls . . .

It's confused in my head now. This afternoon feels like a long time ago, and all blurry. She said she felt kind of powerful, though, and I do too. Except I've killed bad guys. And I could kill more bad guys now I know how easy it is. Maybe the dead girls will come back and help me! When I tune back in from this thought, Chief Inspector Macintyre is talking.

'The problem with this tape, Thera, is that, yes, it shows Eve killed Billie, but it also shows that you planned to kill Eve, and then executed that plan when she was defenceless, in cold blood.'

'Well, it wouldn't have been very clever to attack her when she could defend herself, would it? She's bigger than me.'

'*Why* did you kill Eve, Thera?' Macintyre asks.

'Because she deserved to die.' I don't understand why he doesn't get it.

He pauses, rubs his lips together and looks at Georgie. She seems nervous, standing near the door, balancing with her hand on the back of a plastic chair and one foot scratching the back of the other. He turns back to me. 'Did you feel threatened by Eve when you decided to kill her?'

'Not really. She was tied up.'

'So there wasn't a possibility that she could kill you?'

'Well, if she wasn't tied up, obviously she would have tried.'

'Were you worried she would break free?'

'Oh, no. I used three nylon cable ties around her wrists and ankles.'

'Where did you get those?'

'From the hardware shop near Nanny and Grandad's.'

'And why did you use cable ties instead of rope?'

'I went to look for some rope, but they were in the same aisle, and they looked like they'd be more effective.'

'We know that you were in a bunker in the woods.'

'That's right. Did you find it okay? Because I didn't move her or anything. And I left the door open so you could get in.'

'We did. How did you end up there?'

'She drove me there. Then when she drove down the track to the car park, I knew for sure she was going to try to kill me.'

'What happened then?'

I smile and lean forward over the table. 'I bashed her on the head with my brick-in-a-sock, and then I took the sock off and taped it in her mouth. I should have brought another sock, but I didn't think of that,' I add. 'Then I tied her up and dragged her to the bunker.'

'And the tape starts from when you arrived at the bunker?'

'Just about, yeah.'

He sighs. He seems to be taking issue with something, but I don't understand what. When I told him about the brick-in-the-sock I expected he would be glad, and tell me how well I had done. I mean, I went up against two killers and I didn't die! And I'm eleven and smaller than both of them. *And* they've killed plenty of girls my age. I frown.

'You know they killed Jenny Ann Welder, right?'

Macintyre looks at Georgie and then back at me. 'Why did you think that Thera?'

'It's obvious! From the tape. Eve is totally lying.'

'Yes, well. We'll look into that. But what I meant is why did you *originally* suspect that they had something to do with her disappearance?'

Well . . .' I hesitate. I don't want to tell the police about the dead girls. Adults won't believe me about them, unless they are cool, like Grandad. They might think I'm going crazy if I say the ghost of Jenny Ann Welder and Billie's ghost and a bunch of her dead friends told me to kill Nick and Eve. In the end, I say, 'I saw about Jenny on TV. Ages ago, when she went missing. So I thought . . . maybe . . .'

'We don't know if it's connected in any way, Thera,' Georgie says quietly.

'But they never found her killer, right?'

'No, but they had a suspect. He fled the country.'

'I'm pretty sure they did it. Check Nick's wallet. Check the pictures.'

'We're searching their house now. We'll find evidence if they did kill Jenny, or other girls,' Georgie says.

'Why do they suspect this other guy?'

'He . . . killed a young girl before. He served a prison sentence. He was quite old.'

I gape and then bang my fist on the table. 'So he's still out there? Another perv who kills girls?'

'Calm down, Thera, this is a police interview,' Macintyre says. 'We need you to stay calm.'

'Well, who's looking for this other guy? Is someone going after him?'

Georgie and Macintyre exchange a look. 'Why, Thera?' says Macintyre. 'Would you?'

'Me? Well, I would if no one else is doing it. He needs to be stopped! No wonder—' I was going to say no wonder there were so many dead girls haunting me, but I stop myself just in time.

'No wonder what?' Macintyre asks.

'Nothing.' I smile. 'I forgot what I was going to say.'

Maybe he's understanding more than I think, because he says, 'Why did you say you weren't alone, at the end of the tape?'

'Um . . . I wanted to scare her,' I lie.

'Were you referring to Nathan Nolan?'

'Oh!' I sigh with relief. 'No, no, he just told me about the jeep.'

'But did he plan the killing with you?'

'No, he didn't know what I was going to do. I feel like he'd have been freaked out about it. He's a bit jittery. He's not as tough as me.'

'I'll tell them to let him go home with his mum,' Georgie murmurs, and leaves the room.

I frown. 'Is Nathan here?'

'He was worried about you and rang us, but you were already with us by then,' Macintyre says. 'So we brought him in for a little chat. He's been here for a good while, like you.'

'Why, what time is it?'

'It's nearly midnight.' Macintyre is being really snappy

and short with me. I shake my head, annoyed at him. What is his problem?

When Georgie gets back, he starts asking me more questions.

'What did you kill Eve with?'

'A knife.'

'Was it her knife?'

'No, it was my mum's Japanese veggie-chopping knife.'

'Did you bring it with you?'

'Yeah.'

'And why did you bring it with you?'

'Because it's really sharp and Dad confiscated the one I bought at the shopping centre.'

Macintyre sighs. 'Did you know you were going to kill Eve when you got up today, Thera?'

'Sure.'

'Think about this before you answer,' Georgie says, talking over me.

'Waters!' Macintyre snaps at her, then turns back to me. 'Thera?'

'I've known I was going to kill the murderer pretty much since I found Billie dead,' I tell him. 'I just had to make sure first to find out who it was who murdered her. I didn't want to kill the wrong person. Or people, in this case.'

Macintyre frowns. 'Do you think killing people is wrong, Thera?'

'In general, yeah.'

'Do you think killing Eve was wrong?'

Now it's my turn to frown back. 'Look, maybe *you*

think that, since you're behaving so weird and moody with me, but I don't care what you think. Killing bad people makes kids safer.'

'If we let you go now, and Nick and Eve were free, or even bad people generally were free, would you go after them?'

I shrug. 'Sure. If you weren't doing your job properly.'

He leans forward in his chair. 'Why didn't you go for help? When you found out about Nick and Eve, why didn't you come and get us?'

'Because you wouldn't have believed me. No one believes kids, or listens to them. I had to take matters into my own hands. And I had to get Eve's confession, to be totally certain she was the killer, and to make Mum and Dad, and you guys, believe me. Besides, it would have been dumb to be like "Oh, you're the killer? Cool, I'll just turn my back on you and walk, because obviously I can't drive, all the way to the police station." This isn't a film. I had to be realistic.'

'If you had left them both alive, they would have been sent to prison. Children wouldn't be in danger. Justice would have been done.'

I raise my eyebrows. 'Oh, would it?'

'It would,' he says certainly.

'Justice, maybe, but not vengeance. Vengeance wouldn't have been done. Billie would have died for nothing.'

'Vengeance?' He seems like he's totally not following. 'Why did you want that, Thera? Is this something you've seen on television? Why did you have to take revenge?'

I blink slowly at him. 'Because Billie was my best, true,

forever friend. You don't let your best, true, forever friend die and not find and murder her killer. It's like you didn't even really care about them if you don't do anything. I promised her, anyway. I promised her.'

There is a short silence, and Macintyre blinks back at me. 'You were gone a while this afternoon, and this tape is only an hour long. How long did it take Eve to die, Thera?'

I sigh impatiently. 'Ages.'

'How long is ages?'

'*Ages!*' I shout at him. I'm annoyed now. 'I took my time about it too! I didn't want it to be over quickly for her. I wanted her to think while it happened. That's why I stopped the recording halfway through the killing.' I look up at Georgie, explaining. 'It was almost full, and when you get to the end of the tape there's a danger it'll rewind and start recording over what you've got. I didn't want to record over her confession.' (I'm proud of this. I thought of everything. Well, everything important anyway.)

'And afterwards, you walked here?'

'Yeah. You know that already. Look, this is all a waste of time. Look, it's done. The killers are dead. Justice, vengeance, whatever you want to call it, it's done. You're welcome. Can I go home now? 'Cause I've had a long day and I'm really, really sleepy.'

Macintyre stands up.

'Wow, you're tall,' I comment.

'We'll find out about where you can go, Thera,' Georgie says. 'To make sure you're well looked after.'

'I don't need a hospital or anything,' I say, exasperated.

'I'm fine! A good night's sleep'll put me right. I mean . . .'
I feel bad for snapping at her. 'Thanks, though, Georgie,'
I add sincerely. 'For the tea and putting the tape into evi-
dence and everything.'

She nods and gives me a weak smile. You'd think they
would be happier. I mean, I just caught a serial killer.

'You can't go home, Thera,' Macintyre says.

'What? Why not?'

He shakes his head.

'Why?' I say.

Macintyre ignores me and says, 'That'll be all for now.'
He looks at Georgie and opens the door for her. She goes
out in front of him. Outside, there is some bustling in the
corridor and a lot of noise through in reception.

I stand up, knocking my chair back. 'Why can't I go
home?' I cry after them. 'I'm tired!'

'It's a lot to go through, for a child that age,' I hear
Georgie say pleadingly, as the door closes. Chief Inspector
Macintyre holds up his hand to shut her up.

I wait there for what seems like hours. Why aren't they letting me go home? Why are Mum and Dad here but don't come in and see me? I'm getting pissed off now. Eventually a lady comes in. She isn't in uniform. She's wearing a dark-red patterned blouse and black trousers. She is almost as old as Nan and is holding a steaming cup of tea and some toast.

I sit up, lifting my head from the table. 'Is that for me?'

'Yes, it is,' she says.

'Good, I'm starving.' I start in ravenously, and she sits down in the empty chair, and takes her bag off her shoulder.

'I want to go home,' I say through chewed bread. 'Who are you?'

'I'm Dr Anita Kapoor, I'm a forensic psychiatrist,' she says. 'Do you know what that means?'

I think about the word 'forensic', and sigh. 'Something to do with evidence?'

'In a way. I'm here to talk to you and give the police some advice about what we should do. Sort of just having a chat to see what you're thinking and feeling. I also have to say whether you're a risk to the public.'

'Great, okay,' I say, settling into my chair, yawning, holding my tea. 'Let's get on with it.'

'Are you tired?'

'I've had a nap. I just want to get all this over with and go home. For bleep's sake, I only came here to hand in the evidence tape.'

'I thought Chief Inspector Macintyre explained you couldn't go home?'

'He didn't say why.'

'Well, you killed two people, and the police have to look at the evidence and listen to what you say—'

'But they've done that already. I identified Billie's bag and stuff.'

'They have to look at the evidence from where Eve was killed and where Nick was killed, and then they have to decide if they are going to charge you with a crime.'

'*Me?*' I say, incredulous. 'What about them killing Billie?'

'Oh, the police are certainly looking at all that evidence too. But you did kill people, Thera, and you have to expect there will be some punishment.'

'But they were bad people! They killed Billie and Ellie and Jenny Ann Welder and—' I cut myself off before I reveal I know about the other two dead girls. They'll find the pictures in Nick's wallet anyway. I checked for them after I killed him and before I went down to Mrs A. Their pictures were all there. I guess it's why he took mine – as a souvenir. 'They deserved to die!' I sit back in my chair, astounded. 'This is crazy. The police are idiots if they think that's a crime. They should be thanking me. What about this don't you all get? I got the bad guys! I'm the *good guy*. Why am I having all these stupid conversations? The police didn't find the killers or anything. How come they seem surprised and ungrateful that I went and did their job for them?'

'Thera, it's against the law to do what you did. Vigilante justice is—'

'Isn't killing little girls against the law? Doesn't the fact that they did that cancel out me killing them?'

'Thera,' Anita says, more loudly because I'm shouting, 'think about this logically. If you don't play ball, you'll be here a lot longer. You have to talk to me before anything is decided, so perhaps you can talk to me and clear this all up and you won't be charged with anything. But you won't be going anywhere until I do my report on you. So what are you going to do?'

I put my hands on my hips and think about this. Then I throw my hands up in the air. 'Why not? Fine.'

'Good, let's begin from the beginning, shall we?'

Despite me being tired and thinking all of this is pointless, Anita and me actually have a reasonable chat. She asks me if I know the difference between good and evil, and I scoff and explain the definitions, and she says I'm very smart. I say thanks. She asks if I've been feeling well, and how my mental state has been after Billie's death. There are loads of questions, about forty. She even asks if I've been hearing any voices, and specifically if I've been hearing Billie's voice, but I keep shtum. I put on my good-girl act and answer sweetly, but without expression: 'No. I wish.' She tells me I'll probably be taken somewhere secure until they decide what to do with me. She seems to want me to say killing Nick and Eve was bad, but I'm not going to do that. I shrug when she asks me if I feel bad about what I've done, and I get a bit moody with her. 'Whatever,' I say when she tells me about a children's home in Lincoln. She tells me she has to go away to make a medico-legal report and a risk assessment, but I'm too tired to even ask what they are.

She leaves me alone for ten minutes and I feel jittery, but there are a number of old tape recorders for recording interviews in the room, so I flick them on and off and figure out how they work. I play with the one Macintyre used to tape our interview earlier. I am just walking past the door to go and play with the oldest-looking machine, when Georgie, Mum and Dad come around the corner. I see them through the glass bit in the door. As soon as she sees me, Mum bursts into tears.

'Thera!' she cries – I can't hear her, but I recognize the shape of my name in her mouth – and she breaks into a run.

'Mum!' I shout happily. 'Finally!' Georgie unlocks the door and Mum grabs me and hugs me really tight. Her tears make my neck wet. 'Ma, you're squashing me! I can't breathe!' I say, and she lets go, and Dad hugs me.

Georgie walks into the room, looking pale, followed by Chief Inspector Macintyre. She presses 'Record' again on the tape machine, starts to whisper, then clears her throat.

'Thera Leigh Wilde, it is my duty to tell you that you are under arrest for the double murder of Nick and Eve Adamson.'

416

'Urgh!' I exclaim in disgust. 'This is crazy!'

'Thera, shush,' says Dad, putting his arm around me. Mum puts her arm around me on my other side, and we stand in a line of three, listening to Georgie.

'You do not have to say anything, but it may harm your defence if you do not mention when questioned something which you later rely on in court. Anything you do say may be given in evidence.'

'I'm not being questioned again, jeez!' I cry. 'This is all a huge mistake. Think about it, Georgie, I caught the killers!'

Georgie continues, not really looking at me. She seems really shocked, and her voice is quiet and shaky. 'You have the right to free legal advice, to tell someone where you are, and if you feel ill at any time while in police custody, to see a doctor. You may have regular breaks for food and for the toilet, but someone will be with you at all times.

'Because you are almost twelve, the court has decided to charge you as a twelve-year-old, which means you are kept in police custody if it is felt you pose a threat to the public. Because of the seriousness of your crime, the court will not be offering bail. You will be put on remand, which means you will be held at a secure facility for young people until your trial, which will be at the Crown Court.'

'It won't be at a young people's court?' Mum asks. She looks as white as a ghost.

'No, all homicide offences must be tried at Crown Court,' Georgie answers.

'We'll find a lawyer,' Mum whispers in my ear. I frown at her. 'And we'll always be close by, Thera, ask anyone for us. I'll be right outside the station. I'll go wherever they move you, my baby, and I'll love you always.'

'Huh? What? Move me?' Mum looks terrified. 'Mummy, calm down, don't talk like that, it's just a ridiculous accident, they'll see, when they look at all the evidence properly – wait, what's happening?'

Mum and Dad are still holding my hands, but Georgie is trying to manoeuvre them out of the room.

'Let go, please,' Georgie says, and she breaks my mum's hand away from mine. I am holding on, but I think Mum is holding onto me even harder.

Dad squeezes my wrist and looks at me helplessly. 'We love you. Be a good girl, Thera. Don't get into trouble. Just keep your head down wherever they send you,' he says as Macintyre practically pushes him out of the room.

'Daddy?' I say, screeching a bit. 'Daddy?'

'It's okay, Thera, it's okay,' Dad calls back to me, but he's holding his body stiff so Macintyre can't make him budge. I don't think it's so much that Dad is really strong, but that he's young and Macintyre is old. 'Just take care of yourself,' Dad says to me, but it's like he's trying to communicate something else. Georgie blocks the door so I can't get out.

'We love you!' Mum shouts.

'Out – out now. Sergeant Davies!' Macintyre calls. Outside the interview room I see one of the younger policemen, who brought me home when Billie's dad saw me on the road that time, come and take hold of Dad. 'That's enough!' Macintyre shouts at Dad. 'Out!'

'Daddy? Mummy?' I struggle against Georgie.

'Stop struggling!' shouts Mum. 'Just don't do anything. Just be safe and don't talk to anyone.'

'We're leaving, we're leaving!' my dad shouts back at the young policeman. 'Get your hands off me.' He shoves at him, and the guy grabs Dad's arms. Dad looks back at me once before he rounds the corner. I can still see him a second after he's gone, like his body has left an imprint in the air by the wall. His mouth is shaped like my name, and the sound left is a desperate 'Thera', as if he wasn't talking to me or to anyone, just saying my name to hear it.

Mummy is gone a second after him. Her dark-blue eyes look more like the sea than ever, because they are filled with water, and her big bottom lip pouts at me. The last sound I hear from her is a big breath in, like when you're crying and gasping for air.

Georgie pushes me back inside and shuts the door, and the sound is cut off. After a second, she opens it to let Anita back in. 'Until your social worker gets here, Anita will be the second adult present for the arrest of a minor,' she says, talking into the tape recorder.

'What social worker? Why can't Daddy and Mummy stay?' I shout at her.

'Thera,' she says. Her whole body is shaking. 'I understand Eve and Nick were criminals, but it's my duty to make it clear to you that killing them was against the law, and that you have been denied bail, which means we can't let you go home. Please provide us—'

'I want my mum and dad!' I scream.

'Please provide us' – she raises her voice over me – 'with

a written statement of what you told us earlier, and then sign it at the bottom of the last page.' She unlocks the filing cabinet and takes out paper and a pen, and puts both on the table in front of me. I bang my fist on it.

'Which part of what I told you? I've been talking to you guys forever and you still don't get *anything*!'

'The part where you killed Eve and Nick, Thera,' she says.

'Urgh!' I scream. 'Fine!' I write it up really fast, filling four pages.

'Right,' says Georgie when I'm done. 'Am I going to have to handcuff you or will you promise you won't hit anyone?'

'Why the hell would I hit anyone?' I say this, but I literally feel like kicking and hitting everyone in the police station right now and then running home. The dead girls' power isn't in me any more, but I feel like I might just be able to do it.

She grabs my elbow and hauls me off the chair and down the corridor to have my picture taken.

'Why am I denied bail?' I ask Georgie grumpily as the man gets me to stand square. He holds up the camera, and I smile and he takes a photo. Georgie tells me not to smile and makes him do it again, but she doesn't answer my question.

'Four feet eleven inches,' she says to the photographer, then to me: 'Come here. Put your fingers in the ink.'

'Why can't I go home?' I repeat. She ignores me, not even looking at me. 'Why can't Mum and Dad stay? Why is everyone so angry at me? Georgie!' The guy is still taking photos, now of the side of my face. 'Why are you ignoring me?'

'Oh, Thera!' Georgie says, then shakes her head. 'Thera, the crime scene in the woods is horrendous. I told you the court thinks you pose a threat to the public, and having seen it . . . well, I don't want to agree, but I find I have to. I understand why you think what you did was right, but it isn't,' she says shortly.

'You've seen the bunker? When did you go?'

'I've been on all night. I've been to their house too. Macintyre thought it would be good for me, to see your work, so I wouldn't feel so sorry for you.'

'Huh. So do you feel less sorry for me?'

She looks at me. 'Put your fingers on the paper.' She holds my hand and we do my fingerprints, all ten of them. There is still blood on my hands.

'Wait. All night?' I say, just realizing. 'What time is it now?'

She sighs and shakes her head. I think she is still thinking about the bunker.

'Look, I didn't have time to clean up,' I say apologetically. 'I had to get the tape to you. I came looking for you. You, specifically, Georgie. I knew you'd understand. You're on my side, right?'

Georgie changes the subject and asks if I want a banana and some Coco Pops for breakfast.

Later that day, two police officers drive me to a kids' home in Lincoln, where I live for a few months with some right brats, one of whom manages to stab my leg with a protractor when we are doing maths homework. I kick the boy in the head, hard, twice, and he doesn't mess with me any more. I don't even bother telling the adults about it. They won't understand. They never understand. I don't trust any of them, not the social workers, or the foster carers.

Five months after my night at the police station, we go to trial. Outside the court there is a crowd of people, and I wonder what they are here for until I get out of my social worker's car and they all start taking pictures of me, and shouting questions at me. Most of them ask about Mrs A, but one of them, a man with a big nose and a beard, sticks a microphone underneath my face and shouts, 'How does it feel to be famous?'

I frown. 'Famous?'

'Get a move on, Thera,' Ruth, my social worker, says. A policeman comes down the steps of the courthouse, claps his hand on my shoulder, and marches me inside. As we walk up the stone steps, I see a group of women holding banners above them. Out of the corner of my eye, I notice one of them has my name on. I lean back to read it as the policeman drags at me.

'Inside!' Ruth shouts.

'Weird,' I mutter.

The poster is painted on a white background in big, purple capital letters. It reads:

I STAND WITH THERA WILDE

'What's that all about?' I ask Ruth, but she shushes me and nods ahead. 'Mummy! Daddy!' I shriek. We run towards each other and they swoop me up into a hug. I haven't seen them for three whole weeks. I was supposed to see them last week, but a social worker has to be available for me to be with them, in case they run off with me, because Dad got mad one time and threatened to. Last week there wasn't a social worker available so we missed our visit. I'm still annoyed at Ruth about it. She said something about cuts but they can't be out of money, because she went on holiday a month ago. Lame.

We all squeeze each other really tight. Nanny and Grandad come too. It's so lovely to see them, I almost forget why we're all there.

Mum, Dad and my lawyer, Amber, remind me to plead not guilty and to say I regret everything. I do, as soon as I'm asked what I'm pleading, but I'm not sure the judge buys it. He is very frowny and is about as old as Grandad, and wears a red gown and a totally daft wig that looks like it comes from the seventeenth century. My lawyer and the other lawyer are dressed in black gowns and equally dippy wigs. The jury are dressed normally, but they also seem not to like me.

The other lawyer, the one prosecuting, talks about how I planned to kill Nick and Eve, and how I'd do it again if it would prevent other girls from being killed and raped. I'm not allowed to take the stand, so I have to keep my mouth shut, but I don't disagree with anything he says, in principle. Which is weird, because he's supposed to be against me.

Anita gets up and tells the court I'm not insane and I understand morals and that killing people is wrong, which you would think would work in my favour, but it turns out she's on the prosecution's side. Traitor.

We all get shown the crime-scene photos on a big telly, and most of the people sat to the left of the dock, in the audience seats, look away and gasp. In contrast, the jury are all concentrating very hard on the pictures and scribbling notes, but one or two of them look like they're about to throw up. 'This is crazy,' I mutter. 'Why don't they show the photos of Billie?' Ruth, who gets to sit near me, tells me to shush.

That's basically the first week of the trial. Every day, as I walk out, the women are still there, and they start up a chant, saying the same thing the poster said. At the end of the first day, Mum, holding my hand, tells me, 'Don't listen to them, Thera.'

We walk quickly to Ruth's car, and she and Dad kiss me, then Ruth bundles me in the front seat. She gets in and shuts her door, and the noise outside muffles. I peer at the ladies with the posters. 'Why did Mum say to ignore them? They seem to be on my side.'

'They're pro-vigilante justice, Thera. They're hippy hooligans. Mad as bats.'

'Huh?'

'They think what you did was a good thing.'

'How was it a bad thing?'

Ruth's head snaps towards me. She frowns. 'Because you should have called the police and let the courts put Eve and Nick away. Imagine if everyone did what you did when they thought someone deserved to be offed. People would be murdered left, right and centre. No one would be able to sleep at night because maybe some nut at work or at school thinks they have it coming.'

She starts the engine. I'm thinking.

'Oi, Thera,' Ruth says. 'That's bad, isn't it?'

'Yeah,' I answer, nodding. 'Yeah, they're crackpots.'

She nods, but she doesn't look totally convinced. 'Okay,' she says. 'Well. Good.'

The next day when we come in, I watch the women out the corner of my eye. There are other posters too, apart from the first one I saw. They have my face on them. In some of them I'm made out to be a hero, and in some of them I have horns above my head like I'm the devil. I ask Ruth who the men with the devil posters are and she says they are from the church.

The second week is more prosecution evidence – a forensic pathologist, and lots of working through a folder of pictures and names and evidence from the case. It's like we're making a TV show for the jury, and I'm the main character, but it's not my chance to do my scenes yet.

The third week is all my defence. Firstly, I am cross-examined on my interview with the police. I basically confirm everything I said. The prosecution lawyer isn't allowed to ask me any complex questions because in the morning before the jury came in, Amber told the judge it would be too confusing for me at my young age. I disagreed with Amber about this when we discussed it, but it sort of works out, because I get to explain for ages about what I did and why, so the jury will understand. I don't talk about the dead girls, of course. After my go on the stand, there are a lot more witnesses. Mr Kent and all the other teachers I've had since I was a baby, Mrs W, Mrs J and Mrs K, come to the stand, and even *Hattie* sits in the courtroom and says how nice I am, even though she looks very nervous. She's dressed very nice, in a pink dress, with her hair clipped back. Not at all how she usually dresses. I haven't seen her in five months, and I'm surprised to realize she looks younger than the kids I live with, even though we are all the same age. Then, at about three o'clock, the judge says we can go home and have speeches the next day. As I stand up I smile at the jury and a couple of them smile back at me, but cautiously, as if they don't really want to like me. I wave anyway, because the whole point is that they do get to like me, and then I walk out with Ruth.

The next day, the other lawyer gives a speech to the court about how Nick and Eve didn't pursue me, and instead I went purposefully to their house to kill them. He says I am capable of acknowledging that killing is wrong, and that I knew that it was wrong to kill Nick and Eve, but that I believed that wrong cancelled out the other wrong. This is all true, but I find it hard to understand why it is important. He also uses really complicated language, and despite knowing all the words Grandad has taught me, and being very smart, I still don't understand everything he is saying.

I sit back after his speech, totally confused. Then my lawyer gives one more boring speech and the jury go away to think about everything.

It feels like we wait forever for the jury to come back, but in reality it's only six hours, three on one day and three on the next. That's what the court clerk says. The day after the speeches, at three in the afternoon, we are all called back into the courtroom, and the jury foreman says I'm guilty of two counts of murder, one count of false imprisonment, and one count of having an article with a blade or point in a public place (the woods).

The judge tells us he has prepared for this eventuality and is ready to pass a sentence. I don't know what this means – I thought my sentence was 'guilty' – so I keep shtum. He turns to me and looks down his nose at me. He looks mad. He says, 'It was a savage and brutal crime, cunning in its conception and undertaken with a sadistic joyfulness I have seen rarely even in seasoned violent criminals. You have consistently displayed no remorse for your actions. Indeed, you believe you are righteous, and that the public should be grateful to you. This crime, and your demeanour, horrifies even me, with my long tenure in this court.'

The room is very quiet.

'Public debate on this sentence will be lengthy and thorough, and probably should be, but I see no option but to sentence you at Her Majesty's pleasure.'

The people in the audience gasp. I turn to Amber.

'How long's that?' I whisper to her.

'As long as a piece of string,' she says.

I make a face and tut. 'What the fuck does that mean?' Amber shakes her head at me and I clap my hand to my mouth. 'Sorry.' I look at Mum and Dad. Phew. They're not looking at me, just at each other. I know they would be ashamed if they thought I sounded common and rude. It's being around the kids at the children's home. They swear all the time. I guess the kids' prison will be pretty much the same. I look over at Georgie, who is sat in the audience on the other side of the room, and shake my head at her in disgust. She betrayed me. She looks away from me, down into her lap. She gave evidence for the other side. Macintyre is sat with her. I guess they're happy now. Mum and Dad turn back to look at me. Mum is crying.

The judge concludes, 'I am recommending a minimum stay of ten years in a maximum-security facility for juvenile offenders.' He bangs the hammer and everyone starts talking animatedly, but in a hushed way, so it's like a huge, buzzing murmur. All the people Ruth told me were journalists leap up and run out of the room.

They let me hug Mum, Dad, Nanny and Grandad before the men who are going to transfer me to the children's prison take me away. Ruth will go with me and drop me off there. It's nice to see my family, because they haven't been allowed to visit me loads at the children's home, but I'm sad that they didn't bring Sam, because I haven't seen him at all since I was arrested. I haven't seen Nathan either, but Mum and Dad said I won't be able to see him again. They went to the caravan and asked, but his mum didn't know where he was. He's also been taken into foster care. I knew Nathan's mum was horrible. That's probably why he's been sent away. Hopefully Sam at least can come and visit me at the secure facility, which is in an undisclosed location. I wonder what crimes the other kids will have done. Maybe there will be some tough, brave crusaders, killers of bad people, like me.

Nanny and Grandad hug me first. Grandad gives me a book to read, called *Papillon*. 'Use your years in prison to learn, my dear Thera,' he whispers in my ear. 'The active mind can never truly be imprisoned. It is a guarantee of freedom you should guard and foster carefully.'

'I promise I'll read lots,' I tell him. My social worker confiscates the book later, and I never get to read it. I'm finding out more and more not to trust anyone who works for the police or prisons or court. They are most definitely not on my side.

Nanny gives me a big squeeze, but doesn't say anything apart from that she loves me. She kisses all over my arms and her eyes are wet. 'Don't cry, Nan,' I say. 'I'll be fine. I'm going to learn and work on stuff while I'm away, like Grandad said. I'll see you when I get out.'

Mum and Dad give me the biggest hugs I've ever had

from them in my life. I can tell they are sad, but they are much quieter and calmer than we all were at the police station. They tell me they love me and that they will come and visit on the first day they are allowed, which is in two weeks. 'Behave yourself, my little baby,' Mum says to me, before making a weird, choking, animal noise and turning away from me.

'Bye, I love you,' I call as the men lead me away. 'Get Sam to feed my Nano Pet!'

When we leave in a police car to get my stuff from the home, there is a roar of voices outside, and some of the pro-me posters bang against the windows. 'We're with you, Thera,' a lady mouths from outside. Another gives me a thumbs-up. Their breath fogs up the glass. I'm surprised they have been out there the whole trial. It's a frosty January.

28 January 2000

I still don't get why they had to lock me up. It's not like Billie was going to get killed again, leaving me to hunt another murderer, although I have to admit, now I have a knack for it, I'm not afraid of killing. There are plenty of other girls and even little boys who get abducted all the time and never find vengeance or peace. Some of them have started to visit me. Kids who weren't killed by Nick. Who were killed by other men. There are plenty of men out in the world, and many of them are evil, and I know now that some ladies are evil too. Sometimes I imagine all the dead girls' and boys' little ghosts wandering around, crying for their mummies and daddies, sitting next to their buried corpses in shallow ditches or deep lakes, wondering why they can't go home, and why they can't go up in the clouds to play, when I know it's because their stories remain unresolved, their bodies undiscovered. It makes me so sad to think of them, and I realize that it wouldn't be so hard, especially when I'm a bit older, to seek vengeance for a few more of them, maybe even to travel Europe avenging their deaths, strangling the stranglers and dropping them in ditches, charring my prints off them like Eve did off Billie, letting the symbolism and irony speak for me to the dead kids, to let them know they have been avenged.

In the meantime, I'm not too worried about being locked up. On the way, in the little bus, my social worker showed me the brochure, and they have a gym and lots of activities and classes. What better place to learn and train and ready myself for life ahead? I'll miss my family, and Nathan, but those are my only regrets. If being locked up is a consequence of killing Eve and Nick, and of coming through for Billie, well, I guess that's okay. I wouldn't go back and do it differently.

At the kids' prison, I walk down a long corridor with a squeaky, green floor like in school. The walls are white and have nothing on them, not like all the bookshelves, photographs and paintings everywhere at home. We pass a room with four computers in. I can see because every room has a window into the corridor running the length of its interior wall. Another room has a couple of kids a bit older than me hanging out in it. They are playing charades, sat on beanbags. We turn a corner into the bedroom area and they unlock a room for me.

'At first, you'll be confined to several locked rooms at set times, but when we get you settled in you'll have more freedom,' says the plump, nice lady who is showing me around.

'Great.' I smile. 'I like the room.'

It's bare and simple, with enough space to do push-ups and dance about, which is good because I intend to get very strong and work on my muscles while I'm here. The bed is by the window, and the room is on the ground floor, and the window has bars. The door opens outwards but actually there is a metal gate as well, so they can lock you in your room but still hear you and see everything you're doing. The gate retracts into the wall, which is quite cool. The lady, Lou, opens my door wide and holds my gate half-closed. 'I'm going to leave you in here for half an hour, just to settle in. Is that okay?'

'Yep, sure.'

'Got everything you need?'

I pat my rucksack, which is on my bed waiting for me, along with a small pile of new clothes. 'Looks like it.'

'Again, you'll be able to have some of your own clothes and things once you settle in.'

'I don't mind,' I say, shrugging.

'Alright, then,' she answers, sort of strangely, as if what I said was a weird thing to say. 'I'll come back and fetch you for dinner.'

'What are we having?'

'Roast.'

'Chicken, beef or pork?'

'Erm, chicken.'

'Delicious!' I say, rubbing my tummy. 'Mm.'

'Well, er . . . see you then,' Lou mumbles, and slides the gate out of the wall and across the doorway. The bars clank like in all the movies. It's a satisfying sound, like resolution.

Acknowledgements

This novel is dedicated to the dead and missing girls. According to UNICEF, every ten minutes an adolescent girl dies a violent death.

May they not be so defined by their deaths and the short stretch of their years as to rest in the narrative of collective memory as angelic victims.

May we see them as fully formed, even flawed, complex human beings deserving of life without the necessity for canonisation.

May we teach girls not to be obedient, digestible, and decorative, but to fight with teeth and mind and fists; to see themselves as potential victors, and not ineluctable victims.

Thank you, as ever, to my family and friends.

Thank you Sarah Branham, for early, and very useful, notes and encouragement.

Thank you to my patient maverick of an agent, Jo Unwin, and to Isabel Adomakoh Young, for their faith, hard work, and support.

Thank you to the Mantle family and to my editor Sam Humphreys, who truly made this novel what it is, and who loved Thera in all her awkwardness and determination from the beginning.

Reading Group Guide

1) What does having an eleven year old narrate this particular story add to the novel? How would the story differ if it was told from another character's perspective – Thera's parents, Nathan, or the detective in charge of the case?

2) Think about other young female would-be victims in contemporary novels and films. How do they act? What is different and the same about them and Thera? Do authors have a responsibility to portray girls in a certain way in this age?

3) Is Thera a reliable narrator?

4) *'We've got to shield them from the details of the investigation.'* What effect has Thera's parent's overprotection had on her? Should they have been more up-front with her about Billie's death and the investigation? How do we talk to our children about adult concepts like consent?

5) What did your parents tell you about strangers? Was it good advice?

6) The media often paints young female murder victims as 'innocent angels', as if it's their purity that makes them undeserving of death. How does *Dead Girls* take a stand against this in its portrayal of victims and young girls?

7) How culpable is Nathan? How do you think he was affected by what he saw? And what do you think the book is saying about how we learn – and how we *should* learn – about sex and sexuality?

8) Thera comes to understand how much adults try to claim her body by touching and commenting on it. How do we talk to our children about bodily autonomy in a positive way?

9) What can be done to change society so deaths like Billie's don't happen? Should the onus be on adults to prepare girls? To stop male perpetrators? Or to do both?